CW00621070

THE SUMMER

Maureen was surprised at how close Larry and Kathleen had become. Surprised and a bit jealous. She had long ago given up any dreams she had. Her life was over. But Kathleen was a different matter. Hers was just beginning and she was going to have everything that Maureen had ever wanted. She would be clever and beautiful and have her pick of any man. She would travel, and meet royalty. Maureen's dead dreams would be Kathleen's reality. And she would not shrink from playing the wicked mother if need be. She knew one day her daughter would be grateful. Besides, what did this child have to do with the proprietor of a corner grocery shop? Her father was an executive. He was handsome and witty and not unlike Laurence Olivier. She sometimes wondered what had become of Mr Morris. She pictured him at high-level board meetings. He would jab his finger forcefully in the air to make a point as others gathered around the gleaming mahogany table gave him their undivided attention. He would win every argument because he was always right. But then she would decide Mr Morris had no more reality for her than did the celluloid figures she saw on the screen on Sunday afternoons. He was just another part of her dead dreams.

About the Author

Margaret Morley is the author of three previous novels, and two non-fiction books, including a biography of her father-in-law, the actor Robert Morley. She was born in Boston, Mass., and has a B.A. from Emmanuel College, Boston, and an M.F.A. from the University of Hawaii. She has lived in England for twenty-six years and now resides in Berkshire with her three children.

The Summer Woods

Margaret Morley

Copyright © 1990 Margaret Morley

First published in Great Britain in 1990 by Hodder & Stoughton Ltd.

Nel edition 1991

A John Curtis Book

The characters and situations in this book are entirely imaginary and bear no relation to any real person or actual happenings.

The right of Margaret Morley to be identified as the author of this work has been asserted by her in accordance with the Copyright, Designs and Patents Act 1988.

This book is sold subject to the condition that it shall not, by way of trade or otherwise, be lent, re-sold, hired out or otherwise circulated without the publisher's prior consent in any form of binding or cover other than that in which it is published and without a similar condition including this condition being imposed on the subsequent purchaser.

No part of this publication may be reproduced or transmitted in any form or by any means, electronic or mechanical, including photocopying, recording or any information storage or retrieval system, without either the prior permission in writing from the publisher or a licence, permitting restricted copying. In the United Kingdom such licences are issued by the Copyright Licensing Agency, 90 Tottenham Court Road, London W1P 9HE.

Printed and bound in Great Britain
and Stoughton Paper-

I envy not in any moods
  The captive void of noble rage,
  The linnet born within the cage,
That never knew the summer woods

IN MEMORIAM A.H.H.
Alfred, Lord Tennyson

1

The scent of roses, jasmine and gardenia mingled with the smoke from the melting candles, creating an oppressive fog. Maureen was trapped, caged in by the rows of metal chairs that lined the sombre walls. Those sitting on them could barely see each other's faces. The murmuring conversations were carried on with the secrecy of the confessional. It was a long thin room, a door at one end and at the other, bathed in a twilight glow from the candles and discreetly placed dim lights, was the focus of the gathering – an oak coffin with brass handles, open to reveal a blue pleated satin lining encompassing a tiny white-haired corpse. She was dressed in blue which exactly matched the satin lining and merged into it, giving the impression of a disembodied head, framed with a crimped halo of recently permed white hair. Few of those present had seen her asleep either in reality or in this semblance of it and, in death, without her glasses and tinged with a beige make-up, a tasteful splurge of rouge and ever such delicate pink lipstick, most of those who came to pay their respects thought they were in the wrong room. If it hadn't been for the hovering presence of her son, Larry, with his red-rimmed eyes, they would have retreated in search of the proper corpse. Kathleen, who had never worn so much as a shine of Vaseline on her lips in life, looked ten years younger due to the cosmetician's expert hand. The wrinkles acquired during her sixty-six years of life were tucked away somewhere in the recesses of the newly-styled hair. Only her hands remained nearly the same as they

7

clutched her favourite mother-of-pearl rosary. Whoever had done her could not resist some colourless nail polish which shone in the candle light. A large crucifix hung on the wall behind the coffin, and flowers, most in the form of wreaths or crosses with large purple bows, spread behind and around it.

'Doesn't she look a picture?' Bridget Walsh said to her daughter Maureen as they knelt at the prie-dieu and looked at the body. 'Ah, she's at peace at last, God rest her soul, after all that suffering.'

Bridget and the dead woman were near contemporaries. Together, as teenagers they had sailed from Cork to begin a new life in the New World, and settled where the ship had docked – in Boston. Looking at her Bridget felt the sharp edge of her own mortality, even though she was far from the bedridden invalid her friend had been for the past ten years.

'He's a good man, you know. You'll find no better, my girl,' Bridget said, switching quickly to the subject dear to her heart – her daughter's marriage to her old friend's son. Too many of her children had gone wrong and she was determined to take no chances with this, her youngest.

Maureen blushed at her mother's Irish whisper which she was sure echoed around the room.

'And now, poor soul, he is all alone. No woman to look after him,' she continued.

Maureen crossed herself and rose from the kneeling position, a bit unsteadily. It had surely been the other way around. It was Larry who looked after his mother. It was he who washed her and cooked for her and ran hundreds of times a day up the stairs from the store to see to her when she banged on the floor.

The room was nearly full, not surprisingly. Kathleen Thornton was a neighbourhood fixture. She had run the grocery shop since before Maureen's birth and when she took to her bed, Larry had taken it over. Everyone knew them and knew they were good solid people willing

8

to put things on the slate till the money came in.

And Maureen also knew what else her mother wanted. There were just the two of them now and the taxes on the house got higher every year. It would be a sensible move. The three of them could live comfortably over the shop. But Maureen didn't want to marry Larry. It wasn't just because at thirty-eight he was seventeen years older than she was. She had no objection to that. John Barrymore was probably that old – and Douglas Fairbanks. It was simply the feeling of 'is that all there is?' There had to be something more to life than living all the time in the same street. Something more than getting up in the morning and working and eating and going to bed worrying about money. She probably wouldn't have that worry if she was married to Larry. He'd look after her – after both of them. She knew that. But it would probably also mean giving up her job and she liked her job. She did the bookkeeping for Campbell's, the five and ten cent store in Central Square. At least sometimes there, there was someone to laugh with. And of course there was Mr Morris. At thirty he was one of Campbell's youngest managers and she figured one of their best looking. He was always so pleasant and cheerful towards her, even when she made some silly mistake. She knew it wasn't right to daydream about him – a married man – but at times she couldn't help it. Forbidden fruit.

Larry had always been around. He was polite and neat and tidy and not bad looking. He'd never actually taken her out – not on a real date. Mother couldn't be left alone for long and there was the store to run. But sometimes Maureen's mother, Bridget, had organized Sunday lunch for all of them and then sat with Kathleen while they went for a walk. His conversation was always about canned goods or bread delivery or sometimes, if she was lucky, there was a bit of neighbourhood gossip. He had no dreams. Maybe he had no time for them or maybe he felt no need for them. He was a good man but there was no denying he was dull. She didn't want to spend her life with him. No matter what her mother said she would never marry Larry.

Maureen Walsh and Lawrence Thornton married at St Catherine's Church in August 1928, six months after his mother's funeral had been held in the same place. It was an altogether quieter occasion. Larry didn't think it seemly to have a large wedding so soon after his mother's death, but it was impractical to postpone it any longer.

Maureen's brother, William, came from his parish in Revere, having got special permission to perform the ceremony. As well as being her eldest brother he was Larry's best friend. In fact his only friend. They had grown up together, played on the same high school baseball team and Larry had been shattered when Bill entered the priesthood, leaving him alone. They met infrequently after that. After his ordination, Bill's parish duties gave him little time and Larry, with the store and mother, had none.

Maureen had wanted her sister, Elizabeth, to be her matron of honour but Mother said she wouldn't come to the wedding if that heathen were there. She hadn't spoken Elizabeth's name since she had married a Protestant. So Maureen asked her old school friend Nancy. They had, as teenagers, had such plans. They were going to travel and meet rich men and dance on tables. Nancy had married Tom straight after high school. He worked at Armour, the meat packing firm that could be smelled so keenly while waiting at Lechmere station for the trolley into Boston. Nancy said she'd got used to the way he smelled every night and kind of liked it. Pork was her favourite meat. They already had four children and Nancy was pregnant again, but it didn't show a lot.

Maureen's other brother, Michael, was best man and he was nearly sober. His wife cried a lot during the ceremony, pausing only to hit the children when they squirmed. Bridget had said it was a waste when Maureen wanted lots of flowers and a long dress. 'Flowers just die. It's not like a funeral where they are a mark of respect. And you'd

10

only wear the dress once.' So there were two small bunches of marguerites on the altar and Maureen wore her white linen suit and carried a single yellow rose with her prayerbook. She did, despite Bridget's protests, buy a white straw picture hat.

'Didn't I save the First Communion veil?' Bridget had railed. She sulked for two days when Maureen rejected the greying object. 'Young people don't know where money comes from,' she muttered.

'It's a happy day for me,' Father Bill toasted the bride and groom with a drop of porter in the sitting room over the shop while Nancy's children climbed over the furniture and Michael's squabbled in the kitchen. 'A day I've dreamed on. My best friend and my pretty little sister. And it's a good Catholic home I know it will be.'

Michael had a bottle of more substantial bourbon in a discreet brown paper bag. Bridget ostentatiously sipped her tea. She strongly disapproved of liquor of any sort and Father Bill was setting a bad example. She would speak to him about it. But she was pleased to see her new son-in-law decline it and join her at the teapot. There were ham sandwiches which Bridget had made and cole-slaw from the Jewish delicatessen, and Maureen had made a chocolate cake and decorated it with white frosting and sugar flowers she had bought in her lunch hour at Campbell's. Mr Morris had given her the little bride and groom that stood on the top and she was sure that no one noticed that the bottom layer was ever so slightly scorched.

There was a lot of cleaning to do when everyone had gone. The children had left crumbs and half-eaten sandwiches everywhere. There was frosting smeared down one of the curtains. Michael had been sick in the bathroom and had missed the bowl but Maureen didn't mention it to her mother. She knew it would somehow be her fault and she didn't want to ruin the day. She was feeling very virtuous. She had done the right thing. She managed to confine her tears to the locked bathroom where she sat after she had scrubbed the linoleum floor with disinfectant. Larry, Bill and Bridget were having another cup of tea in the kitchen.

Bridget occupied the armchair by the radio. Larry sat at the table with his accounts book while Maureen hovered. She had already moved all her clothes from the single bedroom into Larry's room. The one that had been his mother's. Bridget had taken over Larry's old room. As Maureen had hung up her dresses in the half of the closet Larry had cleared for her, her glance had kept darting nervously to the old mahogany double bed, and the carved pineapples atop the four posts, one on each corner. She had visited Kathleen who lay propped up with pillows in that bed as she slowly died. Larry told her that he had bought a new mattress but she could see that the room remained otherwise unchanged. The heavy six-drawer chest of drawers, three drawers of which were now hers; the mother-of-pearl crucifix over the bed; a Madonna and child framed on one wall and on another a head of Christ crowned with thorns whose eyes followed you. The curtains were Irish point, the drapes a heavy maroon brocade. Speckled linoleum covered the floor and there was a hand-hooked rag rug by the bed – a huge pink rose on a green background. Kathleen had made it. Maureen kept thinking she could see the old lady sitting up in the bed, clutching her rosary. She was smiling. Father Bill had come into the room before he left to go back to Revere, where he had a meeting of the boys' club to oversee, and blessed the bed. Maureen had blushed. She hadn't had to share a bed since Elizabeth had left home.

At nine o'clock, Bridget turned off the radio, said it had been a busy day and it was time to go to bed. Larry closed his book and agreed.

'I'll just wash the tea cups,' Maureen said.

'That's right, my girl,' Bridget said. 'Never leave a dirty dish on the side over night. There will come a morning you don't wake up.'

Maureen stood at the kitchen sink – stalling. She heard her mother close her bedroom door. She heard Larry in the bathroom. Then he went into his bedroom – their bedroom. She dried the cups and saucers and put them on the shelf. She dried the spoons and stood them, handle down, bowl up in the spoon jug. Then she went into the bathroom and looked at herself in the only mirror in the house. It hung over the bath and had pink flamingos in one corner. She washed, and put on her best nightdress. It was sleeveless and had lace trim around the neck. Then she combed her hair and pulled the light off.

The bedroom door was ajar. It was dark inside the room. She pushed the door open and then softly clicked it shut behind her, leaning against it. She could hear Larry's even breathing but as she slowly approached the bed she hesitated. She didn't know which side was hers. She had forgotten to ask. Maureen stood at the foot of the bed and tried to get accustomed to the darkness. Finally she could make out his shape. He was nearly in the middle, on his side, facing towards the window with his knees curled up to his chest. Facing towards the side of the bed that had the rose rug on the floor. Gently she lifted the covers on the other side and eased herself in quietly so that she wouldn't disturb him. She, too, lay on her side, her back towards his back, on the very edge of the bed. Her foot accidentally touched the smooth cotton of his pyjamaed back and she pulled it away quickly.

'He's a good man,' she thought. 'I've married a good man. He'll always work hard. He'll never be drunken or beat me – or run around with other women – or leave me. I'm a very lucky person. Every wife can't say that. Very few can say that.' And she cried ever so softly so she wouldn't disturb him.

It was still dark when Maureen woke with a start. For a few seconds of panic she couldn't remember where she was – or who this was, moaning next to her. Then the funeral and the wedding came back to her.

13

'Is it . . . maybe . . . you want . . . time to eat now . . . I get . . . can't . . .'

It was Larry. He was still asleep but now he was lying on his back. His right hand was in the air, reaching for something.

'Can't . . . try . . . trying . . .' he continued.

Maureen didn't know what to do. He seemed so upset. His eyes were open. What was he looking at? What was he seeing on the ceiling?

'Can't . . . can't . . .' he kept repeating.

Maureen sat up and leaned over him. 'Shh,' she crooned. 'It's all right. You're dreaming, Larry.' She stroked his head. He was wet with perspiration. 'It's all right,' she said. 'Just a dream. I'm here.'

'Can't,' he said. He was shaking now.

She leaned closer, putting her face right down to his. 'It's all right, shh, I'm here,' she repeated, cooing softly.

'Oh, oh,' he reached up and pulled her close to him. She continued to stroke his face. Gradually the trembling stopped. He cuddled her close.

'Mummy,' he murmured as he drifted back to an untroubled sleep. 'Mummy.'

'Well, if it isn't the married lady,' Robert Morris said. 'Good morning, Mrs Thornton.'

Maureen had arrived early at the store, as usual, on the morning after her wedding. Everyone – that is Bridget and Larry – had agreed that it was practical that she continue to work. At first Larry thought he would rather that she helped him out in the shop, but Bridget said he'd managed by himself very well and there was not a full time job for the two of them there.

'And we all know what the devil does with idle hands,' she had concluded her case.

Larry remained uneasy about it. It didn't seem right that a married woman worked. Oh, it was all right in the family shop, or taking in washing at home to bring in some money, but going out to work was a different matter. Still, he had bowed to Bridget's authority.

Maureen was tired after her restless night. She wondered if Larry was always like that. Would she ever again get an uninterrupted night's sleep? Still, she managed to smile brightly at Mr Morris.

'Good morning,' she said, sounding as if she were the happiest person on earth. She was determined at least to try not to dwell on her wedding night. It was altogether too shaming.

'I was going to ask how the bride was,' he said, 'but I can see she is absolutely blooming. Welcome to the club.'

Maureen decided that this remark had something to do with sex so she blushed and busied herself with papers on her desk, while Mr Morris settled into his chair and reached for the phone.

The office was at the back of the store. A twelve-foot-high wooden partition separated it from the rows of counters. The door on the left concealed stairs to the working area and was always locked. Mr Morris had a key and so did Maureen. Inside she had a buzzer on the desk which she could use to unlock the door when someone needed to gain access. When seated she and her boss were hidden from view, but if they wanted to check something on the store floor or summon an assistant they only had to stand up and peer over the partition. By Mr Morris' desk there was also a one-way glass through which he could observe the proceedings below without being seen. All the girls who worked there knew about the glass but by its very nature they could never tell when they were being watched. If there were no customers to serve at their counters the girls were supposed to occupy themselves dusting or tidying. Chatting to each other, although even the manager knew it was inevitable, was forbidden. He let the occasional lapse pass unreprimanded, especially during the early morning slack period, but the girls had learned to hear, above the hubbub of the shoppers or the traffic passing outside, the staccato click of a ruler against

15

the top of the partition. The culprit and most of the others would look up to the icy stare of Mr Morris, chest, shoulders and head above the partition, motionless, and to them very threatening. They were terrified of him.

Maureen was in a no-man's-land. The girls on the floor didn't quite trust her. After all, she was up there with him all day, probably spying on them as well. At the same time most of them liked her and accepted that he was her boss, too. Sometimes they tried to involve her as mediator but Maureen avoided taking sides. She remained polite, even friendly, but kept her distance.

There was a dark room in the basement, carved out of the stock rooms, and furnished with a dilapidated green sofa, stained with coffee, burned with cigarettes and in which most of the springs had been sprung. There were a few tables and peeling folding chairs and here the girls took their breaks – ten minutes in the morning, ten minutes in the afternoon and twenty minutes lunch break. Staggered, of course. Maureen seldom went down there, so as not to get too involved. At first she had, but there were always questions – about Mr Morris, about rumours that fluttered around continually from counter to counter. Had Peggy been fired for shop lifting? Was Martha really pregnant? Had Edith got a raise?

Maureen would have liked to have made friends, anyway with some of them, but her job depended on discretion and the further she distanced herself the easier it was to maintain. She knew Mr Morris wasn't the ogre they imagined. He just had a job to do, and she thought he did it well. It wasn't easy. And of course the girls didn't know head office was continually breathing down his neck. She could always see the tension rising in him when the quarterly visit of the team from head office was nearing. Five or six of them would descend, poking noses into every aspect of the store, from the state of the floor (a single blob of chewing gum resulted in an inquisition) to the girls' fingernails (which should be short, clean and unpainted). Then there were the auditors who came twice a year, not to mention the constant threat of being 'shopped'. Undercover people from head office, usually middle-aged women, came unheralded and unannounced, passing themselves off as ordinary shoppers. Mr Morris only knew that they had been when a report arrived, marking him on the state of the store, the stock and the efficiency of his staff.

Although reports were usually good – hovering between seventy-five and eighty-five per cent, he lived in dread of the shoppers. They always found something wrong. That was what they were looking for. Their job was nit-picking. But if a report ever fell below sixty per cent, he knew he was out of work. And it could happen. A careless or a rude girl, a foul-up in the stock room . . . It wasn't easy. It took constant vigilance to maintain standards. Mr Morris had his eye on head office and knew the reports would have to rise to the nineties before he stood a chance. Maureen never said anything when she could see that he was nervous but she tried to smile in a reassuring way. Early on she had sensed his ambition although he never mentioned it – to her. And she wanted to help in any way she could. Before her marriage she had a fantasy that he rose to the top of the company – beyond the area office, right to the head office in Chicago. And the best part of the fantasy was that he took her with him – all the way – as his assistant. She never fantasized about his home life – his wife, his children. In fact she tried never to think about it. It was his office life she shared and that occupied her dreams. Now, of course, the dream was over, but it had been a long time in the making and she couldn't just abandon it overnight. She would never abandon her fierce loyalty to him. Maybe she would never get to Chicago, but if that was what he wanted that's what she would help him to do.

Married life settled quickly into a mould. Instead of having constantly to please her mother, or rather avoid displeasing her, Maureen found she now had two people who required her acquiescence. Though, to be fair, Maureen thought, Larry didn't ask all that much of her. She finished work at five and managed to have supper on the table by six. Wednesdays were a half day, so she looked after the shop then while Larry had a break. She never knew where he went, or what he did but he would leave at two and come back at five, every Wednesday. He joined the Knights of Columbus after their marriage and they met on the first Tuesday of the month. On Thursday evening Maureen would go out after she had done the supper dishes. It was her regular evening for visiting her friend Nancy, but often she would avoid the hurly-burly of that household and just walk, enjoying the freedom of her imagination. She had managed to get Larry to take her to the movies on Sunday afternoons after lunch. At first it had been difficult but it soon became part of the routine. Larry was good about routine. After a while he even seemed to be enjoying the outing. They always stopped for coffee on the way home and Maureen used the time to ease herself back into the real world, after her celluloid escape.

Larry still had nightmares and would wake her with his screaming three, sometimes four nights a week but he never seemed to remember in the mornings so Maureen never mentioned it. She felt sorry for him and wanted to comfort him but he avoided any sign of intimacy, clinging to her only in sleep as he murmured 'Mummy.' That upset her more than anything in the rest of her life.

Since her marriage she found she began to enjoy her job even more. The sense of relief which she felt when she said goodbye to Larry and her mother after she had tidied the breakfast things grew to a feeling of freedom – which slowly diminished as the time neared for her to return to them.

The store outing was planned for the second Wednesday in August. It was a yearly tradition. After the store had closed for the half day, the buses would arrive and take everyone off to Whalen Park. It was a forty-five minute drive to the recreation park. There, they would have a picnic lunch and there would be swimming in the lake, and boating, as well as walks through the woods. Maureen had never particularly looked forward to the outing. It always seemed as if the jollity was just a bit forced. But this year, as her first wedding anniversary approached, she welcomed the extra time away from her home.

It was a bright, sunny day when it arrived, after days of thundery humidity. Maureen packed her swimsuit – the one she had bought the summer before, before her wedding, but which she had never worn. She also packed a pink skirt and a white blouse with pink rosebuds. Her mother made a few pointed remarks about people who spent their time enjoying themselves with no thought for others, but Larry said he hoped she had a nice time. He never even mentioned the fact that he had to forgo his Wednesday afternoon out.

The girls arrived, twittering in their navy blue overalls, clutching cases which contained their more frivolous clothes. They spent the morning in high anticipation. Mr Morris overlooked the constant chattering which went on on the sales floor. It was only to be expected and it was after all only once a year. Maureen noticed that he looked as businesslike as usual – dark blue suit, white shirt and blue tie. She also noted that there was something different about his hair. It fell across his forehead at a different angle and was most becoming.

'Good morning, Maureen,' he said as he arrived. He, too, was carrying a case.

'Morning, Mr Morris.'

'It is going to be a beautiful day,' he said. 'Temperatures in the eighties and low humidity, the forecast said.'

'Yes, that is nice.'

'Well, Mrs Thornton.' He always emphasized the Mrs in a teasing way which made her blush. 'I hope you've brought your swimsuit. Mustn't waste the sunshine.'

Maureen blushed more deeply. Mr Morris didn't usually make personal remarks. But the blush was really caused because she was remembering him in his own swimsuit

19

from previous years. He had a very handsome body.

The store doors were barely locked to any further customers before the ladies' room was crowded with chattering changers. Despite the noise, the changing was accomplished with alacrity, including the application of make-up and the total reconstruction of many coiffures. The buses were loaded and on their way fifteen minutes after the store had closed. Singing commenced immediately, the soprano voices heavily drowning the baritones, as the total male population of the store came to six – Mr Morris, a trainee manager and four stock boys. Five of them found the atmosphere heady as the girls vied for their attentions. Mr Morris, although now friendly and casual in his open-necked shirt and white flannels managed to maintain an air of separateness. Authority could too easily be undermined in a careless afternoon and could take weeks to recover. It was, he knew, a tightrope he must walk with skill. But each year he felt he became more adept. It was, however, a strain. Some of the girls were most attractive.

The sun glistened on the lake as they tumbled out of the buses. A long table on the water's edge was covered with salads and rolls and a brick barbecue was already laden with hot dogs and hamburgers, white smoke carrying the aroma of the cooking as a greeting. Bottles of beer and soft drinks were in a huge barrel nestling in ice. A mad dash to the changing rooms and soon the lake was full of splashing. The boats had been pushed out and one or two of them, overladen, were soon overturned. Giggling and screaming, the staff were enjoying themselves.

Maureen stood and watched. She was always amazed by the speed and the noise. And she always felt unable to join in. Like Mr Morris, she felt it wouldn't do to be too abandoned. Besides, this year there was the added reason. She was a married woman.

'Just like a pack of kids.' Mr Morris was standing beside her. She hadn't noticed and jumped when he spoke. 'Hey, sorry. I didn't realize you were so far away.' He put his hand on her arm – just a touch at first and then his fingers closed around it. 'Where were you, anyway?'

'Here,' she said quickly. 'Right here,' looking up at him. She hadn't meant it to sound seductive but it had. He continued to hold on to her as if she might float away.

'Aren't you going to change?' he asked.

'No, not yet. I thought,' she hesitated, 'I thought I'd walk for a bit first . . . if that's all right.'

He smiled. 'Hey, you do anything you like, Mrs Thornton,' he said, 'anything at all. I'll just go have a look see at the barbecue.' He released his grip and watched her walk away from the lake and disappear into the pine-wood.

It was cool and shady to the point of darkness as Maureen wandered slowly, ducking now and then to avoid a low branch. Soon the noise from the lake was a distant murmur and she sat down on a bed of pine needles, softened and bleached with age. She looked at her arm. He had gripped it very tightly and she could still make out the marks the pressure of his fingers made. Delicious pressure. If only she could feel the same way about Larry when he touched her. But then he never did, except in his sleep when he held her and called her 'Mummy' and she rocked him back to calm.

It would be different if Robert were her husband. Robert. She had never called him that, except in her fantasies. Maureen decided to indulge herself in one now, while his touch was still warm. She had worked on and perfected a number of scenarios. She chose the one where they are both working late in the store, during stock-taking time. The girls who had been counting have gone home and Maureen is at her desk, head down, filling the stock book's column with numbers. The pencil point breaks and at that precise moment she senses someone behind her. It's Mr Morris. He bends and kisses the nape of her neck. She is frozen with surprise and then he grasps her shoulders from behind, so tightly it hurts, and stands her up. She turns and looks at him and then silently he pulls her close and kisses her. It was her favourite and never failed to bring tears of pleasure to her eyes and a satisfactory tingle to parts of her body she preferred not to think about. She could replay it slowly, over and over again and it always worked. She lay back on the ground and closed her eyes.

Maureen had just got to the point where the pencil breaks.

'Aren't you hungry?' he asked.

No, no, she thought. It is silent. And she began again at the beginning.

'Hey, hello. I'm speaking to you.'

She opened her eyes. He was there. Mr Morris – sitting on the ground, leaning over her. He was smiling.

'Aren't you hungry?' he asked again. 'I've left hordes of them demolishing the food.'

Embarrassed in case he had read her thoughts, Maureen tried to sit up. She could only prop herself up on her elbows as he was leaning over her. Then he put a hand on her shoulder and rather roughly pushed her back down. He moved even closer, leaning on one arm, across her body. His face was now very, very close.

'It is nice here, isn't it?' he said. 'So peaceful, so lovely.' His fingers were stroking her hair, then, slowly, they moved gently, but firmly down her neck to the buttons on her blouse. There was no haste, no speed – just the simple determination of a man who knew what he was doing – and met with no objections. He had undressed her completely before he began to kiss her.

It was the end of September when Maureen realized she must be pregnant. She tried very hard not to panic. She and Mr Morris had not mentioned the outing – nor the pine-wood. Formality had returned at work, although occasionally they exchanged glances which signified that if the opportunity presented itself, neither of them would be averse to repeating the encounter. But it was not practical. There were too many people to consider; too many obstacles. Not to mention the distinct lack of opportunity. Maureen was surprised that she felt neither ashamed of her behaviour, nor guilty about it. It had been a wholly pleasurable experience – so pleasurable that as time went on, she began to wonder if it had not been just another one of her fantasies. The confession of her adultery had elicited only the usual three Hail Marys penance from her rather deaf confessor. However pregnancy was a totally different thing. Actually she was pleased with the notion of having a baby. But as she and Larry had not consummated the marriage it might present a problem. Religious as he was, she didn't think even he'd believe in an angelic visitation culminating in a virgin birth. It was necessary that he made some attempt to sleep with her. But how was she to bring that about? He had shown no interest at all. She would just have to force the issue and quickly.

'Larry,' she said, as she got into bed that night. 'Larry,' she shook him gently. He couldn't have fallen asleep so quickly. Instead of reading or taking her time tidying the house after he had gone to bed as she usually did, she hurried along after him.

He stirred and rolled on to his back. 'What is it?' He sounded neither sleepy nor cross at having been disturbed, merely surprised. They had never spoken in bed before – at least not when both of them were awake.

Maureen was sitting up. 'Larry,' she thought she might as well say it quickly. 'We should be thinking about having a child.' Larry was speechless and looked rather frightened. 'We've been married more than a year now,' she continued, 'and I think it is time.'

Silence from Larry. Silence hung in the air like a blanket. 'But surely there is no rush,' he finally said, in a whisper. 'When we get more settled. Then we can think about it.' He turned over again – his back towards her as usual. 'Go to sleep,' he muttered.

There was no going back now. 'Larry, we are settled,' Maureen said. 'The only way we could be more settled is to be six feet underground, like your mother.'

He sat up again. 'Don't you speak about my mother like that.'

23

'Like what, Larry? All I said was that she is dead.'

'Yes, well, it was the way you said it. Taking her name in vain. I won't have it. As for this nonsense about a child. It is just not practical, Maureen. Be sensible. What about your job? I thought you liked your job so much.'

'To hell with my job.'

In the darkness she could feel the shock emanating from him like a hurricane blast. He had never heard her swear before. She couldn't even remember swearing before, but this was desperate. Now that she had his attention she would have to keep it. She began to cry. She had never done that before either – not in front of him.

Clumsily he put an arm around her. He was frightened by her outburst. Where would it all end? 'Now, now,' he said nervously. 'It's not as bad as all that.'

'Yes it is,' she sobbed. The sobs were real now. 'It's worse.'

'But we've been just fine. You've been fine. As good a wife as a man could want. Why all of a sudden . . . ?'

'It's not all of a sudden,' Maureen interrupted. 'I've been thinking about it for a long time.'

'But now – with all the troubles in the world.'

'Damn the world. It is always full of troubles.' She began shaking violently now and she wasn't pretending. What would she do if . . . it wasn't possible to think about. He had to put both arms around her to stop the trembling. This is it, she thought, and embraced him. Half sitting, half lying she held him tightly to her, working her body along the length of his. She kissed him gently on his face, on his mouth, his ears, his eyes. Surely there must be some basic male reaction – some reaction out of his control on which she could rely. At last she felt the stirring in him she needed. Quickly she settled down, pulling him on top of her and wound her legs around him. There was no time to be coy or delicate. The task was accomplished quickly. It had certainly not been a complete and total fusion of bodies, but it would do. Maureen was calm again. Larry lay quietly, his face on her breasts. She still held him. Now it was he who was crying. 'Sweet mother of God,' he moaned. 'Jesus, Mary and Joseph, forgive me. I'm no better than an animal.'

Maureen tried to soothe him. She found his guilt unspeakable. But it did make a change from his usual litany of 'Mummy.' Finally he fell asleep in her arms.

Bridget was horrified when Maureen told her the news.

'No sense of decency,' she railed. 'Why, you've barely been married two minutes. You'll be sorry, my girl. Children are nothing but pain and heartache and shouldn't I know?'

'Thanks, Mother,' Maureen said and dropped the subject. She gave her notice at work. Christmas Eve would be her last day. Mr Morris said he was sorry to be losing her. She had been so reliable and pleasant to work with.

'It just won't be the same without you,' he said. 'Especially the outing,' he added meaningfully. 'I'll really miss you, Maureen.' He kissed her lightly on the cheek.

'I'll miss you, too,' she admitted and forced herself not to cling to him. 'Goodbye.'

'I hope you'll keep in touch,' he said as she was leaving. 'Drop in and see us occasionally.'

'I'll try,' she said. 'But I expect to be rather busy.' She patted the incipient bulge.

'I'm sure you will,' he said. 'And I'm sure you'll be a wonderful mother. All the best.'

A wonderful mother, she thought. She could be a wonderful wife – to him. It was then that the devil came over her. 'I do hope there are no blue-eyed blondes in your family.' Would he understand, she wondered as the words tumbled unbidden out of her mouth. Did she really want him to?

'What?' he asked, as if he hadn't heard.

But Maureen had gone.

2

Maureen was finding it hard to concentrate and the star's broken English didn't help. She had been keen to come and hear Garbo as the unfortunate Anna Christie, but never imagined how strong the accent would be. At first she had been mesmerized, but now the heavy though occasional pains distracted her attention from the screen. As the grey, wind-swept sea appeared on the screen, she whispered to her husband, and abruptly he whisked her out as the rest of the audience dabbed their tear-specked eyes, tidying themselves up before the lights came up.

Kathleen, their only child, arrived at the Boston Lying-In the same day that Bird's Eye Frosted Peas arrived at her parents' grocery shop – May 12th, 1930. Larry Thornton had been dubious about both arrivals. It didn't seem to him the best time to introduce new products. His business wasn't bad, although most of his customers made their purchases on tick. He could rely on them to pay each week, or at the worst every other week. For them, though, as for everyone else, money was tight and the future was frightening. Jobs were scarce and although Larry knew that they were better off in Cambridge than a lot of people elsewhere – the newspapers wrote scary stories of the Midwest – he found it disturbing to see the long lines of young people outside Woolworths: fifteen, sometimes twenty, recent high school graduates all after a couple of jobs serving behind the counter. He had been approached for work but had nothing to offer. The shop just supported himself, Maureen and Maureen's mother. And now, he thought, there would be another.

Still, people always had to eat. He wouldn't like to be trying to sell cars. But as he explained to the salesman, he couldn't see anyone paying thirty-five cents for a small packet of peas. Sliced bread had been a different thing. His customers found that economical. You knew where you stood with sliced bread, every piece the same size. You could count them out and plan ahead and not worry that one of the kids would cut himself a doorstep and scoff what was meant for three. But those little hard pellets? Who was going to buy them? Still, the agent had persisted. What did Larry have to lose? They kept indefinitely – just like cans. In the western part of the state, where they had gone on sale in March, they had been an enormous success, he told him. People would be asking for them. The taste was just like fresh picked. Larry told him his customers didn't know what fresh picked peas tasted like; they enjoyed their cans. But times were changing, the salesman assured him, and he didn't want to disappoint customers did he?

Larry succumbed but later found that the salesman had been exaggerating if not actually lying. No one wanted them. Occasionally as a diversion they would finger the packet when Larry dug down into the ice-cream freezer and produced one, together with a half-hearted sales patter. But the general feeling was that they certainly wouldn't do you any good and were probably downright dangerous. Only Mrs Weston bought some but then Larry had always regarded her as rather eccentric. She fell on anything new straight away and even seemed to know about new products before the salesman had arrived. She demanded Hostess Twinkies, Mott's Apple Sauce and that spicy Worcestershire stuff in the bottle all wrapped up in paper. She never seemed short of money either.

The other new arrival was much more successful than the frozen peas – although that could be construed as an understatement. One look at his daughter and Larry knew

27

his wife had been right to insist that they had waited long enough. Kathleen was the most beautiful thing he had ever seen. She had his mother's eyes, he thought, God rest her soul, and she was named after her.

Kathleen's presence had made an enormous difference in Maureen's life. Here, at last, was a project worth concentrating on. She felt she could now ignore Bridget's nagging without guilt. Her daughter was the more important – and somehow she took her strength from the child.

'That's not the way to hold her, poor thing will suffocate,' Bridget said, as she watched Maureen put Kathleen to her breast. 'Here, give her to me, let me show you.'

'I shall hold her however I choose,' Maureen said. 'She's sucking perfectly well and it is comfortable for both of us.'

Maureen was surprised when Bridget responded to open defiance not by the expected flash of temper, but rather with meek withdrawal. She was sorry she hadn't tried it years ago. Her life might now be totally different. But it was no use worrying about what might have been. That was past. It was the future she now concentrated on and that was Kathleen.

Her name had been the first bone of contention. Maureen wanted to call her Amelia after her heroine, Miss Earhart, the flyer, but she was outvoted two to one and conceded gracefully in the end. Kathleen was a pretty name.

Nancy was godmother and Father Bill godfather. Nancy, whose youngest was already nearly two and who felt baby deprivation, cooed ecstatically over the new arrival and Father Bill exclaimed she had her namesake's eyes. Maureen was grateful that, like her own and her husband's, the baby's eyes were indeed a deep velvety brown. Larry had been immediately besotted by the baby, constantly running up the stairs to peep at her and rising at night at her very first whimper to cuddle her tight and walk with her around the room.

She was two weeks old when the godparents, Bridget and Larry accompanying, took her to St Catherine's for her baptism on a Sunday afternoon. They were gone less than an hour, but Maureen fretted all the time. She felt naked without the child. She felt she didn't exist without her baby and quickly snatched her back when they returned.

'There now,' Bridget said, 'she's no heathen now. She's safe. Straight to heaven she'll go, should, God forbid, anything happen. Such a beautiful child. Like an angel. Just like my dear Mary. She was too beautiful to stay on earth and so God took her for himself.'

Maureen had heard the story that she knew was about to be retold for the millionth time. She tried not to listen. She held Kathleen close. There would be no stopping Bridget, she knew, once she had started the tale.

'It was, God knows, a difficult birth. I nearly died twice, didn't I? Thirty-six hours . . . thirty-six hours I was in labour. Thirty-six hours, day and night, of hellish agony. I thought, you know, it was the twins all over again. Both born dead. Both dead before their immortal souls were cleansed – may God forgive them and let the perpetual light shine upon them.' At this point Bridget made the sign of the cross and everyone in the room, from habit, followed suit. 'But then when they put little Mary in my arms it was all worth it. Worth every bit of the pain. And sure there was no other name to call her. She was an angel – a pure angel. A darling healthy little girl angel. And never any trouble – sure, not a bit. She never cried, God bless her. But you know, I should have seen it. She was too good. Your brother Thomas didn't he adore her and him a little devil, no more than a toddler himself. Even that small, as he was, he could see how special she was. But the good Lord didn't see fit to leave her with us for long. Not long enough to be tainted by this world.'

Maureen shifted uneasily, trying to smile down at the baby, while Bridget continued her tale.

'I can see it like it was right in front of my face, as clear as I can see you all now. There she was in the cot beside my bed. Something woke me up. It wasn't her, I swear to God it wasn't her. Bless her. I knew that. It was a knock on the door. Your father, he said he never heard it – swore it. But I heard it all right. It woke me up, it did. A loud knock. I shouldn't have opened it. I'd heard the banshees, hadn't I? I had heard them earlier, wailing outside. Your father, he said it was only the wind, may he rest in peace – only the wind! But I tell you I'd heard them just like I heard the knock. And I went, God forgive me, and I opened the door. There was no one there. No one you could see. But I knew, knew as I stood there with the night coming in on me, that I had opened the door to death. I rushed back to her but it was too late. She was pale – white and beautiful like a china doll, more beautiful than ever with a smile on her little dead lips. My darling angel had gone to heaven.' At this point Bridget always sighed deeply and paused, wiping a tear from her eye. 'And you know,' she continued, composed now, 'there hasn't been a day – from that day to this – when I haven't felt she was there, praying for me. My beauty, my little Mary. Too good, too beautiful for this world, wasn't she, my beauty?' Bridget leaned over Kathleen and stroked her cheek with her finger. Maureen shivered and held her daughter closer. 'Not even four months old,' Bridget concluded.

'We all know it was a blessing from God, Ma,' Father Bill said. 'Would I be a priest today if she hadn't been at God's right hand praying for all of us?'

'It's true. One of his mysterious ways,' Bridget said. 'I'll put the kettle on.'

'I think I had better get back to my own brood,' Nancy said. She, too, had heard the story before, often in fact, when she was younger and playing with Maureen; but somehow it had just seemed like a fairy tale then. It was frightening hearing it recited over Kathleen – like a warning.

'Oh, sure you'll stay for a cup of tea,' Bridget said.

'Thanks, but I really must hurry. Himself can't cope for long with the tribe.' She turned to Maureen. 'See you soon.' And she hurried away, trying to shake off the feeling of doom Bridget had managed to create in the room.

*   *   *

The baby carriage became the focal point of the shop. Larry thought Kathleen even increased business, as customers came to peer at her – and they were too polite to leave empty handed. Kathleen was sitting up and waving at the clientele by five months – at least Larry insisted she was waving. Maureen said it was involuntary movement. When Kathleen was weened there was no shortage of prepared baby foods for her. Gerbers were forever leaving free samples and Beech-nut had thirteen different kinds. They were all equally poisonous, according to Maureen's mother. 'Bread and milk,' she kept muttering. 'That's what's good for babies – sure shouldn't I know?' But Maureen was determined to be a modern mother.

By the time she was toddling, Kathleen much preferred to spend her time in the shop, rather than upstairs with her grandmother who seldom left the large chintz-covered easy chair which she had positioned next to the radio. Kathleen soon learnt to sing, 'When the Moon Comes Over the Mountain', and lisped 'Heigh-ho Silver', just like the Lone Ranger, when the ice-man's white horse pulled the wagon down the street. Kathleen thought the old lady never moved. She just sat, listened to the incomprehensible stories on the radio and crocheted colourful little squares of wool which she left for Kathleen's mother to sew together into blankets. They had drawers full of these blankets.

Maureen insisted on her daily walk, though Kathleen would have been happy to spend all her time in the shop. There had to be fresh air every afternoon, Maureen insisted, even when the air was tainted with quantities of rain. Usually Kathleen climbed into her stroller and was pushed along the pavement, but when it snowed it was more exciting because her mother would then pull her on a sled.

There were two routes they always used. Some days they would go past the three-family houses that made up their neighbourhood and on into Central Square where they would stop at the drug store or the shoe shop or the fish shop or at that shop which sold wool for grandma's endless crocheting. Different days meant different shops, but each day her mother would stop outside the theatre and study the pictures and the posters of beautiful women in colourful dresses. Kathleen soon noticed that her mother sighed a lot as she looked at the pictures, and patted her hair. At least once a week they set off in the other direction, which took them to Harvard Square and there was a large park they called a Common. It was full of trees and squirrels. Kathleen thought there must be millions of squirrels there and she loved feeding them. But first, before the Common and feeding the squirrels, they stopped outside a different theatre with different pictures. Still her mother sighed and went quiet and patted her hair and smoothed her dress. The ladies in the pictures were always beautiful – much more beautiful than the ladies who came into the shop or whom Kathleen saw on the street. Except, Kathleen thought, maybe Mrs Weston.

Kathleen was nearly four when her parents first took her inside one of those theatres. It was the one near the shops. After lunch one Sunday afternoon they set off, leaving Bridget alone with her radio and wool, muttering that they were colluding in the work of the devil. Kathleen walked in between her parents, each holding a hand and swinging her up and down when they came to the kerbstones. Kathleen was very excited although she had no idea what happened inside those buildings that made her mother sigh so much. It was obviously something special. But after they had bought tickets from the lady who sat in a glass cage and had gone through the huge glass doors into the lobby, Kathleen began to feel that it was somehow a magic place – like a palace where a princess would live. Chandeliers sparkled from the ceiling; the carpet pile was so deep the buckles on the sides of her Mary Janes disappeared into it. There was on sale every kind of candy they had in their store and some Kathleen had never seen before. Hot popcorn spilled out of its popper and was delivered drenched in melted butter.

The girls who carried flashlights and showed them to their seats wore black trousers and burgundy jackets with brass buttons and golden braid on the shoulders. Square hats perched on the back of their heads. This was indeed a magic place. The seats were huge and soft, covered in red velvet. Overhead was an enormous wheel of lights – five circles, one inside the other – and she watched as these lights went fainter and fainter and then it was dark and in front of her the red curtain opened. On the huge screen there were pictures of trucks and trains and a man was telling a story about the mail. Kathleen looked around but in the dark she couldn't see where he was – then she decided maybe it was like the radio. Then there was a story about a mouse which someone had drawn and then, what it seemed her parents had been waiting for: *Queen Christina*. Her mother read her the writing that was on the screen until it moved too fast. It was a sad story. At least, Kathleen thought it was. And she saw her mother crying. But it wasn't such an unhappy kind of crying as she sometimes did when Grandma said something.

When it was all over Kathleen begged to be taken again. And so she was, each week. At first she longed to be Garbo, and then it was Ginger Rogers, but finally she settled on Bette Davis. Oh, how she longed to be Bette Davis. But that would mean leaving the shop and she loved the shop every bit as much as she loved the movies. Besides, the shop was real and, as her mother told her, the movies weren't. The movies were just pretend. Still, she sighed a lot and patted her hair and when Kathleen saw her with her father at night going over the books and realizing they couldn't afford a new dress – or when Grandma told her she was a lazy woman – Kathleen began to understand why she sighed.

Kathleen was not quite five and a half when she started school. She had often seen the sisters in church on Sunday mornings, so she wasn't surprised by the long black dresses they wore, beads clanging from the waist, nearly to the floor. Stiff white bibs encircled the top part of their bodies and equally stiff stocks covered their necks, seeming to cut into their chins, encircling their faces, covering their foreheads right down to their eyebrows. Their faces peeped out as if from hiding.

Sister Felicitas welcomed her to the sweet smelling room.

'Say goodbye to Mummy, now,' she smiled.

For a while Kathleen stood, one hand held by Mummy and one hand held by the smiling nun. The three of them were motionless in the quiet classroom doorway. She couldn't understand why there were tears in her mother's eyes.

'It's all right, Mummy,' she reassured her. 'I'll be home for lunch.'

Maureen tried to smile back the tears and relinquished her grip.

'Just go quickly and she'll be fine,' Sister Felicitas whispered and led Kathleen into the classroom. They stood facing the rows of desks and chairs. 'Now, Kathleen, where will you sit?'

Many of the seats were already occupied. Then Kathleen saw Patricia, golden hair in tight ringlets, a large blue ribbon over each ear. She knew Patricia. Sometimes she came into the store with her mother. Kathleen liked Mrs Weston – she looked like a movie star – but she didn't like Patricia. She always whined for candy or ice cream and Mrs Weston always gave in to her. Kathleen didn't like to admit it but she also envied her her fair hair and ringlets and those enormous bows. Sometimes she also envied her her mother – but somehow Kathleen knew that was a wicked thought. One of the devil's thoughts as her grandmother would say.

'Can I sit there, please?' She pointed to the empty desk.

'Next to Patricia Weston? Of course, Kathleen.' Sister put the card with Kathleen's name on it into the seating plan on her desk before going to the door to meet the next arrival.

'She's very young, isn't she?' Patricia said as Kathleen

sat down. 'She's only just become a nun. We're her first class.' Just like her mother, Kathleen thought. Patricia seemed to know everything.

The sun was streaming through the windows. The room seemed to glow and sparkle. The desk had been newly varnished and the floor was polished. Kathleen had been longing to start school and as she looked around the room it all seemed very cosy. There was a blackboard at the front behind Sister's desk and over it hung a large crucifix. One side of the room was all windows and on the other side was another blackboard. All along the top of it brightly coloured cards spelled out the alphabet with pictures and words. Aa apple; Bb baby; Cc cat . . . Kathleen could read a bit. She couldn't remember being taught but she could read. At least some words. Mainly on cans. There were coat cupboards at the back of the room. And in the corner, at the front was an American flag. All the desks were occupied when Kathleen finished her survey of the room.

'Now, children, all stand up,' Sister Felicitas said. 'This is how we'll begin each morning. First of all I'll say, "Good morning, children" and then you answer "Good morning, Sister Felicitas."'

They managed that with only a few nervous giggles.

'Good. Now you kneel up on your chairs.'

There was a good deal of scraping and shuffling.

'Quietly children. Now – In the name of the Father and of the Son and of the Holy Ghost, Amen. Dear God . . . repeat after me children and you'll soon know the morning prayer. Dear God, make each action I perform today enhance your glory and that of your Holy Mother, Amen. In the name of the Father . . .'

Maureen tried not to feel lonely on the walk home, but she could only think of it as the beginning of the end. There would be no excuse for the daily walks now. There would only be the shop – and Mother and Larry. There would be no more children, she knew that. Both Larry and Bridget had said one was quite enough – especially considering the times, whatever that meant. Still, there might never have been Kathleen if she hadn't . . . but she wouldn't allow herself to think about that. Larry was Kathleen's father and that was that. Everything else had been a dream. And she vowed to give up dreams – except for her daughter.

Kathleen found break the most difficult part of school. All the other children just knew what to do, but the games they played involved complicated rules which no one seemed able to explain to her. She tried to join in but was desperately afraid of getting it wrong. No matter what they played she was always the first to get three ghosts and be out.

'Can't I stay inside at break?' she finally asked Sister Felicitas. She was tired of getting it wrong. She didn't like to get things wrong. And she was hopeless at skipping too. She didn't know any of the chants the girls recited while they swung the rope and the others leaped in and out on cue.

'Aren't you feeling well, dear?' Sister asked.

'I'm all right, it's just . . .' She didn't know how to explain. 'Can't I help you?'

'I can manage just fine, Kathleen,' Sister said. 'Now you go out and get some fresh air.'

She might be able to manage, Kathleen thought, but I can't. The girls were already involved in their discipline. Yet the boys just rushed about madly. She noticed they only ever played one game and the rules were simple. It was called War. They divided into two fairly even groups and chased each other about. Those that were caught were put into prison. One prison was by the chain link fence and the other in the area by the fire escape. The prisoner always escaped straight away and joined back in the chase. No one ever won or lost. No one was ever out. How much easier to be a boy, Kathleen thought. She edged over towards Francis who seemed to be planning his next dash.

'Can I play with you?' she asked.

He hesitated and then looked shocked. 'Girls can't play War.'

'Why not?' she asked.

'Because. Because they just can't,' and he dashed off and captured Bobby who sure enough escaped straight away.

Compared to break, work at school was easy. Kathleen couldn't understand why Sister kept going over and over the same things. Surely it was enough to say something once. 'I don't chew my cabbage twice,' Grandma always said if Kathleen was foolish enough to ask her to repeat something. As Sister continually traced out a capital S on the board Kathleen's mind drifted back to the shop. Perhaps she had made a mistake about school. It could be very boring. And the agony of listening to some of the others reading aloud was unbearable. It was mostly the boys who hesitated and stammered their way through easy-peasy words. Kathleen read on in her head quickly turning the pages while they struggled. Then she was left with nothing to do. She couldn't lift her desk lid to get another book. Sister would notice. She looked out of the window. Framed as if on canvas she stared at the large chestnut tree, the source of conkers to be collected, polished and strung. The boys made weapons with them and challenged each other in tournaments, but this was another activity denied the girls.

The tree became etched in her mind. She watched as the leaves fell, baring it. She knew the position of each branch and during the winter she watched as the snow clung to it. That chestnut tree was the first thing she drew, really drew. At first winter naked, then she drew in the first spring buds and blossoms and then finally in full leaf. Over and over she sketched the tree at first in a halting clumsy scrawl but gradually with more control. At last she had found something to occupy herself at break. She didn't draw anything else. She didn't even think of it as drawing. She was trying to capture the tree. To hold on to it. But it changed. Everyday she noticed it was different. She envied the birds when they perched on the branches. She would like to sit up there but it was too high to climb. Even the boys couldn't climb that tree.

Sister Felicitas had given out the rexographed sheets, newly printed and smelling strongly. The children buried their heads in them, savouring the aroma. Arithmetic. Easy and, for Kathleen, quickly finished. She put it to one side while the others struggled on and once again began to draw her tree.

'Kathleen,' Sister Felicitas was standing over her.

Kathleen jumped, startled. She hadn't heard the nun's approach. She was in her tree.

'What are you doing, young lady?' The tone was cross. It wasn't a tone the sister had used before with Kathleen.

'The tree, Sister.'

'You are supposed to be doing arithmetic.'

'I did, Sister – look.' She handed the sheet to Sister who noted quickly that it was not only finished but also that it was neat and correct.

'What is this then?'

Kathleen handed her the drawing. She resented sharing it.

Sister Felicitas took it and as she looked at it her expression changed. 'Oh, I see, dear,' and she returned it and went back to her desk without saying anything else.

'Now, children, if you've all finished . . .'

The class nodded as one, except for Francis in the back row who scowled, defeated.

'. . . exchange papers and we'll correct them together.'

Kathleen exchanged papers with Patricia who had pink bows in her ringlets today. Kathleen didn't think she looked at all like Shirley Temple.

Before she went home that afternoon Kathleen was given a note to give her parents. She kept it in her pocket all evening, afraid to deliver it. It must be telling them she was bad. She was doing the tree when she shouldn't have been. But it wasn't fair. She had finished her arithmetic. What was she supposed to be doing? She worried all

38

through supper and later in bed as her mother read her the story of the Little Mermaid, she hardly listened . . . and it was her favourite. She had hidden the letter under her pillow. Her mother tucked her in and kissed her good night. As she turned out the light Kathleen knew it must be done.

'Mummy,' she called after her. 'I forgot,' she lied, sitting up in bed and holding out the envelope. 'Sister said to give this to you.' She quickly snuggled down again and tried to bury herself in the bed.

As usual, Maureen left the bedroom door ajar. Kathleen liked that. She could hear the radio from the dining room and she could hear them talking too, although they didn't usually do much talking. Grandma didn't like it if her programmes were interrupted. Tonight, though, Kathleen was almost afraid to listen.

'Listen to this, Larry,' she heard her mother say. 'Kathleen's teacher says she is a most unusually talented child.'

Talented, Kathleen thought. What was talented? Her mother said it as if it were something good. Not at all like disobedient – the worst thing a child could be.

Larry looked up from his stock books. 'What's that?'

'She is exceptionally mature,' Maureen quoted.

'Well, we always knew she was quick. I certainly couldn't read and write as well as she does at her age. But I expect she'll settle down. It will average out. It always does.'

Undeterred, Maureen continued to read, 'Her drawing has remarkable control and perception.'

'Drawing!' Bridget's voice came into the conversation with a dismissive grunt. 'Drawing, is it? And what, pray tell, is the earthly use of drawing? What a load of nonsense people talk – and her a nun. Now shush and let me listen.'

The angry tone. That's what Kathleen had expected. But she wondered what the rest of it meant as all she could hear now was 'Fibber Magee and Molly'.

* * *

That summer Maureen encouraged her six-year-old to draw, to paint. She took her to the common armed with paper and charcoals, paints and pastels. Kathleen found it strange. There seemed to be such an urgency in her mother's behaviour. And she didn't like it. Dutifully she would attempt to capture the scene on the paper, but it wasn't like drawing her tree. Maureen was disappointed in the results. Gradually the urgency receded and Kathleen was once more allowed to spend time in the store. Now she reached over the counter, just, and Larry even let her handle the money sometimes and make change, under his strict supervision of course, although she never made a mistake.

'I'm very good at arithmetic, Daddy,' she assured him each time.

'Of course you are, pet,' he patted the top of her head and the customer on the other side of the counter invariably smiled.

In August Maureen took her to Sears and Roebuck where together they chose three different kinds of material, which Maureen then made into three dresses for school – 'one on, one off and one in the wash', Maureen said and Kathleen took it up in a sing-song.

Maureen enjoyed making clothes for her daughter. She liked handling fabrics but even more she took pride in the individuality she achieved. The pattern for each dress was the same, but one would have a white collar and cuffs, another a wider belt and the third had a large flat collar in the same material. Kathleen, too, liked the material department. It was, to her, an Aladdin's cave of colour and texture. She'd run her hands over the velvet and dream of wearing it. How soft it felt on her skin. At home, with the scraps she would make clothes peg dolls, dressing them for a ball or declaring one a princess. Maureen noted her dexterity and imagination and encouraged this, too, until Kathleen tired of her mother's enthusiasm and returned to the store where her father greeted her casually and told her to mind her manners with the customers.

One Wednesday afternoon as her mother took over the store and father prepared for his mysterious outing, Kathleen said, 'Can I come, Daddy?'

Maureen held her breath. She had no idea where these excursions took him. At first she had wondered and hesitated to ask because she was too shy, but gradually she just accepted them and refused to allow herself to invade his privacy.

'Now you let Daddy go off,' she said, 'and you help me in the store.'

Larry looked at both of them, side by side behind the counter. They were both so beautiful. He was proud of them. But it was so much easier with Kathleen. There was nothing mysterious about the child, and there wasn't that sadness, deep down, that he could feel in Maureen. That sadness he knew he could never reach – that he tried not to think about. Kathleen had the simplicity he longed for in his wife. She knew he loved her. He could see it in her eyes. There were no questions there. She knew who he was and didn't want anything else. She didn't play emotional guessing games. She was like her namesake.

'The child can come, Maureen,' he said simply.

'Well, let me give your hair a brush, darling,' Maureen fussed over the child to hide her amazement.

'She's fine as she is.' Larry took Kathleen's hand and led her off. Maureen watched them turn into the street and felt pangs of jealousy. But Mrs Weston soon arrived, interrupting the nasty feeling and demanding a Chunky.

'I'm sorry, what did you want?' Maureen thought she hadn't heard correctly.

'A Chunky, Mrs Thornton.'

Maureen wasn't sure where to look. She'd had less and less to do with the shop. Her time was spent encouraging Kathleen's talent. Although she felt she wasn't having much success. The girl could be very stubborn at times.

'It's a candy bar,' Mrs Weston explained. 'Thick milk chocolate with brazil nuts and raisins. It's new and Patricia is dying to try one, the little angel.'

It would be new. Maureen surveyed the candy section. 'I don't think we've got any yet. I'll put it on the list. What is it again?'

'They're square and very thick – Chunky Bars.'

'Right. The wholesaler will be in . . . let me see . . . Friday.'

'Well, I suppose that's the best you can do. But Patricia will be disappointed. She was looking forward to a little treat. They get so restless, don't they, during the vacation? I must admit she is running me off my feet. Take me here, take me there. I'm quite worn out. I suppose Kathleen's the same,' Mrs Weston looked around. 'Where is she? I'm so used to seeing her in the store. I always feel a little sorry for her, but I suppose it is difficult when you've both got the store to run. Haven't much time for outings. And she's so good, isn't she? Always seems so cheerful – long suffering.'

'Kathleen enjoys being in the store.'

'Of course she does, Mrs Thornton. Doesn't know anything else, does she? But maybe she'd like to have a change. Why doesn't she come and play with Patricia? It would be no trouble – give me a bit of relief to tell the truth.'

Maureen wanted to tell Mrs Weston to mind her own business and that Kathleen would never be desperate enough to spend time voluntarily being bullied by the spoiled and snobbish Patricia. But a customer was a customer and Mrs Weston spent an awful lot of money. 'She has gone out with her father for the afternoon, Mrs Weston. Maybe some other time.'

'Yes, of course. Anytime. Just remember to give me a bit of notice. We do lead a very hectic life – on the go every moment.'

'I'll bear that in mind – and I won't forget the . . . Chunky Bars.'

Larry and Kathleen had stopped to buy a miniature rose bush in a pot. It had three buds and two open flowers –

no bigger than half her little finger. Kathleen was carrying it very carefully in both hands as they went through the cemetery gates. White headstones stretched in rows as far as the eye could see. Every once in a while a white stone angel or a cross appeared to break the monotony.

'You should bring a present on your first visit,' Larry told her and led the way through the maze. They stopped in front of a mound of grass. It looked like all the others, except around the white stone at the head of the mound different kinds of pink flowers bloomed. It was a very pretty miniature garden. Larry knelt and dug a little hole, scooping out the earth with his fingers.

'Put the pot in here, pet,' he told his daughter.

But Kathleen stood frozen to the spot. She was staring at the stone – at the writing. Kathleen Thornton it said. That was her. That was her stone.

'Kathleen,' Larry raised his voice – something he never had done with her. It called her back.

'That says it's me, Daddy.'

'What, child?' Larry was confused. Then he followed her eyes. He laughed. Just a small laugh. 'It's your grand-mother. Come, kneel by me and say hello.'

Kathleen handed him the pot and he firmed the soil over the edges, plucking away a couple of weeds at the same time.

'She'll like that,' he said. 'Pink is her favourite colour. It's time you met, child. Come here, by me.'

Kathleen thought it most peculiar and somehow a little frightening but she knelt on the grass beside her father, a large tree shaded the grave and there was a smell of grass.

'Hello, grandmother,' Kathleen said softly to the grass and then not knowing how to continue the conversation added, 'I hope you are well.'

'But I thought Granny was my grandmother,' Kathleen said to her mother as she was tucked into bed.

How like Larry not to explain anything, Maureen thought. She hadn't been sure of the wisdom of taking the child to the cemetery although she was amused to hear that's where Larry spent his Wednesday afternoons.

'Granny is my mother, darling. Your father's mother died before you were born.'

'But she has my name.'

'You were named after her.' Maureen remembered the arguments there had been about that. The argument she lost as usual.

'Did you know her?' Kathleen asked.

'Yes. She was Granny's best friend.'

'Was she like Granny?'

'No, not really. She was very delicate when I knew her.'

'What's delicate?'

'She wasn't very well. She was in bed most of the time.'

'So she didn't shout like Granny does.'

'Sometimes she did. But she shouted . . . quietly.'

'How did she die?'

'She just went to sleep and didn't wake up.'

Kathleen sat up sharply. 'Will that happen to me?'

'No, darling, she was very old. It only happens when you are very old. Now tuck down.' Maureen kissed her lightly on the forehead. Then she left the door ajar as usual so that the light from the hall filtered through.

Kathleen kept her eyes firmly open. She tried to listen to the radio but her thoughts were too loud. Her mind kept remembering Granny's story about her little angel, Mary. She had heard it many times. Only four months old when she went to sleep and didn't wake up. Kathleen was more than six years old. That was surely old enough. She listened for the banshees, while in the shadows she watched the pink rosebuds on the wallpaper turn into grinning faces. Pink rosebuds just like on the mound of grass that covered her other granny. She threw off her blankets. She didn't want to be covered up like the granny who had her name.

3

Kathleen Thornton was seven when she fell in love. It was the day of her First Communion. She knelt in the midst of rows and rows of little girls in white dresses with white veils on their heads. Hers had elastic and was very uncomfortable but she dared not touch it. It might spring off and fly up to the stained glass windows. Next to her Patricia knelt. Her dress was trimmed with real lace and instead of a net veil she had a lace mantilla that matched the lace on her dress. She looked just like a bride, her hair in soft curls decorated with tiny satin bows. Blue for Our Lady. Kathleen wished she were half as beautiful. Across the aisle, rows and rows of little boys knelt, dressed in white suits and shirts. They all wore red ties. Red for the Holy Ghost. Kathleen tried not to think about the net veil which she knew looked babyish and awful. It made her head all flat and came halfway down her forehead where it dug in ferociously. She told herself once more that it was selfish and vain to worry about the way she looked and on this day of all days – sinful. God was going to come into her body, really and truly.

There was so much to remember. Prayers before Holy Communion. Approach the altar, hands just so, kneel and wait for the priest. Open mouth wide, stick tongue out flat – never never touch the host. Only the priest could do that. It would be sacrilege for anyone else. Then give thanks after communion – face buried in hands. Feel Christ inside you. Forget any instructions, make any mistakes and it was sure damnation. The nuns told stories of hosts bleeding.

'Dear God, please make me worthy to receive you,' she prayed in her head. Then she was in line, slowly filing up the centre aisle. They had practised many times. Just the right pace – not too fast, not too slow. Dignified. The choir sang:

> Blood of my Saviour, sanctify my breast
> Body of Christ be thou my saving guest.
> Guard and defend me from the foe malign
> In death's dread moment make me wholly thine.

Kneeling at the altar rail, back straight, hands folded, she awaited the priest's approach. She wickedly lifted her eyes and stole a glance as he moved down the rail pausing before each child to deliver God. The altar boy beside the priest held the gold plate under each chin, to catch God if He fell. At last the priest stood in front of her.

'Corpus Christi,' he said.

Kathleen opened her eyes and looked up as she said, 'Amen.' Her eyes were still, wide, as she opened her mouth. They should have been shut but she forgot and in the most sacred moment when the priest put the host on her tongue she was looking at the altar boy who held the plate under her chin. He looked like the archangel Michael. But she knew him. He was Daniel Towski. He was at school; he'd been in the store. But she'd never seen him so wonderful before, white lace and linen over black cassock. He smiled down at her as he and the priest moved on to the next child.

Over the next few worrying months Kathleen decided that her thoughts hadn't been sinful at all. Surely it was a sign from God himself. She and Daniel were meant for each other. She prayed each night for God's will to be done and managed to be in the store any time Daniel came in. But he barely acknowledged her existence with a 'Hi.'

It was the same at school. She would find ways to pass him in the playground, often three or four times a day. But Daniel was nearly twelve and seldom noticed her.

* * *

Maureen was surprised at how close Larry and Kathleen had become. Surprised and a bit jealous. Larry always seemed to have a joke and kiss and cuddle for his daughter. He eagerly awaited her return from school each day, plying her with milk and with cookies from the barrel. It wasn't Larry's affection for Kathleen of which Maureen was jealous – it was Kathleen's affection for Larry that Maureen resented.

'There's homework to be done, young lady,' Maureen would interrupt them.

'Oh, what's the hurry, Maureen?' Larry always said.

'Come along,' and Maureen would lead the reluctant child to the kitchen table, always noticing the looks father and daughter exchanged, presumably behind her back. But the looks would not deter her. She had long ago given up any dreams she had. Her life was over. But Kathleen was a different matter. Hers was just beginning and she was going to have everything that Maureen had ever wanted. She would be clever and beautiful and have her pick of any man. She would travel, and meet royalty. Maureen's dead dreams would be Kathleen's reality. And she would not shrink from playing the wicked mother if need be. She knew one day her daughter would be grateful. Besides, what did this child have to do with the proprietor of a corner grocery shop? Her father was an executive. He was handsome and witty and not unlike Laurence Olivier. She sometimes wondered what had become of Mr Morris. She pictured him at high-level board meetings, controlling whatever things they controlled at board meetings. He would jab his finger forcefully in the air to make a point as others gathered around the gleaming mahogany table gave him their undivided attention. He would win every argument because he was always right. But then she would decide Mr Morris had no more reality for her than did the celluloid figures she saw on the screen on Sunday afternoons. He was just another part of her dead dreams.

*   *   *

47

On September 3rd, 1939, when after the invasion of Poland, Britain and France declared war on Germany, Larry didn't believe it would have any effect on them. He agreed with Charles Lindbergh that there would be no need for America to get involved in the European squabbles. What did worry Larry that month was the opening of an A & P supermarket just three blocks away. The *Cambridge Journal* was full of it – bands playing, scores of people crowding the aisles, shelves full of stock and free samples everywhere. Larry hadn't been able to bring himself to face the opposition personally, but Kathleen and Maureen had gone. Kathleen came home beaming with enthusiasm, seemingly unaware of the effect it was having on her father.

'Shelves and shelves of breakfast cereals,' she enthused, 'and they've got Kix; remember, Mrs Weston asked for that last week. And I got some little bits of cheese on a cracker and a little miniature ice cream cone and some cookies. And you just walk around and help yourself,' she bubbled on. 'No one has to wait at all.'

Larry got even more depressed. How could he possibly compete? They had even won over his own daughter.

'You don't have to compete,' Maureen told him. 'It's a different kind of store, that's all. People will still want service.'

But the weekly orders began to fall. The store kept ticking over, though, and after the novelty had worn off Larry found most of his customers had returned. The supermarket didn't put things on the slate.

The war came suddenly.

'Yesterday, December 7th, 1941 – a date which will live in infamy – the United States of America was suddenly and deliberately attacked by naval and air forces of the empire of Japan.'

President Roosevelt, newly elected to a third term of office, despite Bridget's opposition, asked Congress for a declaration of war against Japan which he got almost unanimously. Only Miss Rankin, Republican representative from Montana, voted against it, as she had voted against the First World War. The only one with any sense, Bridget said. But such was the overwhelming noise of the abuse that echoed through the House when the vote for a declaration of war on Germany and Italy was taken three days later, she merely abstained. 'And,' Bridget declared, 'it is supposed to be a free country.' Still, she had decreed that they should stay up late on Tuesday to hear Roosevelt's speech to the nation. It didn't start until ten o'clock.

'Easy to see *he's* not a working man. Working men are in bed by that time,' Bridget said. 'But I want to hear his excuses.'

When Larry had read out the details, such as they were known, of the Sunday morning raid on Pearl Harbor, Bridget had dismissed them. 'He's making it all up so he can join up with the Russians. Mark my words, it will end badly. We'll all be heathen commies before the year is out.'

Kathleen tried to listen to the president from her bed but all she could hear were her grandmother's comments. And Granny was the one who always demanded silence when *she* was listening to the radio.

'Well, that's it,' Bridget said pointedly, clicking off the radio. 'They'll be closing the churches before we know what's happened. That is if we're not all slaughtered in our beds first. Worse than the black and tans he is – but too clever to let on what he's really up to. All that talk of God, with his woman preaching birth control. Heathen commies the lot of them.'

The three of them went silently to bed. Kathleen tried not to shut her eyes. If she were to be slaughtered in her bed she wanted to be awake at the time. She shook with fear, knowing that any minute there would be bombs and fire. She'd seen pictures of war in England, on the newsreels. At the time she had been more frightened of the wicked Queen in *Snow White and the Seven Dwarfs*. England was another world. But now the newsreel pictures played in her head. Black and white devastation. Despite her efforts, she fell asleep and was pleased to find herself still alive in the morning.

Breakfast was the same, dropped eggs on toast. Everything looked normal as she walked to school, carefully keeping an eye on the sky for bombers. She was nearly calm when she arrived, but the thumping fear returned when Sister taught them the air raid drill. Everyone down, under her desk, kneeling, head on the floor, arms over head. She hadn't added keep eyes tightly shut, that was a refinement Kathleen brought to the drill herself. They practised every day at first but then as the weeks went by and the familiarity of it became a source of giggles, it was once a week, then once a month.

All the accoutrements of war became commonplace. There were black curtains closed at night so the Germans couldn't see the cities. Uniforms were everywhere and then there were the newspaper lists of the dead. Every morning the newspapers were like geography lessons with maps of battlefronts. Even Bridget entered into the spirit – cheering on the Allies (excepting the Russians).

'I thank God I've got no one in it this time,' she said. 'Tommy was enough.'

'Who's Tommy?' Kathleen asked.

'He was a darling boy, Tommy. Just turned twenty when he died in that foreign muck. A brave lad, though, that's what his commander wrote. And it was a blessing, he died instantly – no pain, they said. A lad to be proud of.'

'Tommy was my older brother,' Maureen explained. 'He was killed in the Great War.'

'No one ever tells me anything,' Kathleen said crossly.

The unusual became the normal. Kathleen would run out of the door when the air raid alert sounded and catch the leaflets the planes dropped, which explained that everyone had just been bombed and how they should have reacted to the sirens. Kathleen didn't always believe everything her grandmother said but she did believe that when the bombs came they would come unannounced. There would be no time for sirens.

There were endless snap shortages of deliveries to the store, but they never lasted long. And even though food prices had risen by sixty-one per cent by the end of the year, some things remained the same.

'Cheerios,' Mrs Weston said. 'They're shaped like the little letter "o". A breakfast cereal.' Exasperation entered her voice as she tried to explain her simple request to Larry.

'Cheerios,' he repeated. 'I'll put them on the list.'

The war had been going on for two years when Larry unknowingly dropped his own bombshell at the supper table.

'Mrs Towski was in today. She was pretty broken up – nearly cried,' he said.

'Them Polacks are always crying,' Bridget said, dipping bread into her fish chowder.

'What was the matter?' Maureen asked.

Kathleen's heart had stopped as she waited for the reply.

'Her son, what's his name?' Larry said.

'Daniel,' Maureen supplied.

'That's right, Daniel. Went off this morning – joined up – the navy.'

'Surely he's not old enough,' Maureen said. 'He's just a boy.'

'Seems he is just old enough, and said he was going.'

'Poor soul. It's hard on her, especially as she's a widow. She'll be all alone now – nothing to do but worry.'

'Sure, it's their own fault,' Bridget said.

'Whatever do you mean?' She looked hard at her mother across the table. Maureen's voice had an unusually sharp edge to it. Mostly she tried to ignore her mother's more tiresome remarks for the sake of peace and quiet.

'The Polacks. They started it all. Russians really, no matter what they calls themselves.'

'Ma, how can you say that?' Kathleen couldn't control herself. 'They were the ones Hitler attacked.'

'If they'd stood up for themselves and not been such scaredy cats they could have stopped the Germans before they got started, seems to me. But did they? As God is my witness, they did not.'

Kathleen had already flung her spoon down. It splashed into the soup as she fled from the table.

'Where's she off to?' Larry asked, ignoring Bridget.

'Oh, she'll be all right, have another drop of soup.' Maureen would have liked to react in the same way to her mother – but what was the point? It wouldn't change anything and just make the atmosphere even worse.

'Don't know what's got into that girl. She's not the same anymore,' Larry said more in sorrow than in anger. The little girl who sat on the counter eating cookies and telling him about school had become sulky and distant. Distant like her mother. He didn't know how to talk to her any more.

Kathleen lay on her bed crying. She hadn't thought of him going off to fight. The war was something that happened to other people. He had still been there – at school. She had gone to every basketball game and watched him captain the team. He was terrific. He had even spoken to her – four times.

'Oh, God. Please let nothing harm him,' she prayed.

It was May the eighth. The war in Europe was at last over. Kathleen couldn't remember when there hadn't been a war. Well, not really. What, she wondered, were the newspapers full of when they weren't about casualties and foreign countries? But there was still Japan to worry about. And, to her, the Pacific war had always been the worst. That's where Daniel was. And where he was going back.

She'd been shocked the day he'd come into the shop. She was alone looking after it, after school and her father had set her the task of tidying the canned goods and restocking the shelves. He was busy with the books. The war had put the extra burden of a very tight inventory on him and there were the ration coupons to deal with, too.

Sugar, coffee and those precious red stamps for cheese. He'd stopped stocking coloured margarine in 1943 when the extra tax was levied on it. No one would pay more for a yellow square when they could get the white block with its little cellophane sachet of powdery food colouring attached. A couple of minutes' pleasurable squelching through the fingers in a bowl and there it nestled all glistening and yellow. Some people told him they didn't even bother to colour it. Just spread it pure white – tasted the same.

The bell tinkled and she looked up, a can of green string beans in her hand, pleased to be interrupted from her solitary task. The fun of the store was in chatting to the customers. Her eyes widened, her smile dropped into a gape and she felt her cheeks burning as she clutched the can closer, her knuckles whitening. A weakness spread through her body and she felt strangely leaden, unable to move, having lost control of her body, but at the same time floatingly, giddily unencumbered by it.

'Hello,' Daniel smiled. He was dressed in navy whites, his hair sun bleached into a golden halo, his face tanned a deep copper brown. He was the most beautiful man she had ever seen and that included a comparison with Alan Ladd. Here she had been, worrying about him, every night praying ceaselessly for his safety, and here he was. Delivered to her.

'You're home!' she said and then blushed again, realizing how stupidly obvious that remark was. 'I mean . . .'

He smiled and the smile positively gleamed. Then he recognized the little girl she had been two years before, when he had last seen her.

'You've grown,' he said, the smile widening.

Kathleen recovered a measure of composure. This angelic creature, too, could make stupid remarks. 'What did you expect?' she retorted.

He hadn't actually expected anything. He had never thought about her. If pressed, he might remember that there had been a rather precocious little girl at the corner grocery shop who had always offered him cookies when he went in and asked endless questions about the basketball team. But she had just been a fixture, not even a nuisance. He searched the past for her name. Catherine? Kathleen? Which was it? He decided to play safe.

'So, Kathy,' he said and couldn't decide how to continue. Suddenly it seemed very important to say the right thing . . .

It sounded so beautiful. No one had ever called her Kathy before. It wasn't allowed. Her parents didn't approve of shortening names. But she couldn't just stand there staring at him like a fool. She put the can on the shelf. It gave her both the excuse and the stimulus to move. But she found she could only do it very slowly, very deliberately. She concentrated on moving her arm, on placing the can on the shelf. And she was pleased when she had accomplished the task.

'Now then,' she pushed efficiency into her tone as she turned to him again. 'What did you want?'

Daniel wanted to kiss her. He wanted to put his arms around her and scoop her up and hold her tightly. She was beautiful. He wanted to stroke her long brown hair and nuzzle his face into her neck. He turned away so she wouldn't see his confusion. He had forgotten what it was he had come in for. Pop down to the corner, his mother had said. And get me . . . what was it? Anyway he knew it wasn't anything important. It was meant as a kind of therapy. He had been nearly motionless in the house since his return five days before. He had been given ten days at home after the hospital. His leg was better now, the shrapnel wound had healed. He'd been lucky. How many of his buddies had been left on that beach at Iwo Jima? Had anyone counted? Had anyone been able to count?

How brave he was, the nurses in the hospital had said. How brave, his mother had cried. He hadn't been brave; he had been scared mindless. The noise, all that racket, the explosions, the screams. He couldn't even remember what had happened, only the noise and the crying and then

54

being moved. Then the ship and a plane and the hospital. He was alive, he realized on one of those days. How strange. He had thought he was dead. Why wasn't he dead? Tim had died. An arm here, a leg there, everywhere blood. The sand was wet as he lay on it. He remembered that, but not wet from the sea. It was red-wet; blood-wet.

He hadn't said any of this. He couldn't say any of it. He didn't want to see anyone who would say how brave he was. He had sat there in the house or in the garden reading *The Lost Weekend* and contemplating following suit. Maybe he could lose some of his chaotic memories. All he wanted then was to get back to the fighting. To pay the price for surviving. To somehow make up for being alive. Another week and his leave finished. He had tried to make the time hurry by sleeping but his dreams woke him.

'Go out,' his mother had said. At last he did and now for the first time since Iwo he forgot to feel guilty about being alive.

Kathleen had absentmindedly moved behind the counter and taken a cookie from the bin marked 'Broken: 15¢ a pound'. She nibbled on it while Daniel looked around, desperately trying to remember what he should be buying.

'That's it,' he said, stopping his search at the wire rack full of bakery products. He bypassed the individually wrapped Hostess cupcakes, Twinkies and Devil Dogs and scooped up the plain sponge cake. 'And a can of peach slices,' he said.

Kathleen finished the cookie without tasting it and reached up but couldn't quite touch the Del Monte can. She looked around for the grip – almost like a mechanical hand on a long pole which her father tended to leave lying where he had last used it.

'Here, let me.' Daniel was beside her, very close. She watched him stretch to reach the can. He put it on the counter next to the sponge cake. 'Peach shortcake,' he said. 'Supposed to cheer me up.'

'Are you home for long?' Kathleen tried to make the question seem casual.

'Not long.' A few minutes ago it had been too long. Now he was no longer sure. 'Report back next week.'

'Oh.'

'Still at school?'

Kathleen nodded. Why couldn't she think of anything interesting to say?

'I was wondering,' he said slowly, hopefully, 'would you like to go – see a movie maybe?'

It was the question Kathleen had been waiting for for many years. How many times had she played this very scene in her head, lying in bed staring at the rosebuds on the wall. In her mind she had always said 'yes' very quickly, but the reality presented her with a problem. She wasn't allowed to date. It had come up before. Matthew had once asked her to a dance.

'You're too young,' her father had said. And she recognized finality in his tone. 'No dating until you are sixteen. That's soon enough.'

'Too soon, if you ask me,' her grandmother had muttered from the corner.

Daniel despaired at her silence. He tried to save face quickly. 'Of course, if you're busy, don't . . .' he began to speak nonchalantly as if he didn't feel crushed.

'No, no,' she interrupted. 'It's not that. It's just . . .' And she made a quick decision. 'Which movie?'

God, did it matter he thought. 'What about the University?' he said.

'OK.'

'I'll pick you up at six-thirty.'

'No,' Kathleen said quickly, 'no don't do that.' She nearly screamed. Then more calmly, 'I'll meet you there.'

'You sure?'

'Yes. I've . . . I've got something to do in the Square first.'

'OK then. I'll see you there at six-thirty.' He wasn't going to lose any valuable time. Then he started to leave, flushed with success.

'What about your peach shortcake?' she called after him.

'Oh yeah, forgot.' He turned back and gave her two quarters.

As she got his change she said, 'Daniel . . .' in a hesitant way.

He worried that she had changed her mind. 'Yeah?'

'Ah . . . this may sound a little . . . crazy . . . but, ah, could you not mention me to your mother, please. I mean about meeting me tonight?'

'Why not?'

'It's just . . . a long story. I might tell you later.'

'OK, if that's what you want.' He would have agreed to anything she asked. 'But I don't see . . .'

'I know it's crazy but I'd rather.'

'Whatever you say. See you later.'

'Six-thirty,' she said and found his parting smile devastating.

Her father came down to help her shut up the shop at five. Supper was at quarter-past, always. Gran complained otherwise. And always it was a quick, quiet affair so that she could get back to her radio. Kathleen could smell that it was Tuesday as she went up the stairs. Boiled dinner . . . corn beef, turnip, cabbage and potatoes, all bubbling away on the stove. Not one of her favourite nights but she preferred it to Thursdays which meant canned sauerkraut and franks. Anyway, tonight she knew she wouldn't taste a thing.

'Saw the Towski boy is home,' Bridget said. 'Wonder what brings him back.'

'He was wounded,' Maureen said. 'Mrs Towski was in the shop the other day. She's real worried about him.'

'The Polacks are always worried about something. Waterworks behind their eyes. Looked the very picture of health to me. Saw him from the window on the way into the store.'

'Really?' Maureen turned to Kathleen. 'How is the boy?'

He's wonderful – he's perfect . . . would her thoughts show, Kathleen wondered as she replied, 'Seemed OK – didn't say much.' She wished her grandmother didn't see everything. Old ladies were supposed to lose their alertness. This one only got sharper it seemed.

'Mrs Towski said that's the way he's been since he got home. Shock, I suppose. Nearly got blown up, poor boy. That's something he'll never get over.'

'Give him an excuse to take to the bottle like his father,' the old lady muttered. 'Probably has already. Those Pollacks start young.'

'Have some more, Larry?' Maureen was standing the instant she saw her husband's empty plate.

Kathleen had to think of something. Some excuse to get out. Who could she trust? Mary wasn't any good – nor Patricia. Both their mothers came in nearly every day. Much too risky that something would drop. Paula; that was it. Her mother only spoke Italian, or so little English it made no difference. There would be no chat over the counter about Kathleen. It had to sound unimportant so as not to arouse suspicion.

'Thought I'd go over to Paula's if that's OK.' She said it very normally although her heart was racing. She hadn't much practice lying. She had never felt the need before.

'What about your homework?' her father looked up from his re-filled plate.

'Did that. Had a free period today.'

'Don't be late.'

'Ah . . . we thought we might take in a movie.'

'On a school night?'

'Oh, Dad, school's nearly over. We've had most of the exams already. Only Latin left and you know how good I am at that. Besides, it is VE Day. We should all be celebrating.'

'We are far from out of the woods yet, my girl. Still got the Japs.'

'But Dad . . .'

'Ten o'clock and not a minute after, mind you.'

'Thanks, Dad,' Kathleen jumped up.

'What about your dessert?' her mother called after her.

'It's jello.'

'No thanks, Mum. I'm full up.'

'Too much freedom, nowadays,' Bridget muttered. 'Too much altogether.'

Why did she have to look so awful? Kathleen stared into the mirror. If only she were allowed to wear make-up. Even a little lipstick would help. But her parents were adamant. She'd changed into her pink dress. Second best. If she had put on her new black check they might get suspicious. It was warm. She threw her pink sweater over her shoulders and grabbed her white shoulder bag. She combed her hair once again and decided it was a hopeless cause.

'Bye,' she called nonchalantly, as she passed the kitchen and hurried down the stairs, not waiting for a reply. They might just change their minds. She could hear her mother clattering the dishes as she worked at the sink but refused to let guilt slow her pace.

Paula had been a clever choice, not only because of her mother but also because they had no phone and their house was on the way to the trolley stop. They lived in the middle of a triple decker. Kathleen didn't stop to press the bell. She just bounded up the stairs and banged on the door. Paula's brother Tony answered it. He was a year older and scowled at her.

'She's in there,' he gestured towards the room Paula shared with her little sister.

Kathleen found her friend curled up on the bed with a book. When she spoke Paula started and shoved the book under her pillow.

'Oh ho,' Kathleen laughed as Paula blushed, 'and what are we hiding away?' She reached under the pillow.

'Get off – it's nothing.'

'Why so nervous, then?' she persisted and dragged the book out. It was Tolstoy's *Anna Karenina*. 'Oh, really Paula, I was expecting *Forever Amber* at least.'

'They've made me return it to the library three times already. I'm determined to finish it this time, no matter what.'

'She throws herself under a train.'

'I know that. It's all the stuff in between. Hey, how come you're all dressed up? And looking like the cat that got the canary?'

'Am I?' Kathleen turned to look at herself in Paula's mirror. Holy cards were stuck all around the frame: The Sacred Heart; both St Francises – the one with the birds and the one with the skull – St Anthony – which reminded her – 'Why's big brother so glum? He even forgot to be rude.'

'He's mad 'cause he's missed the war.'

'What a stupid thing to be mad about.'

'Yeh, that's what we've been saying, but that just makes him madder.'

'Anyway, there is still the Pacific.'

'He says with his luck he'll miss that too. Anyway . . . What do you want to do? Play gin – go for a walk?'

'Paula,' Kathleen interrupted, 'I need a favour.'

'What favour?'

'I've . . . got something to do. And . . . I was wondering, just in case it came up, which it won't, but if anyone should ask – like my mother, or anyone – which they wouldn't, if you could kind of say I was with you.'

'What are you talking about?'

Kathleen wished she could just come out with it. It would be a whole lot easier. But she couldn't tell Paula. He probably wouldn't even be there, and she'd feel such a fool if anyone, even Paula, maybe especially Paula, knew. There would be no end to the teasing.

'It's a secret,' she said. 'I'll tell you sometime, but I've really got to go now. I've been with you all evening, OK?'

Paula looked uncertain, but she agreed. 'OK,' she repeated, actually pleased to be able to get back to her book. It was only a matter of time before someone found it again. There was no such thing as privacy in the house. 'But you had better tell me soon. It's a feller, isn't it?'

Kathleen slipped out quietly so no one would hear her going.

She waited on the concrete island, pacing its length, staring down the tracks. Would the trolley never come? Would it be faster to walk? It was only a twenty minute walk, and if she hurried she could do it in less. She had nearly decided to set off when she heard the vibrations and, peering, she could see the trolley approaching. The doors opened with a clatter and she jumped aboard throwing her dime in the top of the glass fare box, watching it sink through the slot and register with a ping.

'Transfer?' the driver asked as she continued to stand there.

She shook her head and sat on the wooden seat behind him. She looked around carefully. One man in a black suit and a youngish couple. No one she knew. It was going to be all right. But as she neared Harvard Square all kinds of worries began to assail her once more. What if they met someone like Mrs Weston? She often saw Mrs Weston in the Square. Then what about Daniel? What was she going to say to him? She could think of nothing. All those conversations she had imagined as she lay in bed, what had they been about? Maybe one of them would do. But they had evaporated. Nothing. Her mind was just a maelstrom of unconnected rubbish – fear – guilt – half thoughts whirling around and out again. Not a single one settled long enough to be examined or even recognized. Except the short one that persisted. *He won't be there.*

By the time the trolley pulled into the tunnel she was hoping that was the truth. It would solve all the other problems. She couldn't keep herself from running up the escalator, though.

As usual, Harvard Square was alive with people. It always seemed that way, day or night. This evening there were small groups of people in what looked like quiet celebration, but they were like the groups on any other evening. Bicycles, their baskets full of books, were being pedalled in all directions with a disregard for both pedestrians and cars. Albiani's Cafeteria was bright and as usual about three quarters full. It was a mystery. It always seemed to contain the same number of people. She had never seen it full and she had never seen it empty.

Next to Albiani's was the University Theatre. It was much grander than the one in Davis Square. Kathleen remembered the first time she had been there and watched her black patent Mary Jane shoes virtually disappear into the carpet. The seats were red and soft as velvet and she especially liked the ladies' room which was at the top of the stairs that led to the balcony. It was a large room with a thick gold carpet and print curtains that curled around the windows, held back with huge gold ropes that had tassels on the end. There were big, soft armchairs and a gold chaise-longue with a fringe around the edge and three dressing tables, each with a triple mirror so that by moving your head just the tiniest bit you could see yourself from all angles. No one she knew had a dressing table. In fact, she had never seen one before she came here. She hadn't been able to understand what these funny tables with mirrors were for until she had seen them in the movies. When she was little and found the movie boring, or while the newsreel was on, Kathleen would disappear to the ladies' room, perch on one of the round stools and examine her face from every side. Or she would lounge on the golden couch and pretend she was in her boudoir. Sometimes she would be Ginger Rogers preparing for her prance down the carpeted staircase, at other times she was Bette Davis, dreading the confrontation she knew she would face as soon as she left the safety of this private place. It was, to Kathleen, a magical room and she resented ever having to share it with anyone. But most of the women who came in simply walked through, not even seeming to notice the luxury, and went into the white tiled room adjacent, with its prosaic row of cubicles and wash basins.

Kathleen looked up at the marquee – there on the side of the canopy that faced her she read:

62

JEANNE CRAIN
DANA ANDREW
IN
STATE FAIR

And under the canopy? There was Daniel, watching her approach. She tried to keep her pace normal, neither quickening her step nor slowing it. But she couldn't keep an enormous grin from spreading.

'I must look like a lunatic,' she thought. But his responding smile mirrored hers, she noticed – and he still looked wonderful.

'Hello,' he said.

She found when she tried to greet him she was breathless, so she just kept smiling.

'I've got the tickets.' He held them between his thumb and forefinger near her face as if inviting inspection. At the candy counter she chose a Bolster Bar and he a Babe Ruth. An usher showed them to their seats, shining her torch in front of them down the aisle. They were in the middle of the orchestra section – the reserved section. Kathleen had never sat in the reserved section before and she found the seats, the rows of which were roped off from the others by velvet cords as thick as a baby's fist, were wider and even plusher than those she usually sat in.

A black and white film was just ending with a shot of Big Ben. She hadn't noticed what it was. Then it was the bright and noisy *Looney Tunes*. As usual Porky Pig chased Bugs Bunny around with a shotgun.

Daniel was restless. By the time Jeanne Crain was sitting on the swing singing 'I'm as dizzy as a spider spinning daydreams' he could bear it no longer. There was so little time and he didn't want to spend it watching actors falling in love. He put his face close to Kathleen's and whispered, 'Let's go.'

She hadn't really been watching the film. She hadn't really been thinking. She was just sitting there, sitting next to Daniel. She raised no objection when he took her hand and led her up the darkened aisle and out into the bright lobby. He still held her hand when there was no need to guide her and they continued out into the darkness.

'Let's walk,' he said.

'Fine,' she said and then added shyly, 'I have to be home by ten o'clock.'

He didn't try to hide his disappointment. 'Well, then we'll just walk in that direction – slowly.'

'You know,' she said, 'I'm really glad you're all right.'

'So am I,' he said, 'now.'

'Was it awful?'

Daniel didn't want to talk about it. And now he didn't want to go back to it.

'Let's walk through the Yard,' he said.

Larry, Maureen and Bridget sat in the dining room – a room mostly occupied by a huge Victorian mahogany table Bridget had brought from her house. It was covered with an Irish point-lace cloth and that was covered with a clear plastic sheet. A large glass vase in the centre held a bouquet of assorted paper flowers. The room was seldom used for eating as that happened in the kitchen, except on Thanksgiving Day.

Larry was checking over orders in his stock book, Maureen crocheting a multicoloured lace edge around a linen handkerchief and Bridget working on her woollen squares. The radio in the corner was on. They were listening to *Duffy's Tavern – where the elite meet to eat.*

'Kathleen didn't get much inventory done this afternoon,' Larry raised his head from his papers.

'I'll help you out tomorrow,' Maureen said.

Bridget shushed them both and leaning over the arm of her chair, pointedly turned up the volume on the radio.

Maureen wished Larry didn't insist Kathleen help out so much in the store. In fact, she hated to see her daughter in there at all. She had such hopes for the girl and working in a corner grocery store wasn't one of them. Kathleen was bright – really bright. And Maureen was determined she was going to college. She hadn't mentioned it. She knew what her mother would say. After all, she herself had had to struggle to be allowed to finish high school. Bridget had said education was a waste of time. She still said it at every opportunity. They never taught you anything you could use. Michael had been apprenticed to a plumber when he was fourteen and Elizabeth sent to work in a house in Brattle Street at the same age. It was different with Bill – being a priest was something special.

'You know how to read and write and add up. What else is there to learn? School's a place for those too rich or lazy to work,' was one of Bridget's favourite sayings. 'And none of mine is rich or idle,' she would conclude.

Maureen didn't know if Larry agreed with this or not. He'd never said. He hadn't complained about Kathleen's studying, although he did mutter that French was a waste of time and what was she doing studying biology? Maureen hadn't asked him about college for their daughter. What was the point in facing something until it existed?

'Wouldn't mind a cup of tea,' Bridget said without glancing up.

Maureen knew an order when she heard one.

'I'll put the kettle on,' she said, folding up her handkerchief and putting it and the ball of cotton into a paper bag. She put this into the big pocket of her apron. It seemed now she only took her apron off to go to church or to go to bed. They had even stopped going to the movies. Larry agreed with Bridget that they were all rubbish now and Maureen didn't want to go alone. Kathleen always went with her friends. Maureen wished sometimes that she and Kathleen could go out together. But she didn't want to intrude. Kathleen would have her own life without her mother interfering. That was something to look forward to. But hard as she tried Maureen couldn't imagine the future. It was something to come – something with a rosy glow.

She made the tea and put a cookie in each saucer. They

drank it in silence. Then Bridget stuck her crochet hook in her ball of wool and snapped the radio off.

'Bedtime,' she announced, handing her empty cup back to Maureen before putting her hands flat on the chair and pushing herself up.

'The girl's not in yet,' Larry said.

'It's only half past nine, Larry. You did say ten o'clock,' Maureen said.

'If she's a minute late she'll hear it from me.' He was tired and wanted to go to bed. He didn't want to sit around waiting for her. 'Besides, I didn't mean she had to stay out so late and she knew that.'

'Too much freedom, too much altogether,' Bridget said. 'I never let my young go gallivanting at night.'

Maureen knew she was the only one who was still at home when she was Kathleen's age. The others had escaped. But she wouldn't argue. 'You go to bed. I'll do the dishes and lock up.'

'And no covering up if she is late,' Larry said.

'The girl runs rings around you – both of you,' Bridget had the last word.

Maureen knew Larry would fall asleep immediately. He always did. But her mother would lie there, one eye on the clock listening carefully for Kathleen's return.

Maureen sighed with relief when she heard Kathleen's steps coming up the stairs. She looked at the clock – it was five minutes to ten. At least there would not be a scene at breakfast.

'Have a good time, dear?' she asked.

Kathleen was flushed. 'Absolutely terrific,' she said. 'The most wonderful time. Good night, Mummy.' She kissed her mother on the cheek and sailed into her room.

It was then that Maureen began to worry. The girl had not been to the movies with Paula.

4

Kathleen lay on her bed and tried to justify the deception. It wasn't her fault if her parents were unreasonable. It couldn't be culpable if she were forced into a situation where she had to lie. Surely it was better not to cause friction than to be absolutely truthful. None of her philosophising, however, drove away the real reason she couldn't tell her parents. She was scared. Of what, she wasn't exactly sure. It wasn't as if they would hit her. They had never been physically violent – although that might be easier to take than the subtler pressures they applied. Grandma had occasionally lashed out in a fit of temper but that was when Kathleen was little. It was the shouting from Daddy and the sulking from Mummy, and then the days of tension that followed any misdemeanour that she couldn't bear. The atmosphere heavy with her guilt and their disapproval. Anyway, if she was exquisitely careful they would never know. And she would be careful. She shoved the guilt to a corner of her mind and concentrated on the good bit – on Daniel.

Daniel had kissed her three times. The first time it had been almost a surprise – under a tree in the Harvard Yard. They were walking slowly, not saying anything. She didn't even feel the need to break the silence. It wasn't uncomfortable at all. Then he had stopped, or rather they had both stopped walking at the same time. It just seemed to happen. She turned to look at him. He simply put his hands on her shoulders and, leaning down, kissed her, so gently on the lips. She didn't know why her eyes filled with tears, but it was she who put her arms around his back and drew him close, holding him as tightly as she could, his chest pillowing her head. After a while they continued to walk, this time closer together, his arm around her shoulders, her arm around his waist. He said he wanted to be with her all the time – all the time there was left. And she agreed. She didn't mention school. That wasn't important. There were only a few days left before he had to go back.

Kathleen heard her mother pass her door and go into the next room – her parents' bedroom.

'Is she home?' she heard her father ask.

'Five minutes early,' her mother replied.

Kathleen thought how she wished she didn't have to lie to them – but it wasn't her fault. They could never understand. Then she realized her watch must be wrong. She wouldn't have wasted those five minutes if she had realized they existed. Daniel had been so desolate when she left him and rushed up the back stairs.

The next morning, after the usual silent breakfast, the dropped eggs on toast, Kathleen gathered her books together in the green school bag. She was excited but convinced she was behaving perfectly normally. She took her brown paper bag, sandwiches and an apple from the growling refrigerator and prepared to leave at the usual time.

'I'll be late home today,' she said it nonchalantly. 'French Club.'

'OK, darling,' Maureen said, still wondering about her daughter's breathless glow.

'What's this nonsense?' her father asked.

Kathleen turned to her mother for help.

'French Club, dear,' Maureen said. 'You know, Kathleen's been doing it for two years now. It helps with her pronunciation.'

'What about stock taking?'

'I told you I would help.'

It was seven-thirty – time to go. Kathleen knew she must

do everything as usual. Catch the bus in five minutes. She was a regular on it and the neighbours might notice her absence. She would get off at her usual stop, near the school, but then it was only a short walk to the river where she had said she would meet Daniel. She would be there at eight-thirty at the latest. School finished at two-thirty, but allowing an hour and a bit for the fictitious French Club meeting they wouldn't expect her home until after four o'clock. Nearly eight hours. She didn't even mind being in the shapeless school uniform. She knew now that Daniel wouldn't care.

'I still don't understand why it has all got to be so secret,' Daniel said. He was lying on the grass of the riverbank.

'Keep still,' Kathleen said. She was kneeling over him, sketching him.

'I've been still for hours.'

'It's only been a few minutes.'

'Seems like hours.' He sat up quickly, and grabbing her, pulled her down to kiss her. 'Ouch,' the spiral on her sketch book dug into his chest. He threw it to one side and held her close. 'So,' he whispered, 'why are you ashamed of me?'

She pulled back. Surely he couldn't think that. She was so proud. She wanted to shout and show him off . . . Look – at last, Daniel! She had been in love with him for eight years – confident that one day he would love her, too. It was, she always knew, ordained by God.

'It's my parents,' Kathleen said, 'they wouldn't understand.'

'Why should they have to?' Daniel asked. There was a time for parents and time not for parents. 'Let's get married,' he said. He wanted her there. He wanted a reason to stay alive.

'Impossible,' she said, laughing, thinking he was teasing her. 'I haven't a thing to wear.'

'I mean it, Kathy. Let's get married – now. Don't you love me?' He said it in a little boy, hurt voice – but he dreaded the answer.

'Daniel, I've always loved you. You know that. For as long as I can remember I've loved you. It was you who never saw me.'

'And now you want to punish me for being an unobservant twelve-year-old, I suppose.'

'No. Better late than never.'

'Then let's get married.'

'Oh, if only we could.' She snuggled down on top of him. It was what she had always wanted.

'Why not?'

'For a start I'm fifteen.'

'So?'

'I don't think it's legal.'

'Only in stuffy old Boston. We could go now; into town and catch a Greyhound to one of those civilized Southern states where fifteen is a perfectly respectable age.'

Kathleen tried to imagine it – it was all happening too fast. Fast? She had only been dreaming it for years. But the dreams were different. In them the wedding was always in church. The other details were hazy but she and Daniel were at the altar and she only ever saw his eyes, looking into hers when they said, 'I will.' She thought about the bus trip. Could he really be serious? In her school uniform, for heaven's sake? And then there would be the justice of the peace. She had seen it all in the movies. The couple knock on the door in the middle of the night and an old man comes to answer it in his wool plaid bathrobe demanding to know what is going on. He then turns all coy at the sight of the young couple, so much in love, who beg him to marry them right away. His wife, her hair in curlers under a net, plays the piano and everyone has an idiotic smile on his face. But that wasn't being really married. Where was the sacrament? Where was God in all that? Kathleen wanted to marry Daniel but she wanted to do it properly. Maybe if he were able to stay with her; maybe if he weren't going away, she could manage to be married in that peculiar way. But alone, by herself, with her parents horrified and his mother horrified? No she couldn't do that. She tried to explain it to Daniel.

'But if I weren't going away there wouldn't be any great rush,' he said logically.

'You'll be back soon. The Japs will have to give up. And then we'll have all the time in the world. We can do it properly. Where will we live? What will we do? How many babies will we have?'

Daniel remembered the beach and the bodies and the blood. He had to be sure. 'It's not good enough,' he said. 'Plans are not enough.'

'Don't you believe me?'

'I don't think I believe anything.'

Kathleen had not seen before the terrible agony he was in. And she knew it wasn't enough to kiss it better. Long term plans would not be enough to heal the terrible wounds. There would have to be short term ones – and compromises.

The next morning Kathleen didn't even bother with pretence. She used the simple expedient of sneaking out of the house before anyone saw her, having hidden her school books and uniform under the bed so no one would know she was unencumbered by them. She also left a note on her bed.

'Gone to early morning mass – will be late tonight, don't worry, Kathleen.'

Maureen did not show the note to Larry and she was worried. It wasn't like Kathleen to be so secretive. What was going on?

Seven o'clock mass at St Catherine's was always very quick. Never more than half a dozen people were in attendance. In fact, the priest, who went through the ritual alone, without altar boys, never even bothered to turn on the lights for the tiny congregation. Kathleen had always liked the cosy womblike darkness and then the altar bathed in what could pass for a spiritual glow. She and the handful of people were anonymous – she liked that, too, especially this morning.

'*Agnus Dei, qui tollis peccata mundi, miserere nobis.*' How could she possibly pray for forgiveness in advance? When the priest turned to face them, holding the ciborium in one hand and a small white host above it, and said, '*Corpus Christi*' Kathleen rose automatically to go to the altar rail. Then she remembered, hesitated and knelt down again. She couldn't receive communion. She had planned to sin; was still planning to. That in itself was a sin. She had already willed it. But something might happen. She might change her mind. Something might prevent it. No. None of that mattered. Even if she were run down by a bus as she left the church the deed was as good as done. What mattered was the willing. There would be no joy in her sin – that didn't matter either. She would give her life for Daniel. She hadn't realized that she would give her soul. Since she was seven, since that fateful day when she saw Daniel at her First Communion, Kathleen had not been to mass and not received communion. She was glad of the darkness. As the others returned from the altar rail they couldn't see the girl kneeling at the end of the eighth pew, under the stained glass window of the Sacred Heart crying.

Daniel had chosen the Hotel Manger by the North Station. He had even brought his duffle bag. Kathleen tried to look inconspicuous as he registered, but she shifted from foot to foot and her hands, unbidden, kept straightening her collar or twirling her buttons. Their room was on the third floor and looked out over the elevated railway which rattled past every fourteen minutes. Daniel pulled the shade down.

'I do love you very much, Kathy,' he said, 'and I need you to be my wife – not after the war is over. I need you now.'

Kathleen was crying again. This dingy room had never been in any of her dreams. But she looked up at Daniel and shut out everything else. 'I love you. And I am your wife.' She smiled but her hand was still nervously fidgeting with the buttons on her blouse.

'Here,' Daniel came closer, 'let me do that.'

She noticed his hands were shaking too.

It was nearly two o'clock the next morning when Daniel and Kathleen kissed goodbye for the last time. He was leaving for the base.

'Let me come in with you,' he had insisted as they stood outside her house. 'I don't want you to be alone.'

'No.' Kathleen was sure. 'I'll be all right.' She felt now she could face anything – except being without him. Everything else was incidental and couldn't touch her.

'I'll write whenever I can – but you know it's difficult,' he said. 'And don't worry, I'll be back soon. You can start planning that proper wedding you want. That will keep you busy.' His lips were on her eyes, her ears, her neck. She held him as tightly as she could and breathed him in.

'If only you could put me in your pocket and take me with you,' she said.

'Goodbye, darling. You will be with me, I promise.' He gave her a final chaste peck on the nose and pushed her away from him with both hands. 'Now go, before we both start crying again.'

She stood still, at his arm's length from him.

'Go – there's a good girl. Do as you're told,' he turned her around and kissed the back of her head. 'Go . . . darling,' he whispered.

He watched as she walked up the stairs. She stopped at the top and waved and then went into the house. As Daniel turned to walk away he didn't even bother to wipe away the tears that blurred the streetlights, then ran down his face. Now that he had a reason to live he was frightened of going back.

Maureen was sitting at the kitchen table, an empty cup in front of her as Kathleen came through the door. She had been sitting there for four hours, wondering if she

73

would ever see her daughter again. She had worked her way through hurt, anger, resentment and fear. Kathleen's presence brought relief. She looked at her daughter and despite her tear-streaked face she thought she had never looked more beautiful.

'I don't suppose you're going to tell me,' she said softly.

'No, Mummy. I'm sorry. I can't.'

'Well, go to bed quietly. You don't want to wake your father or Gran.' Maureen ached to share whatever it was that Kathleen was feeling but she knew that was impossible. The one thing she had learned was that each person was alone in life – in an isolated solitary confinement. All one could hope for was that the walls were padded when life banged your head against them.

'Good night, Mummy. Thanks.'

When Maureen took her cup and saucer to the sink she pulled the window blind up. Down the street she saw a man, carrying a duffle bag. The man turned, stared back at the house for a moment and then head down, continued to walk away.

Daniel was lying on his bunk, writing a letter to Kathleen. He had written every day since he left her – first from San Diego and then after, when he was shuttled up to San Francisco. He hadn't mailed any of them. There was no point really. They were like a diary and the censors would have obliterated all the details – all those black lines drawn through 'sensitive' material, like where he was – then photographed and diminished to the 'V' form you needed a magnifying glass to read. It took weeks before they were actually dispatched and in weeks, he reasoned, the war would be over. That was one excuse. The other was he didn't relish the idea of anyone else reading them. The bits they wouldn't censor were just too personal. He could visualize a sarcastic voice in an office someplace calling out, 'Hey guys, listen to this – must be *some* broad.'

The war would soon be over – he was sure of that. What he didn't know was that he was one of 1,996 men on board the *Indianapolis* who would contribute to the hastening of the end. He had joined the ship at San Francisco just before she sailed on July 16th – her secret cargo, the atomic bomb. They had made their delivery at Guam. The gossip on board was that it was a very important delivery and they were now once more afloat on the Indian Ocean. Also according to the gossip they were heading home. He would give Kathleen all the letters then, to prove that she had never been out of his thoughts. But he knew she wouldn't doubt him. Kathleen was an extraordinary girl. She had told him about that day she had seen him on the altar – about her First Communion. He had laughed. But maybe she was right. Maybe there was something called destiny.

It had barely passed midnight when Daniel was flung from his bunk with enormous force. Warm sea water gushed in as the alarms sounded. The rest was all confusion – screams, cries.

He was in the water for a long, long time. Then he was in a boat – a small boat. Sun. Heat. Bodies in a blood stained sea. Sharks circled. The thirst, the burns, the crying, the screaming. Was that his voice or someone else's? It was four days before the three hundred and sixteen survivors, if they could be called that, were spotted.

On that same day, when the *Indianapolis* was hit, Kathleen decided she could pretend no longer. She was pregnant. She told herself not to worry, the war would finish any day and Daniel would be back. It would be all right. Pregnancy, despite the circumstances, brought a kind of euphoria. It would be more than all right. It would be wonderful.

First the bomb fell on Hiroshima and then Nagasaki. The following day Mrs Towski received a telegram informing her that her son Daniel was missing in action, presumed dead. She made herself a cup of tea and sat silently at the kitchen table drinking it. She washed the cup and saucer, dried them and stacked them neatly in the cupboard. She took her son's basketball awards from the shelf in the front room, polished them and replaced them, shining, on display. Then she put her head in the gas oven.

Mrs Weston, with the help of Father Flynn, quickly organized the funeral. There was no one else, and Mrs Weston liked to be helpful. She was practically a next door neighbour, though she had seen little of the Polish woman.

It wasn't a suicide, Father Flynn decreed. The poor woman was so sick with grief she didn't know what she was doing. Still, Bridget declared it a disgrace . . . a funeral mass for someone who was damned to Hell.

'Sure anyone can kill themselves,' she declared. 'Don't you think I thought about it myself many's the time. The troubles I've seen, been through. But it is a sin against Almighty God. Like spitting in His Face. Sure haven't we all lost a child? Me more than most. What else is life, but a vale of sorrow?' She boycotted the funeral.

Kathleen had been in a stunned silence since she had heard the news. It came, of course, from Mrs Weston in the store. Kathleen and her father were unloading some cases of beans and speculating about how life would change now that things would be getting back to normal.

'But this has always been normal for me,' Kathleen explained. 'There has always been a war.'

Her father laughed. He was pleased with his daughter again. The last few months she had been the cheery little soul he loved desperately. No more of that nonsense about going out at night. That had worried him; but it had been brief. She was her old self again, though he had to admit that she wasn't a little girl any more. She was a beautiful woman, suddenly with a kind of glow about her.

'Good morning, Mr Thornton, Kathleen,' Mrs Weston interrupted them.

'Good morning, Mrs Weston.' Larry stood to attention wondering what exotic request she was about to inflict on him. 'What can I get you?'

'It's for tomorrow, really. I want to be sure you'll have

everything. I'll need three, no, you'd better make it four, loaves of bread, some sliced ham, cheese and a few tins of tuna fish. Then, oh let me see, it is so difficult, isn't it, when you don't know how many you'll be catering for . . .' Mrs Weston dithered uncharacteristically.

'Having a party, are you?' Larry played at being the jovial shopkeeper. 'What's the occasion? Or is it a secret?'

'I wouldn't call it a party. Oh dear, haven't you heard . . .' The rest of the words echoed around the shop and landed on Kathleen like a blow. 'It's for Mrs Towski's wake. It's only going to be one night. I mean she had no one. But I thought the neighbours should be able to pay their respects, even though she had no real friends. Poor soul, she kept herself to herself. I tried to be friendly, mind you, living so close, but she always . . . oh but that's all behind us now. Of course, mind you, if someone had been with her when she got the news, things might have been different.'

Kathleen froze, her back to Mrs Weston, as her father interrupted. 'I'm afraid I don't understand. What happened?'

'Of course,' Mrs Weston continued, 'they shouldn't send a telegram like that out of the blue. Although I suppose it is all they can do when you think of the numbers they have to deal with. Hundreds and thousands killed in a few years, my husband tells me. He knows about these things.'

'Mrs Weston,' Kathleen turned slowly towards her, her face was ashen as she anticipated the answer to the question she had to ask before the woman babbled on any more, 'Mrs Weston, has something happened to Daniel?'

'Of course, you knew him, didn't you? My Patricia told me she saw you together in Harvard Square one night. I'd quite forgotten that. Yes, dear. I'm afraid he was killed in action. That's why she became so distraught. After all, he was all she had.'

'Killed?' Kathleen said it quietly.

'Well, they said missing – and we all know what that

77

means, don't we? – just means they couldn't find the body.'

Mrs Weston continued her monologue as Kathleen slumped against the counter. Larry reached for her but she regained her composure. 'I'm all right, Daddy,' she said. 'Just suddenly a little dizzy.'

'It'll be that summer flu that is going around. Patricia was in bed for two days with it. I thought you looked a bit pale. That girl should be in bed, Mr Thornton. Never get better trying to fight it. Just give in, that's what I say. Then it's over with quicker. Now, do you think four loaves of bread will be enough?'

Kathleen did not protest when her mother tucked her up in bed. She lay there, neither rejecting nor fully accepting Maureen's ministrations. She knew she didn't deserve kindness. To eat was out of the question. Her mouth was dry and she felt constantly in danger of choking, but she sipped the milky tea her mother brought her. Larry made anxious forays to her bedside.

'I can't understand it,' she heard him tell Maureen. 'It came on her so quickly. She was right as rain, blooming really, and then suddenly she just collapsed. Maybe she ought to see a doctor.'

It was the word blooming that stuck in Maureen's mind. She too had thought how wonderful her daughter was looking in the past weeks. Her skin glowed, her eyes were bright. She seemed so happy and somehow more than that. She seemed womanly. Then, unbidden, Maureen's mind went back to that uncharacteristic, mysterious behaviour in May – those three days that had so frightened her. The image of the young man standing desolate under the street light came back to her. And now, there was Kathleen's sudden collapse when Daniel Towski's death was announced so casually by Mrs Weston. All these things added up in Maureen's mind and she prayed her sum was wrong. Kathleen was a child still. She had so much ahead of her.

'Please, God, don't let it be true,' she prayed and put

78

on a reassuring smile as she brought her daughter another cup of tea.

Kathleen lay in bed, staring at the rosebud walls and began to think it had all been a fantasy. Just one of the many fantasies that had occupied her since, as a seven-year-old child, she had fallen in love with Daniel. None of it was true. He hadn't come into the store; he hadn't kissed her; he hadn't made love to her. It was a dream. It had to be a dream. But at the same time she knew that although she could have conjured up in her imagination the day by the river when they laughed and held each other and made plans for the future she could never have invented that hotel room, the trains passing the window. Her dream would have been totally beautiful, and slightly blurred around the edges. She could not have imagined the intensity of the reality nor the ugliness of that room. It was real all right. It had happened and now she was going to have a baby. She was going to have Daniel's baby and Daniel was dead. There were fleeting moments during those days that she lay in bed when she was glad she was pregnant. Maybe, she thought, that had been God's plan. There would be something of Daniel in the world. But then she knew that was wrong. Daniel's death was the punishment for their sin. She wanted to run and hide – but where could she go? What could she do? She didn't want to be a grown-up. She didn't want to be a mother.

Kathleen began to cry – softly at first, silently. Then the sobs grew louder and louder. Her whole body rocked and heaved in torment. Maureen heard the terrible sounds of agony and despair and rushed to her daughter. She tried to hold her, to cuddle her, but Kathleen fought free of her mother's arms. Finally, exhausted she lay still, the sobs subsiding into little painful hiccups, and allowed herself to be held. Maureen stroked her daughter's hair, murmuring softly, sounds more than words. She cooed gently. 'Tell me,' she said, knowing what she was about to hear and dreading it.

The story tumbled out of Kathleen in fits and starts and

all the time Maureen held her, rocking her gently. All the dreams she had had for her daughter splintered in that time as the two clung together in equal despair.

'Shush, now. Try to sleep,' Maureen said. 'We'll manage. We'll all manage together. It's not the end of the world, you know,' but she knew it was, in many ways.

'What will Daddy say?' Kathleen asked, looking at that moment like a very young, very frightened child.

'You let me worry about Daddy.'

Larry said nothing – nothing at all – when his wife told him. He went downstairs to the store and rearranged the canned goods, swapping the vegetable cans for the fruit. Then he put the loaves of bread on a higher shelf and moved the cakes down. He turned next to the freezer section and when he saw the packets of frozen peas, tears began to form in his eyes. He tried unsuccessfully to blink them back. He picked up one of the packets and held it firmly in both hands, squeezing it tightly, remembering the joy he had felt the day his daughter was born. He was glad that his mother was not alive to feel the shame brought on the family by this daughter.

How many sins could she pile up, Kathleen wondered with terror. How long would it be before God struck her down? Her wickedness was inherent and at the same time so obvious. She looked at the sleeping twins. How much more tangible could sin be? Their beauty was testimony to the devil's deception. Gran hadn't spoken to her since her belly swelled. She had spoken aloud in her presence of sin and swore the child would be deformed. Kathleen had believed her. As she grew bigger and bigger she felt she might give birth to a monster. No one had thought of twins. Gran had been wrong about that, although Kathleen knew she hadn't been wrong about her sin.

'Their marks don't show, that's all,' the old woman had said when she was shown the babies, 'but they are marked all right. In their souls.'

Still she smiled over them and cuddled them and poured

out cooing sympathy over their plight. Kathleen couldn't bear it when she touched them. She felt it hard to control her anger when Gran cooed, 'Poor lost souls.'

Maybe, Kathleen thought, she had lost her soul, but her babies were pure and clean. There was only one way they would remain so. She must go away. She must abandon them. They would become her mother's children instead of her grandchildren. That would be an unselfish act, Kathleen told herself, but even as she thought it, she knew she was lying. She had to go away. She had to get away from Gran's eternal disapproval. She had to get away from the sorrow in her parents' eyes whenever they met hers. All their lost dreams and hopes. Well, they could reinvest them in her children and with luck they would have more success the second time around. The odds were better. They would now have two daughters instead of one.

The anger she felt subsided. And the guilt returned. They had given her everything. They had loved her and even through her shame they had been kind. The kindness hurt more than Gran's fury which had been unleashed on them, too, as if it was their fault . . . They had spoiled her, they hadn't been strict enough, she had warned them – Gran would go on and on.

The streetlight outside her window cast shadows on the wallpaper. She remembered lying in the bed, oh, how many years ago, when she was a child and still relatively sinless and loved. She turned the rosebuds on the walls into faces in her mind. Sometimes the faces would frighten her and her mother would come and hold her and tease her tears away. She would do the same with the babies when Kathleen had gone. Although she didn't know where she would go or indeed if she would be strong enough to bear the separation once she had closed the door behind her, Kathleen put some clothes in a bag. Once more she looked at her babies. She couldn't even kiss them goodbye. They might wake up. Then she tip-toed out, closing the door silently. She had left no note. There was nothing to say. She went downstairs and through the shop where she had spent her childhood. She took a cookie from the barrel, not because she was hungry but because it reminded her of how it was when her father's customers had fussed over the pretty little girl rather than eyeing the pregnant schoolgirl with distaste or even worse, with pity. She looked back at the shop and closed the door. The dawn was just beginning and upstairs she heard one of the twins begin to cry. She stopped and listened, once more torn – then walked on slowly and steadily.

That was how, on a very early Wednesday morning in May 1946, Kathleen Thornton, self-acknowledged failed daughter, sixteen-year-old mother of twins and desperate sinner, found herself alone.

Maureen wanted to call the police.

'There has never been a policeman in my house and we are not having one now. She'll be back when she's hungry and if not good riddance to her,' Bridget said.

Larry agreed – although not in so many words. In the past few months he had spoken less and less. He was ashamed, deeply ashamed, of his daughter. He could barely look at the customers when they came into the shop. They were all laughing at him, he knew that. But mainly he knew it was all Maureen's fault. She had a sexual streak in her that his daughter had inherited. And she had spoiled the girl, put ideas into her head. Each month there were fewer and fewer customers. Larry didn't blame the A & P down the street. He blamed Kathleen – the disgrace she had brought down on them. And he blamed his wife. 'She's gone and that's that,' Larry said.

Maureen didn't argue. She was numbed by events. And by the task that now faced her. All those wasted years raising a daughter who would be wonderful, who would have all the things Maureen had always wanted. All that effort for nothing. She looked at the twins. Could she start again? What was the point? Would it work out any better this time?

The physical activity of caring for them by herself occupied her completely – feeding, washing, soothing, airing. Larry said nothing, even when she moved from their double-bed to Kathleen's room. Occasionally the twins cried, but not often because she anticipated all their needs. The only sound in the house was the radio and Bridget's grumbling – she grumbled at the radio, at them, at the world in general. When the first sharp pains of her daughter's defection eased, Maureen began to think that maybe she hadn't failed after all. Kathleen had got away. She was free. Good for her. Maureen's only wish was that she hadn't been lumbered with what was left. She wished she had the courage to go too. But that was impossible – someone had to cope.

Kathleen had not gone very far. She sat by the river where Daniel had asked her to marry him and watched the sun move into the sky. This was not the way she had envisaged it. It made no sense. If God had planned it this way then He had a rotten sense of humour. And if He hadn't, why had she felt so sure He had. Maybe they should have waited. If they had waited maybe Daniel would have come home. She should have been stronger – but he needed her so much. Still, no good blaming God – though she determined not to rely on Him so much in the future. There was no one to blame except herself. That much she agreed with grumbling granny.

Kathleen rejected the lure of the water which had seemed so welcoming when she first arrived at the river's bank and decided she had better set about her own redemption. She had some clothes in her bag and two dollars and sixty-eight cents. That wouldn't last long. With the sun now high in the sky she gathered up her case and crossed the bridge, continuing on into Boston.

By nightfall she had a job and place to sleep. Kathleen was hired as a chambermaid at the Ritz-Carlton Hotel and the tiny cell and cot came with the job. The walls were a dingy green paint. She was thankful she would no longer have to stare at the rosebuds.

🐾 5 🐾

David DeCosta's war had been in Europe. Not in his ancestral Italy but in France and Belgium in the mud. He had written out his nightmares and the play which opened in Boston had been hailed by the critics as the best war play since *Journey's End*. That, however, didn't finish the nightmares. Praise rolled off his back. He didn't feel successful. He had only told the truth. He had thought it would help, but it hadn't.

David knew Boston well. He had been born in the North End and spent his summers playing in the streets with the other boys while their parents moved chairs out on to the pavement and re-created Naples. Italian was his only language until he started school, when he approached English as a foreigner. And he fell in love with it. It didn't have the musicality of the language his parents preferred. It was cooler, quieter, somehow crisper. He refused to go back to the old ways, so communication at home was limited.

He had not been back to his home to stay since the war had mercifully given him the excuse for leaving, and after the fighting there was money to live on in New York while he wrote. It was funny. He had always wanted to write something beautiful and now he was about (maybe) to become a success because he wrote about the ugly, the horrible, the unspeakable. Of course, he told himself he had done it in an acceptable way. That was the miracle, according to S. T. Morton, the critic. He had gone on to say that DeCosta presented the unspeakable in terms that did not repel the audience but at the same time sacrificed none of the truths. He did not prettify nor gloss over the horrors of war; he communicated in terms that made the audience fully aware. He touched hearts as well as minds.

This time he had gone to see his family. They knew success was in the air, but they had neither seen the play nor read the reviews. They had refused the tickets he had offered with a shrug. 'What do we know about the theatre?' His father and brothers had their own construction business. His sister's husband was in it too. And his mother and sister thought only of food and babies, while the men, when not dealing in concrete, played cards and drank wine.

'Here, there is real work for you, when you want it,' his father said. 'Man's work.'

David didn't argue. He couldn't explain. He sat and ate while Fran alternately slapped and hugged her children across the table from him. And Mama hovered at the stove. He had never seen his mother sit at the table for a meal.

'Take the kids out, Fran. We have to talk,' his father said.

David knew what was coming. More of the 'time he was married; time he was a man; family was everything'.

'I've got to go,' he had said. 'A couple of scene changes to rehearse this afternoon. They need me there,' he lied. There were no changes but he knew the talk would end in shouting and tears. Always in the house there was screaming, rage and tears. The scenes blew up like tornadoes and disappeared as quickly. None of them seemed to notice the path of destruction. That was life, they thought – but it wasn't his.

'*Ciao*, Mama; beautiful meal, as always,' he kissed her on the cheek but she drew him close, hugging him to those bosoms he had thought as a child would suffocate him. It was always thus, a suffocating embrace or a slap on the head that set his ears ringing. They were equal expressions of her love.

'You bring your girl to see me, huh,' she said. 'I'll make a nice ragout.'

'Sure, Mama.' He was tired of explaining there was no girl. Mama refused to believe him.

He walked through Scolley Square, avoiding the winos being sick in the gutters, and on to the common. Through that he went into the public gardens where he stood on a bridge and watched the swan boats slowly pedalling around the tiny islands. There were few people about. Soon the boats would be tidied away for the winter. It was September and the leaves were falling. He would soon be back in New York where, Monty the play's producer assured him, he would be the biggest thing on Broadway.

'Believe me, my boy, I know,' Monty had said. 'I could smell it as soon as I read the play – that sweet smell.'

What did it matter? Who cared? He wandered along the neat pathways, kicking at the crisping leaves. He passed a blue-haired lady with a snow-white peke on a lead. She smiled; he smiled back. Then an elderly gentleman with an umbrella smiled at him and again he smiled back. Two gardeners were lifting geraniums from a bed. They smiled; he smiled and nodded. The smile was still set on his face as he passed a girl sitting on a bench, sketching. She looked up and returned his smile and then went back to her concentration.

He stopped. Not just because she was extraordinarily pretty and he was immensely lonely, but there was something . . . he felt foolish but he had to say it.

'Excuse me.'

She looked up again.

He found himself stuttering. 'Excuse me, but don't I . . . I mean, haven't we met?'

She laughed.

He blushed. The oldest line in the book. But he meant it. Here he was, a 'brilliant' writer and that's what he came up with to express himself. There *was* something very familiar about her.

'I'm sorry,' was all he could think to say, but he didn't move on.

'Well, Mr DeCosta,' she said, 'I have been making your bed for a week.'

He was puzzled.

'. . . and vacuuming, and hanging up your clothes as well as . . .'

'In the hotel,' he said. 'That's where I've seen you. I knew I wasn't wrong.'

'I didn't think guests ever noticed the staff . . . only the uniforms.'

'That's why I couldn't place you. The uniform.'

'Well, I don't always dress in black.'

'May I sit down?'

'Of course.'

'What are you drawing?'

'That elm. I always seem to find myself drawing trees. I don't know why.'

'It is good. Very . . . alive.'

'Yes – it is. A whole world to itself really.'

David sat quietly while Kathleen continued her drawing. This was what he wanted. After the turbulence of home, the constant noise of war, it had been good when he got to New York. He had found a studio apartment in the Village and when he shut the door there was perfect peace and quiet. He shut out the cars and the hot dog salesmen. Often the noise from other people's worlds drifted through the walls, or up from the floor or fell from the ceiling but that wasn't to do with him. He could ignore it. But once the production had started the noise became personal once again – producers, directors, actors, publicity; questions, interviews, discussions. Now, here on the bench, it was quiet again. He had never realized it could be quiet with someone. He had thought he would have to be alone.

Kathleen began packing up her sketch pad and pencils into a bag. 'Well, time to go to work,' she said.

'Do you get much time off?' David asked her.

'A fair amount,' she said. 'A couple of hours in the

afternoon and then I finish at ten. It's not a bad job.'

David wondered how she came to be doing it, but only asked, 'How about having supper when you finish?'

'At ten o'clock?'

He smiled. 'We theatricals eat late,' he said.

'And where in Boston do you eat at ten o'clock at night?'

'In the hotel usually. Room service. You can join me. You already know where I am.'

'I think not.' Kathleen got up with a movement which could break glass and moved on down the path. The leaves echoed crossly under her quick step.

David watched her, confused by her reaction. It had been so peaceful and then . . . he realized what she had thought. Oh, God, the master wordsmith had garbled his intentions.

'Hey, wait!' he called after her.

She didn't slow her pace. In fact, if anything it became more determined.

David ran after her and caught up. He walked silently beside her for a bit. The autumn sun caught his face, making him squint uncomfortably.

'I didn't mean . . .' he began slowly.

'I think I know exactly what you meant, Mr DeCosta, and I would like to make it perfectly clear that no matter what you might have heard about chambermaids, I am neither interested nor available for night duty.'

Both the words and her tone slashed into him, stopping him. She walked even faster and he stood watching.

The next morning there was a note on the rumpled pillow:

Dear Chambermaid,

I'm very sorry, but I really meant supper.

An embarrassed playwright

Kathleen smiled and tucked it into her pocket. Perhaps she was becoming overly suspicious, but since taking the job it seemed to be nothing but propositions from bus boys, waiters, window cleaners, travelling salesmen and reception clerks, not even to mention lonely guests. She didn't know what the other girls did. She was too embarrassed to mention it. Maybe it was only her. Maybe everyone recognized 'a girl like that', as Bridget would have put it.

Kathleen didn't see much of the other girls anyway. Conversation was frowned on by the housekeeper as they collected the linen or cleaning supplies and after that each girl worked on her own, had her own rooms and her own bells to answer. They passed in the corridors sometimes with the odd remark on the habits of guests, disgusting or otherwise, but Kathleen had built a protective wall around herself. It wasn't impregnable, at least she hoped it hadn't seemed like that. She thought of it more as a flowering hedge, dense but cheerful. It was merely to protect herself from personal questions. She didn't want to discuss her past. She smiled a lot and thought she was amiable, if not aggressively friendly. But perhaps the hedge was getting just too thick. Perhaps she was turning sour inside it. It was difficult to judge your own actions – and it wasn't a manoeuvre Kathleen attempted often. She had taken all her emotions, all her feelings that morning she had left home, and wrapped them up tightly – liberally sprinkled with metaphoric mothballs and shoved them into the attic until spring came again. But she hadn't even allowed herself to anticipate its arrival. Just concentrate on the job, concentrate on sketching – one day at a time. It was easy. Except at night. Then, waking or sleeping, all the faces were there . . . her mother looking wistful, Bridget fiercely condemning her, the twins sleeping peacefully and Daniel – Daniel was always there. She never cried though. The walls were too thin. Even on the first birthday of her daughters she didn't cry. She longed to see them. To see if maybe they were beginning to look like Daniel. But she remained firm in her decision to give them up – for their good.

Kathleen changed the bed, smoothing the sheets,

humming softly to herself. Then, on the dressing table, as she began dusting she found:

> Dear Chambermaid,
>> Please speak to me.

She laughed aloud when she got to the bathroom and taped up on the mirror was:

> Dear Chambermaid,
>> Three thirty, same bench – pleeeeeeeeese.

David had found it easy to write the notes. It was always easier with a pen and paper than trying to speak – but as he sat on the bench waiting he felt a fool. What could she have thought? She had probably laughed at him and shown the note around as examples of typical male stupidity. Then another thought assailed him. What if someone else had done his room that day? What would she think? He didn't know which was worse, but had convinced himself that the whole episode was a disaster when he saw her coming down the path towards the bench. Was that determined step angry or eager? He couldn't decide. He stood up as she approached, half expecting a maternal slap in the face, prepared to duck, a defensive gesture he had nearly perfected at home.

'I'm glad you came,' David said to her.

'I always come here in the afternoons,' Kathleen said.

'And sketch the same tree?'

'Yup. Always the same tree.'

'Will you come to supper with me tonight? Chinese. Chinatown is open late.'

Kathleen said yes.

Each night after the curtain calls, which never ceased to elicit a standing ovation from Boston's notoriously difficult audiences, David was bursting with new ideas. Everyone, it seemed, was satisfied with the play – everyone except

David. There was always a line he found wrong, a word he wanted to change.

'Leave well alone,' Sebastian, the director, told him that night. 'You've got a hit – never interfere with a hit. I'm happy, the producer is happy, the cast is happy, the audiences are happy and the critics, God bless them, are happy. What more do you want?'

They were standing by the side of the stage and as they talked the actors, now changed into street clothes, bid them good night as they passed, two or three together to return to their hotel rooms, or wander the streets or whatever they did to wind down, David thought. He liked actors, which was just as well, but they made him a little uneasy. He could never tell what they were thinking – and sometimes wondered if they knew themselves.

'Come on,' Sebastian said, 'let me buy you supper and tell you what a genius you are – or even better I'll regale you with tales of theatrical disasters I have known – that will cheer you up.'

David wondered how tales of disasters could possibly cheer him up and then he remembered Kathleen had promised to meet him, to eat with him.

'Thanks,' he said, 'but I'm meeting someone.' He hoped it was true. She might have changed her mind – or never meant to meet him in the first place. Just said yes to shut him up.

'Someone nice, I hope,' Sebastian said.

David blushed. 'Yes, I think so.'

They reached the stage door at the same time as Paul Fredericks. Paul was eighteen and it was his first professional job. He hadn't been in the war; he was too young. He was, however, perfect casting for the second lead. He was the sensitive private who somehow gives all the others the strength to persevere because he is the one who truly understands both the futility and the necessity of it all. The character was himself, David thought – or really the character he would like to have been. All the words that came from Private Edwards' mouth were David's own ideas and thoughts – the majority of them hatched after the event. He had made Private Edwards a WASP and indeed had given him more courage – physical and moral – than David himself had ever been able to muster at the time. He was himself as the playwright wanted to be. He also looked the way David wished he looked. He was very tall, six two or three, whereas David was barely five foot ten. He was fair and his blue eyes flashed an intensity that David's dark brown could only hint at.

'Another wonderful evening,' Paul said. 'You have written the most perfect play.'

'You see,' Sebastian said, 'not only are the actors uncomplaining, they are actually full of praise. Savour it. It's rare.' He bid them good night and went out into the alleyway.

'I meant it,' Paul said. 'The characters are just so real it isn't difficult at all. They just take over.'

'That is thanks to some wonderful performances,' David said, 'including your own. I've been lucky with my cast.'

'I don't think luck has anything to do with it, Mr De-Costa.' They now stood silently outside the stage door for a moment. The single light in the alleyway bathed their faces in a soft glow. David thought Paul looked like an angel. Up ahead they heard Sebastian loudly hailing a taxi and cursing as it sailed passed him. The curses broke the spell which had locked them together for a special moment. They laughed and walked slowly in the direction of the curses, catching up with Sebastian at the same time as a cab pulled up to the curb.

'Want a lift?' he asked.

Paul looked at David as if expecting him to make a decision for both of them.

Sebastian saw the look. 'He's busy,' he said. Then he looked at the two of them again. 'At least, that is what he told me.'

'I'm meeting someone back at the hotel,' David said, not noting as Sebastian did, the disappointment on Paul's face. 'I think I'll walk.'

'Come on,' Sebastian said to Paul. 'I'll show you some of the less salubrious sides of this fair city. It is not all beans and cod you know.'

Paul joined him in the taxi as David quickened his pace towards the Ritz-Carlton, wondering if Kathleen would really be waiting and at the same time remembering with a kind of affection the angelic look Paul had taken on in the glow of the streetlamp.

Kathleen was indeed waiting, as she continued to be each night after that. It was with horror that David felt the time slipping past. The end of the Boston run signalled the Broadway first night, and despite constant reassurances, David was terrified. But now there was something else. He needed Kathleen to be with him. Each night as he lay in the hotel bed after they had parted he went back over the supper they had shared. The time they had been together. He could remember nothing they had said. He couldn't remember what they ate – it was just a time of being. He could luxuriate in the great sense of calm that came over him the moment he saw her. He would arrive agitated from the evening's performance. Why could no one understand the need for changes? Why was everyone so damn confident? Was it just that Sebastian recognized it as a failure that no amount of reworking would save? But then there was Kathleen. It wasn't anything she said. It was just her – her presence. Her strength seemed to draw out all his fears and absorb them. She remained an enigma, never talking about herself. But to David the mystery didn't matter. He felt he knew her completely – knew all that mattered. And what mattered was her being there. Her presence was as necessary to his survival as breathing. He couldn't be alone again.

To his relieved astonishment she agreed. She would go to New York with him. He had been so afraid of putting the question to her. Deep inside he felt she knew he needed her – he also felt she accepted that. He felt they belonged together and that she also knew that – but what if he was

93

wrong? Somehow he knew it didn't even need expressing. And moreover, he didn't know how to express it. He had just blurted it out over the chicken chop suey.

'Kathleen – you will come to New York with me, won't you?' It was half question; half statement.

She had looked at him, her eyes wide, not with surprise but with a searching gaze. He felt she was looking into his soul. And what he wondered would she find there? Oh God, he prayed, let her see how necessary she is to me.

'OK,' she said softly, 'why not?'

David, in his relief, started to reach across the table for her hand, but something stopped his movement. He had never touched her. He felt if he did she might evaporate – vanish into some other dimension.

'Do you mean it?' he asked. But he knew she could not be so cruel as to tease him.

'I always mean what I say,' she said. 'And say what I mean.'

The opening night was a Tuesday. On Monday there had been a run through – which did nothing to reassure David, although everyone else connected with the production was serenely confident. Too confident, David thought. It will end in disaster. To take his mind off it, he took Kathleen shopping and bought her a white satin dress for the opening. It was simply cut with tiny pearls embroidered haphazardly, as if she had been caught in a shower of jewels. He hired his tuxedo.

'If the play's a hit, I shall buy one,' he told her.

Monty was throwing a first night party at Sardi's – naturally. David didn't want to go.

'So much depends on me,' David said. 'You know it's not a very good play. It's not right. I should never have allowed it to be produced. It is not ready. In the third scene . . .' he paced the floor, fully dressed, shouting to Kathleen who was still in the bedroom, dressing. 'This will flop. I know it. My name will be mud. I'll never get another chance.'

'Nonsense, David,' Kathleen smiled. 'Look at your Boston reviews.'

'They mean nothing. Boston's . . . well, more academic . . . highbrow. Different. This is Broadway.'

Kathleen appeared in the doorway, her dark hair brushed till it shone, tumbling over her bare shoulders. The vision of her stopped David's prattling. She threw a satin stole around her shoulders and held out her hand.

'Come on, I'll hold your hand all night.'

Tentatively he took her offered hand. It was warm and soft – and very real. He was delighted to see that she didn't vanish.

'Don't worry so,' she said. She wasn't sure where her calm had come from. She still had dreams – but it was as if they belonged to someone else. Someone she used to know. It was all the time as if she were outside her body, watching herself. Since that day in the shop when she had heard that Daniel was not coming back, nothing more terrible could possibly happen to her.

The taxi drove past the Lyceum Theatre where the lights proclaimed:

JUDY HOLLIDAY   PAUL DOUGLAS

Gary Merrill

in

Garson Kanin's

BORN YESTERDAY

'Now *that* is Broadway,' David said. 'That is real Broadway – not gloomy tracts about war and dying.'

Kathleen squeezed his hand. She said nothing.

The curtain fell on *Somewhere in France* to stony silence. Kathleen could feel David freeze beside her. His hand turned to ice. But then applause exploded like a cannon shot. The audience was on its feet. The curtain rose and fell so many times as the cast took its calls that David lost count.

Applause seemed to follow them all the way to Sardi's, the echo ringing in their ears, only to become real again as they made their way through the tables to the section Monty had reserved. The aura of success had come with them and diners rose and applauded as they passed. Strange hands were thrust in front of David and he took them and murmured, 'Thanks.'

'You see, my boy,' Monty clasped him tightly, 'I am never wrong. Two years – two years at least – we will run. Have some champagne.'

David was dizzy enough already. The noise was overwhelming; parades of people congratulated him. Strange faces smiled and invited him to lunch. Monty made a speech. The leading man toasted him. Through it all David managed to eat and drink, reaching out constantly for Kathleen, who smiled and seemed to say the right kind of non-committal things to the strangers. At last the papers arrived.

This is it, David thought, the moment of glory has passed – now for the truth.

But Monty was on his feet again – reading aloud. David heard words like truth, reality, sensitivity and genius. He turned to Kathleen. 'They liked it?' he asked.

Kathleen had spent the evening feeling like one of those actresses in a film she had seen when she was a child. But she couldn't decide which one. Was she the pretty, rather simpering consort who constantly looked into the hero's eyes, laid her head on his square shoulders and told him how wonderful he was? Or was she the strong, power-behind-the-throne figure without whom the hero would disintegrate? Or were they really the same part?

'They adored it, David,' she said. 'Just think – you are a real, grown up successful playwright . . . Enjoy it.'

Paul Fredericks had spent most of the evening floating from one plane of existence to another. His part was so draining that by the time the curtain fell he was exhausted both mentally and physically. Then there was that applause, a wall of applause, strong enough to lean against, reviving and invigorating. It had risen in a massive wave as he had been coaxed forward from the cast line, up to take his solo bow. He knew actors spoke of it as love – love coming across the footlights – but Paul didn't feel it like that. It was more like a crutch, a support, a prop for his inadequacies. It was something on which to lean and feel less alone while he searched for . . . what? That special person who would embody an entire audience? That one person who could give him all the love, the approval he sought now from any and every direction? It was, he knew, a lot to ask. But in the past month he thought he knew where he could find it.

'So that is what jealousy feels like,' Paul thought, as the emotion cut deeply into him when he saw David come into Sardi's with what Paul could only describe as a floosy on his arm. A floosy with a pretty face and a vacant empty smile. 'He deserves a lot better than that,' Paul told himself as he accepted proffered congratulations on his performance and Monty slapped him on the back once more.

'You'll be a star, my boy.' It was part of Monty's litany.

Throughout the evening Paul avoided David and the woman. He did not trust himself to control his feelings. And this was not the right time to betray them.

When the reviews came through Paul once more found himself at the centre of a group of well-wishers, he supposed he could call them fans. The critics praised the play, they praised the production, they praised all the performances, unanimously, and what was more, each and every one of them also singled out Paul Fredericks for a special mention. His name, coupled so successfully and repeatedly with that of the only other person in the large room who mattered to him, gave him the courage he needed, and smiling, acknowledging all the compliments, graciously he made his way across to where he could see David and the woman were preparing to leave.

'So, it is confirmed,' Paul said, interrupting a minked and diamonded woman, whom he took to be a backer, as she congratulated David. She moved her champagne smile on to one of the other actors.

David looked at him quizzically.

'Your genius, it's confirmed by all the noble scribes.'

David laughed. 'And you haven't done so badly yourself, have you now?' He turned to Kathleen. 'Meet Paul Fredericks – rising star in the firmament.'

Kathleen could see that this young man didn't like her. Despite the devastating smile, his eyes were cold as they met hers. 'A wonderful performance,' she said, extending her hand, which the actor seemed not to notice as he said, 'Thank you' and turned his attention back to David.

'So – what's next?' he asked.

'Hey, slow down,' David said. But he was pleased for Paul. The reviews seemed to have given him a new confidence. The diffidence had vanished. He was more man now than boy – at least moving in that direction. 'We've barely got this one off the ground.'

'But it is only the beginning, isn't it?' Paul said. He put his hand on David's shoulder – somewhere between a pat on the shoulder and an embrace. 'Only the beginning.' And then he left them.

David felt bewildered by Paul's intensity – his hand had seemed to burn right through the fabric of his dinner jacket. But then actors were a different breed – and, David thought, this particular actor was special. He didn't know why, but he could feel it as intensely as he could feel the hand still on his shoulder.

'He'll do well, won't he?' Kathleen said.

'I think so,' David said. 'I hope so.'

'I think,' David said in the morning, as he buttered his toast, 'we can afford a bigger apartment now.'

All the papers were on the table in front of him, folded neatly to the theatrical section. He had read and reread them to make absolutely sure it hadn't all been a wild mistake. 'I'm getting tired of sleeping on the sofa.'

'I knew it would go to your head,' Kathleen said teasingly. 'Were you thinking of Park Avenue, Mr Successful Playwright?'

David blushed. 'Thanks for coming with me. I couldn't have got through last night without you, you know.'

'I don't know about that – but thank you for the trip, and the bed, and the dress and a wonderful night. I'd always wondered what it was like on the inside.'

'And what did you think?'

'Nervy and noisy – but fascinating. I don't think I would care for it every night.'

'Me neither.'

'But, Mr Successful Playwright, you've got dozens of those nights in front of you. You're not planning on being a one play wonder, I hope.'

The phone rang before David could tell her just how frightened he was of that prospect. He felt drained. Would he ever be able to write again?

'Hello,' he answered the phone.

'Dear boy, dear boy.' It was Monty. 'I thought you should know. The lines are forming at the box office – right down the block already. A beautiful sight, my boy – the best sight in the world. Come and see.'

David laughed and thanked him and hung up.

'Monty says we should go and look at the lines at the box office,' he told Kathleen.

'What's the rush? They'll be there for weeks – months even.'

'You're very confident.'

'So are you . . . deep down.'

'No. I don't think so. I'm full of hope, but that's not the same thing – is it?'

'Sort of. Hope is a really good thing to have.' Kathleen controlled her voice which was beginning to shake and was in danger of breaking into tears. It was a danger with which she constantly lived. Every so often the teenaged mother of twins, disgraced and alone, came through the veneer she had learned to assume from all those films she had seen. All those films which taught her how to react and say the right thing. How to dress, how to move. How she would love to have hope. Something to believe in; something to work towards. But there was only getting on. And she should get back to it or her whole life would be this play acting.

David noticed the sadness that came into her eyes. He had seen it momentarily flit across them before but he had never commented on it. He was afraid of a rebuff. But now he asked, 'Kathleen, what is it?'

She shrugged. 'Hereditary depression. The Irish melancholia, don't you know. Just great shrouds of gloom that descend like a fog. Don't worry, they blow away as quickly. Poof, and they are gone – you see?'

'Why are you so determined to be mysterious? You know everything about me – the whole boring life story. And I know nothing about you at all.'

'Nobody ever knows anyone else.' Then she thought about Daniel. 'Well, very occasionally, maybe. But usually all we know are things, moments, events. You've told me the events of your history, but that's not you. If I told you the events of my life that wouldn't be me. They are accidents, that's all, accidents of time and place. If I had been born in ancient Egypt all the events would be different but I'd still be me.'

'Sartre might have something to say about that, but I think it's too early in the day, after all that champagne last night, to argue philosophy. Let's just say I think you're wrong and one day I'll prove it to you. But for the time being let's do something practical to lift the Shannon mist. Like apartment hunting.'

'David,' Kathleen began slowly, 'I . . . have to thank you for introducing me to New York – in a most extravagant way.' Then to hide her shyness her tone turned mocking. 'Imagine me, a simple Irish chambermaid, on the arm of the playwright himself on the first night of a Broadway smash – sure, and sipping champagne with the best of them.' It was a faultless imitation of Bridget's brogue. Then once again she turned serious – it only seemed fair to him. 'Really, David, it has been a kind of a fairy tale, and thank you. But you don't need me to hold your hand any more – if you ever really did – so, I think it's time I was moving on.'

'Moving on to what?'

'Oh, David, I don't know yet. Just getting on.'

'Why can't you stay with me? I'll look after you.'

'I don't want to be looked after. I don't want to be an appendage. And . . . I'm not ready for . . .'

'Hey, hey, hang on. Don't get all excited. What's so awful I've said? Just think. Where will you go? What will you do?'

'I'll get another job. I think maybe I'll stay in New York. That way we can still see each other sometimes. I'll get a job in a hotel again – or in a shop. Wouldn't mind working in Saks.'

'Well, why can't I hire you? What's so awful about working for me?'

'As what?'

'How about personal assistant?'

Kathleen looked dubious. 'I don't know,' she said.

'Look, have I done anything to make you dislike me?'

'No – of course not. You've been too good to be true. Well, maybe a bit jumpy – but otherwise . . .'

'Right then.'

'But we can't go on living like this.'

'That's why I'm suggesting a bigger place.'

'But still . . . living in the same apartment. We can't. It's . . . not done.'

'What are you worrying about? What people will think, is that it?'

Kathleen half nodded.

'What people?' David asked.

'I don't know. It's just . . .'

'Look, Boston . . . New York isn't like that. No one gives a damn. No one even notices. But if you want we'll get married.' He said it jokingly but as he heard it come out of his mouth he realized that that was what he wanted.

'No,' Kathleen screamed with such horror at the idea that David laughed.

'OK, so that's not such a hot idea.' He became serious again. 'Kathleen, you are the first person I've ever met that I felt completely comfortable with. Maybe it's your damn mystery. Maybe it's your . . . serenity. Maybe it's half because you're so good to look at. Maybe it's because you don't frighten me. I don't know what it is. And maybe I am being selfish, but I want you in my life – and close by. All the time. As my very dear friend. Hell, I've just made a success. If I can't share it, what's the point?'

Kathleen thought about it. She didn't quite understand. She knew what he meant about feeling comfortable together. She felt that too, but what about . . . She'd never heard of a man who didn't demand more. According to the nuns that's all they did demand – more. She would have to say it.

'David, what about . . . I don't want you to get the wrong impression – I'm not available for . . .'

'Have I given you any cause to be worried on that score?' David interrupted her. 'Have I once made what you could call an improper suggestion?'

'No.'

'Well, there you are then.'

'But everyone . . .'

'I guess I'm not everyone. Neither are you, it seems. I'm talking about real friendship – not moments of uncontrollable passion.'

'You'll save those for your plays,' she laughed. And the laugh sounded so real he forgot to be afraid of touching her. He put his arms around her, hugged tightly. She found she liked it. It felt warm and snuggly like a blanket on a cold night. She looked at him and smiled. He kissed her lightly, chastely, platonically on the forehead.

'Deal?' he asked.

'Let's give it a whirl,' she agreed. 'Pass me the property pages.'

6

Kathleen loved New York. She loved the skyscrapers and the wide pavements and the elegant apartment blocks that surrounded Central Park. It hadn't seemed strange for a moment. She had seen it all in the movies. When a film began with that shot of the New York skyline and the pizzicato music she had always known immediately she was going to enjoy it. And she always had. It would be peopled by characters who knew exactly what they wanted and got it; who always had a witty remark and made it; and who were always dressed to perfection. And here she was now, living a movie. She particularly liked living in the Village, with its narrow streets that twisted and turned and its corner shops and small subterranean restaurants, it created a cosy setting. David agreed with her and they confined their apartment searches to that area. But the searching dragged on to a full time job. Kathleen insisted that David spend his mornings writing while she did the preliminary leg work. It was discouraging work: everything was too small, or too awkward, or too dingy or just badly laid out. Kathleen wasn't at all sure what she was looking for but she knew she would recognize it when it appeared.

Then, one morning in early December, she found herself standing in front of a wrought iron gate through which she could see a small paved area surrounded by white painted plant pots. Her imagination immediately brought them into a profusion of bloom. The sturdy evergreens provided a subtle background. Straight across the paved area she could see a glass door. She couldn't believe what she was looking at and checked the list the estate agent had given her once more with the number on the gate. It tallied. She searched for the bell and found it hidden beneath the ivy that grew over the stone wall. She pressed it and a voice from beneath the ivy demanded her name. Bemused, she searched again and found the intercom.

'Kathleen Thornton. The Pilger Agency sent me,' she told the metal grate.

'Come on in,' the voice replied and was followed by a buzz and a click that released the gate.

Kathleen pushed it open and went into the garden. It was bigger than it had looked at first, with a table and chairs nestling in a corner. It was a lovely secret garden in the middle of the city.

A blonde woman, dressed in a white silk shirt and black slacks, greeted her at the door. A number of gold chains hung round her neck.

'Just step over the trunks,' she said. 'As you can see, I'm just about packed up. But I'm still able to produce a cup of coffee, if you would like one.'

'That would be nice,' Kathleen said, her eyes darting from one feature of the house to the next. The door led directly into a huge pine panelled room with an enormous fireplace.

'I've already shipped the furniture,' the woman told her, 'and all this,' indicating the trunks and packing cases, 'is going today. Tomorrow I follow, leaving the place in Pilger's hands. I'm not leaving my husband out on the West Coast by himself a day longer than necessary. I know him too well. How do you like your coffee?'

'Black please.'

'Well, have a nose around. I'm in the kitchen with the coffee when you've seen enough.' She pointed to a door.

Through the leaded windows of the room Kathleen could see the garden and the wall beyond but nothing else. Not a single building was visible. It was amazing isolation in Manhattan. She went out into the hall – another door led to a room, also with a view of the garden, which would be a perfect study. Here, too, there was a fireplace, though it was smaller. Open pine steps led from the hall up to the second floor which contained a large bedroom with bathroom attached, another large bedroom and a smaller one and then yet another bathroom. Here, above the trees, the front rooms looked out on to the shops and the back ones on to a little square. But still, she could not hear a sound. It was perfect. She would never have believed such a place could exist.

Kathleen retraced her steps and found her way to the kitchen, trying hard to conceal her enthusiasm. This was exactly what she had been looking for, or would have been if she had conceived of its existence.

'I'm leaving this table and the chairs – and that roll-away cot upstairs,' the woman said. 'Go on – sit down and have your coffee. I know it's not much of a family house. And who wants a house in Manhattan if they haven't got a family? Service apartments, that's what everyone wants – nothing to worry about. Any problems ring the super and let him handle it. But my husband is a romantic, it seems, and he likes his privacy. So instead of ringing the super I unplugged the pipes and fixed the sash cords. But never mind. California here I come – sunshine and serviced swimming pools. Want a cookie?'

Kathleen declined. 'Has your husband been gone long?' she asked.

'Two weeks. Two weeks rampant among the starlets. God knows what he has got up to; as I said, he is a romantic. But I'm getting on that train in the morning. Wouldn't have let him go on his own if I could have helped it. But offers like that don't grow on trees – especially in California. He was off before his agent could hang up the phone.'

'He's an actor?'

'George Pierce.'

'Oh, of course,' Kathleen had heard the name but hadn't made the connection.

'He has decided his life is in films. He has given up the stage. He had been muttering about it for years – well, since *Tomorrow and a Day* flopped. So when this part came up he literally jumped at it. "Sell up," he said, "we're going West."' Mrs Pierce began nibbling another cookie.

'I think it's a wonderful house, Mrs Pierce. Really wonderful.'

'You don't have to be polite, honey, but if you want, just deal with Mr Pilger. You got a husband or what?'

Kathleen wondered if it would be just easier to lie. What did it matter anyway? But it did. 'A friend asked me to find a place for him.'

'I thought you looked kind of young – an older friend I suppose. Well, never mind, kid, you enjoy yourself while you can. Like I said, I'm off to the land of the eternal suntan in the morning.'

'I hope everything goes well out there.'

'Oh, it will when I get there. I'll just swat the girls off him like mosquitoes. Has your friend got a wife?'

Kathleen stood up. 'Thanks for the coffee. I'll be in touch with Mr Pilger.'

'Didn't mean to offend, honey. Can you find your way out?'

'I think so.'

Kathleen left her sitting at the kitchen table reaching for another cookie. She wondered if she looked like 'that kind of girl' or if the woman just had that kind of mind. She pitied her poor husband. Then she stopped briefly to admire the main room again. Leather furniture, she thought, pushing the woman's remark out of her head. What did it matter? But it did. And a big white rug in front of the fireplace. It would be like a hunting lodge. Then she hurried, fairly skipping through the garden, back to tell David.

They moved in in good time to put a Christmas tree in the corner of the big room near the window. David even strung lights around the garden so that when the cast of *Somewhere in France* arrived for a Christmas party the effect was as much a fairytale as anything Macy's could have contrived. Kathleen had made pots and pots of what her mother had called American chop suey – macaroni, hamburger and onions in tomato sauce, but she had added garlic and oregano so to David it smelled like home.

Monty and his friend Eunice had arrived early. She looked spectacular, as usual, and her diamonds threatened to out-sparkle the tree lights. David made them cocktails while Monty joined Kathleen in the kitchen. He looked around approvingly.

'It's nice, it's very nice,' he said. 'You've done good work – real good, but,' he sighed heavily, and moved closer to her, 'but my dear, it's all such a waste.'

Kathleen was spooning the mixture into serving bowls. She had a red checked apron over her silk dress.

'Nonsense, Monty.' She looked at the food. 'I'm sure all those starving actors will wolf it down.' She frowned as it overflowed the fourth large bowl. 'Well, anyway it keeps.'

'That's not what I mean, my dear, the food is wonderful.' He picked a piece of macaroni from the top. 'Superb. No, my dear, it's you. We never see you and here I find you shut away in a kitchen when you should be glittering – glittering out there.' He waved in a non-committal way that seemed to imply the whole universe.

'Don't be silly, Monty, I'm not shut away.'

'What are you doing then? You weren't at Avril's party last night, and I know for a fact that you were invited.'

'Well, David had been working hard all day. You know,' she said, 'he thinks he's got the first act nearly right. And, well, it is cosy here.'

'Cosy! Cosy? What is this cosy? Cosy is not for little girls like you. How old are you – nineteen, twenty at the most? You don't fool old Monty. Cosy is for old. Plenty of time later for cosy.'

Kathleen laughed. She did fool old Monty. Maybe it

was premature aging. Six months to go before she was eighteen.

'We are very happy as we are, Monty. You are sweet to worry but I've heaps of things to keep me busy. Moving, shopping, decorating – it all takes time, you know.'

'Piddle. I still say it's a waste. And what is there for you? You're not even a wife. Wives, they have some rights. And I tell you a secret, little girl. David I love. Like he was my own – but the boy is not for you. I know, I tell you. You don't know; I think he doesn't know – but I know.'

The other guests began arriving. Saved by the bell, Kathleen thought, as she hurried to press the buzzer to release the gate.

'All right,' Monty said. 'So you don't want Monty's advice. But still I give it. Don't be so old, little girl. One day it will be too late to be young. Cosy can wait.'

The snow started to fall just after midnight on Christmas Eve – right on schedule. David and Kathleen had been to mass at St Patrick's. Neither of them could remember suggesting it. It was a mutual decision of which there seemed to be more and more lately. They had lunch at the Golden Bowl Chinese Restaurant on Christmas Day which was proudly serving Turkey Chow Mein, and in those two gestures they summed themselves up. Hard as they tried to be new, individual people, defining themselves, refusing to be defined by their backgrounds, it would not have been Christmas without mass. But they would not admit that. It was a lark, they told themselves. Well, after all, they went on to prove how different they were from their families. Who ate Chinese on Christmas Day? The gold and red restaurant was jammed with individualists. After lunch they considered going to the Ziegfeld to see *Brigadoon* but they stopped outside the theatre and the groups of chattering families put them off.

'We wouldn't hear anything but the rattle of candy bar wrappers and the high-pitched "Where's the bathroom,"'

David said. So they walked on to the village – home.

David gave Kathleen a small gold bracelet watch. 'It suits you better than that schoolgirl one you wear,' he said, shrugging off her gratitude. She gave him a picture she had drawn of the house, as seen through the fence.

'Hey, you've moved on from trees,' he said. 'I knew you could do it. It's wonderful.'

Kathleen blushed. 'I still draw trees,' she said. 'This is specially for you.'

'It is really special,' he said. 'I am honoured, my lady.' He kissed her lightly on the cheek and then rushed around deciding where to hang it.

It might have been because it was Christmas, it might have been because the fire glowed with a romantic intensity, it might have been because he remembered a lot of things he had been taught as a boy about families and commitment and how not to be alone – it might have been any of those reasons or maybe none of them, but that evening, David again asked Kathleen to marry him.

This time she agreed. She didn't know why. It might have been because of the things Monty had said. It might have been because she didn't like people like Mrs Pierce thinking she was 'that kind of girl'. It might have been because she was used to his being there. She couldn't imagine life without him now. It might have been because she couldn't think of any good reasons not to. Daniel was dead.

'Then we can turn that spare room into a studio for you,' he told her.

'Is that meant to be a bribe?'

'Why not? Now how shall we commit the deed? A huge theatrical bash in St Pat's?'

Kathleen thought about that. She pictured herself walking down the aisle in white, with a pure lace veil and a long train. And waiting at the altar taking her hand in his would be . . . for too long the person in that scenario had been Daniel for anything else to be possible. Besides, that would mean families. No, not that, surely. She didn't intend him to find out about her family – and her twins.

They were a dream in the past and much better off that way. She couldn't imagine how he would react to the knowledge of their existence. Or how they would react for that matter. And she didn't really want to find out.

'Not a big wedding,' she said. 'I mean, it would look so silly – after all this time. I'm sure people think that we're living together already.'

'We are.'

'You know what I mean.'

'Oh, the old sex raising its ugly head again. Why, is sex so very important to you?'

'How can you ask that? It obviously isn't.'

'It is usually more important to people who don't indulge in it than to those who do. Vastly more important.'

'And what about you then?'

'What about me?'

'Well, you don't indulge, as you put it, in sex. Is it so important to you?'

'And what makes you so sure I don't?' David said. He wasn't about to admit he was a virgin. It was too shaming. He'd been through a war; he was a feted playwright; he was an immensely admired bachelor . . .

Kathleen looked at him, surprised.

'Don't worry, Kathleen, it will be all right.' He hesitated and then realized the time had come. He didn't want to lose her. He took her in his arms and kissed her passionately for the first time. Instinctively she responded, but then checked herself. So, he attributed her demeanour to virginal status. Well, she wouldn't disillusion him. Let him be the first, she thought. It will please him. She extricated herself from his embrace, shyly.

'Remember the occasion of sin,' she told him.

'Those nuns have an awful lot to answer for,' he said, half seriously. 'OK – no big wedding. Shall we elope?'

Kathleen remembered the last time that suggestion had been made to her. 'No . . . I think somewhere in between. Let's find a compromise.'

* * *

It was indeed a small wedding – in the Cathedral, but at the side altar of the Sacred Heart. Monty was there and so were Paul and Sebastian, their only witnesses. The priest had understood their desire for a quiet wedding. He was used to dealing with theatricals. The only problem had been the baptismal certificates. Each wrote to their home parish and hoped word would not leak out to their families.

'I just couldn't take all those cousins,' David said. 'I think I have more cousins than anyone in the world.'

Kathleen laughed but gave no explanations for her reticence about her family, and David, true to form, requested none.

It didn't seem real, and Kathleen shivered when the priest got to the point about, if anyone can show just cause why these two should not be joined in matrimony, but she carried on. It wasn't as if there were a real impediment to their marriage. At least not a legal one. But a moral one? An ethical one? She wouldn't allow herself to think about it. She'd become rather expert at that – not thinking about things. Life was becoming a fantasy. She wondered if that was dangerous or eminently healthy in the circumstances.

Father O'Connor had a Barry Fitzgerald twinkle in his eye. He was a small man and thin, but wore his robes with a certain élan and, moreover, he was decidedly stage struck. As chaplain to a number of theatres he found his autograph book overflowing with celebrity signatures. He preferred actors and actresses but a celebrated playwright would do. The emphasis was on 'celebrated'. Father O'Connor himself enjoyed musicals and comedies but was not unaware that fame and literature could coexist. After all, Eugene O'Neill, God save his soul, had achieved celebrity. This young man might become more than a writer. He might one day be a star. But he had more faith in the girl. She had that quality – that charisma. Oh, Father O'Connor had seen them come and go. And he knew what it took all right. Kathleen had it. He would stake anything on it and Father O'Connor knew as much about gambling

111

as he did about the nature of stardom. Many a Tuesday found him at the Saratoga race track, where, more often than not, he doubled his stipend. He would not however have wagered so much on the success of this union. But he was philosophical about it. They were both young and he ventured neither of them knew who they were yet. He hoped that when life brought them that knowledge it would be a joyful discovery rather than a tragedy. But that was really up to them. How they handled it was more important than the knowledge itself. Again, he would wager she was a survivor. Him? He wasn't about to place bets on him.

Red roses decorated the altar and Kathleen carried a bouquet of miniature blooms. As David put the ring on her finger she glanced up at the statue of the Sacred Heart and thought, 'He'll forgive; he understands. David needs me.' She saw this as an unselfish act – one which would perhaps expiate the past selfishness. It would have been easier to tell David everything. Easier and more selfish. She could lift the cloud of guilt from her own soul by transferring the knowledge to him. But it would most likely overwhelm him. No. She would bear her secrets. She was better able. She was practised in it.

David could not remember feeling happier. Even the success of his play had not brought this euphoria. This beautiful woman was his. His life was settled now. There would be no more uncertainties. No more loneliness. He was a married man. He had found exactly what he sought. A companion. A companion to be proud of. She was good, as pure as she was beautiful. But above all, she was serene. That serenity was what he prized most. All women before Kathleen had been somehow a challenge to him. A threat. Not that he had known many outside his family. But that had been enough to make him frightened of the species. They sought constantly to devour him. To own him. He shrank from them in terror. Kathleen was different. With her, he could be in control of himself. With her he wasn't frightened. She would be a support to him a – what was the old fashioned word? – a helpmate. She was gentle and soft and kind. He thought of his mother, of his sister, of his brothers' wives and could hardly believe his luck. The pure chance of finding Kathleen in the park sitting on a bench. What if he had taken a different path? A different route? They would never have met. He believed now, almost, in fate.

Away from the altar in the semi-light, Monty shed a noisy tear. Marriages always moved him. He had had three himself – all very moving occasions. Paul found himself unable to watch as David took Kathleen's hand in his – why had he come? Because, he told himself, seeing is believing. Sebastian was not unaware of Paul's distress. Surreptitiously he took his hand to comfort him.

'Don't despair,' he whispered. 'Love finds a way.'

They had booked into the Plaza for the night and found they had a corner suite overlooking the Park on one side and Fifth Avenue on the other. Suddenly Kathleen felt shy. The easy comradeship had vanished as they shut the door behind them. They were two strangers suddenly, uncertain, unsure. Where had the friendship gone? Washed away by marriage vows? Now choice seemed to be taken away, replaced by duty. Uneasily, they roamed about, commenting on the furniture, the flowers, the magnum of champagne in the ice bucket, sent by Monty. Even the carpet was a subject of intense interest – and, of course, the view. They moved from one window to the next, pointing out to each other, in tones of great excitement, the obvious. Mercifully, snow began to fall. The heavens had sent them a new topic of discussion.

'It makes it all look so clean,' Kathleen said fatuously.

'Until the exhaust fumes turn it mucky,' David replied predictably.

'And slushy. I hate the slush,' Kathleen gave the standard reply.

'So do I. Snow would be all right if it just came and then disappeared. But it takes so long.'

'Oh, yes, weeks of yuck – so slippery. It's the slush that

113

causes the accidents you know, not the snow. I mean you can get a grip with snow, kind of crunch along.'

'It is pretty, though. Like a fairytale.'

And so the exchange ground on. Each was aware of the desperation as they sought for words, for topics; each utterance sounding more stupid to the utteree. But it scarcely mattered. Neither of them was listening.

David opened the champagne, hoping the liquid would dampen down the electrical charge in the atmosphere. Their hands touched as he handed Kathleen a glass and both recoiled from the intimacy.

Individually they spent a good deal of time arranging the few possessions they had brought with them. Each had simply an overnight case. They remarked on the sturdy wooden coathangers in the wardrobe, on the opulence of the towels in the bathroom, even on the shine on the taps. Kathleen arranged her comb and hairbrush on the dressing table and changed the position of her tube of lipstick five times. David agonized over the best arrangement for his toothbrush and paste. Neither wanted to be first for a bath. They deferred successfully to each other for a quarter of an hour until finally Kathleen lost and locked the bathroom door behind her. She soaked and washed as if she had been deprived of water for a month – or was about to be. She kept glaring at her nightdress which hung on the back of the door. Although her wedding outfit had been simple, even severe, a lightweight white woollen dress, new look Dior nipped in at the waist, full skirt nearly to her ankles, she had been rather exotic in her choice of negligee. If her wedding dress could be termed Joan Crawfordish, her negligee was definitely Linda Darnell. Against the rules she had chosen a fuchsia pink, virtually transparent long nightdress with unlined lace at the breasts and minute spaghetti straps. The matching robe to wear over this confection was minimal also in its design, being mostly lace and filmy as moths' wings. Now, in the bath, she reclined and wondered what on earth she had been thinking about when she bought it. But now she had no choice.

114

She either emerged from the bathroom totally nude, wrapped in one of the extravagant towels which she reasoned would be more modest, but probably more provocative – or she wore the peignoir. Why, she wondered, was she so desperately embarrassed? If you couldn't be provocative on your wedding night when on earth could you? It was not only legal it was probably compulsory. But a lifetime of caution is not easily overthrown. Years of indoctrination cannot be wiped out in one afternoon. Permission may be given but it is not always readily accepted. And of course there was Daniel.

Kathleen emerged, skin wrinkly from the bath, and dried herself meticulously, averting her eyes from her naked reflection in the oversized mirror. Although completely alone, she wrapped the towel around herself, securing an end under her left arm and proceeded to brush her teeth – one at a time. Finally she slipped on the nightdress and looked at herself in the mirror. Her nipples showed darkly through the fuchsia lace. The outline of her body was clearly visible through the fine fabric, even without the assistance of backlighting. She paused only briefly before slipping on the matching robe. The silky touch felt marvellous on her back and shoulders but did nothing to obscure her body. Holding her breath, she slowly opened the bathroom door, not knowing what to expect. Would he be romantic? Would he be shy? Despite her fear, with Daniel it had been natural.

The bedroom was empty. Silently she padded barefoot through and opened the door to the sitting room. There he sat on the sofa, his back towards her, reading a book. She wondered whether she should go in. She pictured herself standing in front of him, removing the book from his hands and then . . . then what? Instead she merely called from the slightly open door.

'Bathroom's free, David.' Should she have said darling?

'Oh, thanks,' he replied, not looking up.

Kathleen stood in the doorway for a while and watched him. Here was one scenario she hadn't imagined. **Total**

115

indifference. Should she go in there? Should she remain in the doorway, waiting, provocative? Should she call again? Kathleen removed the robe and got into bed. She sat back against the plump, firm pillow, hands neatly folded outside the covers. She hadn't brought a book. Well, on her wedding night she hadn't thought it necessary – even appropriate. Her heart was thudding somewhere in her throat. She felt a sudden rush of inexplicable fear. Her hands began to shake and she knotted her fingers tightly together, willing the shaking to stop. She smoothed the blanket over her thighs and reknotted her fingers.

This, she thought, is ridiculous. Absolutely ridiculous.

Fifteen minutes passed and there was no movement from the other room. Her fear transmogrified itself into anger.

How dare he, she thought. How dare he leave me like this.

But she softened her anger with reason. He's just got stuck into a book, that's all that's happened. It's no crime, surely. Done it myself many times, into another world really. Time just flies, she told herself.

Not on your wedding night, another voice in her head said. Not on your wedding night, it repeated. What was he reading anyway? What was she competing with? She had been sitting up in bed for nearly half an hour trying to cope with her confusion when she flattened the cushions and turned out the light. She gave the pillow a vicious thump in the centre and lying down, cradled her head in the depression she had made. But her eyes were fixed open. What's the hurry? she thought. Well, he could show a bit more enthusiasm. After all getting married was his idea, she answered herself.

If Kathleen had stayed in the doorway she would have noticed that in that half hour David hadn't turned a single page. Not one. He sat paralysed. He had wanted this marriage. He loved Kathleen. He wanted to be with her always. He wanted to share his life with her. But . . . he couldn't face this night. He didn't know what to do. Oh, he knew what to do in the technical sense – at least he thought he did. But he possessed only theory and he wasn't sure how much of that was right. He felt drained and tense at the same time. Cold and hot. Shivery. He stared at the book, his mind a jumbled mass of incoherence. His mother's face, smiling, her hand slapping him across the ear. His face stifled as she pulled him roughly to her enormous bosom. The darkness, the smell of sweat, the fear of pulling away that would tell her he didn't love her.

And that night – a particular night or was it many nights or maybe just a memory of a memory – a disjointed dream, a series of images, sounds, feelings that never added up to much except a feeling of guilt. Somehow he was responsible for the knowledge of things that should remain unknown. It was his fault – a blue light flashing on and off, a muffled light from through the window blind – a hot muggy night, wet muggy. Shadows of the bars rising and falling as the light came and went. The soft noises from the big bed – soft at first and then gentle slapping noises, the quiet laughter and then the breathing noises – no, breathless noises like he had been running. But Papa didn't run. He had no need to. David had to run to keep up with his Papa's long strides. His Papa was strong, his breath was strong, but now he was gasping, pulling in the air. Was he sick? Was Papa going to die? Then his Mama – quick frightened panting gasps. He sat up and held the bars. The blue light flashed on and off, on and off. His Papa was moving to the same rhythm, like a dance, on and off and on and off. And his Mama . . . where? Under Papa. What was he doing to her? She cried quiet little yelps, like a puppy. Like a frightened puppy and Papa held her down with his body. His angry body beating Mama. Now faster and faster – faster than the flashing lights. She stopped breathing. His Mama stopped breathing. Papa had killed her. But he kept beating away – angry bearlike grunts. David screamed. He screamed and screamed and the beating stopped.

His Mama wasn't dead. She picked him up and held him

117

against her. His face buried itself between her breasts, her skin was all wet and salty. He licked her skin and his hand held tightly to her breast. His Mama wasn't dead. He lay between them now in the big bed. His mother stroking him. He said nothing but David knew his father was angry with him. He had done something wrong and his father was angry. But David had saved his mother. She would surely have died if he hadn't screamed.

The grown-up David tried to laugh at the baby fears but over and over the blue light flashed in his mind. Just the neon sign from the bar across the street but to him it merged with the blue flash from exploding shells on the night in that horrible mud where his buddies lay dying. The light that steals life – on and off, faster and faster, draining the soul from the body, leaving an empty shell, exposed, naked, vulnerable . . . spent.

David knew his fear was irrational. He had read all the books. He knew he should not have been sharing his parents' bedroom. He knew that witnessing sex at an early age could scare a child who couldn't understand. It was his parents' fault, not his. He was a knowledgeable man who knew all the answers. He was a famous playwright. An intellectual almost. It was really comical. But the blue light flashed ominously. He forced himself to put the book aside.

As he slid into bed beside Kathleen he assumed from her regular, soft breathing that she had fallen asleep. He assumed wrongly. She had lain there, emotions ranging from hurt to anger and back again as the time slowly drifted by. But now he was here. Marriage, after all, she told herself, is about compromise, about being in tune with the other person, each modifying his needs in response to the other's needs. There is no place in marriage for selfishness. Begin as you mean to go on, one of her mother's easy aphorisms echoed in her mind. She reached out and gently touched David. Was it her imagination or did he briefly recoil from her touch? David pushed the blue light from his mind and gathered her in his arms.

'Hello, my wife,' he said softly as his hands moved tentatively up and down the soft fabric of her nightdress. He searched for the role of lover as gleaned from the pages of literature. 'Shall we discard this, lovely as it is?' he said in what he hoped was a provocative tone and slipped the straps from Kathleen's shoulders, gently moving the lace and silk down her body. She kissed him deeply and passionately. She kissed his eyes, a sensation he found surprisingly pleasurable, and her hand moved delicately along his thigh.

It was going to be all right, he told himself. There had been no need to worry, he thought, as he felt himself hardening. He felt exhilarated, freed. He clutched her body to his and kissed her mouth and her throat. He explored her body with his hands and kissed her shoulders. Sliding his body on to hers he felt her legs encircle him. He throbbed against her. But the joy dissolved as in his enthusiasm his mouth moved to her breasts, his face buried in the softness and the blue light began to flash on and off, on and off. Withered he rolled off her and lay deflated by her side. This time she could not mistake the definite recoil from her touch.

'It's all right,' she said and, leaning on one elbow, she kissed his cheek. 'We have plenty of time.' She snuggled cosily up to him, but he turned his back to her, so she would not sense his tears. Her arms encircled him and they lay close like spoons in a drawer. With a great effort he controlled his breathing until his simulated sleep became a reality.

Kathleen could perceive the difference and when sleep engulfed him she released her hold and slipped noiselessly from the bed and from the room. Naked she stood by the window and looked down at the lights on the street below. New York, it was said, never slept, but now it appeared to be napping.

'There is no hurry,' she reassured herself. 'We have a lifetime ahead of us.' She couldn't begin to imagine the years stretching ahead of her. She could only feel a lonely emptiness, like the street below. She tried not to remember what it had been like as she lay in Daniel's arms. As he had quashed her fears. As he had hungrily needed her – as they had needed each other. She tried not to remember how happy they had been – briefly, but completely happy. She tried not to remember because she could only remember the emptiness when he had gone. Even greater than the emptiness she now felt. 'At least with David there is hope,' she thought, 'and time.'

7

'Poor little bastards. First bastards then orphans. Never any father and then no mother. I wonder who the trollop's run off with now.'

'Ma, I wish you would stop using words like that in front of the children. I don't want the first thing they say to be bas . . . the word that begins with B.' Maureen smiled brightly at the twins who sat up in their high chairs, wearing identical pink dresses which she had made for them, and bows in their wispy hair made from the same material. 'Now watch this, girls,' she struck a match and lit the two candles – first on one little cake and then on the other. The birthday cakes stayed on the table well out of reach of the tiny fingers which grabbed the air. 'Happy Birthday to you,' Maureen sang, as the twins stared fixedly at the candles burning just out of their reach.

'They'll know soon enough who they are and what their mother is,' Bridget said.

Maureen continued singing happily, brushing the tears quickly from her eyes. The twins clapped their hands and laughed.

Kathleen spent the day trying to forget the date. She and David went to the opening of Hugh Martin's new musical, *Look Ma, I'm Dancing*. Kathleen barely saw the play. She was not distracted from her thoughts by Nancy Walker's antics. She just wondered about her daughters. Were they happy? Were they well? God, what if they were sick?

121

What if they were dead, like their father? She kept the panic away by picturing her mother fussing over them. She pictured her father showing them off in the store as he had shown her off. But would he? Was he still so ashamed that he couldn't look at them?

'I'd give it a six-month run,' David said. 'The tourists will keep it open throughout the summer.'

They sat in front of the fire, eating the chicken Kathleen had prepared.

'This is delicious,' David said. 'What is it?'

'Oh, bits and pieces.'

'I can see that. Bits and pieces of what?'

'It's called Spanish chicken and consists of opening lots of cans and pouring them on top of the chicken and putting it in the oven. An immense labour really.'

David began separating the ingredients with his fork. 'I can find corn and olives and onions . . .'

'Oh, do stop playing with it and eat,' Kathleen said crossly.

'OK, OK, I was only teasing. No need to bite my head off.'

'I'm sorry,' Kathleen was truly sorry. It wasn't his fault and she was taking it out on him. 'It's just . . .' she wanted to explain but how could she? If she told him now – well, that would be the end. The one person in the world who thought she was good.

'Kathleen, what is it? What's wrong? You've been so jumpy – it's so unlike you.'

'Is it? Is it really unlike me? What do you know? You don't know anything about me at all and if you did, you wouldn't like it.' She could hold back the tears no longer and rushed out of the room. She ran up the stairs and slammed the bedroom door behind her, collapsing on the bed. She tried to shut out the memories. But then she just let the guilt take control.

David sat stunned by the outburst. Then he followed her upstairs. He knocked softly on the door. Then more loudly to make himself heard over her sobs.

122

'Kathleen,' he said, 'Kathleen. Please, I want to help. Whatever it is you can tell me.'

She could never tell anyone, she thought. 'Go away,' she said.

It was great unhappiness in her voice but to David it sounded like anger and it frightened him. Remembering his upbringing, he did as he was told.

All through that late winter time hung heavily on Kathleen. There wasn't that much to do around the house. David was obsessively tidy. He was also immersed in his new play and often worked through the night. Untired, Kathleen lay in bed unable to sleep and turned to brooding over her life. For a time, for a short time, she had thought she had found a companion in life. Someone with whom to share – share what? Whatever there was. She thought she had found a future that could wipe out the past. But marriage had changed all that. Fully involved in his writing, he seemed to have no further need for her. She walked a lot. She still found that a pleasure in Manhattan. A pleasure but not a life. And then occasionally she sketched, now as obsessed by skyscrapers as she had once been by trees. But drawing out of doors in New York could never be considered a private pursuit. Her shoulder was constantly being peered over.

'Not bad,' a man in a heavy tweed overcoat with his hat pulled firmly on to his head à la Bogart pronounced. Kathleen was sitting on the edge of the winter sleeping fountain outside the Tyler building trying to capture its towering splendour in the sharp biting sun and the man loomed over her menacingly judgmental. 'Not bad at all. Hey, Al, come see this.' He was joined by a replica of himself. Kathleen ignored them and tried to concentrate but she couldn't help but be distracted by the interference.

'Ya, you're right,' Al said. 'She's not bad at all.'

'The picture, dummy. The picture I'm talking about.'

'Oh, yeh, I see – it's the building. That's OK too – but it's kinda crooked ain't it?'

'That's called artistic licence, Al. It's not supposed to be just like a real live photo.'

The two of them continued to discuss Kathleen's work, the nature of art and photography and whether or not photos were better than drawings, as if she were deaf, before they got bored with it and moved on. But she was never short of spectators. Some approved. Some clucked disparagingly. Very few expressed no opinion. Such was the nature of New Yorkers.

She thought about going to art school but rejected the idea. Drawing, painting – they were things that came from inside her. Personal things. Too personal to allow them to be manipulated, changed by someone who thought they knew better. She knew what she wanted to produce on paper or on canvas and that's what she strove to do. Perhaps she could be shown shortcuts to the results she wanted. Perhaps others' experience would be useful to her. But she wanted to get there by herself. She wanted to make all the discoveries. Although it kept her occupied, it did nothing to alleviate the loneliness she felt. The isolation. And the loneliness only led to more brooding. She brooded over the past, over the present and over the future. She sometimes wondered if it was her moodiness that kept David away from her. Maybe he wasn't as involved in his writing as he pretended to be. Perhaps he just used that as an excuse to avoid her. Although he didn't seem to notice how dispirited she was.

He did, however, seem perfectly content to leave his typewriter when Paul came round. And Paul came round with more and more frequency. After the curtain fell on *Somewhere in France* he would drop in – at first only briefly for a cup of coffee. He said he passed on his way home, but Kathleen never asked where he lived. She had a feeling he was not telling the whole truth and reckoned he made a fairly long detour to 'find himself passing'. Although Paul was always warm and friendly to her she felt that too was not quite honest. She didn't analyse it. She didn't want to dwell on it. It was just a feeling. It was definitely David he wanted to be with – and he put up with her because he had no alternative. He became a regular visitor, three or four times a week and David had suggested that they delay having supper until his arrival so they could all eat together. That served two purposes. He had longer uninterrupted at his work – and they would not have to make conversation on their own. Kathleen could see no reason to object. For all her misgivings about him she could not deny that Paul's presence brightened the atmosphere in the house. It relieved the tension that hung threateningly in the air.

It was on one of these nights that the question of what she should do with her time came up. She had tried to make a joke of it. 'Oh, I just do what all housewives do, Paul,' she told him when he had asked politely how her day had been. Paul was always polite to her and she felt he did his best not to make her feel excluded. He did his best but he did not succeed. 'Some light dusting, then curl up on the sofa with a novel and a box of chocolates. A pleasant life, if the novel is exciting enough to take me away from reality.'

'Kathleen is not finding life very exciting at the moment, I'm afraid,' David said. 'And I'm also afraid that is my fault.'

'Nonsense,' Kathleen said. 'When have I complained?'

'You don't have to,' David said. 'I'm not blind, though you may think that I am.'

Kathleen didn't care for this discussion and she especially didn't care for having it in front of Paul. She didn't want anyone to think that theirs was a less than perfect marriage. Besides, Paul was a terrible gossip. He had just spent a good hour relating – in a most entertainingly bitchy way – the goings on backstage of *Somewhere in France*. She supposed it was a two-way street and he would be backstage tomorrow relating the supper table conversation.

'You need an occupation,' Paul said. 'Something to get you away from this selfish genius occasionally.' He looked at David with his most charming smile. Kathleen thought that totally unnecessary. Coming from his lips there could be no mistaking that even 'selfish' was a term of endearment.

'Kathleen has her painting. She'll be a famous artist one day,' David said, concentrating totally on Paul – speaking as if they were alone.

'No doubt about that – she's good. But,' Paul paused for effect, 'I think she should take up acting.'

'Acting?' David was interested.

'Yeh, why not? Look at her. The way she looks, the way she moves. She's halfway there already.'

David realized that Paul had just expressed the idea that had been in his mind all along. Kathleen was a natural actress. In fact, he thought, she is acting most of the time. He thought about his play – it was as if Paul had read his mind.

'You know,' David said, 'you are absolutely right.'

'She's a natural. A bit of training, smooth out the edges, that's all she needs.'

'Where do you think she ought to go?'

'The Studio, of course.' Paul had trained at The Studio. 'She'll have to audition, but I'll give her a hand with that. It's a cinch.'

Kathleen listened to the exchange, absolutely fascinated. Between them, in a couple of seconds they had reorganized her life – and without a single reference to her. Well, she supposed, one of them was her husband. He was footing the bills. If he wanted her to go to acting school, why not? She didn't have anything to lose – and she didn't have any better ideas.

'That's settled, then,' Paul said and finally turned to Kathleen. 'I'll look out some audition pieces tomorrow and bring them round after the show. Then we can get down to work.'

Kathleen wondered what Paul's plan was. He was up to something, but she couldn't figure out what. Still, she was not about to argue with him. 'OK,' she said. 'Thanks.'

'Want some coffee, Paul?' David asked.

'Thanks, that would be great.'

David looked at Kathleen, who was wondering if she would really have the nerve to stand up in front of a bunch of people and show off. How many times at home, at school, working in the hotel, had she been warned not to make herself conspicuous?

'Kathleen,' David interrupted her thoughts, 'yoo hoo, Kathleen,' he gave an exaggerated wave across the table which Paul seemed to think was the height of wit.

'Oh!' she jumped.

'Welcome back,' David said. 'We thought we would like some coffee.'

Kathleen got to her feet, picking up the dishes as she rose. 'Oh, sorry. I'll just make it.' As she disappeared into the kitchen she wondered if she could possibly be good at anything. She was certainly a failure as a mother, a daughter, a wife and now she was even a bad hostess.

The Studio met in a basement hall a few blocks from the house. The working day was neatly divided up – first physical exercises, then vocal training and breathing exercises. After lunch there was improvisation and finally textual interpretation – mainly Chekhov. After that a select group worked on a production and the newcomers were encouraged to stay and watch. Three teachers ran The Studio and occasionally working actors or directors dropped in, usually in the afternoon, and contributed the wisdom of their experience to the proceedings. At first Kathleen was enthralled by it all, and impressed by the labours of the older students, but soon she began to see that for the majority of them the lessons were an end in themselves. They were not really preparing for a career. Two, Alix Sharp and William Fry, she thought had the right combination of talent and drive, but she didn't hold out much hope for the others who were never so happy as when discussing ad infinitum one esoteric line from a play and decrying the commercialism of the stage. They would never sacrifice their integrity on the altar of the box office, they constantly proclaimed, and Kathleen decided that most of them would never be given that opportunity.

She took classes at The Studio during the day and spent many evenings taking private dance and voice lessons. She began to be excited by it and fantasized that she would be a great success. She would pay David back for all that he had given her, she would go off on her own, she would send for the twins. She would owe no one. It would all be fine. It could never be perfect. Daniel was dead. But the constant activity filled not only her time but also her mind. Each night she dropped exhausted into bed and was too tired even to dream. Too tired to resent the fact that David slept soundly far over on his side of the bed. She didn't feel she was neglecting David. After all, it had been his idea. And besides, Paul had taken over the functions which she had been able to perform for him. She would come home to find David reading him his day's work. Her arrival always seemed to surprise them – as if she were an interloper. Paul had also taken up cooking.

At the end of August she came home one night to find David and Paul acting more than usually pleased with themselves.

'David has an announcement to make,' Paul said with a flourish. 'Da Dum . . .'

David rose to his feet solemnly. 'It is with great pride – and only slight trepidation – that I announce –' he grinned at Paul, 'the completion of my latest work of genius, *Friendly Enemies.*'

'Oh, David, that's wonderful!' Kathleen forgot the reserve that had grown up between them and, hurrying across to him, threw her arms around his neck. 'That's really wonderful,' she said. Did she for a moment feel him draw away from her? But then he hugged her, lifting her off the ground and whirling her around.

'And furthermore,' Paul interrupted.

'Oh, yes.' David put her down and took a step back, separating them. 'I am declaring a vacation. We all need a vacation.'

*　　*　　*

128

Cape Cod was perfect in September. The sun was still hot, the ocean was warm after the summer, the beaches were deserted as the children had returned to school and the evenings were long and mellow. They had rented a small beachhouse with no difficulty at all. Kathleen was pleased now to have a break from her constant activity and just to swim or walk or laze on the porch. Paul had left the cast of *Somewhere in France*, after ten months, and the three of them had hired a car and driven up to Hyannisport. They found the cottage clean and airy, the fridge stocked with food and the view out to sea incomparable.

Since the play had finished, David was altogether more accessible. He was even cheerful. But she couldn't say he was the old David. The one who had convinced her so totally of his need for her just a year ago. He had decidedly changed and she attributed these changes not to her own devotion – but to Paul's. David had lost his timidity, gained confidence. He joked. He teased. He had even begun to dress differently. Colour had entered his wardrobe. Most of the changes she thought were for the better but the constant bantering between them annoyed her intensely.

Kathleen sat on the porch in the afternoon sun and put down the manuscript. She had just finished reading *Friendly Enemies*. It was very good. Very different from *Somewhere in France* – just as David was now a very different person. Paul, she knew, was to have the lead in the play. A coup for him. But also good for the play. He would be very good in the role. It would consolidate his success. Show his versatility and the critics would say that he fulfilled the promise he had shown in his début.

She looked at the two of them now, racing back and forth across the beach, frolicking in the surf like puppies. She wondered about his motives. But there was no doubt that Paul's presence invigorated David. Yet she felt left out. They always seemed to have a secret.

That evening they were on the beach barbecuing, or rather Paul was barbecuing and they were watching him struggling with the flames. At last the chicken was scorched to Paul's satisfaction and they settled down to eat. Darkness had engulfed them and the moon shone on the breakers. It was still, except for the sound of the sea, and the occasional crackle of the dying fire. Kathleen wished she were alone with her husband.

'Well,' David said to her, 'you've said nothing about it.'

'The chicken? Sorry, Paul. It's delicious – as usual.'

'No, not the chicken –' David said. 'The play. I saw you reading it this afternoon.'

Kathleen was surprised. She thought David was oblivious to all her actions. 'That's wonderful too, as well you know.'

'Shall we tell her?' he asked Paul, suppressing a giggle.

'I don't know, maybe not yet. Maybe after she has tidied up,' Paul said; his tone, too, was teasing.

'Tell me what?' she asked. There were times when their bantering annoyed her terribly. This was one of them. All she wanted was her husband to herself.

'If I tell you then you'll know, won't you?' David said.

'I'm bored with your secrets,' she said. 'Tell me or not, I don't care.' She made no effort to control her annoyance.

'Oooo,' Paul said. 'Temper, temper.'

'Sorry, Kathleen,' David said. Then after a pause, 'You know the part of Adele in the play?'

'Of course I do – the lead.'

'What do you think of it?'

'I told you. I think the play is wonderful. She's a great character – witty, wise, totally sympathetic. How much praise do you need?'

'How do you feel about playing it?' David had no doubts about her abilities. He had, after all, written Kathleen down on paper. Adele was Kathleen. Maybe in different circumstances, but they were the same girl, as far as he could tell.

Kathleen didn't say anything. This was another one of their jokes. She could feel them waiting for her reaction, so they could have a good laugh.

'Oh, that would be great,' she said. 'But I'm afraid I'm committed to Arthur Miller for his next play – and after that I've been invited to London to play Hamlet.'

'I'm serious, Kathleen,' David said.

She looked at him in the glow from the fire. He looked serious. She looked at Paul. He nodded. They were serious. They wanted her to play Adele.

'David,' she finally said. 'It is very . . . sweet of you, but let's be realistic. I've never set foot on a stage. I've only been studying a couple of months.'

'Everyone has to start somewhere,' David said.

'I don't think the lead in a Broadway show is the place to begin.'

'Oh, don't worry about that. We'll open out of town first.'

'David – stop it. No producer in his right mind would take me on.'

'I'm not prepared to vouch for Monty's mental stability but he has agreed.'

'You mean you asked him already?'

'Of course. No matter what you may think I'm not a complete idiot. I wouldn't want to get your hopes up and then say, sorry no can do. Monty said, and I quote the man himself: "My boy, the girl is perfect. As long as she doesn't fall over the furniture she will be a hit."'

'But . . . names. Even I know you need names up in lights to sell tickets.'

'At the risk of sounding arrogant, Kathleen,' David said, 'Monty reckons my name looks very nice in lights.'

'Thanks a lot,' Paul finally spoke.

'And yours, of course,' David quickly added.

'You two have been planning this all along, haven't you?' Kathleen said.

'Us three –' David said. 'Don't forget Monty.'

Kathleen remembered his little speech in the kitchen at the Christmas party.

'That's why you sent me to The Studio,' Kathleen said.

'So that you wouldn't trip over the furniture,' David

said. 'That's settled then. We open in Philadelphia, then on to Boston before we take New York by storm.'

Kathleen didn't know if she wanted to be an actress. She hadn't expected to have to make a decision so soon. It had just been a way of filling the time. But everyone else seemed to think it was a good idea. Why not? she thought. What did she have to lose?

Larry found that the same number of customers bought less and less. They came into the store for a can of condensed milk and a loaf of bread when a year before it would have been for a week's groceries. They went to the supermarket now and he was only a stop gap. He didn't know how much longer he could go on with constantly falling profits. It was a mad circle. He had to put up prices when the volume fell and the customers complained and more of them went to the supermarket. And he was very tired. He didn't understand how Maureen just seemed to get younger and younger. She thrived looking after the twins, on whom she doted. Every time he looked at them he was just reminded of his shame.

'I think we'll just close the store on Wednesday afternoons,' he told his wife. 'No one will even notice.' He had thought about it for a long time. He couldn't bear Maureen being there with the girls, displaying them for all to see. He had noticed more people came in then – to get a look at them he supposed.

'Nonsense,' Maureen said. 'It's one of our best days.'

And Larry knew why. 'Well, then maybe I'll just stay myself. You've got enough to do.'

'After all these years, Larry? What has come over you?'

So arrangements stayed as they were and the girls toddled around the shop on Wednesday afternoons as their mother had, playing with the cans and eating broken cookies from the barrel. It was harder now to get loose cookies delivered. Everything seemed to be packed and sealed to line supermarket shelves. Nabisco, however, was co-operative with their small customers – especially ones so close to the factory.

'We mustn't try to compete with supermarkets,' Maureen had said. 'We'll only keep our customers by providing old fashioned service. That's what they want.'

Larry doubted the wisdom of that. What they wanted was to pay the lowest price. But he didn't argue. He had no choice. It was impossible to compete. 'What's left of them,' he muttered.

It was a Wednesday afternoon in early November. Maureen was behind the counter, clucking at the girls.

'Now, Eileen, stop that.' One twin was busily encouraging the other to roll cans of corn the length of the store. 'You'll dent them and no one will want to buy them and take them home.' Strange, Maureen mused, it was always Eileen who thought up the naughty things to do while Geraldine just followed meekly.

Mrs Weston came in and Maureen donned her brightest smile as she wished her a good afternoon.

'Aren't they just delightful?' Mrs Weston cooed over the twins. 'I expect you are very proud of them – all things considered. Still you can't blame them, can you? It's not as if it were their fault. It is amazing, I always say, how out of the depths of trouble come blessings in disguise.'

'What can I get you, Mrs Weston?' Maureen asked.

'Well, I don't suppose *you*'ll have it either, but I thought it was worth a try. There's a new juice – a mixture of tomato, carrot, celery and, let me see, oh beet and spinach – all kinds of vegetables. It sounds absolutely delicious and I'm dying to try it.'

'I don't think . . . what's it called?'

'V-8 cocktail.'

'No, we haven't had that. But I'll see if we can get some for you.'

'You are wonderful. It comes from Campbell's. I don't know what I would do without this store. Honestly. You know, at the A & P they wouldn't even consider ordering it for me. No call for it they said. No call for it. Well, I was calling for it, wasn't I? I don't know how they expect to keep their customers when they treat them like that. It took me a full ten minutes to find someone to speak to about it – and then he tells me there is no call for it.'

'I'll see what I can do. Now, what else can I get for you?'

'Oh, that's all. I managed to get everything else while I was at the A & P – it is amazing how much cheaper it is.' Mrs Weston turned her attention back to the twins. 'Aren't you just the cutest things, though? And I bet you are just so proud of your Mummy.'

Maureen stiffened. Customer or not, Mrs Weston went just too far.

'Of course,' Mrs Weston turned back to Maureen, 'they're too young to understand. But I'll bet you and Mr Thornton are fit to burst. Keeping it to yourselves like that. Imagine, having a star in the family and keeping it to yourselves. Of course, I wouldn't want Patricia to be on the stage. It's well, not for her kind of girl. Did I tell you she has decided to become engaged to that nice Watson boy. He's joined Tech Enterprises. Has a great future, I'm sure. They're looking at homes in Billerica. Did you know, there's a whole new country development going up there?'

Maureen hated to ask. She hated anything that prolonged conversation with Mrs Weston. But it had to be done. 'Mrs Weston – forgive me for asking, but what were you saying about Kathleen?' She found the name strange on her tongue. She hadn't said it aloud since Kathleen had abandoned them. Nor had anyone else in the house. 'That girl' or 'trollop' was all Bridget could manage.

'Just that I think it's wonderful for her. I really must try and see it, but you know – going into town, it's so tiring. But Patricia and Francis, that's her intended, went to the Colonial last night. They like to keep in touch with the theatrical world. They couldn't believe it was the same Kathleen Thornton. Well, you can imagine her surprise when on to the stage walks the girl she sat next to at school. Not something you'd expect. I mean, especially not from a parochial school. I said to Patricia, you have to give her

134

credit – after her . . . mistake. She's found a life for herself. Theatrical people – I mean, they don't mind things like that, do they?'

'No, indeed, Mrs Weston. I'll see about the V-8 for you.'

'You are wonderful. A real saint, I always say. Taking so much on to yourself. Well, give my . . . regards to Kathleen. And do tell her I admire her spunk.'

Mrs Weston finally began her departure with a wave of her fingers to the twins. Geraldine waved back and Eileen rolled a can of peas which bounced sharply off Mrs Weston's ankle.

Maureen was delighted. She wished she had done it herself. She was trying to bring herself to apologize when Mrs Weston said, 'Don't give it a thought. What can you do with children?' and hurried through the door as Geraldine bowled another can, in imitation of her sister, at the departing figure.

The theatre was a perfect place for Kathleen to hide, Maureen thought. It was a world completely unknown to any of her family – she might as well have been in Timbuktu as onstage at the Colonial. But she had forgotten the social-climbing Weston family. Maureen knew she was lucky to get a ticket. The theatre was packed as she made her way down the centre aisle to her seat, rather unsure as to how to behave. She had never been to a theatre before but she had seen them in the movies. There, people always seemed to be in long dresses and furs and the men always wore tuxedos. Maybe that's just in New York, Maureen thought, pleased to see that this audience didn't conform to her image. She had put on her best dress in any case. Bridget had not been pleased when she said she was going out.

'What about the babies, then?' she said crossly.

'They're asleep.'

'Sure, they're asleep now. What if they wake up?'

'Ma, you've had enough to do with babies to know what to do for a couple of hours.'

'I'm an old woman and they are not my responsibility,' Bridget said. 'Poor orphans – abandoned by the trollop and now you go and walk out on them.'

'Ma, it's only for a couple of hours.'

'And where do you think you might be taking yourself all done up like Mrs Astor's pet horse?'

'There's something I need to do,' Maureen said. She was not about to give her mother more ammunition. 'I won't be late.'

Larry said nothing, as was becoming his custom. He just ran his open hand back and forth across his chest and shut his eyes and lips tightly.

The curtain rose on a pink and cream living room. The characters laughed and cried and fought and loved. They could not live together, they could not live apart. They ate away at each other but there was no other food for them. Maureen watched her daughter. It was Kathleen, but at the same time it wasn't. This wonderful, proud, untouchable figure who dressed and moved with such elegance. She could not take her eyes off her and waited impatiently for her to return when she was offstage. Although the play had a happy ending, Maureen sat and cried. Her daughter had become everything Maureen had wanted to be – and she was left holding the babies. She imagined the people her daughter now knew. She imagined the restaurants, the parties. Kathleen would be dancing on tables. Maureen was very jealous. Kathleen would now be going out to dine with handsome and witty admirers. Oh, Maureen knew what it was like. She had imagined it for years. And here she would have to go back to the hated house over the store and put her daughter's daughters on the toilet. And there would still be wet sheets to wash in the morning. Maureen looked at her hands. They were red and wrinkled. The nails peeled. Her hangnails were painted with iodine to stop the pain. Kathleen's hands were white and smooth, her nails were long and painted crimson. It simply wasn't fair. Anger welled up in her on the trolley-ride home. Maybe she would just take those babies and dump them in her daughter's lap. Then we would see how long those hands remained elegant. Then there would be no time for prancing about in silk dresses. And Maureen. What would she do? She would be free. Free to do what she wanted. But what was that? What could she do? With these hands? It was too late for her. She felt no embarrassment crying softly in the crowded transport. She knew no one would notice. She wasn't the kind of person people noticed . . . ever.

Kathleen found it very strange staying in the rooms which not very long ago she was earning her living cleaning. However it was a nice kind of strangeness. And in the afternoons, when David wasn't hysterically calling for another rehearsal, she went to the bench and sketched her tree. It had grown, she decided. But not as noticeably as she had. But then trees had more time.

It was difficult remaining calm. Everything was happening so fast – rehearsals, new scenes to learn. David had gone mostly silent again. But one afternoon he joined her on the bench. 'The last time we sat here, I was the rising young star,' he said. 'Now it's your turn.'

'And I don't believe it any more than you did,' she said.

'Well, it is true anyway. You are magic on that stage.'

'If I am, it is all your doing.'

'Nonsense, I've never seen myself as Svengali.'

'Maybe you should – first Paul and now me. Where is Paul by the way?' It was so seldom she saw David without Paul.

'He's taking a nap. Just because you don't need your beauty sleep doesn't mean others don't.'

'You know what I think?' Kathleen asked.

'No, what?'

'I think you should go and see your family while we're here.'

David looked pained. The idea had obviously been in his mind too. 'No, there's no point.'

'What's the point of anything? It would make them happy. You could show them your new wife.'

'No, Kathleen – I couldn't do that.'

'Ashamed of me?'

'No, of course not. It's just . . . well, I don't need them and they don't need me. We have nothing in common.'

'You may not have anything in common – except of course blood – but I think you are wrong when you say you don't need them. I think you need to make some kind of peace with them.'

'Peace? My family don't know the meaning of the word.'

Kathleen had sown the seed and her idea had prevailed. On Sunday morning David announced that they were going to see his family.

'The three of us?' Kathleen asked.

'Nope.' It was difficult enough taking Kathleen – he didn't know what they would think. But he couldn't subject Paul to his family. 'Just me and my wife.'

'Shouldn't we tell them we're coming?' Kathleen asked.

'No, it'll be a surprise,' David said. Besides, he felt safer if he could still change his mind at the last minute.

'More a shock than a surprise, I should think.' Kathleen imagined the expression on her mother's face if she should walk through the door. 'Hello, Mum, Dad – this is my husband.' Oh, so much she wanted to walk through that door. She wouldn't even mind Bridget's presence if she could just hug Mum and be cuddled by her Dad – and the babies. She couldn't even imagine them. She had tried to so many times. She wanted very much to hold her daughters. But she couldn't do that. It would hurt them too much. It would be selfish of her and she had already hurt them enough. It was better she was out of sight and out of mind. 'What if they're not at home?' she asked David.

'On Sunday, after mass? Where else would they be?' Where else, David thought, but around the kitchen table, Mama at the stove dishing out equal portions of food and guilt. Kathleen didn't know how lucky she was. No family. But how could you have no family? But that's what she had told him. 'There's no one, David.' An orphan? Deserted? But each time he tried to ask her she looked so pained he hadn't pursued it. There was obviously so much she wanted to forget. Years of neglect probably. Maybe that was why she had been so keen to meet his family. So keen that he at least make contact with them. Maybe he owed her that. Maybe he owed his wife a chance to meet his family. Perhaps she believed that fantasy of warmth and love that was supposed to exist behind closed doors. Mama and Papa and babies – like the three bears. She was Goldilocks searching for a home; the fiction of family life. Mama in her apron – cooking, cleaning, cuddling; playing games and soothing hurts. Papa being strong, going out to work in the morning and returning each evening full of hugs and kisses for his babies. She didn't know about the shouting and the hurting that couldn't be stopped.

Above all, she could not know about the expectations. Expectations that were so great no one could ever fulfil them. David knew for certain he couldn't. Still, now he had done at least one thing that was expected of him. He had got himself a wife. And all those memories had made that painful too. Since the day they had married, David watched constantly for signs of Kathleen turning into Mama.

The North End seemed oddly quiet to him – but then it was winter. Somehow all his memories were summertime with mothers hanging from windows shouting down into the streets to their children to come or to stop that, or be quiet or leave him alone. There were always chairs and tables on the pavements where the men sat and played cards and drank Chianti as if they were in Rome – a place most of them had never seen but which was buried somewhere in genetic memory. The stoops were always full of children playing jacks, or pitching cards and there was always hopscotch chalked up on the pavement by the girls. Winter meant snow and sleds and snowballs; but now it was winter and there was no snow – no children. The windows were closed and the chairs had been brought inside from the pavements.

David told the taxi to stop about a block from his home – outside a bakery. He could smell the aniseed as he stepped from the cab.

'We'll bring Mama some cookies,' he told Kathleen, 'and maybe she'll forgive us for not inviting her to the wedding.' Although he knew there was little chance of that – maybe she'll forgive me for being me, he added mentally. 'Mama likes cookies.'

They climbed the stairs to the middle section of the three-family house. 'Fran lives down there,' he told Kathleen as they passed, 'with her lot.' He slowed down, waiting for her to catch up. 'But as it's Sunday,' he added, 'they will all be here, as usual – and so will Tony and his family and Gino and his. All of them – as usual.' The last two words were uttered despairingly under his breath.

Through the door they could hear a variety of noises which didn't so much blend together as clash off each other – children's shrieks, the occasional deep male shout, a squabble of female voices. David heard the sound of the doorbell cut through all of it as he pressed the button. For a moment there was silence, followed by a renewed cacophony of questioning voices and a dispute over who was free to 'go see'.

It was Mama, wiping her hands on her apron, who opened the door. Her expression changed from one of annoyance at being summoned from her sauce to one of surprise and then immediately to one which could be called delight.

'Davy!' she shrieked. 'Thanks be to the Mother of God – my Davy. My baby is here.' And she enveloped him in her huge arms, taking as was usual, his breath away with the violence of her embrace. 'But where have you been to? You don't write to your mama, you don't call your mama, you don't come see your mama . . . you could be dead.' And then she noticed Kathleen who stood a few paces behind her husband, feeling very much an intruder. 'Who's this?' Mama asked, pushing David aside as violently as she had enveloped him.

140

Now out of Mama's reach, David put a hand on Kathleen's arm and encouraged her forward. She shyly held out the white box tied with string. 'We brought some cookies,' she said quietly, feeling like a child at a strange party where she knew no one. She wanted her mother to take her away.

Mama looked at her. She looked hard at her, up and down and, Kathleen felt, through as well. She knew she was dressed totally wrongly. She knew no matter what she had on she would feel that. Or was it her hair?

Mama crossed herself. 'Sweet Mother of God,' she finally pronounced, 'she's a beauty. Davy you've got yourself a beauty.'

Kathleen's hand was still outstretched, offering the cookies.

'Come, come,' Mama grabbed her arm, ignoring the offering and pulled Kathleen past David into the hallway. 'Papa, Fran, everybody come look,' she yelled. 'David's brought his girl. Come see.'

Kathleen found herself surrounded, children at her knees, women touching her, men surveying her and this crowd seemed to want more than her autograph. She peered through them to David who stood outside the door; still, poised for a flight he knew he couldn't make. He did not look at all happy.

After lunch they not so much left as escaped. The whirlwind of questions, statements, children crying, men demanding, clanking crockery submerged them. The talking, for it could not be called conversation, switched from English to Italian and back again and Kathleen could follow none of it.

'Now do you understand?' David asked her as the crisp air began to refresh them after the heat of the family, the pervading aroma of garlic and tomato gradually began to dissipate.

'They're extremely . . .' Kathleen searched for the non-judgmental word, '. . . lively.'

'Suffocating is more apt, I believe,' David said, 'or

141

maybe torrential – like a warm sticky monsoon. Either way, by asphyxiation or drowning, they take your breath away. But then that's families for you.'

Kathleen could indeed now begin to understand David's shrinking from close contact. He feared it would end like that. 'I don't believe all families are like that,' Kathleen said. 'It depends on the people.' She thought of the aridity of her own. The dry, brittle exchanges; the monosyllables of communication; the antithesis of the DeCostas. She understood now David's need to be a separate person – he had never been before. And her own need to be a part of someone else. She had never been. She had always, except for that brief time with Daniel, been separate. She would have to earn David's trust. Trust that she wouldn't swallow him up if he let her near him. But could she make that promise even to herself? Still, it wasn't her he was afraid of – it was oblivion. It would be a very delicate process. It had to be approached with care. She would have to teach him that all love was not destruction. At least she hoped it wasn't.

A year, she thought as they kicked their way noisily through the crinkled leaves back to the hotel. Those leaves had sprouted, bloomed and died in that year. They had lived their time. And in her life? A year had changed it completely. Still, a year was a small thing in a human life – usually.

'Let's cleanse our palates with a hot fudge sundae at Brighams,' David said.

'After all that food?' Kathleen was astonished.

'That wasn't food,' David said, 'that was Mama's idea of love. It always leaves me feeling hungry.'

Kathleen took his hand. That was the only answer to his isolation.

'Let's drop into the hotel first, though,' he said, 'and see if we can rustle up Paul.'

Kathleen fought back her resentment of Paul – and recommitted herself to the struggle to win David's trust. It was, after all, her duty. She was his wife.

142

8

When the first cheque arrived Maureen considered tearing it up, but then thought better of it. Why shouldn't Kathleen pay for all the trouble she had caused. It was probably just a drop in the bucket for her, while for them the store's profits constantly diminished. She became more and more bitter. Yet on some days she was proud of her daughter. She felt a kind of happiness that Kathleen had done so well – a happiness that at least she had got away. But then on other days she despised her, echoing Bridget's condemnation. Why should she have everything her own way?

After a few cheques, one each month, arriving in an otherwise empty envelope postmarked 'New York', Maureen went out and bought a television set. The tiny screen in the big wooden cabinet replaced the radio in the corner of the room. Bridget vowed she would never go near it.

'It gives you cancer,' she announced with certainty, but she was lured to take a look at *The Goldbergs*, one of her favourite radio shows when they transferred to television, and soon, deciding to take her chances with cancer, resumed her position in the sagging armchair, watching *The Pinheads* with the twins and continuing immobile until she declared bedtime and switched the set off.

It was Sunday night. Maureen had tucked the twins up in bed. Larry was sitting at the table rubbing his chest and grimacing over the accounts. Bridget sat as usual, crocheting her woollen squares, one eye on the *Ed Sullivan Show*. He was one of her favourites.

'A good Irishman and a good Catholic,' she declared, 'but poor soul he has the map of Ireland on his horse face, God help him.'

She was chuckling over the antics of Dean Martin and Jerry Lewis and muttering 'fools' when Maureen came into the room.

'A cup of tea would be nice,' she said, without looking at her daughter.

Obediently Maureen went to the kitchen and lit the gas under the kettle. She could hear the television from the next room. Although she wouldn't admit it, Bridget was getting deaf.

'And now, ladies and gentlemen,' Ed was saying, 'a special treat. Here we have a scene from the hottest ticket in town, *Friendly Enemies*. Here are Kathleen Thornton and Paul Fredericks playing Adele and Tom. In this scene he has a suspicion that she isn't telling him the whole truth about her lunch date. Let's give them a really big welcome, folks – *Friendly Enemies*.'

Maureen went to the doorway. Larry looked up from his books.

'Jesus, Mary and Joseph, will you look at this?' Bridget said, dropping her crochet.

Maureen watched their astonishment as the kettle whistled in the background.

'You see,' Monty was saying, 'didn't I say? Wasn't I right? She photographs like a dream. Magic. You make the movie and she's your star.'

'I'm still not sure,' one of the men said. 'Broadway and movies – there is a big difference. We need a movie name. The public . . .'

'Piddle the public,' Monty interrupted. 'You tell them she's a star. They'll believe you. What do they know? Look at that face, those legs.' He didn't need to say that. All eyes in the room were fixed on the small screen.

* * *

Larry was rearranging the shelves. He had decided to introduce a modified self-service in the store. It wasn't big enough to display everything properly, like a super-market, but he had to do something. He carried box after box out of the backroom, the niggling pain in his chest swelling like a balloon, forcing out his breath . . .

Mrs Weston found him lying on the floor when she came into the store to buy a Sara Lee Cheesecake and with her usual tact shouted up the stairs. 'Mrs Thornton, come quickly. Your husband seems to be dead.'

Maureen saw no reason to contact Kathleen. She had her own life to lead – it would only be an inconvenience. The wake was well attended by the neighbourhood and Father Bill said the funeral mass. He shed a tear as his old friend was lowered into the ground next to his mother.

'It is where he has wanted to be for years,' Maureen thought. 'He'll be happier now.' She shed no tears.

Maureen was glad now for the presence of the twins. She couldn't bear the idea of once again being alone with Bridget, and bearing the full brunt of her mother's general approbation. The house seemed no quieter with Larry gone. He hadn't spoken in years, but in a way Maureen missed his presence. She realized that now it would be up to her to tend the grave, but felt that attendance every Wednesday was excessive.

The real problem was the store. It was barely keeping them and Maureen didn't want to run it by herself. It would mean neglecting the twins and she had no intention of doing that. Nor did she plan to leave them in the care of Bridget. Although approaching eighty-six the old woman showed no sign of mellowing with age. If anything she became progressively more misanthropic, directing her rage at Maureen and the twins. Mercifully, some of it was deflected by the television set. The only one to escape her wrath was Hopalong Cassidy. His exploits she cheered on.

Maureen knew something would have to be done, some decisions made. But between servicing the twins, attending to the store and looking after her mother, she had no time to think. Luckily the cheques from Kathleen were cushioning them, but she must, she knew, sort things out. Each day, however, was totally filled with trivia and each night she fell exhausted into bed. Bridget grew more and more reluctant to leave her chair by the television but Maureen insisted she come into the kitchen for supper as usual.

'I don't mind delivering your lunch to you,' she said, 'but I will not serve supper on a tray as well.'

Bridget muttered but did as she was told. 'The ingratitude of a daughter,' she said. 'After I've given my life for you. Dedicated that's what I've been. And what thanks do I get? You got what you deserved with your slut.'

Maureen didn't know how it happened. It was just two months after Larry's funeral. Her mind was still in a state of confusion. She was at the stove heating the corn chowder for supper while Bridget, complaining about having to move, came into the kitchen to sit at the table across from the twins. There was a crash and Maureen turned to find her mother sprawled on the floor – and, for once, silent . . .

After the stroke, Bridget was virtually paralysed and she never regained her speech. Maureen, with great difficulty and the help of the doctor, who said there was nothing he could do, moved the television into her mother's bedroom, and there Bridget stayed – helpless. In the mornings Maureen sat the old woman up, washed her and combed her hair then tried to feed her breakfast. But usually the food was spat back at her. Three or four times each day Maureen changed the bedclothes, heaving the dead weight as Bridget stared at her with a look of hatred, as if Maureen had been the cause of this.

Through her exhaustion Maureen tried to remain cheerful for the sake of the twins, who, at nearly four couldn't understand what had happened to their daily walks or why the old lady had shut herself away with the television. Still, they soon found playing in the store a pleasant enough diversion. And they had each other.

146

Maureen thought of closing the store. It would probably save money. It would certainly save work. But she couldn't bear the thought of spending each day upstairs. At least in the store there were people to talk to occasionally – even if only about the weather or the shocking price of bread. She was too tired even to cry when she saw the future stretching out before her. Bridget, although immobile, seemed to grow stronger by the day as Maureen grew weaker, as if the mother were sucking life from the daughter. The only thing of which Maureen was sure was that her mother would live to be a hundred, if only out of spite. But she was wrong.

One February morning Maureen rose and raised the blind to see a gentle snow falling from the still dark sky. She longed just to walk out into it. There was no place to go, but then there had never been and probably never would be. There was only away. Away was a better place. Maybe like the Little Matchgirl she could curl up in a doorway and peacefully freeze to death while enjoying splendid visions. Is that how Kathleen had felt, she wondered . . . But there were responsibilities, and Maureen always shouldered her responsibilities. She shivered into her clothes and went first to the kitchen. At least she could savour a peaceful cup of tea before attending to the needs of others. Then she made up a tray for her mother's breakfast, knowing even as she spooned the hot cream of wheat into the bowl that she might as well throw it at the walls herself. It was bound to be spat out. She put on her apron. Balancing the tray, she slowly opened her mother's bedroom door, dreading the beginning of another day. Immediately she sensed the emptiness. Guilt overcame her as she put the tray down and hurried to the bed. She knew at once that her thoughts had killed her mother.

'Sure it is a blessing,' Father Bill said. 'She had suffered enough. Now it is our turn to suffer on alone without her. A great woman she was – a grand mother to us all.'

He vetoed the idea of Elizabeth coming to the funeral.

'Our mother would not want the renegade daughter there,' he said.

'Who'll be next?' Michael wondered. He had become excessively maudlin due to his high consumption of bourbon, brought on by the knowledge that he was now an orphan.

'Next?' Maureen murmured and then remembered. Bridget always said deaths come in threes. First Larry, then Bridget – and now – which of them?

'It's in the Good Lord's hands,' Father Bill said. 'Not for us to question his Almighty will.'

'At least you're well provided for,' Father Bill said to Maureen. 'She's left you well off. And Larry's left you the store. You'll want for nothing. You and the girls.'

'More than anyone ever gave me,' Michael said.

It was then that Maureen realized she was expected just to carry on – carry on in the same house, running the store, raising the children until it was her turn to join her husband and mother in the graveyard. And it was then that she asked herself, why? Who was there left to tell her what to do? Well off? That depended on how you looked at it. She would never want for a roof over her head or a meal on the table – as long as she carried on in the shop. But was that really what she wanted to do with her life – with however much of her life was left. She would soon be forty-three years old. She had no husband, she had no mother, she had no daughter. The twins were in her care, but only by default.

'You're going to see your mother,' Maureen told the twins as she buttoned up their coats.

The girls looked at each other, confused.

'Ma said we haven't got a mother,' Eileen said.

'Haven't got one,' Geraldine echoed.

'Well, she was wrong. Wrong about a lot of things was my mother,' Maureen said.

The three of them were wearing completely new clothes, and Maureen had brushed the girls until they gleamed.

They were a pretty pair in red coats with velvet collars and black patent shoes. She had even managed fur muffs and matching hats for them.

Maureen still wasn't sure exactly what her plans were, but she had shut the store for the funeral and never opened it again. She figured she would probably sell it but at the moment she couldn't be bothered. She was gaining momentum that she was afraid she might lose if she stopped to think. Directly after the funeral she had set out on a shopping expedition.

'But the mourners will be expecting a collation,' Father Bill had protested.

'Then give them one,' Maureen said, and, armed with the money Kathleen had been sending, she took a twin on either side of her and set off on the trolley bus for Boston. There, in Jordan Marsh, she bought everything new, from underclothes to hats, new nightdresses and bathrobes and a small suitcase in real leather.

She looked at the girls and then her own reflection in the mirror, adjusting her new hat so that the feather perched at an angle.

'Well, at least we won't embarrass her with our appearance,' she said to the mirror. She pulled on her new fur-lined kid gloves.

'Come on, girls,' she said. 'We're going on a train.'

'Train? Never been on a train,' Eileen said.

'Neither have I,' Maureen said. 'But don't you think it's about time? I think we will like it.'

Even Pennsylvania Station didn't faze Maureen for long. She had seen it all in the movies and quickly guided the twins through the crowds to the taxi rank. She settled back in her seat, Eileen to the left of her, Geraldine to the right, and gave the name of the theatre to the driver. The girls each stared out of a window, open-mouthed in awe of the towering buildings and crowded pavements. The cab drove quickly, bumping over the manholes from which geysers of steam rose.

149

'Welcome to New York, lady,' the cab driver said. 'First time?'

'Certainly not,' Maureen lied. She knew they drove tourists the long way round to push up the fare. And there wasn't a lot of money left. She didn't dare to think what would happen if Kathleen refused to see them.

'Miss Thornton comes in at six-thirty,' the stage-door keeper told Maureen.

'We'll wait in her dressing room,' Maureen told him, without a hint of doubt in her voice.

'Oh, now look, lady,' he protested. 'That ain't allowed. I can't just let anyone wander in . . .'

'Please show us the way,' Maureen interrupted. 'I assure you it will be all right. In fact, Miss Thornton will be most upset if you don't.' Maureen was determined not to lose her resolve. There was no going back now.

He capitulated, although shaking his head sorrowfully, and, taking a key off the rack behind him, he stepped from his cubbyhole. 'Follow me,' he said meekly and led them through damp concrete corridors, up iron steps and finally unlocked a door.

'MISS THORNTON' the card on the door read. Taking a dollar from her handbag, Maureen handed it to the man. 'If you could arrange a cup of coffee for me – regular – and some milk for the girls, please, I would be grateful.'

'Hello, Jack,' Kathleen greeted the stage door man brightly. She was feeling very chirpy. Monty had just told her that afternoon that the movie deal was finally in the bag.

'Evening Miss – ah . . .'

'Yes, Jack, what is it? Something wrong?'

'I'm not sure. I mean I probably shouldn't have, but she was so sure it would be all right.'

'What are you talking about?'

'The woman – she's waiting in your dressing room.'

'What woman, Jack?'

150

'Good looking woman – she said it would be all right. Two kids with her – cute kids. I'm sorry if I . . .'

'That's all right, Jack. It's fine,' Kathleen said.

Kathleen walked down the corridor and up the stairs, knowing there was no way she could prepare herself. It was the moment she had most longed for and at the same time most dreaded. She wondered if the years she had spent on her own had given her the confidence to handle the encounter. The last few yards stretched out in front of her like the last mile the condemned man walks to the electric chair. Like him she could face the end of her troubles or the beginning of worse. It was the uncertainty that pained. She stopped dead outside the door unable to open it. It was an exercise in acting class: St Joan, offstage, preparing to walk on and face her inquisitors.

'These characters have a life offstage, you know,' Belosky had constantly intoned. 'If you don't know that life you are merely pretending when you walk on stage. No magical transformation happens when you walk from the wings, no Clark Kent telephone box, no magic rays to bring on the reality. Only you can do it. And if you don't, you're not going to fool anyone. Technique, sure, that's important, but that should be like breathing, automatic. It's the quality of mind that counts. You have to believe. You have to know who you are.'

He made it sound difficult, but Kathleen found it easier to understand, to live the character than to live her own life. The character was written down. You could know her past and her future as well as her present. There were no surprises, no decisions to make. If only she could be handed the script of her life it would be so simple. No matter what it contained she would play it impeccably. It was the ad libbing she hated.

Kathleen planted an almost genuine smile on her face before she opened the door. She would not be surprised. She would not be apologetic. She hoped they wouldn't be deafened by the thumping in her chest. She still had no idea of her lines when she opened the door.

The three of them were sitting on the sofa in a row and three faces turned and stared at her as she stood framed in the doorway. In each of those faces she could see herself – in one her eyes, in another her mouth. It was a curious reflection, muddled in a time warp.

There were no words in the end. Maureen stood up and the eternity of silence ended as they embraced each other.

'Why are they crying?' Geraldine asked.

'Dunno,' Eileen said. It wasn't often she failed to have an answer for her sister.

Somewhere in France had run for two years, overlapping a year with *Friendly Enemies*, now in its second year, and David was in a state of shock. His first two plays were both Broadway smashes. He was interviewed seriously by *The New York Times*; he was interviewed cosily by *The Saturday Evening Post* and he was enshrined on the cover of *Time*. His opinion was asked on topics as diverse as George Orwell's *1984* and potty putty. He was quizzed on his attitudes to the famine in China and his attitudes to frozen orange juice. Instantly and at length, he responded. He accepted lunch from any wandering journalist who offered it in exchange for a few glib quotes. And when no journalist arrived he took himself, and usually Paul, off to whichever restaurant was most fashionable at the moment. Occasionally Kathleen joined them, but, although David couldn't understand why, she preferred going to lessons – movement, singing, dancing. Since her success in *Friendly Enemies* he thought, she seemed to be obsessed with self improvement – as if the success was merely a fluke which might vanish if she didn't punish herself with work.

Evenings were more difficult to fill at first, with both Kathleen and Paul on stage. But he was soon on the lists of everyone who gave a party in New York and he accepted all invitations, sometimes managing as many as four parties in one night. He told himself he didn't want to let his admirers down. The truth was that for the first time in his life he felt safe only in crowds of people. He, who had wanted nothing so much as to escape from the demands of the people who were his family, felt content to be surrounded by strangers who praised his work. And that was the operative word: strangers. He was content with anonymous affability. It occupied his mind as did Paul, with gossip and inconsequential conversation as they solved the problems of the Kefauver Committee, the UN and China. With other eminent partygoers he passed the time putting the world to rights – anything to escape his typewriter; because the truth David was afraid to face was that he was mentally frozen. He had no ideas he was capable of pursuing past a page of dialogue. He had no characters who could communicate with him or with each other. He was frightened that if he tried – if he pushed it – he would fail. People, he knew, critics especially but others in the business, envious of his success, would be out to get him. There was nothing they liked better than toppling an acknowledged success. And in the theatre at the moment there was no success greater, more tangible than his. Every time he sat down at his desk, every time he rolled a fresh sheet of paper into the typewriter he could feel them, massed together out there somewhere, willing him to fail. Nothing would be good enough; nothing would satisfy them. And that's what he had in his mind: nothing – except the fear of never writing again.

But no one knew this. All the strangers he spent his evenings with still thought he was a successful playwright and treated him accordingly. As long, he reasoned, as he was not seen to fail he would be all right. Everyone would be able to see a play flop. Everyone could read bad reviews. Everyone could see a theatre go dark. But no one could see him sitting frozen, eyes blankly staring at empty sheets of paper. No one could see his hands shakily poised over the typewriter, refusing to strike the keys. No one could see him each day failing to write. No one except Kathleen.

David had at last found a temporary solution to both his problems. His writing and Kathleen. He was required in California to begin work on the screenplay of *Friendly*

Enemies. Here was a plot he knew; characters he knew. They were, after all, his. Only the technique required for a screenplay was different. Surely he could master that. And he hoped the very act, the physical act, of writing might help him to overcome the inertia that held him in its grip. And he would be getting away from Kathleen for a while. Every time he looked at her he felt guilty. Guilty that he wasn't living up to her expectations. Where had the successful writer she had married gone? Gone to parties everywhere. And he knew she didn't approve. She didn't have to say anything – he could sense her disapproval, and he resented it. What right had she to disapprove of him? He had given her everything – a home, a career, a life. If it hadn't been for him, for God's sake, she would still be changing other people's sweaty beds in Boston. But still he felt guilty. He couldn't work to suit her and he couldn't suit her in bed. He had given up even attempting the latter. There was no point in trying. She expected too much of him. Like his mother. Of course, Kathleen would be coming to California too, but not for a while. She had another two months in the play before her replacement took over. Maybe a couple of months apart would help the relationship. Give them a chance to get their perspective back. Maybe they would remember just why they had decided they needed each other.

Paul was not coming to California. That, too, might be a help. David knew that Kathleen resented their friendship. It was most foolish of her and unnecessary. But actually he knew she resented it for the same reason he resented her lessons, her success and her painting. His friendship with Paul was something she couldn't share. When the three of them were together it was obvious she felt the outsider. David didn't know why that was – he just felt it. And there wasn't anything he could do about that. So perhaps it was just as well that Paul had not been part of the picture deal. The producers were being difficult enough about Kathleen. They flatly refused to have two movie novices in the picture. Paul's role was to be taken by George Pierce who had made a name for himself already. David found him acceptable in the role – not that it made any difference, he did not have any say in the matter. Pierce was a bit too old for the part but he was a solid, stage-trained actor, unlike many of the glamour boys they could have thrust upon him. It was a funny coincidence that the house he now rented had been George's. Well, it would give them a talking point, anyway, if the going was sticky. Paul was staying on, which was good for the play, and he would be taking the house on when Kathleen went to the coast. They had decided that in no circumstances were they giving up their New York base. Hollywood could be a fiasco and they wanted to be able to beat a dignified retreat if need be.

'Beside,' Kathleen had said, 'this is your town now. This is where you belong – writing real plays for real actors.'

David wondered about that, but he didn't tell her he doubted if he would ever be able to write properly again.

Paul went to Grand Central Station with him. Kathleen had a voice lesson and had bid him a safe journey before leaving to keep her appointment.

'See you soon, darling,' she said and kissed him lightly on the cheek before stating she really had to dash and disappearing out of the door.

'Sometimes,' David said to Paul, 'I don't know whether I'm talking to Kathleen or Adele.'

'Well, you're the Dr Frankenstein,' Paul said.

David felt he should leap to Kathleen's defence. How dare you imply my wife is a monster? But the feeling was not very strong. Instead he just laughed.

At the station Paul helped him stow his luggage in the compartment. David would be changing trains in Chicago for the Zephyr with its Vista Dome coaches. All the better to see America. Who knows, he thought, it might even inspire me.

'Well,' Paul said, standing close to David in the tiny compartment. 'I guess this is it.' He fought back the tears which clouded his eyes.

155

'Thanks for everything, Paul,' David said, a hand on his friend's shoulder. 'Look after the play for me.'

'And Adele,' Paul said.

'And Kathleen,' David added.

They stood silently facing each other. Unable to control them any longer, Paul felt the tears begin to glide down his face.

'Hey, hey,' David said. 'It's not the end of the world. I'm only going to California. We'll see each other real soon.'

'Not soon enough,' Paul said. 'I'll miss you.'

'And I'll miss you, too,' David said, hugging him close while patting his back with a comradely gesture.

Paul clung to him. They stood locked together in a close embrace and David too began to cry. Frightened by the intensity of his feeling he let Paul go and gently extricated himself from the other's arms. Separated now, he held out his hand, to shake Paul's in a proper parting gesture. Paul ignored the outstretched hand. He took David's face between his hands and pulled it towards his own. He kissed him deeply and passionately. It was a kiss which David found himself eager to return. And he did.

There was nothing to say after that. Paul turned quickly and left the train. He stood on the platform and watched as the train began to pull away, taking David out of his reach.

David sat, his head buried in his hands, sobbing. He didn't know if he was crying for what he had lost, or for what he had found.

Maureen tucked the twins up together in one of the beds. They both rejected the roll-away cot so Maureen told the chambermaid to take it away again. Then she prepared for bed herself. It was only eight-thirty but it had been an exhausting day – emotionally as well as physically. Was it what she had expected? She didn't know what she had expected, but she had been surprised by the happiness she felt when Kathleen had walked into the room. Every drop of resentment had ebbed away when she had looked at her daughter and pride flooded in to fill the void. What would happen next? Maureen had no idea – just a feeling that it would be good. The girls had fallen asleep immediately. Maureen climbed into the other bed and switched off the light. Another first – she had never slept in a hotel before. How many miles had they travelled today, she wondered idly. About a million – into another world.

After Kathleen had arranged the hotel room for her mother and daughters and seen them off in a cab, instructing them to order anything they wanted from room service and promising to see them first thing in the morning, she returned to her dressing room to prepare for the evening's performance. As she stared into the mirror, turning her face into Adele's, she could only wonder at how calm she felt. How . . . was it happy? The twins were gorgeous. Shy of course, but that was only to be expected. She was, after all, a stranger to them. She had been wise, she thought, to resist the impulse to gather them up in her arms. She must proceed slowly. It was strange. There was no question but that they were together again now.

There was a problem, of course – David. How was David going to take it? There once was a David, the one she first knew, the one she met on a bench in Boston, who would have found them a delight. The David who would have been so happy that she was happy. The David who would have understood. Perhaps she should have told that David. But she had thought then that the past was best abandoned. She had been wrong. But now – the new David, the suspicious David, the frightened David? How would he react? Accuse her of deception before he poured another drink? And he would be right. She had deceived him. But only with details. She had never lied – just neglected to tell him things that were best forgotten. How would the new David take it? Anyway, her mother's timing had been perfect. David was even now on his way towards the sunshine. She had time to make a plan.

There was a knock on her door.

'Come,' she called, as she mascaraed her lashes. In the mirror she could see Paul, in costume and ready to go on.

'Gosh,' she said, 'am I late?' Had she lost track of the time?

'No,' he sounded despondent. 'I just got ready early.'

'Did you see David off all right?' Whatever would she do if for some reason he delayed his departure? Keep her family hidden in a hotel and behave like a character in a French farce?

'Oh yes, train left on time.'

'Oh good.'

'The compartment was pretty poky though.'

'Well, I expect he'll spend most of his time in the club car anyway.'

'Yeh, sure.'

'And the Zephyr is supposed to be lavish.'

'Yeh, I suppose so.'

She turned to look at him. He was standing there as if he expected something from her.

'What is it, Paul?'

'Kathleen,' he hesitated.

'Yes?'

'Kathleen – do you love David?'

'Paul, what a strange question.'

'Not really. I mean I know you like him – but do you really love him?'

'Of course I do,' Kathleen said.

'Good. I mean that's all right then. See you on stage.' He clicked the door shut behind him.

What a strange fellow Paul is, Kathleen thought. Then she thought about his question. Had it really been so odd?

In the wings, Kathleen took a deep breath, told herself everything would work out for the best and, leaving Kathleen's confusion behind, confidently, Adele walked on to the stage.

Kathleen slept fitfully. It was like the night before her first day at school. She was excited, looking forward to the morrow and at the same time frightened by it. She didn't know what to expect and she didn't want to make any mistakes. The dawn came slowly. She wondered what her mother expected of her. Was Kathleen now to take charge of all their lives? She didn't know what she was going to do and she could certainly not make any plans until she knew what was expected of her. What did she want to happen? That was immaterial. They would stay for a while anyway. She would prepare rooms for them. That would keep her busy in the early morning hours until it was time to meet them at the hotel. The girls could sleep in the guest room – there were two beds there, and she would tidy the studio and make room there for her mother . . .

It was cold and crisp and sunny next morning and the March winds blustered down the artificial canyons of the city, but Kathleen found her family dressed warmly and waiting for her in the lobby. There was so much to say. Four years of conversation – how could she begin?

'Ooh, it is cold out there,' she said. 'Have you had breakfast?'

'In the coffee shop,' Maureen said. She was feeling shy, out of place, not having any dishes to wash or any beds to make.

'We had pancakes and maple syrup,' Eileen said. 'And there were paper mats on the tables to put the plates on.'

'And lots and lots of knives and forks and spoons,' Geraldine added.

'Did you have pancakes too?' Kathleen asked Geraldine.

The little girl nodded.

'And two little sausages,' Eileen said. 'Mummy had bacon and toast and coffee.'

'No, Eileen,' Maureen corrected her, 'this is your Mummy – and I'm *her* Mummy.' Maureen had tried to explain this to the twins before but they were so little and she had just let them call her Mummy. They seemed to understand that she wasn't their mother – but Mummy was a different thing. It was very confusing for them. But it

159

was just a name. She remembered when Kathleen had first gone to school and when she came home in the afternoons out of habit she called her Sister. But although she knew it was just a habit, she didn't want to hurt Kathleen.

'So we call you Mummy?' Eileen said to Kathleen.

Kathleen looked over her to Maureen. Then she crouched down, bringing herself level with the twins. 'You can decide what you want to call me. But you don't have to decide right away. There's plenty of time.'

'Have you always lived here?' Eileen asked.

'For a while now,' Kathleen said.

'Why?' Geraldine asked.

'Because . . . well, because it's where I work.'

'Grandma said we had no mother – she said we were orphans,' Eileen informed her. 'She's dead now. So is Dad.'

Maureen had given her daughter a brief résumé of the events which had led up to their arrival the night before. Kathleen had not felt touched by the deaths at all. They had all been dead to her for so long. She could imagine Bridget's nagging on at the twins. Well, at least that was over now.

'She made a mistake,' Kathleen said simply. 'Now, what shall we do? Shall I show you the city?' Take it slowly, Kathleen reminded herself. The future will emerge.

They walked down Fifth Avenue. Maureen and the girls were overwhelmed by the opulence of the window displays. They went into St Pat's Cathedral, a shelter from the winds for a while and the twins tried not to make their heels click in the dim silence.

'This is where I was married,' Kathleen told her mother as they passed the Sacred Heart altar.

'Married?' Maureen whispered. She watched as the twins walked in front of them.

Kathleen gave the girls a couple of dimes and told them to find their favourite statue and light some candles, as she directed her mother to a seat and sat down beside her. The girls wandered off, happily clutching the coins and

160

examining the towering statues carefully before making any decisions.

'I married David DeCosta. He's a writer. He wrote the play I'm in.'

Maureen considered the information. DeCosta – Italian. At least he was a Catholic. They had married properly.

'But where did you meet him?' she asked.

Kathleen tried as quickly as possible to fill her mother in on the details of her absence. Just the facts, of course.

'A chambermaid?' Maureen was full of questions which Kathleen answered as matter-of-factly as possible.

'He's in California now – or will be soon,' Kathleen finished.

'You didn't say how he feels about your . . . about the girls.'

'I didn't tell him.'

'Oh dear,' Maureen said.

The girls returned. Geraldine began to skip but Eileen quickly stopped her with a fierce look and an admonishing, 'You're in church.'

'Come and see,' Geraldine whispered and they followed the girls to the altar of St Joseph.

'There,' she pointed to two candles twinkling in front of it.

'Is that your favourite?' Kathleen asked.

'Eileen chose,' Geraldine said.

'He didn't have any candles,' Eileen explained. 'He looked lonely, sad; like Dad used to look.'

Larry they meant, Kathleen thought, and looked at the statue. She could see what they meant. His eyes were sad, like Larry's, as if searching to understand something he couldn't even begin to comprehend.

'I know where there's a zoo,' Kathleen said.

'Really!' Forgetting where she was, Geraldine shouted.

Eileen shushed her. 'With real animals?' she whispered.

After Central Park they went to Rumpelmayers for hot chocolate.

'We should check you out of the hotel,' Kathleen said.

161

'Are we going back home now?' Eileen asked.

'You're coming to my home,' Kathleen said. She looked at her mother. They had talked about the past but not the future.

Maureen nodded. She was in no hurry to make a decision. And she rather liked New York so far.

Kathleen wondered if David would phone her when he arrived. Or if maybe she should phone him. She knew he would be staying at the Château Marmont for a while until he found some place to rent for both of them – or the studio did. Was a transcontinental phone call any way to tell him that he was a stepfather? There was really no choice. She didn't plan on being separated from the girls again. She could not abandon them twice. Already she had missed so much. Their first steps, their first words . . . hundreds of bedtime cuddles. From the way her relationship with David was progressing it didn't look like she would have any more children. Besides, there was no need to lose them again. She had a career, a marriage. She could afford to look after them properly. She was sure now that David would be pleased. When he was not physically present only his virtues remained with her. She lived in imagination with his kindness, his sensitivity, his intelligence, his love. His faults receded into minor irritations. The sleepless nights were forgotten, the vivid nightmares that left him cold and shaking in the bed beside her. His solitary moodiness, his blaming her for his inability to write – his blaming her for everything that he found wrong with himself and his life – all that was forgotten. She remembered holding his hand and kicking at dried leaves, and Christmas in Chinatown, and how proud she was of him when people rose and clapped as they went into Sardi's – and how much he said he needed her.

She had no doubts that he would be pleased and a loving and kind father to the girls. It was just the shock she wanted to spare him – and besides, she told herself, she could never work out what time it was on the Coast.

She couldn't understand why he didn't phone her, but figured he was extremely busy.

Kathleen arranged matinee seats for her mother and the girls. She knew the girls wouldn't understand much of *Friendly Enemies* but they kept asking her what her job was.

'Do you sell things to people?' Eileen asked. The store was the sum of the knowledge they possessed about working.

They came to the dressing room where Kathleen had organized tea between the matinee and evening performances. There, they were briefly silenced by the sight of the cakes and cookies and milk-shakes.

'Did you enjoy it?' Kathleen asked her mother as the girls sucked at straws.

Maureen nodded. 'You were beautiful. I saw it before, you know, in Boston.'

Kathleen was amazed and Maureen told her about Mrs Weston breaking the news.

'Well, she hasn't changed, has she?' Kathleen laughed.

'Mummy,' Eileen said, putting her milk-shake aside.

In unison Kathleen and her mother responded.

'Real Mummy I mean,' Eileen said.

Maureen deferred to her daughter. It wasn't going to be easy to give up the girls.

'What is it, darling?' Kathleen asked.

'I thought you were called Kathleen.'

'That's right.'

'But everyone called you Adele.'

'I was pretending to be Adele.'

'Why?' Geraldine asked.

Kathleen noticed it was her single most uttered word. Usually Eileen had an answer for her but this time she didn't.

'Because that's my job. I'm an actress. I pretend to be other people.'

'Then you're not real.' Eileen summed it up.

'Well, I'm real. Adele isn't.'

163

'But you are really our mother,' Eileen said.

'Not just pretending,' Geraldine added.

'I'm really your mother,' Kathleen said.

The girls looked at each other as if they had been planning something. They nodded to each other. 'Then,' Eileen said, 'I think we should kiss you.' Geraldine followed her sister into Kathleen's outstretched arms.

Maureen could not deny she felt a pang of jealousy as she watched her daughter and the twins embracing. But the joy in Kathleen's face drove out the selfish impulses. Besides, she reminded herself, she was free now. That was what she had always wanted, wasn't it?

A knock on the door interrupted the emotional moment. Kathleen released the girls but they remained close by her.

'Come in,' she called.

It was Paul, who hesitated, hand still on the door knob, when he saw that she was not alone.

'Sorry, I didn't know you were busy.'

'It's Tom,' Geraldine said.

'No,' Eileen corrected, 'it's the person who pretended to be Tom. Isn't that right?' She turned to Kathleen for confirmation.

'That's right,' Kathleen laughed. Eileen is very quick, she thought. If bossy. 'Come in, Paul. Have some tea. There's plenty. Girls, this is Paul Fredericks. Paul, I'd like you to meet my mother, Maureen Thornton.'

'How nice,' Paul said as he crossed the room and shook Maureen's hand. He could see the resemblance. Kathleen had inherited her mother's looks.

'And,' Kathleen continued, 'this is Eileen and this is Geraldine. Shake hands, girls.'

They performed nicely.

'My daughters,' Kathleen said proudly.

Demonstrating what a splendid actor he was, Paul showed no sign of the shock he felt.

'I'll bet you are proud of your Mummy,' he said.

The girls nodded, overcome by shyness for a moment. Then Eileen said, 'You pretended very good too.'

'Acting, darling, it is called acting,' Kathleen corrected lovingly, maternally. She was learning quickly.

'I won't interrupt. You must have a lot to talk about,' Paul said, retreating towards the door again. 'Nice to meet you,' was his final understatement.

What in heaven's name was going on, he wondered as he went back to his dressing room. David leaves town and no sooner has the train pulled out of the station than suddenly Kathleen conjures up two children. He knew now he had always been right about her. That first time he met her, the way she clung to David at that party. She was a phoney. Oh, she was a good phoney. She had almost won him over, too. Almost fooled him the way she had fooled David. 'Of course I love David,' she had said, eyes wide with innocence. Poor David. He had fallen for her performance. Well, Paul would certainly have news for his friend when he phoned that night. David phoned him every night without fail.

9

David, from his seat in the club car, had greatly enjoyed the wheat fields and the Rocky Mountains and the plains as they had swept past, exhibiting themselves like a synthetic glass-enclosed mural. They were much too elaborate to be real. The train was comfortable, the food good. A number of his fellow passengers, recognizing him from his appearance in magazines, had treated him with a mixture of friendly awe and obsequious deference. And the barman mixed him perfect old-fashioneds – often. The lack of activity, the endlessly changing landscape and the barman's skill together produced in David a general feeling of 'couldn't give a damn' by the time the train pulled into San Francisco. He had forgotten the unease he had felt about the work facing him. He had forgotten the dissatisfaction with his marriage, he had even managed to shove to the back of his mind the terror of recognition he had felt when Paul kissed him. What was Bogart's line? 'The troubles of three little people don't amount to a hill of beans'; before he and Claude Rains walked off into a starlit adventure. David felt now he was on an adventure and whatever happened, it didn't really matter. He would observe and take mental notes and there might at the end be a play in it – but it didn't really matter. He changed trains once again in San Francisco and watched the Pacific, as improbably vast as the Rockies, sweep past the windows on his journey south.

Phil Hornbeam, from the studio, met him in Los Angeles. He was an effusive man who talked a great deal without imparting much information as he installed David at the hotel.

'You should be comfortable here,' he said, 'but if there's anything you want, anything at all, here's the number. You give me a tinkle and I'll have a look see what can be done. Oh, yeh, the car will be here for you,' he consulted his little book, 'ten a.m. Don't want to get you going too early after the long journey.'

He treated him, David thought, as if he had walked from New York.

'And he'll bring you right on down to the studio so you can have a look round. Set up a few meetings, generally get the feel of the place. First time on the Coast? Oh, yeh, of course, you said. Well you are going to love it here, just love it – can't be avoided. Now tomorrow, nothing strenuous, you understand. No ideas expected on your first day,' he gave a dry throaty chuckle. 'Seriously, you're going to have a ball out here, believe me. Anything you want, anything at all, you just give me a tinkle.'

Mercifully, Phil Hornbeam eventually exchanged the heavy-rimmed glasses he wore for an identical pair with dark lenses and departed into the Californian sunshine.

David poured himself some whisky from the bar which had been thoughtfully provided and flung himself on to the sofa, trying to figure out what time it was in New York. Perhaps he should phone Kathleen and let her know he had arrived safely . . . but she was most likely at one of her endless lessons. He would just, he worked out, have time to catch Paul before he left for the theatre. Just time to . . . hear his voice.

There hadn't been much time to talk that first night, so David took to phoning Paul later, when he had returned from the play. It was something to look forward to, some-one to share his novel experiences of studio life with.

'They're all crazy here,' he told Paul. 'Every single one of them. They all talk all the time and then they all agree with each other and no one has listened to a single word.'

David had been installed in the writers' block, a concrete

167

building with a dozen or so offices on each side of a corridor. Only about four were occupied he had decided from the sounds which emanated from them. His window looked out on to the costume block and he could spend hours watching ordinary people go in and emerge as Mohicans or sixteenth-century French aristocrats or wide-lapelled gangsters, complete with two-toned shoes.

His room was sparsely decorated. A desk and phone, two chairs, a small filing cabinet. Writers didn't take meetings in the block. They were summoned to meetings in the main building where the offices were carpeted and the furniture stuffed.

David put his typewriter on the desk and a couple of bottles of Canadian Club in the filing cabinet. No one visited the writers' block and apart from the first day when he had been given the grand tour, ushered into the Chief's plush office where the tiny bald man had welcomed him to the team, assured him how much they valued his work and told him to come and see him with any problems – 'Anything, anything at all. I'm here for you' – and issued him with an identity pass which allowed him through the guarded gates, he hadn't been spoken to by a soul. Hornbeam had nodded to him across the commissary but that had been the extent of his social contact in three days. He had bought a car – a Chevie convertible, pure white – but so far had used it only to trundle between the hotel and the studio. Hornbeam's secretary had assured him they were on the look out for a rental for him when he had decided to see if the phone worked. Otherwise he had spoken to waiters in the hotel and once wished the receptionist a good morning. He had only returned the studio guard's grunt with a similar noise.

But to Paul he made it sound the most exciting adventure every night. Then one night, in reply to David's question,

'What's the news your end?'

Paul said, 'I don't know how to say this.'

'What do you mean? Is something wrong? Is Kathleen all right?' Although he couldn't bring himself to phone her yet – why hadn't she phoned him if she cared? – she knew where he was. His memory had taken on a rosy glow and he sometimes thought that maybe, just maybe, some of their troubles had been caused by him. Maybe she wasn't as impossible to live with as he thought.

'No, she's fine. I mean she's not sick or anything.' Then he told David about the scene of domesticity in the dressing room.

David didn't know whether to laugh or cry. He was literally speechless. So much so that when after a full minute's silence Paul shouted down the line, 'David, are you all right?'

'Yeh,' David forced the syllable out. 'Yeh, it is just . . .'

'I know,' Paul said sympathetically. 'It is kind of a shock.'

'How old are they?' David asked.

'Gee – I don't really know a lot about kids. Three, four, maybe five.'

'And twins – you are sure of that?'

'They were the same size. Didn't look the same though. Not really the same.'

Recovering from his shock, David began to find the revelation fascinating.

'Were they just visiting do you think?' he asked. Would they be whisked back under the carpet, he wondered.

'I honestly don't know. She seemed pretty pleased with them.'

What a silly girl, David thought. Didn't she think that Paul might just mention to him that he had met her daughters? Or hadn't she expected Paul to see them and for a moment forgot herself? Or perhaps she hadn't expected that he and Paul would be in nightly conversation . . .

'Don't tell her I know, OK?' David said.

'What are you going to do?'

'I don't know. Just wait and see what she does, I expect. It could be very interesting.'

'David,' Paul said very softly across the continent.

169

'Yes?'

'David, I'm really sorry; I mean to have to be the one to tell you. I mean. I know how you feel about Kathleen.'

'Do you, Paul? I don't think so.' David himself didn't know how he felt about her. 'Now don't worry. Look after yourself. I'll phone you tomorrow.'

'David . . .'

'Yes, Paul.'

'I love you.'

'I know, Paul,' David said gently. 'And I need that. Good night, sleep well.'

David waited until he had heard the click from the other end before putting the phone down. Good night, he thought. Paul could go to bed now. He could go to sleep. But in California it was too early. Besides, he wasn't tired. He hadn't done anything all day except watch the endless costume parade outside his window. It was preferable to staring at blank paper. He still couldn't write – not even a simple adaptation. His glass was empty. He got up and rectified that.

So, he thought, her secrets were coming out in the open. And they weren't the simple girlish secrets he had imagined. He wondered what else she was hiding. In a way he admired her audacity – picking him up like that, wheedling her way into his life, getting him to make her a star – and even that wasn't enough to satisfy her. She had to trick him into marriage. The complete hold on him. She was very clever indeed. But not quite clever enough. Her hold, he reminded himself, was not total. He had always known deep down that there was something – that she couldn't be trusted. There was no doubt in his mind that although she had gone a long way, she hadn't tricked him completely. His body had recognized her treachery instinctively. His body had refused to respond to her cunning. She had pretended to be so distraught by that. Oh, he had heard her crying in the night. He had even felt guilty about it. But he had foiled her devious plan. She had wanted him to make her pregnant. That's what it was all about. She wanted him bonded to her totally, with his child. Then she could spring the others on him and he would have no choice but to accept. Or abandon his own flesh. And she knew there would be little chance of that. Italians don't abandon their sons.

He finished his drink, plopped another three fingers of Canadian in the glass and drained that in one gulp.

David manoeuvred out of the parking lot. He switched on the radio. Teresa Brewer urged him to 'put another nickel in, in the nickelodeon' and continued to scream out her need for him and 'Music, music, music' as he turned the car on to Sunset and drove in the direction of nowhere in particular. It was a cool night. The sky was clear but the stars were overpowered by the neon along the strip. It was probably snowing in New York and here he was amidst the palm trees and lights, top down, cruising along. He had a job, plenty of money, respect – life wasn't bad he told himself. Occasionally he turned a corner and guided the car effortlessly down another wide, straight, endless boulevard. So by the time he pulled into the parking lot of a bar that proclaimed itself 'Dino's Place' he had no idea where he was. There was no particular reason why he chose that bar. It just happened to be in the right place at the right time. He felt his alcohol level in need of topping up.

'Canadian, double,' he told the bartender as he perched himself up on a stool and grabbed a handful of nuts from a dish on the bar. Solid food, he told himself. Must keep my strength up.

'You're new in town,' the bartender, tall and lean with a red checked shirt, said.

'How can you tell?' David said.

'Your voice. Back East, isn't it?'

'Yup.'

'And, besides, I know my customers.'

'You Dino?'

The bartender laughed. 'No. There ain't no Dino. Just liked the sound of it. Kind of butch, you know what I mean?'

'Yeh. Solid,' David said.

'Make yourself at home,' the barman said. 'I think you'll find the company pleasant and new faces are always welcome at Dino's.'

From the jukebox Teresa Brewer here too was still demanding 'Music, music, music'. David managed to sip his drink as he looked around. It was dim, but gradually his eyes focused. Except for the music it was a quiet bar, unusually quiet. He accidentally caught the eye of a fellow at the end of the bar. He was tall and blond and for an instant David's heart stopped. It was Paul. But that was stupid, David told himself. He had just spoken to Paul. He was asleep now, in his bed, thousands of miles away. The fellow smiled at him. Automatically, David acknowledged him and watched him call the bartender over and go into a huddle of conversation. David continued his survey of the room. Suddenly the blond fellow was on the stool beside him.

'Welcome to the Coast,' the fellow said. 'You're from back East, I hear.'

'That's right.'

'Me, too,' he said. 'But that's a while back now. Hey, your drink's gone. Let me get you another.'

David protested but Francis, who had by this time introduced himself, insisted.

Half an hour and three drinks later David had learned that Francis came from Connecticut but had come West to escape the dull bourgeois life-style he saw there. He worked, he said vaguely, in the car trade. David found him very likeable – like a puppy, eager to be friendly, wanting to be liked. And he reminded him so much of Paul – his build, his colouring, his mouth, David thought, remembering Paul's mouth on his. He focused on his companion's mouth, his firm full lips, the slight stubble shading the top lip.

'Another drink, or shall we go now?' Francis asked, his hand resting gently, now, on David's thigh.

'I think,' David said, unable to tear his gaze from his companion's, 'we'll go now.'

'Enjoy yourselves,' the man who wasn't called Dino said as they left.

The girls liked Kathleen's house very much. They especially liked the secret garden. Maureen at first felt out of place. It was like living in a magazine; everything was too perfect – the cream carpet, the beige leather furniture, the splash of colour introduced by the vase of irises that Kathleen kept replenished. It was all such calculated good taste. But it was her daughter's house and Maureen did not criticize. There was really nothing to criticize, just that the perfection made her feel uneasy. She wasn't used to it. Maureen was surprised to find herself organizing the girls as she always had. She had expected that Kathleen would want to take charge, that she would find herself redundant – but on the contrary; Kathleen had become a daughter again and treated the twins rather like little sisters. When she was about she played games with them. She delighted in taking them shopping and dressing them up, but she did not alter her schedule because of them. The daily round of lessons continued. She disappeared for hours with her sketch book and of course in the evenings she was at the theatre.

Maureen found herself carrying on her usual tasks in the kitchen, in the laundry and with the vacuum cleaner, as well as keeping the twins occupied and disciplined. She had merely acquired more elegant surroundings. She was still in the business of servicing people. Kathleen had said nothing about what was going to happen – about the future. She seemed, Maureen thought, to be avoiding the subject. Then one morning, a few weeks after they had moved in, she heard her talking with the girls.

'It's a beautiful place. The sun is always shining and you can pick oranges off the trees. You can have picnics all year round,' she was saying.

'We're moving again,' Eileen said more as a question than a statement.

Geraldine sighed. She liked New York and she hadn't even got used to missing the store yet.

'Not right away,' Kathleen said, 'but look how pretty it is.' She showed the twins the postcard David had sent. It showed a glossy, overcoloured view of the Hollywood sign on the hills. 'All is well, wish you were here – D.' was all it said. It had been the only communication she had had from him and she guessed the cliché was meant to be a joke.

'When?' Eileen asked.

'Oh, weeks yet; we've still lots of things to see here,' Kathleen said. They had been to the top of the Empire State Building and ice-skating at Rockefeller Center but as yet not to Radio City Music Hall, nor had they done the tour at NBC she remembered. She mustn't forget; they would love that, especially the sound effects. She herself had been fascinated when she saw them making the sound of galloping hooves with the coconut shells and a sand box. And she was a grown up. And the show at Radio City was a wonderful spectacle. She couldn't wait to see their faces when they saw the Rockettes.

'That's all right then,' Eileen said. Weeks was a long time. 'Let's play in the garden,' she said to Geraldine who immediately got down from her chair and followed her sister.

'Don't forget your mittens,' Maureen reminded them as she came in to clear the breakfast things.

'Why don't you sit down, Mum?' Kathleen said. 'There's another cup of coffee in the pot.' She shook it to reassure herself. 'Honestly, you never seem to relax.'

How could Maureen explain that she couldn't change her habits overnight, as much as she might like to. But she did as she was told, another habit, and poured herself a cup of coffee.

'You'll be taking the girls to California then?' Maureen said. She would miss them.

'What do you mean?' Kathleen was genuinely surprised. 'We're all going to California – aren't we?' She hadn't thought it needed to be said.

174

'All of us?'

'Of course, why not? You will come, won't you? The girls wouldn't be happy without you. And neither would I, if you want the truth. I don't know how I managed without you all those years.'

'And what about your husband?' Maureen asked.

'David? Oh, you'll like him.' Kathleen had totally reconstructed the relationship to her liking his absence.

'What does he think about it?' Maureen said.

'He's absolutely delighted,' Kathleen lied. Well, she reasoned, he will be when I tell him. She decided to write; better than telephoning she thought. She would do it today. After all, they would need a fair-sized house for the five of them. They would all get on just fine. And deep down the thought persisted, the thought she didn't want to acknowledge – that she didn't want to be alone with David. Not in California, not anywhere. It would be much better as a family.

Somehow Maureen had thought it would look different, but as she turned the key in the lock and went into the store it was as if nothing had changed at all. She stood in front of the counter and expected Larry to appear from the storeroom – but he didn't. And upstairs, when she saw the empty armchair by the television she was overcome with a sense of loss.

She didn't know how long she sat there and cried, but it was dark when she returned to the real world. How, she asked herself, could she miss them so much when for as long as she could remember all she had longed for was escape? Well, now she was getting her wish and all she wanted was Bridget back, crocheting her woollen squares and demanding her cups of tea and dear Larry sitting at the table, going over his books. They had loved her, she thought. In their way they had loved her very much and she loved them still. She had agreed to go to California with Kathleen and the girls. They belonged with their mother but Maureen knew they still needed her, for a while

175

yet anyway. They had already had so much disruption in their lives. At least she could tide them over, with a bit of continuity. But she had left them in New York. There were things here to be settled. A lot of things to be done.

Kathleen had assured her mother she would be perfectly able to cope with the girls.

'You go home and sell up the old homestead,' she told her. 'And then we can get on the wagon train West with no loose ends. We'll have fun on our own, won't we?' she said to the twins.

They nodded. Weren't they ever going home again, they wondered in mental unison.

'But you have to be in the theatre at night,' Maureen had said.

'They have baby-sitters in New York, Mum. Honestly, stop worrying. We'll be just fine.'

So Maureen had just packed her own things for the trip back. 'I don't know how long it will take,' she said as she left. 'Depends on how quickly I can find a buyer.'

'As long as you manage it by June. Then we can all travel together,' Kathleen said.

June, Eileen thought. June was summertime and it was still winter. June was forever away.

'Can you bring back Fuzzy?' Eileen asked Maureen.

'Oh, yes, please, and Wuzzy,' Geraldine piped up. She missed lots of her toys, but especially their twin teddies. Although Kathleen had bought them splendid dolls at FAO Schwartz they weren't the same as Fuzzy and Wuzzy, especially at night.

'Of course I will. Big kiss now. I have to catch my train.'

They ran into her arms and she gave them a big hug. Then Maureen turned to kiss her daughter goodbye.

'Uh,' Kathleen said shyly, 'I wouldn't mind seeing Teddy-One-Eye again, if you've room in your case.'

Maureen looked at her and she was a little girl again. How had she managed without her mother all this time? She laughed and hugged her tight.

'Now, be good with your Mummy,' she told the twins one final time as her taxi arrived.

Kathleen was pleased to be alone with her children. It was the first time and she filled their days with walks and stories and games, and tucked them up at night before leaving them in the care of the sitter the agency had found and going off to the theatre.

On the third day of this new regime Kathleen was so exhausted she was on the phone to the agency again and within an hour the full-time nanny she had requested arrived. She was starched, uniformed and a genuine English nanny.

'What do we call you?' Geraldine asked.

'We call her Mummy, of course,' Eileen said.

'You most certainly do not. You call me Nanny,' Nanny said. 'Now, come along and wash before tea.'

Kathleen's letter had arrived. The desk clerk stopped David as he walked through in the morning on his way to the studios.

'Letter for you, Mr DeCosta,' he called.

David had put it in his pocket without even looking at it. He knew it was from Kathleen. In the office he propped it up on the keys of his typewriter and looked at it. He hadn't noticed before how schoolgirlish Kathleen's handwriting was. Perfectly formed Palmer method script . . . without character, individuality or soul. There was nothing there for a handwriting analyst to work on. It was so controlled, everything was hidden. On second thoughts maybe that is how an analyst would characterize her personality, he thought. Controlled and deceptive. Or did he mean deceitful?

The letter remained unopened through the morning as David sipped his Canadian Club and looked out of the window. The procession today consisted of soldiers: American soldiers and German soldiers. He was getting bored by the steady flow of uniforms when suddenly a beautiful girl in a red taffeta, full-skirted, floor-length off-the-shoulder ball gown appeared. Her hair was caught up in ringlets, Southern ante-bellum style. He amused himself by trying to fit her into a movie with all those soldiers.

At lunchtime the letter was still in place on the typewriter. Still unopened and unread. He didn't want to go to the commissary. He wasn't hungry. He refilled his glass and noticed that his cache in the filing cabinet was running out. He would have to go to the package store and replenish it, before he met Francis. What, he wondered, would Francis have organized tonight? He didn't want to know. He didn't want to know Francis. But he couldn't help himself. That first night with him – the pleasure he had found in that meticulously tidy apartment. Pleasure that he hadn't even imagined could exist.

'I live alone now,' Francis had explained. 'My friend went back to Detroit.'

'Your friend?'

'He's dead now. They found him in the car – pipe from the exhaust. He shouldn't have gone back. I knew it was a mistake. He was married – he felt guilty about his family. But he couldn't . . . oh, what the hell.' Francis went to a cabinet in the corner of the room and poured David a drink.

'What about you?'

'No – I don't think . . .' Their fingers touched as Francis handed him the glass. They stood. Eyes locked. David was mesmerized. Those eyes, so like Paul's, that mouth. He felt lonely and bereft and at the same time excited and eager. He inclined his face towards his companion's and Francis met him halfway.

'I'm going to shower,' Francis said as they parted. 'Remove the city's grime. Make yourself at home, I won't be long.'

David sat on the sofa uncharacteristically nursing his drink. He didn't want to think about it. It was wrong. He should get up now and leave. He could hear the shower pulsing. He thought of the water caressing that body, that

178

lean muscular body. He drained the glass and put it aside. Just get up now and walk straight out of that door he told himself. He followed the sound of the rushing water, unbuttoning his shirt as he went . . .

His clothing lay heaped on the floor as he pulled aside the shower curtain. Francis, glistening with water smiled and opened his arms embracing him in the torrent . . . .

A couple of nights later two other guys from Dino's had joined them in the apartment. David knew he was making a mistake. But he was powerless to deny himself the physical pleasure. Pleasure he had never missed because he had never even imagined its existence.

Alone in the office, the guilt returned, alternating with the desire for the hours to hurry and pass. Longing for the exhilaration of the evening – for another encounter with pure joy. Well, maybe not pure – David laughed at himself. He told himself it was only temporary. Just an experiment. The experience would help him grow as a person, as a writer. 'Oh, God make me a saint,' he prayed in imitation of Augustine, 'but not just yet.' Soon, well soonish, Kathleen would arrive and Dino's would be history. He would have his wife, his work, a family. That's what life was about. He would have a ready-made family to keep him on the straight and narrow. When he wasn't alone, the temptation would cease . . .

He reached out and took the letter from the typewriter. It had suddenly become his salvation. It was a long letter, but so many things were left still unsaid. She told him about the twins, but made no mention of their father, as if there had never been another man in her life. Through it all, he realized how difficult it must have been for her. How she must have suffered. It didn't excuse her deceit, her manipulation, but it did explain it. There, David told himself, I'm able to understand her now – now that I have secrets. Francis has already helped me to become a more sympathetic person. He would never tell her of his evenings at Dino's.

David dialled Hornbeam's extension. He got the girl.

'Mr Hornbeam's taking a meeting,' she said.

'It's just about the rental,' David explained, 'I'm going to need something bigger than I anticipated.'

He planned to phone Kathleen that night. He planned to tell her he had got the letter, that everything was going to be all right. But he didn't. He didn't phone Paul either.

Francis met him at five at the studio. There was a party at Malibu – a big house on the beach. David never found out whose house it was. It was a large party and no one exchanged names. They had brought no identities, only bodies, and required only bodies.

Maureen finally found a buyer. No one was interested in a corner grocery store. That didn't surprise her. She knew all too well how much the weekly takings had dropped in the past few years. Small retailers were a thing of the past. But in the end a Mr Galliano, God bless him, had arrived and decided it was the perfect position for a dry cleaner and cobbler's shop. He had no need of the stock and was only interested in obtaining the premises – empty. Maureen called up the St Vincent de Paul league who sent their battered van on numerous trips and cleared the place. She brushed aside their effusive thanks, but accepted their offer of prayers. They were doing her a favour, she said. There wasn't anything there she wanted, nothing at all. She was going to California.

As she walked, for the last time through the now empty rooms she bid goodbye to all the ghosts. She wasn't going to take them with her – and she begged them not to follow.

10

Hornbeam had brought the studio stills photographer to meet the train. Thank God I didn't give it to the papers, he thought, as he watched Kathleen alight from the train, one small girl on either side of her. He had thought something was up as DeCosta vetoed house after house that the studio proposed.

'Bigger,' he had said simply, 'much bigger.'

Hornbeam hurried forward and virtually grabbed the girls from Kathleen's hands. Mother and daughters were too surprised to protest.

'Welcome,' he remembered to say, clutching a twin in each hand. 'Now if you just back up a bit . . . that's it, back up on the step, hold on to the rail and lean this way a bit. Fine, great. If you could just look a bit happy to be here – that's it.' He said to the photographer, 'Grab me a couple of those.'

The photographer moved in, at the precise moment Maureen appeared behind her daughter.

'Found it,' she said. She had been searching the compartment for Geraldine's bracelet which had slipped down behind the seat.

'Oh, good.' Kathleen turned to her mother just as the flashbulb popped.

'Oh God.' Hornbeam approached again, girls still clutched by the hand, swept along in his movements. 'Who is this?'

'This is my mother,' Kathleen turned back to her – 'Mummy, this must be Mr Hornbeam, from the studio.

181

He's looking after us.' She descended once again to the platform with Maureen following.

'No, no,' Hornbeam nearly screamed. 'We haven't got it yet.' Then he lowered his voice, someone might be listening. 'Nice to meet you Mrs . . .' he hesitated, '. . . Thornton.' Dippy name; have to do something about that. 'Could you come this way and Kathleen, sweetie, if you could get back on the step.' He eagerly handed the girls to Maureen. 'That's it – like before. Head out this way – smile. OK, get that, Tony. Uh,' he said to Kathleen, 'you haven't got anybody else there have you? No aunts, uncles . . .'

'Nope – this is all of us.'

'Good, great, wonderful – OK, Tony, that's the shot we want.'

'Where's David?' Kathleen asked when she was at last allowed to join the others on the platform.

'He's back at the house making sure it's all ready. You'll love it – you and your little sisters. And you too, mam,' he said to Maureen.

'They are my daughters, Mr Hornbeam,' Kathleen corrected him.

He had been afraid of that. He looked around nervously. In this town you never knew who was listening. 'Shhh,' he said. 'We had better have a think about that one. Chief wouldn't like it. Anyway, we don't have to decide right on the spot,' he said, his mind racing for a solution. 'You don't like sisters, huh? How about nieces? That's it. Sister tragically killed in a car crash. You take them on – wonderful. Chief could go for that.' He turned to the girls who were clutching Maureen's hands. 'You can call your Mummy Auntie, can't you? It's a kind of game.'

The girls nodded silently. Why not? Mummy, nanny, auntie, what difference did it make?

'Mr Hornbeam –' Kathleen began to protest.

'Good, that's settled then,' he interrupted, 'much the easiest. Now, we are not all going to fit in the car? Tony, why don't you take the uh – relatives. Grab a cab and follow us.'

'Now, we want to get the reunion,' Hornbeam said as he stopped in the drive of a two-storey white and pink house, hacienda style. 'Let's just wait until Tony catches up.'

Kathleen didn't object. Even if she had thought it would do any good in the face of this dynamo, she wasn't in any hurry for the reunion. She didn't know what to expect from David. She hadn't spoken with him since he left New York – and the only reply she had had to her letter telling him about the girls was a telegram that said: ORGANIZING HOUSE LARGE ENOUGH FOR ALL STOP DAVID.

She had tried to pay attention to Hornbeam as he rattled off the sights but her mind was really on the meeting. How would it be handled? In the end she needn't have worried. It was taken out of her hands. Tony arrived.

'Right, here we go,' Hornbeam said, getting out of the car. He turned the rear view mirror towards Kathleen.

'You just freshen up your make-up while I get Hubby.'

And so Hornbeam orchestrated the reunion: arms around each other on the doorstep; framed in the doorway for a kiss; huge smiles. Tony followed everywhere, flash-bulbs popping as David showed Kathleen around the house, introduced her to the cook and housekeeper – and posed.

Maureen had kept the girls out of doors, wandering through the garden, out of the way of the camera.

'Look,' Geraldine said, pointing at the orange tree. 'It's true, they grow just like apples.'

'There's a pond,' Eileen said.

'Where are the ducks?' Geraldine asked. All ponds surely had ducks.

'Out flying, I suppose,' Eileen said.

Maureen laughed. 'It's a swimming pool, silly, not a pond.'

Geraldine looked at her in amazement. Not a pond. Eileen had made a mistake.

'Does he never stop talking?' Kathleen asked when Hornbeam had finally decided he'd had enough.

'I'll be going then, let you get together properly.' He flashed a knowing grin which Kathleen found distinctly salacious. 'But try and get some rest as well, you hear. Busy day tomorrow, lots of work to do.'

David smiled in agreement, although he hadn't seen the man, except across a room, since that first day. They all seemed to be letting him get on with it on his own. He wasn't getting on with it, but kept telling himself that it would be all right. Any day now it would be all right.

'You must have an awful lot of questions,' Kathleen said that night when, at last, everyone else settled, they were alone in their bedroom.

'I think,' David said, 'the girls are delightful and your mother is a honey.'

'Oh, David,' Kathleen looked at him, tears welling in her eyes. 'Do you really mean that?'

He crossed the room and took her in his arms. 'Of course I do.' Her body felt strangely soft and pliable. There was no strength in it. She would, he thought, never realize how much he meant it. What a stroke of luck had hit him. Not only did he have a beautiful wife and a 'happy' marriage but he also had twin daughters. Even if the studio insisted on the fiction of them being nieces everyone who was important in the town would assume they were his. That would be the focus of the gossip, the whispering. And that was just fine with him. He didn't plan to spend the rest of his life in places like Dino's or at Malibu beach houses, but for the moment that is where he wanted to be – and now with Kathleen safely installed in the house and the bonus of the twins, he would be free from suspicion.

'But don't you want to know . . . ?' She pulled her head back from his chest and looked up at him, still enclosed in the circle of his arms.

'You keep your secrets,' he told her gently. 'I'll be satisfied with the present and the future.'

You keep your secrets, he thought, and I'll keep mine.

Kathleen was disappointed with the twin beds in the master bedroom. She would have been more disappointed if she had known that David had specifically requested that the king-size was removed and these installed in its place.

Unlike his treatment of David, whom Hornbeam just allowed to get on with it – whatever 'it' was, Hornbeam thought he really didn't care. Who could understand writers? – Kathleen was never left alone. He overwhelmed her with his continual flow of ideas. It was a machine which was taking charge and Hornbeam was the chief cog in that machine. They were going to make her a star – and in return she was going to do what she was told. Everything that could be captured, photographed and used was captured, photographed and used. Her life, it seemed, was to be one big publicity stunt.

'Now, the name – the name is wrong,' Hornbeam had said and the minions around him agreed with simultaneous nods. 'We want something classier – something with more style.'

'Amanda,' the lady in the straight skirt and the bun said.

'Not bad, not bad – has a certain kind of Britishness about it. That's it, Britishness, that's what we're looking for.'

'Cynthia,' the woman said.

'Cynthia . . . Cynthia, I like it. Cynthia . . . Lonsdale. How about that?' He looked delighted with himself.

Kathleen was appalled. She mustered all her dignity. 'Mr Hornbeam . . .'

'Just Hornbeam, sweetie, everybody calls me Hornbeam.'

'Mr Hornbeam,' she continued, 'I think I should remind you that I have been brought out here on the strength of a certain success I had on Broadway. My name is known. I have already made it known.'

'Broadway!' Hornbeam laughed. 'Who knows Broadway? A couple of New Yorkers, and they've got short memories. Soon as your name comes down, sweetheart, soon as those lights dim you are forgotten – nothing. Anyway, we are talking Atlanta and Wichita and Hoboken here. We're talking real people. Broadway – a couple of intellectuals. We're talking Public.'

185

Kathleen felt he always said Public with a capital P, as if it were a proper name, a real entity with a head and a body and arms and legs. A huge giant that might walk through the door any minute. It reminded her of something. She thought back to the religious classes – there was something there. Then she remembered. Of course, Hornbeam's Public was the secular version of the Communion of Saints – a living body, she had been taught, with God at the head and all the believers, living and dead, the members. She wondered who or what composed the head of Hornbeam's Public? Himself? The studio? Or maybe it was Hollywood itself.

Kathleen was adamant. She was going to star in *Friendly Enemies* as Kathleen Thornton, just as she had on Broadway.

'Ah, yes, well that's another thing,' Hornbeam said. 'We've got a couple of things for you to do first – you know, while we're waiting for *Friendly Enemies*. I mean the script isn't ready yet anyway – what a crappy title. Need something zappier than that, that's for sure. Note that down will you Edith.'

The woman in the straight skirt and bun made a note on her pad.

'No one told me . . .' Kathleen began.

'Yeh, well we were getting to that. You signed the contract.'

'I thought that was just a formality. Monty said they really only wanted me for *Friendly Enemies* but they always like to cover themselves and they wouldn't hold me to it.'

'Yeh, well, Chief changed his mind. He decided that you might just really have the stuff. Isn't that great?'

'I don't really know . . .' Kathleen was confused.

She stopped arguing. Publicity invented a totally English background for her – just short of the aristocracy. She had, according to them, been born in London, the daughter of an art historian and his concert pianist wife, both of whom were tragically killed in the Blitz. She had sailed across the Atlantic on a ship which zig-zagged the sea, narrowly escaping torpedoes and arrived in New York where, spunkily unused to such deprivation, she had worked in Saks selling gloves. It was there she was discovered by the Broadway producer who, recognizing her natural charm instantly, cast her in the show and made her a star. Her favourite colour was old rose and her favourite drink Earl Grey tea. She had married her playwright after a whirlwind courtship and breaking off a former attachment to a duke who was of course heartbroken.

'What about my mythical sister?' Kathleen asked. After all, what they had invented was probably more believable than the truth. Why not?

'Ah,' Hornbeam said, 'well, she's kind of shadowy. A tragic figure. You can't bear to talk about it.'

'Don't tell me you have run out of invention?' Kathleen said.

'Just stick to the essentials. It's easier that way,' he replied.

But when it came to changing her name, she held firm. Somewhere in the midst of what was happening to her, what had been happening to her, she had to cling to something. She was Kathleen Thornton. She threatened to take the next train East, contract or no contract and they could sue her to kingdom come as far as she was concerned, but she was not going to be Cynthia Lonsdale or anyone else. She was surprised when they capitulated. Hornbeam insisted it was a mistake and only agreed when the Chief said he would take the responsibility himself. He rather liked Kathleen's obstinacy – it made a nice change – and such a pretty girl.

The victory gave her confidence and the strength to fight when a poodle hair cut was suggested, and a definite thinning of the eyebrows. She emerged from those early meetings, with publicity and make-up and the Chief and planning, virtually intact. Except for one cap on a slightly crooked front tooth and a fictitious biography.

Not bad going, she thought and David congratulated her.

11

The studio wasted no time in putting Kathleen to work. Virginia Wilkins, who was scheduled to play the young widow in *Remember the Dawn*, was pregnant. The rumour was that the condition was definitely planned in order to get out of the project. Virginia thought of herself as a comedienne, while the studio insisted on casting her in emotional roles in multiple handkerchief pictures. In her last three she had been a deserted wife, a manipulated mistress and a dying concert pianist. Plucky widowhood was the last straw, and pregnancy (according to the contract, being an act of God) was preferable to confrontation and suspension. Kathleen's tests were fresh in the chief's mind – she was immediately cast. The script of *Friendly Enemies* was nowhere near ready, a fact Kathleen had been amazed to learn.

'The transition to the screen is trickier than I thought it would be,' David explained to her. 'Opening up – all that kind of thing.' He neglected to tell her that not a single page existed.

Kathleen was not exactly thrilled with the script when it was handed to her. She found *Remember the Dawn* maudlin in concept and simplistic in execution but there seemed no point in arguing. It would give her something to do besides pose for publicity shots. And she was curious about her ability to act for the camera. She had been given the complete studio tour – all the departments from carpentry through editing and had stood on the sidelines and watched

Van Johnson go through a scene. It didn't seem as real as she knew it would look on the screen.

She was surprised at how quickly she had settled into California, the house and indeed the family. The girls were a delight, except when they squabbled over trivialities, but mercifully the squabbling was brief. Her mother managed them beautifully, just as Josie managed the house and Raphael managed the garden and the pool, leaving very little for Kathleen to do other than fret about David. Usually in his absence. He disappeared to his office in the morning and seldom returned before midnight. Often he neglected to return at all. He volunteered no explanations and Kathleen asked no questions. It was only fair after his acceptance of her surprise. Still she felt very lonely and despite the constant movement of people through the house, she felt very alone. At no time did she feel more alone though than on the nights he did return and they had dinner together. She talked about the girls and the photo session and he retold studio gossip. Then afterwards in the bedroom, beyond the bedside table on which rested the two-way lamp, the phone and two separate alarm clocks, she listened to his sleepy murmurings. It will sort itself out, she told herself. So much has happened in such a short time. We love each other, she told herself, blotting out the Plaza, the wedding night and thinking of the park bench in Boston, the play's first night and the evenings in Chinese restaurants. It's a difficult patch to ride out, she told herself, his work is going badly. It only requires patience, tact and caring. So in a way she was grateful for *Remember the Dawn*. It might not be the greatest movie ever made – or indeed even a good one – but it was something to occupy her mind and body.

Surprisingly enough, George Pierce was to be her co-star. Or really her leading man, as the main part was hers. His role was to coax her back to life and love after her tragic bereavement. Hers would be the close-ups, although they shared the billing. As it was a contemporary drama the costume fittings went quickly and easily, as did the make-up and hair tests. So they would start on schedule despite Miss Wilkins' defection. The only thing that pleased the studio more than starting on schedule was finishing on schedule. Kathleen wondered about her ability to deliver the goods. It was a big part to take on, and she was a novice. But she had got on well in the preliminary shots, taken purely for the sake of checking how the costumes and make-up showed on the screen. Just standing still, or walking, turning and sitting, without as yet a character to play, she thought she saw in that girl on the screen a naivety, a vulnerability that she certainly didn't feel. Was that the way others perceived her, she wondered briefly and then locked her musings away. It wouldn't do to become self-conscious. That was a crippling disease for an actor.

George Pierce was introduced to her on the set during the prelims, together with his wife, who, true to her word, left his side only when he was on camera. If her protectiveness irritated him he gave no sign of it. He hardly acknowledged her presence.

'Of course,' Mrs Pierce said as she faced Kathleen, 'you're the girl who bought the house in New York. George,' she turned to her husband, 'you remember I said there was something familiar about Kathleen Thornton when I saw those publicity stills.'

'Such a lovely house,' Kathleen said and remembered the joy in finding it. And the happiness at the beginning. 'We've let it while we're out here, to friends. So we won't have any trouble getting it back when Hollywood tires of us. Don't expect it will take long.' She said it as a joke, but it was what she believed.

'I wouldn't count on that.' George looked at her very carefully, appreciation shining in his eyes and Mrs Pierce moved in closer.

The studio car fetched Kathleen at five each morning to take her to hairdressing and make-up. The shock of the dawn soon gave way to a warm camaraderie. The bustle belied the early hour. Norma Talbert, who was in a costume drama, was already in her chair, her hair being piled high into ringlets when Kathleen arrived the first morning. Without any make-up and indeed no eyebrows at all, Kathleen failed to recognize her, but as she settled into the chair next to her, the voice, familiar from so many epics, jolted her.

'Ah – the new girl in town.' The husky tones were unmistakable.

Kathleen caught her breath. Hollywood grew increasingly, rather than less, unreal.

'Miss Talbert,' Kathleen said.

'Norma, honey, Norma will do fine. We're all in this together. Loved your bio – pure genius I thought. Hornbeam, I expect.'

Kathleen nodded into the mirror. A pink plastic cape was being draped around her by a boy who didn't look a day over twelve. He completed his task and disappeared.

'So where you really from?' Norma asked.

'Back East. Boston actually.'

'Oh well, so there is some class there. You must tell me about it when we are all awake. Freddy!' She called the impresario of hair who was dashing about overseeing the dozen chairs – most of which were occupied. Kathleen strained to identify the occupants, trying to appear nonchalant.

'Yes, sweetie.' He came rushing.

'Are you sure this is right?' Norma asked, indicating a single curl that dribbled down her forehead.

'Let me see, let me see – the pictures . . .' He was impatient with the young man who was working on the coiffure and who seemed to incur his wrath by hesitating a mini-second before producing the pictures from a nearby stand. Frederick held them up, examining them. He turned to Norma's image in the mirror. He screwed his eyes in concentration and then opened them full.

'Sweetie, you are right.' He turned to the young man, Charles, who stood poised, comb in hand, to rectify his mistake.

'Look,' Frederick said, pointing to the picture. 'Further

to the left – do you see?' He grabbed the comb from the man's hand and with a flourish moved the offending curl a fraction, before standing back to survey the effect in the mirror.

'There, you see . . .' his voice dropped off as he admired his own expertise.

Charles nodded, humiliated.

'Never mind, my boy,' the master was now prepared to be generous, 'we all make mistakes.' He patted him on the shoulder. 'But precision is everything in this business – remember that, precision. Miss Talbert's face will be ten feet high. That curl will occupy two feet of the screen at times. Can't have it floating about her forehead from one scene to the next.'

Watching this exchange in the mirror Kathleen could see no difference at all in the positioning. She certainly had a lot to learn she reminded herself.

'Ah, now,' Frederick turned his attention to her. 'Miss Thornton, *Remember the Dawn*.'

'That's me,' she sighed.

He turned away, clicking his fingers. 'Carol,' he called. A young woman appeared instantly, paper cup of coffee in her hand.

'When you have finished your breakfast perhaps you would be good enough to get the working pics of Miss Thornton – *Remember the Dawn* file.' He tutted a bit, clicking his tongue as Carol scurried off. 'Young people,' he clicked. 'But she's a good girl really, talented.' He shuffled through the pictures Carol produced. 'As I remembered, straightforward,' he said as if to himself. 'No problems here.' He fingered Kathleen's hair. 'Lovely hair, no problem – a smidgeon of Autumn glow, I think, Carol – that's all.'

Kathleen didn't remind him that it was he who only a few weeks before had suggested cutting it all off and permanent waving it into tight curls.

Frederick consulted the schedule which was in the file with the hair designs.

'They're starting with the staircase set up,' he said to Carol. 'That's the swept-up do.' He stuck the photo on to the mirror. 'There, now,' he looked at his watch. 'Good heavens, nearly six. Hurry along now.' And he circled the room, chivvying everyone on.

As Carol washed and set her hair, Kathleen closed her eyes to shut out the bustle all around her and tried to concentrate on the lines for the scene she would soon have to do – but her mind went blank. Soon she would have to face the cameras for the first time in her life – the first time that really counted – and her mind was blank. She could only think about the flutterings in her stomach, which felt not so much like butterflies as a plague of locusts. She willed herself to be calm, but as Carol settled her under the dryer with a cup of coffee she could barely bring it to her lips, her hand shook so much. The noise of the dryer drowned out Norma's comments as Frederick approved the completed coiffure.

'She's a cool one, Freddy,' Norma said, indicating Kathleen with a nod of the head. 'A real cool cookie.'

Two hours later Kathleen began her film career. But as she walked on to the set she was not feeling it was a momentous occasion, a milestone; she felt, rather, very, very small and very, very shy as she picked her way around flimsy painted walls, terrified she would send them toppling, and trod very carefully over the myriad cables that snaked everywhere. All around were carpenters, hammering, sawing and stapling with what sounded like machine guns; overhead men swayed from beams, positioning lights according to instructions being shouted from the studio floor. Kathleen felt she had wandered into a foreign land – a land where she had no function, no place, no friends. A land where she neither spoke nor understood the language. Whichever way she moved she felt she was in someone's way. Everywhere voices shouted meaningless instructions. She froze in place, letting the maelstrom whirr about her for what seemed an hour but was only a few minutes, until she was rescued by a sandy-haired young man with a clip board.

'Miss Thornton . . .' The voice spoke her name and edged its way through the din like a sliver of light.

She turned in the direction of her name, staring blankly into the freckled face that seemed to be trying to communicate with her. The face smiled tentatively. 'It's always a bit of a shock at first,' he said, 'but it is exciting isn't it? All this creativity. You never quite get used to it.' He spoke as the veteran of two pictures.

Kathleen nodded to him, seeing no creativity – only chaos. She very much wanted to be someplace else – on a park bench drawing a tree.

'Mr Kelper is ready for you,' he continued. 'This way and watch out for the cables.'

How could she do otherwise? The floor was covered with wires – thin wires, thick wires, some as big as water hoses. Metal connections provided even more traps for her high-heeled shoes. She picked her way through the maze behind the young man to an oasis of relative calm, beyond the cameras. From this perspective she looked back on to the set on which she had felt marooned and saw a substantial entrance hall seemingly transposed piece by piece from an elegant mansion. The floor was obviously marble, the wall panelled in the best mahogany. The curved staircase swept, carpeted, up to a gallery of portraits – it looked from her new angle as if they were painted by Singer Sargent. All this from plywood and paint – it was truly magic.

❧ 12 ❧

The studio was pleased with *Remember the Dawn* and immediately scheduled Kathleen in to *One Last Night*. This time she was the other woman – of the nicest possible, misunderstood kind. George Pierce was once again her leading man. The studio had decided the chemistry between them worked well and the studio motto could well have been 'never try to improve if it works'.

George, this time, was an unhappily married man. His wife, a shadowy figure, more talked about than seen, was a drunk and a bitch, constantly taunting him about his lack of success. Miriam Telford played the wife and had only one scene, but it was a beauty; she got to scream, throw things and be generally nasty. Kathleen was the quiet nice girl working in the office to whom George confides his unhappiness. Naturally they fall in love but after many soul searching, heart-breaking romantic scenes they renounce each other. He must stand by his wife and children in the for-better-or-worse tradition. After the one last night of the title Kathleen leaves her job and dissolves into the distance out of his reach and out of his life.

Friendly Enemies was still not ready. It was more not ready than even the studio realized, although they appeared not to care all that much – seemed even to have forgotten about it completely and, indeed, about David, who nevertheless continued to occupy his office and to collect his salary. But what David perceived as amnesia on the part of the studio was in fact merely indifference.

At one of the regular meetings between the Chief and Hornbeam the subject of David had come up.

'What is happening with that writer guy who came in on Thornton's coat tails?' the Chief asked. 'How long's he been around?'

'More than a year – and nothing good is happening,' Hornbeam informed him.

'How so?'

Hornbeam hesitated. He was the Chief's eyes and ears, but part of his job was to handle things himself. Picayune details were not to interfere with the Chief's grand schemes. He had the vision, the plans, the ideas. Hornbeam was the executor and sometimes the executioner. But hell, he thought, he wasn't going to be able to keep this quiet much longer. David had all but abandoned discretion. Now that he had Kathleen and those girls in residence he felt safe. Hornbeam had seen it all before. Writers were trouble, he thought – especially fancy East Coast writers who thought they were better than anyone and usually turned out to be drunks or queers, or, as in David's case, both. If it were up to Hornbeam his contract would be cancelled, bought out if necessary. It would save money in the long run. And then David could be put on the next train back East where he belonged. He was going to be nothing but trouble and, Hornbeam suspected, big trouble at that.

'The usual story,' he told the Chief. 'Queer as a coot and half as clever.'

The Chief showed no surprise. 'Kathleen know?' he asked.

Hornbeam shook his head.

'Well, you'll just have to keep it under wraps, won't you? Can't have the little lady upset. She's good, that girl – valuable property. Besides they look good together – in the biogs – golden couple, all that crap – makes a change from the eligible bachelorettes. That's the way I want it to stay. Have you tried putting it to him? The way it is?'

'Don't think it would do any good. As usual, he has a

196

smart ass attitude. Thinks he's clever. Thinks I don't know he spends his days with the bottle and his nights at the beach house.'

'*The* beach house? At Malibu?' The Chief now looked surprised.

Hornbeam nodded again.

'The idiot! And I thought he had class. Not a hell of a talent but plenty of class. Hasn't anyone told him that the beach house is real no-no? I mean there are places and there are places. Do you remember when Maxie got mixed up with that crowd?'

Remember, Hornbeam thought, how could he forget? He had arranged Maxie's funeral – and the coroner's report. Death by drowning, it had read, after Hornbeam had paid plenty for him to forget to mention that he had been tied up and beaten to death before being dumped into the Pacific. How Maxie's fans had mourned the All-American boy who had drowned so tragically just before his most important movie had been released. Of course the money hadn't been in vain – besides saving the reputation of the studio, the movie grossed plenty. It became a cult classic and would probably go on forever, as would Maxie's boy-next-door image, frozen in time and space and celluloid before his tragic death.

The Chief tapped his fingers on his desk. 'Couldn't you steer him towards Johnny?' That, he thought, would be ideal. Johnny Cartwright, the cowboy star had just been left by his lover. The public, of course, thought he was in love with his horse but in reality it had been a lighting man with whom he shared his life. Unfortunately the lighting man had gone off with the latest beefcake heartthrob who wasn't, the Chief was glad to say, contracted to his studio. Johnny was distraught and, in honesty, the Chief liked him. He might be queer but he was no trouble. Gunslinging and mean on screen he was a pussycat in reality. He did what he was told. He never questioned a script or a photo session and kept his private life private. You wouldn't catch him at the beach house.

197

Hornbeam, too, liked Johnny, for much the same reasons as the Chief did. He shook his head. Even if it were possible, he thought, he wouldn't wish David on to Johnny.

'The writer is not interested in going steady,' Hornbeam said. 'He likes plenty and it seems he likes rough.'

The Chief slapped his hands palms down on the desk in a gesture of reluctant acceptance. 'Well, try and avoid major disasters. I've got Thornton scheduled for *Goodbye to Yesterday* as soon as we wrap *Night*. You've seen the cards from the sneaks of *Dawn*?'

Hornbeam nodded; he had indeed.

'They love her,' the Chief continued. 'That lady is a very, very valuable property and we don't want that stupid little bastard queering the deal, do we?' He gave a grunt of appreciation as he recognized his unintentional pun. 'Queering the deal . . .' he murmured again.

'Right, Chief,' Hornbeam said, as usual, but he hadn't any idea how he was going to carry through. He did, however, have a feeling that it was not going to be easy. The best thing for all concerned, he thought would be to kick the fruitcake out of town – best for the studio, best for Thornton and probably, although he didn't care about that part, best for the bugger himself. At least he stood a better chance of staying alive and reasonably healthy.

The trouble began even sooner than Hornbeam expected. The phone rang in the middle of the night – three-twenty-four to be precise, as Hornbeam noted on his bedside clock.

'Got one of your boys here.' It was Sergeant Bill Evans, calling from the station. 'Didn't think you would like seeing him up in court in the morning.'

'Who?' Hornbeam focused quickly. Years of experience had made him instantly alert.

'Says he's an important writer.'

Hornbeam didn't need to hear the name. 'What's the charge?' he interrupted.

'Could be drunk and disorderly – could be morals. It

198

was some do – a dozen or so of them slugging it out in the buff on the beach. At least I think they were slugging it out.'

'I'll be right down.'

'You'd better bring some clothes with you,' Evans said. 'Police blankets don't leave the station.'

God Almighty, Hornbeam thought, as he dressed quickly – this one will be expensive.

He brought David, still drunken and unrepentant back to his apartment in which he had lived alone since Miriam had left with the words, 'You're married to that goddamn studio. You don't need me as well.'

She had, he supposed when he thought about it, been right. He hadn't missed her at all. He installed David in the spare bed and watched him snort into a drunken sleep. He was filled with disgust but not surprise. Nothing about human nature could surprise him any more. And it was, after all, what he had expected from this particular human. The standard lecture about discretion would have to be postponed until the morning or probably, from the look of the miscreant with his bloodied face, until noon. Hornbeam had no doubts about the lecture's efficacy – it would be zero. This particular wise guy thought he had all the answers and he knew he held the trump card – Kathleen. Well, he would just have to learn the hard way – if he lived so long. Maybe the booze would get him before the boys did. Maybe not.

Anyway, Hornbeam put the organization into action, money changed hands, favours were promised and the incident, despite the near death of one of the participants, a car jockey from the Brown Derby, went unprosecuted and unreported. Hornbeam thought David decidedly unworthy of all the trouble but there was the studio to protect from embarrassment and of course there was the new star who just happened to be the bastard's wife.

David remembered little of the incident and couldn't understand what all the fuss was about.

Remember the Dawn was, as predicted by the Chief, an

enormous success when it was released. The critics, while declaring the script rubbish, hailed Kathleen's beauty, style and performance. The audiences wept rapturously.

Kathleen had had only one week's break between finishing *One Last Night* and beginning *Goodbye to Yesterday*. That week was spent giving interviews and travelling to personal appearances. She was exhausted and seriously contemplating following the example of Virginia Wilkins and pleading Act of God but her chances were negligible. David barely touched home base and when he did he certainly didn't touch her. If only she could have some time with him, she thought. Some time away from everybody and everything. If only they could both relax and talk – but there was no time. The studio and David between them made sure of that. She knew he was staying away because he still hadn't forgiven her for her deception. She couldn't really blame him – it had been a whopper. He had said he had forgiven her, but she knew differently. Perhaps in time he would, she thought – she hoped.

Because of her work-schedule Kathleen saw very little of the twins. They were always asleep when she left for the studio and asleep again when she returned. On Sunday, her one free day, she had little energy left to expend but what she had was spent on them. She cuddled them unmercifully, as if they were dolls. She learned to swim, alongside them in the pool, sharing their tuition. Maureen thought she behaved more like their older sister than their mother and that couldn't be right. As for herself, well, she liked California, at least she liked the climate and she liked the house and of course she adored the twins and was pleased to be with her daughter once more. But still, it wasn't right. She saw no one except Josie and Raphael and she spent all her time doting on the girls. No, she thought, none of this is right. This was definitely not the way she should be spending her life. Besides, if she remained looking after the twins Kathleen would never become their mother and from the way the marriage appeared to be going these were the only children she was likely to have, so she had better take advantage of them. Anyway, they were going to be starting school soon so then what was Maureen going to do with herself? No house to keep, no shop to mind, no aged husband or mother to look after and no children. It was time to move on; she wasn't needed. She remembered having that feeling when she had taken the twins to New York with every intention of leaving them with their mother. What had happened? They all seemed still to need her too much to let her get away. Or perhaps she had needed them to need her? It was a frightening idea, setting off on her own. But this time it was definitely now or never – she was ready and this time she wouldn't stop. She was about to be forty-five. If the saying was true her life should have begun five years ago. And here she was, still living other people's.

Before she told Kathleen of her decision she called up Sandra, the nanny the girls had had in New York. She was pleased to learn that Sandra's latest temporary job was coming to an end and that she would be free and there was nothing she would like better than to come out to California and look after Geraldine and Eileen. That would be good for the girls – someone they knew. It wouldn't be another upheaval. And so Kathleen was presented with a *fait accompli*.

She felt lost when her mother told her. Everyone seemed to be abandoning her – first David and now her mother.

'Nonsense,' Maureen told her, feeling as frightened as she knew her daughter felt. Wouldn't it be easier, she thought, if I stayed? Easier, she answered her own doubts, in the short term but not what she wanted and, assuaging her guilt, Maureen reminded herself that it was for Kathleen's own good. She may have become a Broadway star, she may even become a movie star, but Kathleen had still not grown up. Neither, thought Maureen, have I. Kathleen still thinks that life consists of responding to other people's expectations. I may now know that's not the way it should be, but I'm still terrified of behaving otherwise. Still frightened of being thought selfish. Still striving to be a good obedient little girl. She decided to keep that her secret and maintained a firm, calm, confident tone of voice.

'You'll get on just fine. Besides,' she added consolingly, as a mother should, 'I won't be far away if any of you need me.'

Sandra arrived and the girls were delighted to see her again. They loved the funny way she talked – and Kathleen decided it would be useful having her around. The accent might just rub off a bit – and Sandra could help her with her research if she played English roles.

❧ 13 ❧

Maureen found herself an apartment in a curious court surrounding a swimming pool. There were fifteen apartments on three sides of a rectangle. They were lodged in three separate single storey buildings and each apartment had its own entrance. The janitor showed her to number twelve in the right hand side of the rectangle.

'Miss Oklahoma finally gave up and went home,' he said, barely moving the lips which clenched a cigarette between them. The pool was deserted and a murky green colour, with leaves floating on it. That didn't matter to Maureen. Unlike her daughter and granddaughters she had not learned to swim. The janitor opened a screen door and unlocked an inner door, leading the way.

'Yup, they usually give up – some later than sooner. Some leave it too late,' he said.

He switched on a light. Despite the sunshine, the room was dark and all over brown nicotine stained. It was a medium sized room but contained a sofa, and an arm chair in one section and a small kitchenette on the far side, with a square table and two kitchen chairs.

'Them that cares about that kind of thing puts up a screen to kind of divide up the room,' the janitor said. 'We don't supply none, though.'

He led the way through to the bedroom. A double bed and a chest of drawers took up the entire room and next to the bedroom a tiny bathroom contained a pitted bath with a shower attachment on the wall.

'There are some hooks on the walls already, for hanging

up mirrors or pictures or whatever,' he said, the ash clinging precariously to the stub still between his lips. 'No hammering nails into the walls, that is a rule,' he said.

The sound of a typewriter came through the wall from the next apartment. Whoever was causing it was not a trained typist, Maureen thought. It came in fits and starts. Rhythm was non-existent.

'I'll take it,' Maureen said. It wouldn't do to be fussy. She knew she should be grateful. There was a housing shortage in every city in the country.

'There's some papers to sign up in the office,' the janitor said, 'and it'll be a month in advance plus a deposit in case of damage.'

Formalities completed, he handed Maureen the key and she hurried around the algae ridden pool and into the apartment, giddily. It was hers – all hers alone! She could do as she liked. No one would be there to expect anything from her! She could get up when she wanted – eat or not eat as the mood took her – anything – without having to explain to anyone. She was free – at last!

Maureen sat at the kitchen table and began to make a list of all the things she needed to buy for her apartment. She savoured the thought of that – her apartment. At the top of the list she wrote sheets. Then a wonderful idea came to her. She would buy purple sheets. Bridget had always said that coloured sheets were sinful. And Bridget hated purple. Giggling she decided to buy purple towels as well and a big purple throw pillow to brighten up the sagging sofa. It was all going to be such fun!

It was not long before Maureen found herself a job. It was in the china, glass and giftware department of Mendel's Department Store in Beverly Hills. Of course she didn't really need it. There was still plenty of money from the sale of the house and the shop and even if that didn't last her forever she knew Kathleen would always help her out – but she wanted to meet people, on her own and not through her daughter. She was determined to lead her own life, not someone else's. And she very much enjoyed being surrounded by Royal Doulton, Wedgwood and Baccarat crystal. It made the most wonderful change from baked beans and Twinkies.

Maureen had also reformed herself. She had decided that strawberry blonde was exactly the right colour for her hair and now she dressed rather elegantly in black and white for her job. She still hadn't decided on the perfect clothes for her social life but she spent her lunch times and coffee breaks perusing the designer section of Mendel's dress department. There was no hurry, she could plan thoroughly because as yet she had no social life. This, however, didn't worry her. It would come. Anything, she now felt, was possible. She luxuriated in her independence. There were so many things to catch up on, so many wasted years to be redressed. Maureen learned to drive and bought herself a red Buick with a black stripe down the side and on her days off she headed it out of town and explored the countryside or she went to the coast and walked by the sea. She thought about building herself a house similar to the ones she saw hanging precariously above the high water mark. Maybe she would. Anything was possible.

Maureen was constantly amazed as she watched herself build a new life. She was amazed by her abilities. She found at Mendel's she had fitted in immediately. There were two other women in the department not including Miss Simmonds, the buyer. Freda Hoffman had been there for three years. She was from somewhere in the Middle West, somewhere unspecified, somewhere she never talked about. What she did constantly talk about was Sam. Sam was a car dealer in Santa Monica who was by all her accounts, 'going to be really big'. He had a General Motors franchise and the cars were really moving. He also, according to Freda, had film-star looks – a cross between Robert Taylor and George Montgomery. (Maureen kept trying to imagine him, but couldn't.) He also, it seemed, had a wife and four kids, but Freda said he was sorting that out. She planned her working life, indeed she planned her whole life, around trips out of town to motor shows.

Shirley Moran, the other woman, was much younger but already had a middle-aged set to her face and a rather middle-aged waistline. She had been engaged to Peter Squire for four years. They had been more or less promised to each other for years before that and they were saving up to get married. Every Sunday they drove somewhere to examine the show houses on the new tracts that were becoming suburbs.

'Although,' she explained, 'I'm not sure that we will stay in California. There is so much competition here.' Peter had been a garage mechanic, a waiter, a taxi driver and now he was working in a supermarket and taking night courses in photography.

'He says there's good money in photography,' she told Maureen, 'but I wish he would settle for something . . . steadier. Like a job in an office, you know?'

Miss Simmonds, Maureen thought, was maybe a few years older than herself, or maybe not, it was hard to tell. There was a kind of timelessness about her. She was a big woman, not just tall but big all over, though certainly not what anyone would call fat. Statuesque. Imposing. Severe. She wore her hair scraped tightly back from her face and gathered into an enormous chignon at the back which she surrounded with a black velvet ribbon that had a discreet flat bow at the bottom. Her lips were always scarlet, outlined, Maureen noted, with lip pencil. She wore false eyelashes and blue eyeshadow and her eyebrows were shaved and immaculately re-drawn with tiny strokes. Her nails, impossibly long, were the same shade of scarlet as her lips. She also always wore a long strand of pearls that stopped at the most prominent point on her bust and large pearl clip-on earrings. Maureen wondered if they were real but thought not. Miss Simmonds also wore black stockings, sheer – and extremely high heels. Hovering over the pearls, her butterfly-framed glasses dangled on a black cord around her neck, ready to be swept in a quick movement into place when it was necessary to check a price, an order or a china mark. Maureen thought any of these features, the eyelashes, the lipstick, the nails, taken separately would be considered vulgar, but somehow the overall effect was dauntingly sophisticated – very Joan Crawford. Maureen would have loved to have imitated it if she thought she could carry it off – but she knew she couldn't. So she settled for her more natural look, with just a touch of pink lipstick and the merest hint of eyeliner. And of course, the strawberry blonde hair colour she had acquired could be taken for natural. The less to go wrong the better. After all, she was still finding her feet in her new life – she was still deciding who she was.

Miss Simmonds did not chat. She had a desk in the stock room, behind a wall of Waterford crystal, to which she retired if she was not needed on the shop floor. There she kept her order books, her inventory ledgers and packets of Kents. Maureen also noticed, although this was some time later, that she also kept a bottle of Jack Daniels and some mouth refreshers in a drawer there.

On the floor itself Miss Simmonds had another desk. This one was much more elegant with curved legs that ended in brass claws. It had a single drawer in which she kept customer order forms and bridal lists. There was a glass top on which there was a brass plate that said, 'Miss Simmonds, China and Glass' and two pens in marble pen holders. An armchair, delicate and also with curved legs and brass claws and a cream and brown wavy patterned Bargello woven seat, was behind the desk and on either side, for privileged customers, there were two chairs with matching seats, but armless.

At first Kathleen was frightened of being alone with the girls and despite the nanny she felt alone. She wasn't sure what caused the fear. Was it just a lack of confidence or was it because she had abandoned them once. Did they blame her for that? Or was she afraid of what she might do? Would she let them down? She was daunted by the responsibility but knew, really, that she had always felt responsible – even in absentia. Gradually that responsibility became a daily caring rather than an abstract guilt. The nebulous worry, now that the twins had become a defined worry, transferred to her mother. Whatever was she doing? Kathleen had been to visit her, as Maureen refused to come to see her. Actually, Maureen was afraid of her reaction at seeing the twins – she missed them terribly and she needed more time before she could be a grandmother and no longer a mother. But that wasn't what she said.

'Don't want to interfere in your life,' she always said to her daughter.

Kathleen had found an elegant creature, a Greer Garson clone, serving her tea in china cups, seemingly unaware of her seedy surroundings. Maureen had spoken brightly of unspecified plans with an optimistic twinkle in her eyes. It was true she looked much younger than her years, but Kathleen could not help thinking that her mother was losing touch with reality.

'You've made it very nice,' Kathleen said, looking around the room. Maureen had hung reproduction Dutch Masters on the nicotine walls, but the subtle browns and golds of the prints were totally overpowered by the blaze of purple that shone through the room. A lilac cloth covered the table and similarly coloured material was thrown over the sofa, teased into place by velvet cushions in a darker shade. Huge paper lilacs filled vases and nylon fur rugs in deep purple were dotted around the floor. A tasselled purple shade covered the bulb which hung from the ceiling. Maureen didn't very much like the decor she achieved – but she knew Bridget would have hated it and that's what mattered.

'Milk or lemon?' Maureen had asked as she poured tea from her purple and gold pot into the delicate china.

'Lemon, please,' Kathleen had said, not knowing what to say next. Her mother looked like a duchess who had innocently wandered into a brothel and hadn't noticed.

'I'm glad you like it,' Maureen had said.

Kathleen joined her at the purple table and sat on the other chair – which wobbled.

Maureen noticed and said, 'Oh, dear, yes – that chair is a nuisance. One of those rubber things has come off the leg. It was already off when I moved in – but the janitor has promised to do something. He is a nice man. He really likes what I've done here. Said he could hardly believe his eyes.'

The sound of typing came through the wall.

Maureen looked at her watch. 'Right on the button.'

'You mean it always starts at the same time?' Kathleen asked.

'Four-thirty to eight-thirty every day,' Maureen said. 'Then the door slams and it starts again at ten. I don't know how long it goes on because I usually fall asleep pretty quickly. Usually it has stopped by the time I wake up in the morning though – except a couple of times I heard it then.'

'Doesn't it annoy you?'

'Oh, no. I find it rather soothing. Company, you know, in a funny way. And I'll tell you something strange. I can tell when whatever it is he is writing is going well – it takes on a kind of rhythm.'

14

Maureen adjusted the purple velvet cushions. Perhaps her mother had been right, she thought. After all, she must have been right about something. Purple was a mistake. Three months at Mendel's and her taste had changed radically. Although the purple *had* been a revolt rather than a choice . . . She glanced up at the clock. It was quarter to seven and there was silence. She had come home earlier, for the first time to silence – every day when she returned from the store there had been the welcoming sound of typing. The lack of it worried her. Maybe he was ill. She had caught a glimpse of him a couple of times as he left at eight-thirty. Not at all bad looking. In fact he was quite attractive in a dishevelled sort of way. He could use a hair cut and then his face wouldn't seem so thin. But being so tall, with a slight stoop, the longish hair seemed part of the design – artistic, consumptive even, but she had heard no coughing through the wall, and certainly not terminal coughing. Still, she couldn't help worrying. She tried to assure herself that it was no concern of hers. If he didn't want to work that was his business. She had absolutely no responsibility and wouldn't be thanked for poking her nose in where it didn't belong. Besides, she hadn't even met him.

By seven o'clock she had convinced herself that he lay dying on the floor. Nonsense. He was out. He had an appointment or a date or something. People were, after all, allowed to break with routine occasionally. But she couldn't relax until she was sure. She listened, her ear against the wall for sounds – any sounds – but there was complete stillness. Absolutely certain that there was no one in, she went next door, opened the screen door and knocked tentatively on the inner door. It sounded hollow. She wondered if her own door sounded like that. No one had ever knocked on it. To her horror she heard footsteps from inside – and a kind of shuffling noise. What in heaven's name was she going to say? Should she try the cup of sugar routine? No, that was too . . . She decided to bolt back inside her own door, but it was too late. With a slight creak of the hinge the door opened inwards and he was facing her.

'Yes?' he asked. There was no impatience in the question; in fact there seemed a kind of hopeful anticipation in it, as if he were expecting her to do something for him – to bring him good news.

'It's just . . . I was wondering . . . I live next door and . . .' Maureen did feel a fool as she babbled on.

He looked at her quizzically, with the beginnings of a smile in his eyes. They were very dark blue.

Maureen breathed deeply. A sigh really. 'There was no typing,' she blurted out.

The smile fulfilled its promise and dazzled her with its brilliance. It sparkled from every facet of his face. 'And you worried about me!' he exclaimed. 'How wonderful!'

For a moment Maureen thought he was making fun of her. He thought, she decided, she was a silly busybody – but no, she realized, that smile was real. He was really pleased. And she also realized that despite her resolve, she still felt good about pleasing people.

'Come in, come in,' he said, although he continued to block most of the doorway, his head slightly bent to fit under the lintel. He held his hand out to her. 'Hank,' he said, 'Hank Martin.'

She took his hand and he shook it vigorously.

'Maureen Thornton,' she said, having caught his smile.

Maintaining a grip on her hand he stepped sideways and ushered her into the room.

'Goodness,' she said. It was empty except for a table and a hard wooden chair with three stiff round dowels, like broom handles, for a back. On the table was a typewriter and two boxes full of paper – one box blank, the other covered with writing – and an Anglepoise lamp. The floor – wall to wall – was covered in screwed-up bits of paper, ankle deep. Maureen tried to avoid stepping on them, but it was impossible.

Seeing the look on her face, he explained, 'Had everything else taken out. I'm easily distracted, you see.'

'I see,' she said, mesmerized, and noted through the open door that the bedroom was also empty. 'But where do you sleep?'

In the doorway of the bedroom, Hank pointed to a darkened corner of the room, 'I've got a roll-away cot stashed there and I keep it folded up so that I'm not tempted to avail myself of it – not until the four pages are done.'

'Four pages?'

'That's my target. Every day. Four pages that satisfy me. Of course I usually lose about three of them the next day.' He kicked some of the paper out of the way. 'Gets like this by the end of the week. Saturday is clear out day, you see. Sweep up all the dross and dump it. Here, sit down.' He pulled out the chair and held it for her.

'Oh, I don't think . . .'

'Come on, come on,' he interrupted, 'it's such a pleasure to have visitors. I mean *a* visitor.'

Maureen sat down and Hank perched on the edge of the table, sweeping more screwed up paper on to the floor with the back of his hand. 'Sorry I can't offer you anything. Don't keep anything here, you see.'

'Distractions?'

'Right. I mean, I'd be making cups of coffee for myself endlessly, and then drinking them and well, you see anything is better than writing.'

'Then why do you do it?'

'That's a question I often ask myself. I just do – don't

212

have a lot of choice in the matter, I guess. Oh, here –' He reached into his pocket and produced a pack of assorted Life Savers. 'Have one.' He held the opened packet towards her. The end one was green. Maureen didn't particularly like green but it seemed rude not to accept his hospitality and she couldn't bring herself to say, you first, although she knew that the next one along would be her favourite grape flavour.

'Thank you,' she said, popping it into her mouth, watching wistfully as he helped himself and began sucking on the purple one. Probably his favourite too, she thought. Probably everyone's favourite. But then lime wasn't too bad. She wondered if she would have had the courage to reject a yellow one? She positively disliked yellow ones. But then she had been used to putting up with things that she disliked and the reconstruction of her personality was still incomplete. Sometimes she thought she fell back into old habits with a certain relief.

'A screen play?' she asked, indicating his work.

'No, a novel. I must be the only writer in Los Angeles who isn't working on a screen play. Kind of perverse isn't it? But then maybe I'm not a writer – who knows.'

Maureen wondered what else he could possibly be with all that paper strewn about. And she had heard him working – he certainly wasn't a professional copy typist.

'How long have you been next door?' he asked, and then mused on before she had a chance to answer. 'Funny, isn't it? A writer is supposed to be observant but sometimes I'm so occupied looking into myself – into the past – that I miss everything around me.'

'A little over three months,' Maureen said casually, not indicating that they had been probably the most important three months of her life. Three months in which she had got herself her very own home and her very own job. They had been three months in which she had been responsible to no one except herself. And now, she looked at him – maybe she had found a friend. But she reminded herself she mustn't intrude – only respond.

'And I've been driving you mad – tap, tap, tap.' He poked the air with his fingers. He could have been playing a silent piano.

'No, no – not at all,' she said quickly. 'I've gotten used to it. It's like company.' She could have bitten her tongue off. That sounded desperate and she didn't mean it to. He would feel sorry for someone who was so alone she listened to typing with pleasure. 'I mean, you type very nicely.' Now that sounded really stupid. She wasn't used to talking to people – socially. And she could tell it showed. 'I mean you type so well – it's kind of soothing.' She decided to stop – it was just getting worse.

'Now that is nice to know,' he said. 'It would be even nicer if I could think that the words I was typing were as good as my mechanical technique.'

'I'm sure they are,' she said quickly – and secretly hoped they were a good deal better.

'Now how could you possibly know that –? For all you know I'm typing "The quick brown fox jumped over the lazy dog" over and over again. Maybe I'm just a looney who thinks he's a writer.'

'I . . . I kind of feel it,' she said and that was the truth. He looked kind and gentle and understanding and from his routine he was certainly dedicated. That should add up to something, she thought. If there was any justice in the world it should add up to something but whether there was was questionable. There was silence then and for the first time since she had come into the room she felt awkward, uncomfortable. She was not used to being the centre of attention, even of an audience of one and he was staring at her, very intently, as if he was looking inside her, maybe to see if she was indeed telling the truth. She shifted a bit – the chair was every bit as uncomfortable as it looked.

He seemed to have found whatever it was he was looking for. 'Have you eaten?' he asked.

'Eaten?'

'You know, supper. Have you supped yet?'

'I was just about to make –'

'Come out with me.'

'With you?'

'Do you question everything?' He laughed and it was a friendly laugh. He wasn't making fun of her, she thought, though she did seem to amuse him in a nice way.

'No, it's just that . . .' she looked at her wristwatch – it was twenty past seven. 'It's work time still. For you I mean.'

'The hell with it. Let's be devils,' he paused. 'Besides, as you so astutely observed, I'm not working this evening.'

'Why not?'

'There you go again with the questions. Come on, it's a long story. Maybe I'll tell you over a steak and some Californian red. Maybe I'll tell you the story of my life and you can tell me yours.'

Maureen doubted very much whether he would be interested in hers – but she had to admit to herself that she was very curious about him.

'If you are sure I'm not intruding,' she said.

'You do underestimate yourself,' he said seriously. 'Do you always do that?'

Maureen stood up. Did she? Underestimate herself. What could that mean? She thought maybe she knew – and she thought maybe she knew the answer. Maybe she used to, but not any more, not lately. She did have a kind of confidence now – it was a fragile confidence easily dented, but that was only to be expected. After all, it was a new thing, a baby.

'I'll get a sweater,' she said, 'and lock up.' She shuffled her way through the papers. It really was a most extraordinary room.

15

They did the unheard of in Los Angeles and walked down the street, past some bars and shops and the occasional house. The traffic streamed past, tune mingled with beat as radios blared out from sharp-finned convertibles cruising the road. Caught between the sea and the desert Los Angeles had a distinct chill after dark, but it was refreshing, almost, Maureen thought, like an autumn evening in Boston, except it all seemed so much bigger here – wider, longer, more spacious. There was nothing cosy about this city. Anonymity stretched into the horizon.

They walked silently, whether from choice or design she couldn't decide. They would have had to shout to converse, not only because of the noise but also because of the disparity in their heights. Freed now from the restrictions of doorways and ceilings, Hank towered over her. She noticed as they walked that the stoop straightened with every stride and he stretched to his full height in the open air. Back and neck erect she decided he must be six four or five. She needed two steps to his every one to keep up, but he seemed unaware of her struggle as he effortlessly strode along.

'Been here?' he paused in front of a neon-lit bar. 'Ladies Welcome' the sign in the window declared.

Certainly not, Maureen thought, and then immediately felt shame at her prim reaction, which had sprung unbidden except by years of habit. She said, 'No, no, I haven't,' in as non-judgmental a tone as she could muster. She had never been inside a bar in her life and she would never have even considered this one, which despite the Christmassy effect of the Budweiser sign flashing red and blue, looked decidedly unwelcoming to ladies. Still, she reminded herself, this was a new life and she did want it to be different from the old one.

'It's OK,' he said. 'Good steaks.' He pushed the door open, standing back at the same time, his great reach forming a pyramid between ground, door and his body. She had no choice but to step in ahead of him.

Seated on red leatherette in the high-backed booth one step up from the floor at the far corner of the room they were, she felt, comfortably private, cocooned. She had kept her eyes averted as he guided her from the door past the bar to this particular booth. The formica table which separated them, she immediately noted, was clean and smooth. She was surprised. If she had thought about it she would have expected it to be stained with circles from beer glasses and sticky. And the light, though dim, was restful rather than sinister. There was a soft murmur of voices – not the 'one for the road' drunken slurring she had expected from too many gangster movies.

'Hi, folks, what can I get you?' A pretty blonde girl in black slacks and a white blouse, buttoned up to the neck, arrived at the table. From their perch they came eye to eye with her as she stood, pencil poised over her order pad. 'Oh, hi Hank,' she said, 'you're early tonight.'

'Don't remind me, Betty. I'm not here to think about work.'

'Tough day, huh? Never mind. It can only get better as they say. Can I get you some drinks?' She looked at Maureen with what Maureen interpreted as a slightly surprised expression. Obviously she was used to seeing Hank on his own.

'Let's have a bottle of your very best Napa Valley Beaujolais – then we'll think about food.'

'Okey dokey – you want menus?'

'Has it changed?' Hank asked.

'Not since I've been here. Not since the Ark I think.'

'Then I shall entertain my companion by reciting it from memory.'

Betty grinned at him and went off with not the slightest trace of the barmaid wiggle Maureen had been led to expect.

'What a pretty girl,' Maureen said.

'Actress hopeful – like just about everybody in this town,' Hank said. 'Waiting to be discovered. But she seems to be surviving all right. Not like some.'

'Are you native?' Maureen asked.

Hank's eyes widened and he gave her an 'are you serious?' look and then burst into laughter. 'Me? A native of LA?'

'I don't see what's so funny about that,' Maureen said.

He stopped laughing. 'No, of course not. You wouldn't. That wasn't fair. It is just, well, my father would be so horrified that his eldest could seem so at home in the City of Angels, that he could be taken for a native.'

'What is wrong with that?'

'Absolutely nothing, unless you happen to be my father.'

'I'm afraid I'm not following . . .'

'Well, like I said, it's a very long story.'

Betty arrived back with the wine, slightly chilled and already open, and two glasses which she placed side by side in the middle of the table.

'Ready to order?' she asked, pencil poised.

'Not yet,' Hank said, 'give us five minutes.'

'Okey dokey, give me a shout when you want me.'

Hank poured the wine and pushed a glass across to Maureen with a flourish. Taking his own he smelt it and then sipped it ostentatiously.

'An unpretentious little wine, I think you'll agree, with just an undertone of Californian facetiousness.'

Maureen tasted it, finding it slightly sour at first, but then she wasn't used to drinking wine and was unsure whether it was supposed to taste like this or not. She just smiled at him and the second sip tasted better than the

218

first. Just a question of getting used to it – like everything else, she told herself.

'Now the menu,' Hank said. 'There is *soupe de jour*, which everyday is Campbell's cream of mushroom. I think someone sold them a truckload. There is shrimp cocktail with an amazingly bland pink sauce but it's OK if you put a lot of pepper on it. They do a good Reuben sandwich, a gargantuan cheeseburger and the turkey club is good too. However, as this is a special occasion I'd recommend the steak, fries and onion rings with a side order of cole-slaw.'

'Good heavens, that sounds like too much to me.' Maureen wanted to bite her tongue again. Why did she have to sound so prim? And it wasn't just nervousness. She knew she was prim. Hard as she tried she couldn't break out or back to that girl who all those years ago had wanted to dance on tables.

'We'll just have one order of cole-slaw then and share it.' He beckoned Betty to the table and ordered.

'Rare steaks?' she asked.

'Of course,' Hank said without consulting Maureen.

She didn't correct him. Rare steak. Just one more thing to get used to. Well-done steak was unsophisticated, provincial, bad taste. She only liked it because that was the way she had been conditioned. And here she was facing someone who obviously knew what was what. He was everything she was not – sophisticated, worldly, even a bit bohemian – but under it all, yes, well-bred. He was definitely Beacon Hill and Park Avenue. She could tell now, that despite his present surroundings, he was used to the best. She didn't know why she was so sure. Something about the way he joked about the wine, about the food, about his work. The well-bred always took life very lightly she had been led to believe. And by the time the food had arrived she knew for certain that her instincts had been right.

After Betty had laid a paper place mat, fork and steak knife and white paper napkin with the Budweiser eagle in front of each of them, he talked easily, and even more lightly about himself, as if he were talking about a slightly strange acquaintance he had known briefly years ago, whose life was a source of wonder and amusement. In that well-bred way he glossed over pain and frustration that had brought him from partnership in his father's law firm in Shaker Heights, Michigan; brought him from a marriage which produced two now grown-up children and twenty-five years of misery for both himself and his (in his words) understandably unfaithful wife.

Hank's story was interrupted by Betty's arrival with two overflowing plates which she hastily and with little ceremony deposited on the mats with a clatter and an admonition.

'Careful, they're really hot tonight. I'll just get the cole-slaw – anything else?'

'Another bottle, please Betty,' Hank said, 'and mustard and ketchup.' He turned back to Maureen. 'Might as well have the works.'

'So, you see,' he continued, when Betty had quickly satisfied his requirements, 'that's why I'm not so sure whether Hank Martin is a writer or just someone who, like all the kids in this town, is waiting for a break, is living in a dream world. Henry Walter Martin III, attorney at law, was sure as hell no writer and sometimes I don't have a lot of faith in metamorphosis.'

Maureen cut into her steak, pretending not to notice the blood oozing from it. She didn't know what to say. It was all so embarrassingly personal. But she had many questions so she chose the least emotive.

'What kind of lawyer are you?' she asked.

'Henry Walter Martin III, like Henry Walter Martin Jr, and indeed the first Henry Walter Martin, was an excellent, highly overpaid corporation and tax lawyer with many valuable and valued clients – on whom he walked out one day, leaving total chaos in his wake.'

'But why?' Maureen asked. 'I'm afraid I don't understand.'

'Because, I suppose, it was never me there in the first place. You probably couldn't understand what it is like just fitting into a place which had been structured for you before you were even born. An independent lady like you – you probably wouldn't know it's the easiest thing in the world. St Paul's, Yale, Harvard Law, marriage, the firm, kids, golf, bridge – all there, all waiting. I just had to fit in – which I did beautifully with only a slight rebellious hiccup. But dear mother soon sorted that one out, bless her.' Hank's voice drifted off in memories. He shook his head, as if to awaken himself. 'Where are you from?' he asked Maureen.

'Me? Oh, back East.' An independent lady! He had called her an independent lady! Was that how she seemed? It couldn't be possible.

'Aha, mystery!'

'No, no mystery – just dull. You were right; the steak is very good. Tender and tasty at the same time.' And Maureen meant it. All those years of thinking steak was chewy and dry and hard and all because she had been afraid of a little blood. A metaphor for her life. 'This rebellion,' she said. 'What happened?'

Hank refilled their glasses and stared for a moment into his. 'It was so long ago,' he said, 'I don't even know if I remember it or just remember a memory. It was a year before the crash – that dates me – and I was at Harvard Law. It had been planned that I should be there, as I said, and I was fitting in nicely. Then I went up to Sears and Roebuck in Porter Square.'

Maureen leaned forward – so close to home – but she didn't interrupt. He had a look in his eyes that made it impossible to interrupt anyway. She watched him slip far away, into the long ago when he was young.

'I wanted new curtains for my room. I don't remember why. There were curtains there, but they were old and faded and I felt I wanted something bright, something new. It was funny I didn't usually notice things like that. I suppose I could have got them in Harvard Square but it

221

was a bright, crisp day and I felt like a walk – something more than just through the Yard, and, yes, somewhere different. It was such a closed society – students and professors, all intellectual, or at least pretending to be. I suppose that just shows that I was already restless, looking for something besides curtains. Anyway, there she was – seventeen, tall, dark haired, velvet brown eyes and somehow full of excitement. She agreed with me that all the ready-made curtains were wrong for me. They all had flowers or Japanese ladies or were heavy brocade. They were totally wrong. There was some material – a rich golden linen, full of sunshine. I don't know why it was so important to me – it was most uncharacteristic – but I simply had to have that yellow linen. They could be made up for me, she said – but it would take two weeks. I couldn't wait. Suddenly having those golden curtains on my windows was the most important thing in the world to me – silly wasn't it? I couldn't remember wanting anything more. I must have gotten the urgency across to her because she offered to do it for me. Just something simple she said – a hem on each end, tidy the selvages. It made me so happy that she would actually do this for me. So I bought the material.

'I could barely sleep that night; I was so excited. But when I went back the next day I realized it wasn't the curtains – it was her. I found myself going back daily. I bought sheets I didn't need, towels, pillows – just to be with her for a few minutes. I started giving things away to startled friends. Until one of them said, "Look, why don't you just ask her for a date; it would be a lot cheaper." And I realized that was what I wanted. But if I asked her and she said no then I couldn't ever go back and I couldn't face that. Just buying things from her gave me something to look forward to. Even I realized that this nonsense couldn't go on forever; I asked her to have dinner with me. She hesitated, obviously unsure, and I hated myself for asking. In those few minutes while she contemplated the offer, I wished the ground would swallow me up; but, miracle of miracles, she agreed.

'That semester was the happiest time of my life. We dined, we went to football games, we walked – I had never met anyone before who was so enthusiastic – so sure that life was immeasurably enjoyable, so certain that anything was possible. I probably fell in love with her that first time I saw her, but I didn't realize that's what it was for a couple of weeks. That that was why I felt so good about waking up. And her home – it was just so different from mine. We'd sit around the table sometimes, eating franks and beans – her father was a plumber full of tales of domestic disasters. They weren't constantly wondering what kind of impression they were making or looking behind everything that was said for some sinister meaning. Everything was what it seemed, you know?'

Maureen wondered if he wasn't perhaps being just a bit romantic in his description of this girl's home life. And maybe just a bit stricken by the glamour of simplicity that the well-to-do seemed to find so charming.

'For the first time in my life I felt I was me, you know what I mean? And that was when I first thought about not trying to be what my family took for granted. I started to write. There was just so much in life that I wanted to share. I wanted to tell everyone how wonderful it was to be alive. To wake them up. I had, I thought, seen the light.'

'And then what happened?'

'The light went out.'

'Why?'

'I suppose my overly enthusiastic letters home made my mother suspicious. One evening she telephoned me.

'"Henry," she said, "How are you?"

'It wasn't just a cliché greeting. She wanted to know what was going on. I pretended I didn't notice. "Just fine, Mother," I said innocently, "absolutely fine."

'"We've been just a bit worried dear – your letters. You don't seem yourself."

'"Everything is just fine and dandy," I assured her.

'"Are you sure? I know you don't want to worry me,

dear – but are you sure? Mrs Havers was saying the other day that Thomas hadn't seen you for weeks."

'Tom was my best friend from home,' Hank explained to Maureen. 'He was studying at the business school. "Been busy," I lied to my mother. I had been avoiding him. Deep down I knew he wouldn't approve of Ann – that was her name. I knew he would try to tell me I was making a mistake and I didn't want him spoiling things. He was like my family – he wouldn't understand.

'"And this girl you've been seeing," mother continued – she let it hang in the air for a while, having emphasized "girl" and "seeing" as if there was something unclean about it. And I realized Tom had been reporting back. "What's her name?" Mother asked.

'"Ann," I said, "Ann O'Malley" and you know I felt good even saying her name. But the silence from mother weighed heavily on the phone lines. I could picture them sagging all the way from Michigan to Cambridge. Then there was a sigh, "O'Malley," she said. "A Boston family?"

'I knew what she meant, the land of the cod and all that, but I deliberately ignored her. "You'll like her," I said and knew she wouldn't.

'"Catholic I expect."

'"Ah . . . yes."

'"Is she at Radcliffe, dear?"

'It seemed that being at Radcliffe could outweigh the disadvantages of being Catholic. Perhaps that was the time I should have started lying – but I didn't.

'"No, actually, she works," I said.

'"Really!" At least mother found that concept fascinating. Fancy a girl working. She had never had a job in her life.

'"In Sears and Roebuck." I definitely should have lied.

'There was another lengthy pause during which time I was expected to realize the depths of her disapproval before she spelled it out.

'"Do be careful, Henry," she said, "Irish Catholic *shop*

224

girls can be well . . . there is no nice way to put it – they can be troublesome. Don't see her any more, Henry. Promise me?"'

It was strange, Maureen thought – her mother would have said that smarty-pants rich college boys would be trouble and stay away from them. 'And you did as you were told?' Maureen found that hard to believe. She would have – but then she always had done what she was told. She would have expected him to be made of sterner stuff.

'Mother's reaction worried me at first, but not for long – I mean, I did respect her judgement but out of sight, out of mind you could say. Anyway, I was living in the present, not, for once, needing my parents' approval.'

'So what happened? How did it go wrong?'

'Christmas vacation came and reluctantly I went home – it was expected. I knew it would be difficult. I mean I knew I would miss Ann like crazy – but I didn't know how difficult it would be. I didn't know that snares had been carefully laid.'

'Snares?'

'Singular, really. Snare. Caroline Dobson, attractive, well-bred daughter of a Dupont vice-president. I had known her all my life and it was expected, as they say, that one day we would marry.'

'Raise little Dow-Jones indices and live happily ever after at the country club,' Maureen said.

'Until death placed us side by side in the Episcopalian cemetery. Yeh, that's it exactly.'

'But you had spoiled all the plans by falling in love with this unsuitable Irish girl.'

'As I said – there were traps set. To draw an end to this interminably sad tale, suffice it to say that on New Year's Eve, after a few too many glasses of champagne I found myself in a bedroom with Caroline and . . .'

'The well-bred Miss Dobson seduced you?'

'You could put it like that.'

'How else?'

'No way else,' Hank laughed. 'And when she told me she was pregnant, well, I couldn't be a cad could I? We announced our engagement to the delight of both families and I settled for the inevitable. Henry Walter Martin III put his feet firmly on the treadmill of life.'

'How did Ann take it?'

'I never saw her or spoke to her again. I couldn't, you see. I couldn't bear it.'

'Poor girl,' Maureen said. 'So you married in haste.'

'No, actually. That was the funny thing. We didn't get married until the following summer.'

'But there must have been an unseemly bulge by then. Whatever did Mummy say?'

'Caroline had a miscarriage right after we announced our engagement. The morning after our engagement pictures were in the newspaper, in fact.'

Maureen looked at him in astonishment. 'You mean . . .'

'I fell for the oldest trick in the book.' He laughed.

'Well, why didn't you become unengaged?'

'Because I was a coward. How would it look if I said oh, I'm not going to marry you now that you're not pregnant? If indeed you ever were. What would people think? I guess I cared an awful lot about what people thought of me.'

'That is a very, very sad story, Hank,' Maureen said.

'Well, I told myself it probably wouldn't have worked with Ann anyway. My family would never have accepted her and I would always feel guilty about that.'

'But you don't now?'

'Feel guilty? I feel guilty all the time, but now I just accept it. I got to the point where it was cut and run or leap out of a window. I think, marginally, I made the wiser choice.'

'Why California?'

'There were no memories here. No good memories, no bad memories. Isn't that why everyone comes to California?'

'But you packed all your memories and brought them with you.'

'Here in the sunshine I pretend they are someone else's.'

Even in the dim light Maureen could see that Hank hurt a lot – that he wasn't as inured to the hurt as he pretended. In fact if he went on thinking about it all, she thought, he would probably cry. 'What's your novel about?' she asked, changing the subject, she hoped.

'Oh, the usual – life, death and marriage; hope and despair and of course money.'

'Why of course?'

'Because that is what everything is about really – money. All of life is about money.'

'How very cynical.'

'Truthful. You think about it. If everybody had the same when they were born; if someone said "Here's your share, now get on and do what you want. You can farm or paint or build houses, or bridges or anything you want and it won't make any difference." Think how happy life would be.'

Maureen laughed. 'Pleasant idea, but no one would do anything if they didn't have to. Everyone would just sit around.'

'That's not true. Oh, maybe for a while but it is very boring doing nothing. I'll bet everyone would be busier than ever.'

'But if there are no rewards for hard work . . .'

'You have fallen into the trap. There are no rewards now for hard work. It is the people who work the hardest who are the worst off. Think about women who raise children and take in other people's washing and clean other people's houses and who put in twenty-hour days before falling exhausted into bed for a few hours' oblivion. What are their rewards? Material? Bare survival. Spiritual? They are too tired to even wonder if they have a soul.'

'But no one would do the awful jobs unless they had to.'

'That's a different argument. And if you believe that

227

then you're saying it's right to exploit your fellow man. People should be able to do what pleases them without restrictions. There will always be those who take pleasure from tilling the soil, as it is so romantically put. People enjoy making things with their hands, people enjoy fishing, although I personally hate it. People enjoy raising animals – some people even enjoy raising children.'

'What about street sweeping?'

'If there were no people who enjoyed street sweeping, which I contend, all things being equal, could be a satisfying occupation, then everyone would have to do their bit – that is if they decided clean streets were a necessity. You see, it is the compulsion that makes certain occupations odious. If you do it because you want to, then it's enjoyable.'

Maureen was certain there was a flaw in his utopia.

'Just think,' he continued, 'with a stroke mankind could wipe out all crime. There would be none because all crime stems from jealousy and greed. If everyone were given the same . . .'

'There are people who would want a little more than everyone else,' Maureen interrupted.

'You are a hard, cynical woman, Maureen Thornton,' Hank laughed.

'Is this all in your book?' she asked.

'Good heavens, no – it's a novel not a political tract. I'll get around to that later and prove you wrong by my perfect logic. I think you were right about the food though. This has defeated me.' Hank put down his knife and fork and pushed the plate towards the table's centre. On it were two french fries, half an onion ring and a little pool of ketchup.

'But I think I could manage some coffee,' he said. 'How about you?'

'Yes, please,' Maureen said.

'So,' she stirred sugar into her coffee, 'what happened today?'

'Today?'

'The lack of typing.'

Hank stared into his coffee, breathing in steam as if it were an inhaler to clear his mind. He looked up and across the table at her. His eyes were very serious now – the teasing look had gone. 'I just kind of froze, I guess. Most days I can sort out the jumble in my head – all the ideas, the memories. Or at least I can override them, disconnect bits and pieces for a few hours at a time – examine them, try and bring some kind of order to the chaos. But today . . . well, I suppose it's because it's my birthday.'

'Today? This very day?'

'Yup, that's right, mam – forty-seven today. And you know how it is about birthdays. It's the one day you can go right back through your life with. I mean, Christmases and Thanksgivings, they kind of merge into one another – but birthdays . . . You can remember who you were with on certain ones, where you were, what presents you got, even. And they all just kept jumbling in on me. Happy birthdays, sad birthdays and in the last few years each one I was convinced would be my last. The weirdest thing is that it was the memory of the happy birthdays that I found most depressing.'

'That's not so surprising. Will you ever be happy again, that's what you wonder.'

'Or is there any such thing as happiness when you are a grown up? And at forty-seven you can't kid yourself any longer that it is all ahead of you, can you?'

'Oh, I don't know.' Maureen certainly did feel just that most days. She didn't know what it was but it was there somewhere ahead of her. 'You could say you were in your prime.'

'Or my second adolescence. And it seems a hell of a lot worse than the first. Then, I knew what I was doing. I may have been wrong, but I didn't know it then.'

'That's only because time has softened the edges of your memories. You probably went through agonies then.'

'Maybe,' he said. 'Maybe.' Then he seemed to force himself into brightening up. 'You realize,' he continued, 'that you are now going to be part of those memories – my indelible forty-seventh birthday memories. Spent with a lovely lady about whom I know nothing except that she is called Maureen Thornton, that she comes from back East and she too is running away from something.'

'What makes you think that?'

'Because you're in California. Everyone in California has a past somewhere else. You are alone, listening to me typing, and you are so convinced that you have done the right thing. You have such hopeful confidence that the future can only be better than the past that I infer the past was not a very happy one.'

'You are observant.'

'Thank God for that, maybe there is hope for me still.'

'But,' she said, 'you are wrong about one thing. I didn't run away from anything. No decisions at all. Everything just kind of slipped away from me. Everything and everybody, and I wasn't needed any more.'

'And you are very glad of it.'

'Oh yes; most days.'

'When you're not feeling guilty about being free.'

Maureen laughed. Was she really so transparent? Or was it just that everybody was the same? A little bit hopeful, a little bit guilty, a little bit confident, a little bit frightened?

Hank looked at his watch. 'What shall we do now?' he asked Maureen and called to Betty for the bill.

'Now?'

'Will you stop with those one-word questions – they are most disconcerting.'

'Sorry. But isn't it time you were getting back to work?'

'Nope. I have decided this is a free day. I shouldn't work on my birthday. Let's go to the movies. There must be something to see – after all this is Hollywood.'

❧ 16 ❧

Kathleen had been in David's office only once and that had been when she was given the obligatory tour of the studio on her arrival. The writers' block was on the very edge of the lot and when Kathleen was working there was never time to make the trek. Making movies, Kathleen thought, was very like the old army saying, 'hurry up and wait'. The trouble was that you never knew how long the wait was going to be. It could be five minutes while some lights were adjusted or half an hour because a vital prop had gone missing. Very occasionally the director foresaw a lengthy hold-up and told the actors to take a break. Usually, grateful to get away from the noise, Kathleen just retreated to her dressing room and went over her lines. It was important that she could be found quickly when the cameras were ready to roll.

'Damn,' the chief electrician said, as once more the Kleig lights began to flicker. 'Harry, check out that main connection will you?'

Harry scuttled, but relative darkness ensued nevertheless. It was the third time since lunch the fault had brought the studio to a halt. They waited restlessly but the minutes dragged on. The electrician and the director went into a huddle and Kathleen could see the director was far from happy. He, after all, got the blame when productions went over schedule. It was four-thirty, an hour and a half left of shooting, officially, although they often went on to seven o'clock.

'OK,' the director shouted reluctantly. 'We'll have to

call it a day, people, while they find the goddamn gremlins.'

He didn't need to say it twice, as the actors responded with the alacrity of children being let out of school unexpectedly.

'But be ready for a long haul tomorrow,' he called after the fleeing figures.

Kathleen changed quickly out of her costume and into her sweater and slacks. She scrubbed her face clean and brushed her hair loose. Her first reaction was that it would be nice to get back to the twins, but she realized there was something more important that she had to do. She had to talk to David and not at home, where, if he did turn up, there were always others present – the twins, Sandra, Josie. Kathleen had taken David's monosyllabic bad temper, on the few occasions when he was present, as a righteous punishment for her deception. Yet surely he had by now made his displeasure clear and it just couldn't go on forever. They would have to come to some kind of accommodation. Moreover, recently she had begun to suspect that, though that could be his excuse, there was some other reason for his behaviour.

David sat at his desk, as he did each day with the bottle close at hand, staring from his window. He no longer even saw the motley parade which passed by. Sometimes he wondered why he even bothered to come in to the studio. No one noticed. The phone remained silent. Occasionally he lifted the receiver just to listen to the dialling tone, to make sure it was connected. He came here, he knew, because he couldn't stay in the house, for many reasons. One reason was that it would look suspicious. But the most important was that he simply couldn't bear it there. All that homely atmosphere made him feel unclean. The pure joy the twins found in life; that goody two shoes Nanny, Josie, humming her way through domestic duties. It was all so apple pie. But Kathleen was the worst aspect of the house. She was so serene, so self-confident. She had so much. Well, it was easy for her, he thought. She was successful. She could work. She had everything she wanted. He hated being in that house. And there was nowhere else for him to go but to his office – during the day. The nights were different. With his companions at the beach house all his mental anguish disappeared. At night, the moment was all that existed and indeed all that mattered. There was no thinking, only the intensity of feeling.

He was so far immersed in the chaotic shambles of his mind that David didn't even hear Kathleen open the door. She stood looking at him, as he remained oblivious to her presence. The totally vacant expression on his face frightened her. His eyes were wide and staring but they were the eyes of a man who could not see.

'David,' she said softly, as if to a sleep walker, so as not to startle him. It seemed he was deaf as well as blind. Walking with measured steps, she approached his desk. She remembered the untidy piles of paper on his desk in New York when he was writing *Friendly Enemies*. How he could work in such seeming chaos had always amazed her, and she used to tease him about it. Here she saw nothing . . . no tumble of papers, no lengthy diagrams, no chewed pencils, no crumpled, rejected sheets. There was just a naked typewriter and the playscript of *Friendly Enemies*, unopen, between the typewriter and a bottle of Canadian Club. He was automatically reaching for the bottle to replenish his glass when he finally focused on Kathleen.

'Ah,' he said quietly, guiltily, like a boy caught with his hand in the cookie jar.

'David,' Kathleen said, bemused, 'what's going on?'

'As you can see,' he replied, 'not very much. It hasn't been a very productive day.'

She wondered about the honesty of the singular. Had any days, any months been productive?

'I'd ask you to sit down,' he said, 'but as you can see –' he gestured extravagantly around the room, bare but for the filing cabinet which was itself empty except for his emergency supply, 'the prisoners here in the cell block are not expected to socialize.'

Kathleen could no longer ignore what she had been refusing to see for months. David was in a very sorry state.

'You can't go on like this,' she said. 'If you can't tell me what the matter is – there must be someone you can talk to, someone who can help.'

'I don't know what you're talking about. For God's sake, can't a guy have a bad day without you making a federal case out of it? What are you doing here anyway? The whole goddamn studio will go bankrupt if you're not out there wringing the tears from the hicks in the boondocks.'

'David, how far have you got with the screenplay?' She must, she told herself, remain calm. Was all this her fault? Probably, she thought. And if that was the case, it was up to her to rectify it, somehow.

'It's all right; it's coming on.' He refused to look at her.

'Let me see,' she said gently.

'No.' He plonked his glass on the desk and stood up, unsteadily pushing his chair back. 'It's none of your god-damn business, Miss Smarty Pants. I don't come on to the set and tell you how to act, do I? What gives you the right to come in here and tell me how to do my job? I knew how to do it, and pretty damn well, too, when you were making beds for a living.' David strove hard to keep up the attack. He advanced towards her, coming round the desk. 'Now get out of here and leave me alone. Go on. Get going and do your bit as a perfect star, or a perfect mother or whatever of your goddamn perfect things you've got to get on with. I sure as hell don't need you.'

Kathleen found it hard to believe that this was her husband. What had happened to David? How could that sensitive, gentle, yes even slightly frightened person be-come this . . . loud-mouthed drunk? She knew it was all her fault. How could she have done this to him?

'Get out,' he screamed into her face. His breath was so heavy with the smell of whisky she could taste it like fear. She shrunk back.

234

'Go on,' he shouted as he picked up the bottle to finally replenish his glass.

Kathleen mistook his action for aggression. He was, she thought, about to become physically violent as well as verbally aggressive.

'It's all right, David,' she said, her voice pleading, breaking. 'I'm going. I'll let you . . . get on with it.' She turned and walked to the door, tears blurring her vision. What else could she do? Her mind frantically searched for an explanation and a solution at the same time. If only there was someone who could help. Someone she could turn to for advice. But there was no one. Her mother wouldn't even be able to begin to comprehend it – and she knew no one else. It was out of the question to talk to anyone at the studio. Word would get out no matter how discreetly she broached the subject. It would be a betrayal of her husband. She would never be disloyal. There had to be a solution, she told herself, and she would have to work it out by herself.

David stood still and watched until Kathleen had closed the door. He felt ashamed. But it was the bitch's own fault; he justified his behaviour. No one asked her to come here. Then he sat once more behind the desk and put the confrontation out of his mind. As if the interruption had been a dream, he continued the action she had interrupted and poured a couple of fingers of whisky into the glass. He then quickly drained the glass, gulping the liquor to erase the dregs of memory that still remained. Then he looked at his watch. The numbers were hazy in his vision, the hands of the watch wiggly. Finally he focused. Thank God, he thought, nearly time to head to Malibu.

It was the morning after Hank's birthday that Maureen arrived in the department and was surprised to find that she was the first. Although she usually preceded Freda and Shirley by about ten minutes, Miss Simmonds was invariably already installed at her stock-room desk.

Maureen was humming, 'Good morning, good morning,

we've talked the whole night through,' and replaying in her mind the scene with Gene Kelly, Debbie Reynolds and Donald O'Connor dancing over the sofa which was in the film she and Hank had seen the night before. She smiled to herself as she removed the dust sheets from the merchandise and remembered Hank on the walk home, dancing around the lamp posts and leaping in and out of the gutter in imitation of Gene Kelly *sans* umbrella. The slightly moody introspection that had come over him at the bar (she wanted to think of it as a restaurant, but she had to be honest, it was a bar) had been blown away by the delightfully uplifting movie. She had asked him in for coffee and they had sat on the sofa, leaning back against her purple pillows and giggling over the movie until it was no longer Hank's birthday.

'Thank you,' he had said, as he stood in the doorway, butting the screen door open with his shoulder, 'for making my birthday happy and,' he paused, 'for bringing me back a future.' Then he had kissed her, a peck really, ever so gentle, on her cheek. She felt herself flushing, as the screen door closed. He looked through the screen at her for a moment, his hand on one side, hers on the other, fingertips almost touching through the mesh and pursed his lips in a final chaste kiss. A few moments later, as she was preparing for bed, she could hear him singing, 'You are my lucky star,' and she wondered if he had meant her to hear.

'You are looking very cheerful this morning,' Freda arrived and grabbed the end of the dust-sheet Maureen had been struggling to fold on her own.

'Am I?' Maureen asked, looking wide-eyed and, she knew, coquettish.

'You are indeed. Are you going to tell me or should I guess?'

'There's nothing to tell,' Maureen said. She much preferred listening to other people's stories than telling her own. Her life was – had been, she mentally amended – so dull.

'I don't believe you. You look to me like a lady with a secret.'

'Me? No, I was just thinking of a movie we – I went to see last night. *Singing in the Rain*. Have you seen it?'

'It's a musical, isn't it?'

Maureen nodded, taking Freda's folded end and tucking it under her chin in a final flourish.

'Sam doesn't like musicals. He says they're for kids. Sam likes meatier things – you know, more intellectual, like the one we saw last weekend. His wife had taken the kids to visit her mother in San Francisco. *High Noon*. Gary Cooper is one of his favourites. Sam reminds me of Gary Cooper a lot. You know, strong, forceful.'

Robert Taylor, George Montgomery *and* Gary Cooper, Maureen thought. She really must see this Sam.

They moved along as a pair now, removing dust covers, folding them and slotting them away in their special drawer for the day and as they reached the last counter, the Wedgwood, Shirley came panting in.

'Has she noticed I'm late?' she whispered, cocking her head towards the stock room.

'You're in luck,' Maureen said. 'She's not here yet.'

The other two were shocked.

'What?' Shirley cried. 'That's impossible.' And Freda stuck her head round the opening to the stock room to check.

'She's right, you know. Dragon lady has not arrived.'

At that moment the store bell rang. That meant that down on the ground floor the uniformed commissionaires would have finished polishing the brass door handles and would now be unlocking the plate-glass doors, unhinging the revolving doors and setting them in motion. Mendel's was open for business, officially, although the store's clientele were not the kind who rushed in at nine o'clock in the morning. They tended more to saunter in around eleven, after the hairdresser and before their luncheon appointments. For the next hour or so there would be a bare trickle of customers. Mornings were more usually spent

237

on displays and arrangements and general stock taking. But there was no Miss Simmonds to organize her staff.

'Shall we tell someone?' Shirley asked. She looked about to panic.

'Like Mr Hickox,' Freda said referring to the store's manager.

'Or Miss Pally,' Shirley said. Miss Pally was the personnel manager and everyone thought it such an apt name.

Maureen thought about it. Although the most junior – in terms of time there – member of the department; the other two did tend to defer to her.

'I don't think so,' Maureen said. 'Let's just wait and see. She has probably called him already herself and he'll be along to tell us when he has a moment.'

'Oh, he wouldn't come himself,' Shirley said. 'Not just to give us a message. He'd use the phone, or Helen would. Most likely Helen.' Helen was Mr Hickox's secretary.

'Well,' Maureen said, 'let's just leave it. Let's just wait and see.'

'But what shall we do?' Shirley foundered like a boat without a captain, so Maureen assumed the bridge.

'Dust the Baccarat wine glasses, Shirley,' she said, and hesitated before issuing instructions to Freda. But Freda stood motionless, waiting.

'Why don't you have a look at the Rosenthal?' Maureen said. 'I think those demi-tasse cups are in need of a wipe out.'

Pleased to have the weight of personal responsibility lifted from their shoulders, Freda and Shirley set off about their appointed tasks.

Maureen herself watched them and wondered if she had the courage to do what was forming in her mind. She hadn't liked the centre display table at all. She hadn't liked it when Miss Simmonds had bid her to set it up last week. It was an oval table laid for a dinner party of six. The setting was changed about once a month under Miss Simmonds' instructions. Maureen had disputed her latest choices, but only mentally. It wouldn't have been her place to voice

238

her ideas. But somehow this morning she had a feeling that she could get away with just about anything. Could it have been Hank? Nonsense, she told herself. She was just finding her feet, that's all. She wanted more than anything to see the table laid with the new Lenox, the one with the swirl of pink roses, and in the linen department on one of her forays through the store she had seen exactly the tablecloth to set it off. Not the fussy lace one Miss Simmonds preferred. This one was cream coloured Irish linen with just a few threads of pink to catch the colour from the plates. The silver was all right and she would use the Waterford glasses and the Royal Worcester single rose place-card holders. All she needed was the tablecloth and napkins from the linen department. She went to Miss Simmonds' desk in search of the requisition form. That's when she noticed the Jack Daniels.

Rosemary Simmonds had woken very slowly that morning. Her head was throbbing, her mouth was parched and her stomach felt as if it were hopping up and down from its proper place to the base of her throat. But this she was fairly used to lately. If she could just manage to wash her face, brush her teeth and swallow a pepto bismal with a bourbon chaser she would be ready for Mendel's. What she couldn't understand was how cold she felt and that terrible pain. It was not the usual pain – but where was it? She finally located it in her arm – but which one she wondered? Concentrate, she told herself, concentrate. But it was difficult. Her physical symptoms were taking priority over thought. It was definitely her arm – her right arm she decided, just there under her chest. She shifted her complaining body a bit to take the weight off it and then realized that she was not in bed but sprawled on black and pink tiles. The colours floated together in front of her eyes. She was in the bathroom – and she was naked. No wonder she was cold. Naked and cold on the hard tiled bathroom floor. She hadn't liked pink and black tiles. They had been Sally's idea and she never liked to argue with Sally. Sally always got her own way – no matter what the cost to Rosemary. It was only to be expected. She had been spoiled all her life. Anyone that beautiful was used to being spoiled. And they didn't even know they were. It was just the way life was. Rosemary had actually enjoyed spoiling her – giving her her own way. She liked to see the delight in her big blue eyes and the way she tossed her blonde hair like a beautiful pony frolicking in a meadow.

Tears came to Rosemary's eyes as she thought about Sally and the tears mingled with those caused by the pain she felt now – the physical pain. Above her loomed the wash basin and her knee was jammed into the base of the toilet. She managed to roll on to her back. The movement made her head throb even more and the ceiling, as she glimpsed it, swirled threateningly close. When she tried to prop herself up she realized that her aching arm was useless. It just lay there sending out signals for he'p.

'Broken, damn it,' she said out loud and her voice was raspy and echoed in the room.

It was late afternoon at Mendel's before the message came through that Miss Simmonds had had an accident, a fall. She was in hospital overnight for observation after they had set her arm. It would be a few days before she would be back, unfortunately.

'I see, Mrs Thornton,' Mr Hickox had said to Maureen, 'that you have had some experience beyond selling.'

She had been summoned to the fifth floor and was sitting in his carpeted, oak-veneered office. He swivelled behind his immaculate desk and she sunk into the visitor's chair facing him. She had tried to perch but the soft fabric engulfed her. This was the first time she had actually been face to face with the manager. Well, he had nodded to her abstractedly and occasionally when he strode through the department, but this was the first time he had seemed to be aware of her name. He was an attractive man, hair slightly greying in the cliché of maturity. For a brief moment she remembered Mr Morris and the cramped

240

conditions of the office all those years before. Would he now be dramatically greying and had he, by now, she wondered, surrounded himself with all this luxury and, yes, she supposed it was power.

'Yes, Mr Hickox,' Maureen tried to keep her voice from trembling. She was very nervous. 'I kept the books for a few years in a Five and Ten Cent store – before I was married.'

'And after that?'

Surely she had written it on her application form. Hadn't Miss Pally rather sneered when she said, 'I'm sure you'll find Mendel's a million miles removed from a corner grocery shop.' But then, having taken in Maureen's sleek appearance, she had added, 'However, you do look as if you will fit in.'

'I helped my husband in his business,' she said and left it at that.

Mr Hickox put down the papers, her papers, which he had been leafing through and peered at her across the desk.

'It is temporary, of course, until Miss Simmonds is fully fit, but I would like you to keep an eye on things in China and Glass. Stock, reordering – just the day to day basics of course. Don't want Miss Simmonds to return to chaos, do we? And things can get out of hand very quickly in the retail trade, as I'm sure you are aware. And of course there is the look of the department. Mustn't let standards slip. Mendel's has, after all, its reputation to uphold. Any problems, any problems at all and you just come to me.'

Later, after the closing bell had rung and they had begun putting the dust sheets back in place, Mr Hickox had strolled through the department. He paused at the as yet uncovered display Maureen had changed that afternoon.

'Nice,' he said to her. 'Very nice indeed, Mrs Thornton. Good work.' And he carried on.

17

The call came at ten-to-four this time. Hornbeam noted the time on the luminous dial of his bedside clock as he picked up the phone.

'It's Evans,' the police sergeant said.

Hornbeam prepared himself mentally for the drive to the station. It had become a habit – once a month regularly since that first time. A few cuts, a few bruises that DeCosta explained away with stories of falls. Maybe it has something to do with the moon, Hornbeam thought idly. Maybe queers were like werewolves.

'I'll be right down,' he said.

'No, not this time, Phil.'

'What do you mean?' He thought he probably knew. Evans was stalling. It would come more expensive.

'DeCosta's not here. He's in LA General.'

Hornbeam sat up. 'How serious is it?' Maybe he's dead. Maybe he's off my back. It wasn't a wish; just a tidy solution.

'Not a pretty sight, I'll tell you that. Cigarette burns.'

'What?' How could anyone be in hospital with cigarette burns?

'All over. Looks like when my kid had chicken pox.'

'My God!'

'There's no accounting for some taste. Anyway you had better get over there before he starts chattering and someone puts two and two together and calls the papers. Unless you don't give a damn any more.'

Hornbeam admitted to himself that he didn't give a

damn. Not about DeCosta anyway. He was no use to the studio; he was no use to anyone, least of all himself. But the publicity would hurt Kathleen and after the gigantic success of her first three pictures he wasn't taking any chances. Besides, that kid didn't deserve this. He hated to admit it, even to himself, but he, who didn't give a damn about anyone, had a soft spot for that kid – she was some worker.

'Thanks, Bill,' he said, 'but we've all got our jobs to do and unfortunately that bastard is one of mine.'

'Good luck,' Evans said, 'and you'll sure as hell need it. Boy, would the papers ever love this one. Even the soles of his feet – can you believe it?'

'They probably started there, Bill.'

Kathleen closed her eyes. She couldn't take in what Hornbeam was telling her. He had arrived on the set just as they were wrapping for the day. She could tell by the look on his face that something was wrong.

'Is it the girls?' she asked before he had a chance to speak.

'No, no,' he said. She had never heard this brash man speak so softly. He put a gentle hand on her shoulder.

'Mother! Has there been an accident?'

'It's David,' Hornbeam said. 'Now don't worry, he'll be all right but he's in hospital.'

David, Kathleen thought. She hadn't seen him for days but that was not unusual. She had got used to his unexplained absences.

'A crash?' She had always thought David was a careless driver. He was so wound up in his thoughts. 'How is he? Where is he? I must go to him.' The words tumbled out as her mind raced in circles. 'Was anyone with him?' There was in David's life another woman. Kathleen was sure of that. She had been sure for a long time. What other explanation could there be for his behaviour – his staying away from home all the time? But who was she to question him, who had given her a new life when she thought there was no hope left?

'It wasn't a car accident. And I promise you he'll be all right,' Hornbeam said.

'Well, what then?' David was young and healthy. It couldn't be his heart, could it?

'Get changed and I'll drive you home. We can talk on the way. It's all right, I've already told your driver.'

'But I want to go to David.' She was his wife. It was her place, her duty, she owed it to him. He needed her. He needed her, even, she told herself, even if he loved some-one else.

'Not yet,' Hornbeam said, 'there are some things you should know.' It was, he decided impossible to keep it from her any more – both impossible and unfair. It was bound to get out despite his efforts and the Chief had agreed with him when they had discussed it after Horn-beam's visit to the hospital.

'She's a tough cookie,' the Chief had said. 'She'll take it OK.'

But Hornbeam had to admit that it was at times like this that he hated his job.

As Kathleen changed into her slacks and sweater, took off her make-up and brushed out her elaborate coiffure until her hair once more flowed naturally over her shoulders, her mind darted from one possibility to another but she could focus on none of them. David would be all right, Hornbeam had said that – but it must be serious. His face, his eyes, his voice, even the way he stood – all of that told her that it must be serious.

But this – what was he telling her as they drove along? This had never come into her mind – how could it? It was beyond her imagination. Hornbeam was looking straight ahead, keeping his eyes on the road, and she realized why he had decided to tell her like this, in the car. It was so he wouldn't have to look at her. It was so she wouldn't have to mask the emotions which showed in her face – confusion, incredulity, disgust . . . and then pity and despair. For all his toughness, Hornbeam, she decided, was a tactful kindly man. But David! What could have happened to him?

How could he have turned to these people? Violence was anathema to him – it was simply not in his nature. He was shy, he was sensitive. Was it, she wondered, her fault? What had she done to drive him to this?

'I have to see him,' she said and she was surprised at how calm her voice sounded.

'I don't think that's a good idea, not yet. You've got a lot to come to terms with.'

'I want to see David, now,' she said firmly.

'At least sleep on it,' Hornbeam suggested. 'He's all sedated now, anyway.'

'But there's shooting tomorrow.'

'I'll take care of that. You haven't missed a day in nearly two years. I think the studio owes you one.'

Hornbeam stopped the car in her drive and looked at her for the first time. Her face, in profile, betrayed nothing. It still shone with the peaceful untroubled beauty that had taken her through all her emotional screen disasters. How, he wondered, could she ride out something like this? This, after all, was real life. But perhaps it was as the Chief had said. She was a tough cookie. He took her hand which lay on the seat between them. It was icy cold. He revised his theory. The Chief was wrong. Kathleen wasn't a tough cookie – she was a great actress.

'Will you be all right?' he asked.

Kathleen turned to him and smiled. 'Of course,' she said. 'I'll be fine.'

'Call me if you need anything – anytime.'

'I'm fine,' she repeated, still forcing a smile into her eyes. It was no use, she knew, if your mouth smiled while your eyes cried.

'If I don't hear from you tonight I'll call you in the morning. We can talk about what you want to do. And don't think about the movie. They'll shoot around you for a while.'

'But the schedule?'

'The hell with the schedule. You try and get some sleep.'

*   *   *

The hospital had rigged David up in a contraption that was a cross between a sling and a hammock. There was not more than an inch between any of the blistering burns which dotted his body, as Evans had pointed out, like a pox. He was still in shock when Kathleen arrived. Hornbeam, at her insistence, had fetched her in the morning. She hadn't slept properly – only dozed fitfully. Why, she had asked herself. How, she had asked herself. Homosexuality – it made sense of all those nights, of David's attitude to her. She found it almost a relief that it hadn't really been her from whom he shrank. It was not something he could help. It probably had been as much agony for him as it had been for her. She realized now that he had been homosexual all along, but he hadn't even known it himself. She thought back – reconstructed conversations, meetings, parties. No, he hadn't known when he married her; she was sure of that. He was too good, too kind to do that to her. Too good to use her as a cover. He hadn't known until . . . until when? She searched her mind, ransacked the past for clues and finally they came. Paul! That was when – that was when he realized. He had fallen in love with Paul.

But that didn't explain this. Why the seedy pick-up bars? Why these people? Why the violence? David didn't need that. He was attractive. He was talented. How had he come to this? And what was she going to do about it?

She stood looking down at him – at his swollen face. She longed to touch him, to comfort him. But she knew his condition prohibited it – besides, she knew from experience he would shrink from her touch.

He managed a feeble smile – boyish and sheepish.

'Hi,' he said, 'guess I'm a sorry sight.'

'You sure are,' she smiled back, 'but I hear you'll improve. Soon be good as new.'

His smile faded and tears welled up in his eyes. 'I'm sorry, Kathleen,' he said. 'You must be so ashamed of me.'

'Shhh,' she comforted. Somehow she knew it was not

his fault — it was hers. If she had looked, if she had seen . . .

'I don't know why,' he said again. 'I don't know why. I don't understand.' His tears flowed and Kathleen bent over him wiping them gently away with some cotton.

'I'm sorry,' he said again. 'It was exciting, Kathleen. It was so exciting. I felt so alive. I had been dead. I couldn't write, I couldn't think — but then I could feel — physically feel for the first time ever. I could feel ecstasy; I could feel pain. Then I guess I just couldn't tell the difference any more — but it didn't matter. I knew I was alive.'

'But this?' Kathleen was gesturing futilely at his prostrate body.

'Just went a bit too far, I guess — I don't remember,' he chuckled ruefully. 'It was just a game, just fooling around.'

'Who was it?'

'Don't remember that either. It was just two of us — and then others joined in. It was exciting . . . so many bodies, so many hands . . .' His eyes actually began to glow with the memory, then the tears came back, 'I'm such a fool.'

'Don't, David,' Kathleen said. 'Don't.' She felt the tears in her own eyes. 'It will be all right.'

'How can it be,' David said. 'I wish I was dead. Really dead.'

'No, no you don't,' she told him. 'You wish you were really alive — not like this and not alone. I know the feeling. Believe me, I know.'

'How?' He looked into her eyes and saw she was telling the truth.

'All those questions you didn't want to ask — and I suppose I didn't want to answer. I lost someone once. I know the despair. We all have to deal with it any way we can. That was your way. I had mine. At least we have both survived — sort of. But,' she said, 'your case is not a hopeless one.'

'I don't understand, Kathleen.'

'You'll see. Leave it to me. You just get well. Trust me.' She stopped and looked deeply into his eyes where she saw all his pain, all his despair, all his fear. 'Trust me,' she said again.

Kathleen knew now what had to be done. And she thought she knew how to do it. She would need help and she hoped she knew who would supply it. But first things first.

'How,' she asked Hornbeam as he drove her home, 'are we to handle the divorce?'

'Easy,' he said, relieved that she wasn't going to insist on martyrdom and stand by her husband. 'Incompatibility covers the metaphorical multitude.'

'And how,' she continued, 'are we going to handle the papers? They could have a field day with this one.'

'That,' he told her, 'is my job. And you might have noticed that I have been doing it for a very long time now – and I'm damned good at it.'

18

After *Friendly Enemies* Paul Fredericks had had another long-running Broadway success. He spent eighteen months in *Charlie's Story*, in which he played the title part. He was a young man who breaks away from a domineering mother only to find himself in the same situation with his wife. It was a drama with touches of wry humour – a combination at which Paul excelled. It was based very closely on *The Doll's House*, with the neat twist that at the end it is the husband who slams the door behind himself and goes off an independent man. Every night the final scene brought the men in the audience to their feet with shouts of approval.

It was a good play, but not a great one and not a patch on David's work. Paul thought of David a lot. He missed him, especially at night after the show when he returned to the little house in the village where there was so much to remind him of David. Would he ever be back, Paul wondered. And if he did come back would he come back to him? Would there still be room in David's life for Paul? He hadn't heard from him for months and ached to pick up the phone and call him but he stopped himself. He had probably gone too far already. He remembered the embrace on the train with a mixture of pleasure and pain.

When *Charlie's Story* closed, he hated having so much time on his hands. He couldn't relax and he resented the loneliness. In a long-running play you felt you were part of a family. There was an amazing closeness, not only among the cast but also with the backstage gang. Not only did you work together but often ate together and frequently slept together, although Paul hadn't gone to that extreme since Sebastian had bedded him in Boston during their time there with *Somewhere in France*. It wasn't any use even trying. He was in love with David and any other encounter was just that – an empty encounter. But once the play was over the family split up – it was worse than divorce. There was nothing unless and until the next time you worked together and then it was as if you had never been apart, no matter how many years intervened – years filled with silence. Theatrical friendships were most peculiar – deeply intense one minute and non-existent the next. And with no theatre to go to each night Paul's loneliness became acute.

When the offer of a television job came up, Paul grabbed it immediately. He didn't stop to think about it. He didn't stop to weigh up the consequences. It could do harm to his career. He did realize that, but he refused to think about it. He simply had to do something and it would most likely be months before another stage play came along. Legitimate actors, especially successful ones like Paul, were highly suspicious of television and not a little afraid of it. Rehearsals were not that different from stage work, but then came the live transmission when you not only had to play the part but also manage to judge camera angles, avoid stumbling over the electric paraphernalia and stay within range of the bobbing boom microphone. Add to that the seventeen million television sets around the country, with a conservative estimate of three viewers each, and with one slip you could blow your career in front of fifty-one million people.

But in spite of all this, or maybe because of it, Paul found working in live television even more stimulating than in the theatre. He found his tape marks on the floor effortlessly and seemed drawn to the camera with the red light on instinctively. The adrenalin produced by the knowledge that you only had one chance at this role, unlike in the theatre where if you were down one night you could pick up the next, made his performance sharp and precise. The weeks of rehearsal were all-consuming and left him no time to brood as he dissected his character and built it up from the inside out. Television close-ups did him no harm either. The camera picked up every nuance he chose to project. It was, he decided, an altogether satisfying medium and the audiences agreed with him. He picked up an Emmy for his portrayal of a conniving advertising executive in *Boardroom Jungle*.

It was with congratulations on this achievement that Kathleen greeted him when she phoned from California. Wanting to ease into the reason for the call, as she had no idea how he would respond, she then asked about the house, which he assured her was in good shape. Then she asked him about his plans.

Paul was mystified. Kathleen never called him. It had been years since they had spoken. And she hadn't even mentioned David. Why hadn't she mentioned David? Paul told her he was in rehearsal for another television drama which would be broadcast the following week.

'And then?' Kathleen asked.

Paul realized she was leading up to something – but what?

'Nothing planned,' he told her. 'In fact, I thought I might take a vacation.' Only successful actors took vacations. The others 'rested', hoping for work.

'What a good idea,' Kathleen said. 'You've been working so much you must be exhausted.'

'I am, kind of – television is very intense.'

'I'll bet it is. I don't think I could hack it.' She hesitated. 'Paul,' she said tentatively, 'why don't you come out to the Coast? I'm sure David would love to see you.' She had decided before she placed the call that the conversation would be nonchalant. Anything David wanted Paul to know he could tell him himself. That was, if Paul was still interested in David.

And when Paul said, 'How is David?' she could tell from the tone of his voice that he was indeed still very much interested.

251

'Oh, David is fine,' she lied. 'Rather homesick though, I think. I don't think all this sunshine agrees with him. You know what a Puritan he is – can't bear being comfortable. He prefers the extremes of climate back home.'

Paul was not fooled by Kathleen's seeming offhandedness. Something was wrong. She was telling him that David needed him, but managing not to say it.

'I'll be there,' Paul said. 'I'll be there as soon as I can.'

Kathleen did not tell her mother of the developments on the home front. Even if she had felt she wanted to she wouldn't know where to begin to explain. Her mother couldn't possibly understand. Kathleen doubted that her mother even knew what a homosexual was. And how could Kathleen explain about David when she didn't even fully understand herself? It was her fault anyway. She was willing to accept the blame but she felt she couldn't yet again be a disappointment to her mother. She had failed her as a teenager, now she failed her as an adult. Mother would have to know about the divorce. Kathleen grimaced. Was there anything worse in her mother's eyes than divorce? Everyone would have to know about the divorce. The golden couple would be no more. She had failed to make the marriage work despite all that David had given her, had taught her. The only thing she could give him now, in return, was his freedom. Perhaps that would be enough to cure him of this sickness he had fallen into. Perhaps freedom from her would be the answer. Then again, perhaps Paul could give him whatever it was that he needed to be whole again – to be able to write. Writing was as necessary to David as breathing. Without his writing David had nothing that he cared for.

She was glad that her mother was so involved in Mendel's. Since she had taken temporary charge of the department she had barely found the time for a once-a-week phone call to ask after the twins. Luckily she never enquired about David. Perhaps she thought it tactful, as she could not have failed to notice that all was not, as she would put it, 'as it should be' between them.

Meanwhile, as David was healing, Kathleen went back to her filming schedule from dawn to dusk. And Hornbeam was looking after things. He had advised that she didn't visit the hospital again. Although no one would recognize David, and Hornbeam had given a false name, there were few who would not recognize her. Kathleen did as she was told. Hornbeam, she decided, knew what was best. She had long ago ceased to be annoyed by his constant organizing. In fact now she was glad of his presence, glad that she could trust someone, indeed lean on someone. She worked on the film, she left her personal life to Hornbeam and awaited Paul's arrival.

Although Rosemary Simmonds' arm healed, it seemed that more than a bone was broken and the mind would take longer to heal. Sally would not return to Rosemary and Miss Simmonds would not return to Mendel's.

'Well, Miss Pally,' Mr Hickox said when he received the news, 'I can't say I'm surprised.'

'Nor I,' the personnel manager replied.

'Do we take a chance with Mrs Thornton?'

'I don't see it as a risk at all, sir. She's been in charge for three months now and there hasn't been a hitch. In fact, the department has never looked better, the sales are up and she handles the girls beautifully.'

'Yes, she sure does that, but there is her age to consider – and, indeed, her background. She puzzles me. Why suddenly come West at her age?'

Miss Pally looked at him. She considered Mr Hickox to be ahead of the game in every sense. She considered him intelligent, astute and most of all observant – surely . . . 'Don't you know?' she asked.

'If I knew then it wouldn't be a mystery,' he said, annoyed. Women, even women as efficient as Miss Pally, could be infuriatingly obtuse. But women were a necessary evil in the retail trade. As for Mrs Thornton it could just be some menopausal quirk – change of life wanderlust. She could be taken funny again at any moment and decide she was going to explore South American rain forests, for heaven's sake, and he would have to start all over again. It was bad enough having to put up with all that at home. Madeline, his wife, was becoming most unpredictable.

'She's Kathleen Thornton's mother,' Miss Pally informed him, with just a touch of superiority in her tone. It wasn't often that she was able to supply Mr Hickox with information and she rather relished it.

'Kathleen Thornton?'

'The movie star. You know, *Remember the Dawn.*'

Mr Hickox did recall that his wife had mentioned it – a woman's picture, not his kind of thing at all. Still he was impressed – if it was true.

'What,' he asked, 'makes you think that? Just because they have the same name. Movie stars are always changing their names anyway. Look at Doris Day – what's hers? Klumpermeyer or something.'

'Kappelhof.' Miss Pally corrected him. She was something of an expert on movie stars and sought out sneak previews to fill her evenings. 'And Thornton is her real name. Besides, they have the same eyes and they walk the same way. There is simply no doubt about it.'

'Have you asked her?'

'Of course not. She would probably deny it.' Miss Pally had not been fooled by the stories in the magazines about Kathleen Thornton coming from England. She prided herself on being able to spot the phoney stories. It was, after all, part of her job to assess people, to be able to tell when they were lying and when they were telling the truth. There was no doubt that Kathleen's vowel sounds were not British – certainly nothing like Ronald Colman. They were definitely East Coast, Boston in fact, and that is where Maureen Thornton came from. Basil Rathbone's Sherlock Holmes would have had no difficulty putting the clues together and neither did she.

'So you see,' she concluded her case, 'she had a perfectly valid, if secret reason for coming here. It was not just a whim and if you must know, Mr Hickox, I find her age irrelevant.' Miss Pally was not far behind, at forty-three.

As he could see no satisfactory alternative, there was no one else in the store who could handle the job and if he advertised he would probably have to wait months before the right person turned up – Mr Hickox decided that he would take the chance.

'Tell Helen to ask her to see me, will you, Miss Pally?'

'I think you should know,' Kathleen told her mother, 'David is going back East.'

'Oh, that's nice, dear. For long?'

'Not just a trip,' Kathleen took a deep breath, 'there will be a divorce.'

Maureen wasn't sure how she was expected to react to the news. Kathleen betrayed no emotion. Maureen had liked David, but she could always see that he and her daughter were not suited. But, then, how many couples were truly suited? Still, it was different nowadays – people didn't feel it was necessary to stay together any more. Whether that was a good thing or a bad thing, she didn't know. All she knew now was that it had nothing to do with her. Kathleen had always made her own decisions and she didn't need a mother interfering now, even if Maureen had a desire to do so, which she didn't.

She supposed she had become very selfish, but she couldn't deny she was happy. Even Kathleen's news couldn't dent her personal happiness. She loved her job, she loved her freedom and although she would not go so far as to say she loved Hank (loving people was a thing she was still wary of; loving people robbed you of all the things she had longed for all her life and had finally achieved), she certainly liked his company and, moreover, she certainly liked the way he held her and touched her and, when she had finally overcome her fear, the way he made love to her. That was a new world of sensation that she very much enjoyed. She had been surprised at how natural it felt and amazed by her lack of guilt. There was no great overwhelming passion, as she had suspected there had to be. There was just a simple coming together for mutual pleasure – a pleasure that was so intense every nerve of her body responded and relaxed so totally that her mind was clearer than it had ever been and she felt suffused with energy and well being. She would have moved from what she now recognized as her seedy surroundings now that she was making such good money as head of the department, except for the fact of Hank's proximity. She had come to rely on that. Could that be a kind of love? Anyway, she was staying put for the time being at least. She did, however, ditch the rebellious purple furnishings in favour of creams and browns.

'Are you sure about this decision?' Maureen asked her daughter. And whose decision was it, she wondered. Kathleen's or David's – or hopefully both?

'Yes, David has never really been happy out here.' Kathleen continued to blame the climate rather than herself when she talked about it.

'Well, you could all go back East.'

'No. I've got my work here now – and, well, it is more than just the place.'

'Do you want to talk about it?'

'No, not really if you don't mind,' Kathleen said. David was now out of the hospital and Hornbeam had found him an apartment for the time being. It was Hornbeam who met Paul at the airport and drove him to David. It was Hornbeam who had told Kathleen of the emotional meeting. It was Hornbeam who had arranged David's flight. He was leaving with Paul in the morning. Then Hornbeam would organize the divorce. Everything was taken care of by Hornbeam. Everything except the personal details like telling her mother and the twins. Everything except the emotions.

Kathleen had not seen David since that brief visit to the hospital. There seemed no point in a meeting. They couldn't talk to each other. Maybe they had never been able to. It only seemed that they had communicated. In fact each had buried secrets and the secrets were the most important things to them. Besides, he hadn't asked to see her. Well, now Mother had been told and Kathleen was glad that she had taken it in such a matter-of-fact way. She had wondered how to do it. She had agonized over it and decided it was best done in public. They met at Mendel's during Maureen's lunch break. Kathleen had finished shooting and was scheduled for a month off; well, nearly off, there was always the publicity, before starting a new picture. Heads turned as Kathleen entered the restaurant and whispered asides echoed around the tables as mother and daughter greeted each other.

'Well, I'm sure you are doing what you think is right,' Maureen said. 'How have the twins taken it?'

'I haven't told them yet, but I can't see it making much difference to them. They hardly know him.'

'That's true and heaven knows they are a resilient pair. All the moving about, the way we go in and out of their lives and they seem as happy as can be.'

'They seem to need only each other,' Kathleen said. She, herself, felt shut out from the twosome.

'Maybe that's just as well,' Maureen said. 'Now,' she consulted the menu, 'the chicken à la king is very good.' She must get on, she thought. She had a busy afternoon ahead of her and she and Hank were going to drive out to the shore after work. Hank had re-arranged his working schedule so that they could spend more time together. And he had assured her that the work was going better than ever now that she was in his life.

David and Paul sat side by side on the plane. David had the window seat and watched as Los Angeles grew small, becoming a toy town in the distance. Then as the plane turned its back on the Pacific and headed east for the real world, David took Paul's hand. It had all been a nightmare. The moment Paul had walked into the apartment David realized that. He had told Paul everything. They would have no secrets.

19

Kathleen was not looking forward to her next scheduled publicity appearance. She and Virginia Wilkins and Isabelle Young were being taken down to the Naval Hospital in San Diego.

'It is just so . . . morbid,' she told her mother when Maureen made her weekly phone call. 'So . . . oh I don't know, patronizing. There we will be all decked out glamorously in our borrowed studio clothes, made up to the hilt, dispensing flowers and candy and pecks on the cheek to all those horrifically wounded men.'

'It will cheer them up, dear.'

'How could anything cheer up those guys? They'll never get any better. How long has it been?'

'The twins were six in January,' Maureen said. She always dated the war by the twins.

'All that time and there are still hospitals full of victims. And there is no hope for them now.'

'We all have our crosses to bear, Kathleen. Some are just more visible than others.' Maureen hated it when she heard herself mouthing clichés which had been dinned into her by the nuns, or her mother. She shivered at the thought. One day she must decide what she really did think for herself. All those years of doing nothing except reacting to others, and now? Well now she was so busy being free she was still not thinking – except about china, glass and Hank.

'It still seems like exploitation to me,' Kathleen said.

'Everything in life has a bit of exploitation to it. Every-

258

one uses everyone.' God, there I go again, she thought. 'Anyway, cheer up. It will soon be over.'

It was a small caravan of stars, photographers, make-up artists and publicity men which made its way south to San Diego. The hospital itself was a large building with magnificent views over the bay and the sun was shining, glistening off the water as they disembarked and arranged themselves around the lawn.

French windows opened and a convoy, a seemingly endless line of wheel-chairs emerged into the sunshine, each containing a blanket-covered occupant. Some of the chairs were pushed by white-clad nurses, starched and rustling, with linen crowns perched precariously on top of short, curled, efficient hair. Others were pushed by pony-tailed teenagers in pink and white striped dresses and few, a very few, came on to the lawn unaided, the muscular arms of the occupants whirling the wheels with an aggressive power. The nurses were erect, bodies seemingly starched along with their uniforms. The candy-striped girls bounced along, leaning over, chatting constantly into the ear of their charges, hair bobbing. But the only smiling masculine faces were those who proceeded across the lawn driven on by their own power.

Kathleen, as she knew she would be, was horrified by the sight, but she had learned enough about acting in the past few years to smile brightly as the lawn filled. Beyond that she didn't know what was expected of her. Was she to approach or was she to wait to be approached? Was she to speak or to be spoken to first? And if she was to speak what was she going to say? Where was the director? Where was the writer? She smiled, as, following the lead of the other women, she began to walk in between the chairs, trying not to look at faces as hands or sometimes just stumps of arms reached out for her hand. Photographers snapped, the girls giggled and the nurses relaxed enough to nod a greeting as the photographers demanded smiles.

'How ya doing?' she would say, with exaggerated cama-

259

raderie, her eyes shining, trying not to see. 'You're looking swell. Great weather, huh? Look at the birdie now,' as she posed.

Some of the men managed a joke or sexual innuendo. They were flirting, showing the brave spunkiness for the camera that they knew was expected of them. Kathleen wondered who had taught them to act. She forced herself to move on, to mingle. The pain made all the faces similar. It was, she thought, not the physical pain, but the mental anguish with which they lived each day, knowing their dreams had been destroyed with their limbs. Still, at least they are alive, she thought. Was it better for them than for all those thousands who had died at their sides? Was it better for all the wives, the sweethearts? She tried to push the memories from her mind. They were still too real, too definite. She could see Daniel's face the day he walked into the store. At first all sad and disconsolate and then she could see it brighten when he looked at her, and then the look had turned to joy. It was so real. So real she could reach out and touch him, grasp the hand he held out to her.

'Hello, Kathy,' he said.

They blamed the strong sun for Kathleen's faint and carried her into the building. The photographers stopped clicking in her direction – discreetly.

The room seemed very clear, distinct, as Kathleen opened her eyes. The vase of flowers on the sideboard was bright, intense. The eyes that met hers seemed to see right inside her.

'It's all right now, Miss Thornton,' the nurse who was by her side, who gazed so intently at her, said. 'You'll be fine. It is the sun on the water that does it. And I'll bet you had no breakfast. There'll be a cup of tea along in a minute. You just rest. You've done enough for the morning. I saw *Remember the Dawn*.' She said it proudly as if it were an accomplishment. 'I thought you were just great. When you came down that staircase carrying the tray –

just after you discovered that he was dead – well, I cried and cried.'

'Thank you,' Kathleen said. 'I'm glad you liked it.'

'You are my favourite,' the nurse prattled on. She was just about the same age as Kathleen. 'I hear you're doing a movie with Rock Hudson.'

'No, no.' Kathleen shook her head. 'I'm not.' She wished the woman would stop talking. There was something she had to remember.

'Oh, yes,' the nurse said definitely. 'I read it in *Photoplay*. Kathleen Thornton stars with Rock Hudson in a new romantic mystery. Should be some chemistry. Shooting begins . . .'

'Maybe, maybe,' Kathleen interrupted. Would she just be quiet.

'I suppose it is a secret. They did say that. It was in the Hollywood gossip column.'

Daniel. Kathleen suddenly remembered. Daniel! She sat up on the sofa where she had been reclining.

'Now, now – you mustn't make sudden movements like that, Miss Thornton.' The nurse put her hand on Kathleen's shoulders to push her back down. 'All the blood will go rushing out of your head again.'

Kathleen did feel dizzy but she struggled to get to her feet. The restraining hands succeeded in keeping her recumbent. Kathleen was amazed by the strength of this slender woman and then realized the weights with which she was trained to cope. All those men. Most of them virtually helpless – and one of them Daniel.

There was a rap on the door.

'Ah – that'll be your tea. Come in,' she called. 'Now you can sit up, but slowly.' This time she eased those strong arms under Kathleen's shoulders and effortlessly brought her to a sitting position. A candy-striped cadet deposited a tray on the table by the sofa as if by remote control. 'Oh, Miss Thornton,' she exclaimed, 'I've seen all your movies. I specially –'

'Shoo,' the nurse interrupted her, 'can't you see Miss Thornton is not feeling well?'

Abashed, the girl backed out of the room, eyes still mesmerized by seeing the movie star close up.

'These kids,' the nurse said, 'they've got no idea. Now,' she approached the tray, 'I suppose you English don't have milk and sugar in your tea.'

'What?' Kathleen was confused. What was this woman talking about?

'You English. Tea and cucumber sandwiches and all that. I've read about it.'

Kathleen remembered her publicity. English, of course.

'Anyway, you'll have your drink the way I say. I do know what's best for you, after all. Plenty of milk and sugar. My Irish granny always said . . .'

Somewhere in the distance Kathleen heard the nurse's voice droning on while in her mind all her moments with Daniel swirled around. She was back at her First Communion with the hated veil cutting into her forehead. She was kneeling there, waiting and looking up and seeing him. Then she was at school – across the playground she would see him talking to his friends and long to go to him, long for him to come to her, to notice her and then . . . then the day he came into the store and then and then . . . she was in his arms . . . and then her arms were empty again. Had she dreamed it? Daniel was dead. He had been dead for years. Sometimes she believed he had never existed – and the girls, they were just some kind of magic. She couldn't remember Daniel – just the memories. She remembered the memories that had grown in her mind over the years.

Somewhere, deep down inside every person there lodges an alarm system. It lies dormant for years and years and then a moment comes when it begins to ring, sending signals to every part of the body. This is the moment it says. This is the moment that will be the most important in your life. How you react to this moment will decide your salvation or your damnation. The alarm system throws the brain into muddle, the stomach into heaving and the nerves into disarray. The reaction is to run, to flee, to ignore the moment, to pretend it doesn't exist – to pretend there is no decision to be made. Some people accept that. They flee into activity or retreat into darkness. They refuse to recognize the alarm. They swallow it back into that corner of themselves where gradually it ceases to exist. It is understandable, because at that moment they are least able to be rational, least equipped to make a decision, least able to assess the consequences of any choice.

This was Kathleen's moment. Everything in her life so far had been inconsequential until now. Everything in her life had just happened. She had not decided to fall in love with Daniel – there had been no choice. His need for her, her attraction to his need that had overwhelmed everything else when he made love to her. That had not been a choice either. The twins just happened – even abandoning them had been automatic. She could not have stayed. She could not have survived if she had. There had been no choice. David had happened. Acting had happened. Up until this moment Kathleen had been on automatic pilot, she had been sleepwalking. But she could not pretend this was a dream. Daniel was alive – and she was faced with a choice. She could get up now, walk from that room, leave the hospital and try to put that fact from her mind. What, after all, was he to her? Did she even know who he was? Had she ever known? And wouldn't he be different now anyway? Daniel was a fantasy, a memory. He had no place in the real world – in her world.

But he wasn't. He was real. He was there in that wheel-chair and now needed her more than ever. Or was he? He had made no attempt to contact her. Maybe he didn't want her. Maybe he had never really loved her. Could she survive that knowledge? Could she survive without it?

With the alarm swirling through her, Kathleen decided that the commitment had already been made years before and that she would see it through. So, although the adrenalin counselled flight, she instructed her hands to stop shaking, her knees to unbuckle and her tears not to flow. Then she instructed the nurse.

'There is someone I must speak to,' she told her. 'Can you ask Daniel Towski to come in here so we may have some privacy?'

20

The doctors advised against it. The problem was not so much Daniel's physical condition – very many men had overcome that to go on to happy, productive lives. It was his mental state. There was, they pronounced, a genetic disposition to manic depression and this had of course been aggravated by his wartime experiences. For months after his rescue he had been in a catatonic state. For a year he had not spoken. At the moment, they told her, it was true he was on an upward swing but any time the depression could return. He was better off in hospital.

Phil Hornbeam advised against it. She had just rid herself of David. Why take on more problems? She was, he insisted, a great actress. She was already a star and she was only going to get bigger. She had her work, she had her girls, she could have any guy she wanted. She didn't need this. It would only be trouble. Besides, what about her image?

Maureen advised against it. She remembered Daniel's drunken father. She remembered his mother's suicide. She told her daughter she owed Daniel nothing. Nothing at all. He had been important a long time ago when Kathleen was really only a child. Now she was a young, successful, beautiful woman who deserved more from life than being tied down nursing a physically and mentally crippled man. This was not the Daniel she had known. Had there ever been a real Daniel? Her Daniel was a fantasy.

The more she was advised to the contrary, the more adamant Kathleen became. To take the advice would be to deny everything she believed. She and Daniel belonged together. They had always belonged together. She had been right all those years ago when she promised herself to him. When she gave herself to him. If that were not true then the twins would indeed be the bastards that her grandmother had pronounced them. There was nothing sordid about their conception. It had been love and love was unchanging. Moreover, theirs was a special love. It had nourished her through her childhood; it had sustained her since then and it would transcend all obstacles. Crippled, he was no less Daniel. As for the other, of course he was depressed. Life had not been good to him. But that was about to change. She could not give strength back to his body but she could give strength to his mind and to his soul. She could give him his daughters and a reason to live.

Kathleen found a house set on the cliffs high above the Pacific ocean. It was one storey, ranch-style, with lawns out to the road and views from the back over the sea that were magnificent. The builders were put to work immediately – constructing ramps, widening doors and generally making wheel-chair access to every room. Hornbeam sighed deeply, accepted the inevitable and began work on his press release. Although it was Hornbeam who had handled the divorce and Kathleen had only to contribute a brief court appearance, it was she who wrote to Father O'Connor. He put her in touch with Father Charles, a local priest who took her statement, questioned her fiercely for two hours and then, satisfied, softened and said, 'It should be very straightforward.'

Father O'Connor himself interviewed David in New York. Perhaps it was Paul's presence during the interview, perhaps it was due to Father O'Connor's original misgivings, perhaps it was because Father Charles, contrary to his expectations, had been totally charmed by Kathleen's obvious sincerity and her devotion to her naval hero, or perhaps it was because, as Kathleen thought, God had planned it in the first place that the annulment came through so quickly. It would have been easy to prove non-consummation had she been a virgin, but as that was not the case their word had to suffice. And she had known that her celebrity would count against her. The church did not like to put itself in a position where it could be charged with playing favourites.

The twins took the latest piece of information with their usual equanimity. A new daddy was introduced. The concept of mummies and daddies had become meaningless.

'How long will this one stay?' Geraldine asked her sister, who just shrugged. Did it really matter she wondered.

'Why was he crying?' Geraldine asked.

'Because he lost one of his legs,' Eileen said. Some things were obvious.

Lost his leg, Geraldine thought. How could you do that?

Daniel had been elated by the news of his daughters' existence but overwhelmed when he saw them. They were such beautiful children. They approached the wheel-chair with a diffidence that seemed to come more from a strong reserve than from a shy confusion. Would he ever be a real father to them, he wondered, as they allowed themselves to be gathered to him, one in each arm with a polite self-control and a perceptible stiffening. Daniel himself was not sure if his tears were of joy at finding them or of sorrow at having lost them. What kind of father would he be? Would it not be better if he had really been dead? Hadn't it really been better for Kathleen as well? He was being selfish coming back into their lives.

Kathleen brushed aside his doubts as briskly as she had dealt with all the other doubts expressed to her. Daniel was her husband. Only the formalities remained.

The wedding was small – just the girls and Nanny, Maureen and her new friend. Kathleen had questioned her mother about Hank, but Maureen had been enigmatic.

'A neighbour,' she had said.

Hornbeam had reluctantly agreed to be best man.

The reception was a different matter. If you are going

267

to make a mistake, Hornbeam rationalized, you might as well go the whole hog. Everyone would be curious about this man. Might as well get it over with so at least the gossips would have some first-hand information. He orchestrated the enormous party. If anyone from the Hollywood community had not received an invitation it wasn't his fault. From hairdressers and runners to Oscar winners and legends they all came to the pink and white striped marquee in the garden above the Pacific to drink champagne, nibble jumbo shrimps and, shaking their heads out of her hearing, declare Kathleen a very brave girl.

In three days' time Kathleen was scheduled to begin a new film, reunited with George Pierce. The script was again minimal – a shipboard romance and then at the end a reluctant separation as they returned to their respective spouses and duty. The filmmakers and audiences alike found a sexual chemistry between George and Kathleen on screen that patently did not exist off. Kathleen found George dull and unimaginative and, indeed, not a very good actor. But he was good-looking and had a kind of gentlemanly confidence in his looks that carried him through. She found it amusing that George's wife, despite her experience, seemed to believe the publicity and clung closely to him whenever they were together.

'It is all so absolutely gorgeous,' Mrs Pierce, George firmly by the hand, said. She kissed Kathleen on both cheeks.

'Well, as you can imagine, it is Hornbeam's doing,' Kathleen said. From the corner of her eye she watched Daniel swirling through the groups, deftly manipulating his motorized chair. She was proud of the speed with which he had learned to operate it. He only needed a reason she told herself. Just a reason to take control of himself. She was glad of the pleasure it obviously gave him now to be in control of his mobility – and that was just the beginning. Since that reunion at the hospital she had daily seen him improve, mentally and physically. The defeated sadness in his eyes had gradually receded and now she could see a glowing anticipation – an acceptance of what was, but also a determination that there was a future and it was not black. He no longer seemed afraid. Now as she watched him, tanned and golden once more, she was extraordinarily proud of him. All those strangers to confront and he was not only surviving, he was, she thought, definitely enjoying himself.

'Have you met my husband?' she asked, pleased at the sound of the word and, catching his eye, she beckoned him over. With a whirl he was at her side, reaching out, taking her hand in his. It was warm and comforting and she loved him very much indeed.

Once more Daniel wondered at the miracles this woman could perform. He felt again as he had that day long ago, when he had walked into the corner shop, his head full of thoughts of death, and her look had swept them away like dust. Now once more his future, whatever it was to be, was bright and shining and Kathleen had done that. He was never going to let her out of his sight again. When she was not there bad things happened to him. Without her he did not exist.

'Darling,' Kathleen said to him, 'have you met George and Maria Pierce?'

Daniel reached out with his free hand, still clasping Kathleen's in his other.

'Nice to meet you,' he said, shaking first George's and then Maria's hand. His grip was firm and strong. 'You are starting work again soon, I understand,' he said.

'Yup. A couple of days and it's back to the coal mines. Better enjoy ourselves while we can.' George said it pointedly as he held out his glass to a passing waiter for a refill.

'Star-crossed lovers again, I hear.'

'Are there any other kind?' George said with a chuckle.

'Oh, I don't know.' Daniel looked up at Kathleen. 'Sometimes there are happy endings.'

'I doubt if we will ever find one, will we Kathleen? At least not on celluloid. The public seems to enjoy watching us suffer.'

Daniel did not like the way George looked at his wife. He searched Kathleen's face to see if that meaningful glance was returned but he couldn't tell. He was looking at her from the wrong angle. However, from the way Maria moved in, gripping her husband's arm, she had obviously felt something too.

'I enjoyed *One Last Night*,' Daniel said. 'If enjoyed is the right word. They showed it at the hospital and everyone was weeping buckets.'

'That's what they're supposed to do,' George said. 'Glad to hear it.'

'You never told me you saw that,' Kathleen said.

'Ah – I saw *Remember the Dawn* too.'

'Why you . . .' she swatted him playfully on the top of his head. 'Can you believe it, George, he never once mentioned . . .'

'Didn't want you to see me as just another fawning fan.' Daniel laughed, but his eyes were firmly on Kathleen, searching for a look that would tell him that George was more to her than just her leading man. She had told him about David – the stupid bastard – still, Daniel realized he should be grateful that was what he was. What if the marriage had worked out? It didn't bear thinking about. Where would he be now? But she hadn't said anything about George. The things that weren't said could be much more important than those that were. Still, he was here now, and he reminded himself that there was no way he was going to lose her again. He would be vigilant.

'Well, I think you were wrong, Danny-boy, to keep it to yourself. We like all the fawning fans we can get, don't we, darling?'

Daniel stiffened at the word addressed to his wife, but he remained smiling.

'You bet,' Kathleen said, unaware that the pressure on her hand had increased. 'Another sack of mail means you're still bankable.'

Hank and Maureen stood away from the others at the top of the cliffs, looking out over the ocean. Far away in

270

the distance, glinting in the sun, it was calm and deserving of its name – peaceful. But the waves broke on the rocks beneath them with a swirling fury, beating the shore with foaming intensity. The glossy serenity was a lie. The truth of the sea's nature was only revealed at its edge when its dominion was threatened by confrontation, when the ground and the rocks challenged its eternal flow. Then it lashed out with passion, wearing away at its adversary.

'You don't seem very happy with this match,' Hank said. He had found the story thrilling – eternal love triumphant. It gave a possibility to the scenario he had constructed and often dwelt upon during the years of his marriage and afterwards, alone in California. It occupied his often sleepless nights. Ann O'Malley. They would meet again, unexpectedly of course. The dream took different forms. Sometimes it would be in a restaurant. He would look across the room and there she would be at another table. Sometimes he would be on a plane, searching for his seat. Then having found it he would concentrate on settling in. As he fastened his seat belt he would glance across the person in the window-seat, paying no attention as he looked out on to the tarmac, noting only that the occupant was female. Only as the engines roared into life would their eyes meet – Ann. Sometimes he would be walking down a crowded street, hurrying to an appointment, threading his way through the infuriatingly slow-moving crowds, and there, coming towards him – Ann.

The outcome was always the same. Their eyes would meet and the years would fall away, as in all good fairy tales. True love would not be thwarted by distance or time. He had always known it was a fiction but it was comforting all the same. He had never spoken of it to Maureen. She had a practicality which he knew would necessitate her pointing out to him the improbability of his dreams. Maybe even the undesirability of them. Or was it just the other side of his nature which threw cold water on to his romantic notions? Still, he didn't want Maureen to laugh at him. He needed her approbation.

'Kathleen's happy,' Maureen said, 'that's what counts.' She wondered if that happiness could possibly last. But, then, she reasoned, happiness was a momentary emotion – it never lasted. Contentment was what mattered and she doubted this marriage could lead to that. It would be, she felt, a constant emotional battle. However, standing there in the sunshine far above the Pacific three thousand physical and several million emotional miles from the place and time when she originally formulated her theories of life, she chided herself. She could never have imagined this moment and here it was. Perhaps the future was just a series of accidents and had nothing to do with human decisions, right or wrong. What was the expression Hank had used when she had expressed concern over their relationship? *Carpe diem.* Well, the sun was shining, the surroundings were heavenly, her daughter was married to the man she had always believed she loved and there was no one she would rather be next to than Hank. *Carpe diem.*

Kathleen, along with many other celebrities, had been invited to bring her family to the opening of Walt Disney's theme park in Anaheim. The twins, already fans of *Disneyland*, which they watched every Wednesday evening on television, were much more excited by the prospect of going there than they had been by the wedding.

'Davy, Daavvvy Crockett,' they sang loudly, 'King of the wild frontier', as Kathleen headed south on the freeway. Even the fact that their mother had insisted they leave their 'genuine racoon hats' at home did not diminish their enthusiasm. Soon the city petered out and the car rolled along as the road cut through orange groves. Daniel seemed to be enjoying the journey, even joining the girls in the *Ballad of Davy Crockett* but by the fifth time round, 'killed him a bear when he was only three', he called a halt, irritated.

'That's enough,' he said sharply and the girls stopped at once.

Kathleen glanced at him, beside her, in the passenger

272

seat. She could see only the back of his head as he stared pointedly out of the window seemingly intent on the rows of trees as they flashed by, but she could imagine the expression on his face. He was far away, inside his pain, somewhere she could not reach him, no matter how hard she tried. She had seen the look before and all she hoped was that it would come with less frequency – that he would accept the love and let it fill up that void within himself which so afflicted him. She tried to tell herself that it had become less apparent since he had moved into their new home, but she was unsure of the truth of that. It was something she wanted to believe. Since that day at the hospital when he had been wheeled by the candy-striped nurse's aide, the only thing she had been sure about was that they belonged together. She had sat on the sofa, he in his chair opposite her. Their eyes were level and only the sadness of recognition was obvious. She held out her hand to him.

'Daniel,' she said softly.

He took her hand and tears formed slowly in his eyes. She watched as, unchecked, they ran down his face. With her other hand she reached out and gently wiped them away, forcing back her own tears. Locked in silence they sat motionless, holding each other in their sight.

Finally Kathleen said simply, 'Why?' There was almost anger in her voice. The unfairness of him allowing her to think he was dead for all those years.

'How could I come back to you like this?' he said. 'It just wouldn't be fair.'

'I love you,' Kathleen said.

'No.' Daniel shook his head. 'You loved someone else – a long time ago. Someone who doesn't exist any more. And I held on to that love. I held on to it, Kathleen, as I floated in that water and when I was pulled mostly dead on to the rescue boat the only part of me that was alive was that bit clinging to you. You saved my life. How could I return that gift with . . .' he indicated the chair, the rug thrown over him, '. . . this.'

Kathleen could control her tears no longer. 'Oh, you stupid . . .' She slid from the sofa, kneeling before him, her arms around his neck, her head buried in his chest. There were no words she could use to show him how wrong he was. There was only touch. She lifted her face to him and gently kissed his lips.

From that moment she was determined to do the right thing. She had never reckoned it would be easy but it would be less difficult for her now than it would have been if she had remained at home caring for the twins – living above the store. That was strange. It had been wrong to walk out on them – anyone would have said that. It had been wrong to deceive David – anyone would have said that. Two wrongs don't make a right. The old cliché, she realized, was not true. It was as if there were a plan which she, unwittingly, had followed. It was a plan that led to Daniel and the means for looking after him properly. Now she had the money for a specially designed house, a car he could learn to drive, a nurse when he needed one. She had the money for a good nanny for the twins so she could give him time and attention. Because she had given everything up, she now had everything.

That, however, was not how Daniel had seen the situation. It was as if when he lost his leg he lost all power over his life. He knew that it was wrong to be supported and looked after by Kathleen. He was a man – he was the one who should look after her. But, like a child, he was helpless in the face of her determination. He had grown used to the hospital. There he was like the others, better than some, in fact. He felt he belonged there where everyone understood. Now in the ordinary world he was a cripple, a freak to be pitied, constantly reminded he was different, powerless. Perhaps the doctors were right. Perhaps he could use an artificial leg and hobble along on a wooden contraption, but the idea nauseated him. He preferred the comparative dignity of the chair to the idea of people thinking how brave he was as he lunged into the room with a Frankenstein gait.

274

There were moments when he caught her infectious optimism. There were even days when he was convinced it would, as she said, be all right. But the doubts pushed through and the blackness descended. He couldn't bear the thought of Kathleen seeing his deformity. When he closed his bedroom door at night, it was the nurse who helped him into bed. And now, in the car as the orange groves flashed past, he looked out of the window but all he could see was the irritatingly handsome face of George Pierce, twelve feet high on the screen, gazing adoringly at Kathleen, and Kathleen's eyes misting with love, returning the gaze. It was the same look she bestowed on him.

✣ 21 ✣

'That guy has got to go,' Hornbeam paced his office, talking aloud to the empty space. 'That's all there is to it – he has got to go.' But how to get rid of him? That was the problem. He was fuming, trying to calm down enough to think constructively. It had started innocently enough. Daniel had wanted to visit the set of *Sea Voyage*. Understandable really. He obviously wanted to see for himself how things worked. Who didn't? Hornbeam would bet there wasn't a person in the world who didn't want to be on a genuine Hollywood film set. Even in Timbuktu, wherever that was, he figured the natives were sitting around in their straw huts longing for a chance to come to California and see the stars close up. So why shouldn't the new husband of a star?

Hornbeam had laid on the grand tour. No trouble was spared – from carpentry and props through costumes and make-up and on to the floor itself. Daniel got the works. The Chief himself even made a rare visit to the commissary and introduced Daniel around. Hornbeam thought Daniel would be happy with that but it turned out only to be the beginning. Every day he was there. Every goddamn day. At first he stayed on the sidelines, waiting patiently nearly out of the way until, after each take, Kathleen returned to him. The first week or so the rest of the cast and crew found it touchingly romantic as Kathleen and her handsome wounded hero held hands and whispered to each other between takes.

What did not become obvious for a while was that they

276

were not whispering sweet nothings to each other. Daniel was, in fact, beginning his takeover. At first he had been content just to be there, to ensure that Kathleen spent as little time as possible in the company of George Pierce, or indeed any other man. He soon realized that George was not the only threat to him. There was Bill Compton, the director, who Daniel felt touched Kathleen a bit too much as he set up the moves. There was Jesse, the chief cameraman. There was the lighting man, not to mention the various young crewmen who were obviously enchanted by his wife. And Hornbeam was altogether too chummy. That, Daniel decided, was more than a professional friendship and merited watching. The only man he was not suspicious of was Frederick, the hairdresser. That one was obviously a fruit; but then he reminded himself that Kathleen had already been married to a fairy.

Each day at dawn he accompanied Kathleen to the studio and waited on the sidelines until the last take, when they returned home together. He had at first been amazed at how much time was spent just standing around, waiting. That convinced him that his presence was imperative. If he were not there to talk to, to sit with, how would she occupy herself? How had she before he married her? Flirting with her co-star? Or perhaps more than flirting. There must be some reason for Maria's constant presence on the set as well, he thought. Was it really likely that Kathleen had been celibate for all those years as she had told him? It seemed unlikely – especially now. She had come to his bed. He had been shy, unsure. It was she who had initiated, she who had caressed him into strength – and she who had hungrily drawn the passion from him. And now nightly she came eagerly to his bed. Could this woman, so wonderfully sexual, have been alone for so many years? He was taking no chances on losing her. And he was definitely not imagining a certain chemistry between her and George. Perhaps that relationship had been thwarted by Maria but there were plenty of other possibilities.

Of course this was not the reason he gave his wife for his eternal presence. He told her he was interested in the mechanics of film making. He thought there might eventually be a job in the industry for him. That was partly true. At that moment, however, the only job he wanted was taking control of Kathleen. He moved in, gradually at first, subtly – a comment here, a suggestion there. It was all very simple – a pair of shoes he disliked, a scarf he preferred. Soon his comments extended to the way she read a line, her profile on camera. There were whispered comments on the side at first, but soon Kathleen was seeking his approval for her every move. Just before the cameras rolled at each scene she would turn to him. Bill Compton could stand it no more.

'Who,' he stormed into Hornbeam's office, 'is directing this goddamn movie?'

Hornbeam tried to calm him. He knew it was useless to try to ban Towski from the set. He had already suggested to Kathleen that it might be a good idea if her husband found other ways to spend his days.

'Oh, no,' she had said, seeming not to grasp his point, or simply not wanting to. 'He adores it all.' She was pleased with how much better Daniel seemed since he had become involved with her work and amazed at how quickly he had picked up the techniques. His advice had become invaluable. And she enjoyed not being alone any more. She loved sharing her life and now sharing her work. The one thing she had feared had not materialized. He wasn't at all overshadowed by her. He had a mind of his own and it was a fine, strong mind. It was, she decided, a much better mind than hers and she wondered how she had managed without him.

It was probably Kathleen's protestations that she had never been so happy that most worried her mother. Like Phil Hornbeam, Maureen could see what Daniel was doing to her daughter. He was becoming stronger by the day, but it was a strength he was draining from Kathleen. There was, however, nothing she could do about it. She had made her protests firmly known when Daniel had come back into their lives and now she must just keep her silence. What good would criticism do, anyway? And besides, who was she to bestow wisdom? How long had it taken her to reach this point in her life? And was she right, anyway? Everything seemed perfect now, but that was just how Kathleen saw things. Funny, she thought, how easy it is to see just where others are going wrong and how to fix it, but how impossible it was to step back and gain a perspective on your own life. Kathleen said she was in love. Maureen could only see a dangerous obsessional infatuation, mingled with some masochistic desire for martyrdom. To what end?

Anyway, Maureen had her own emotional life to work out. The same night he had announced that he had finished the novel Hank had proposed marriage to her. Sitting in the bar which had so horrified her sensibilities the first time he had taken her out to dinner and which had since become like a second home, she had been taken completely by surprise.

Betty, who was still waiting to be discovered, had deposited the steak on the table, and the red wine.

'You're looking pretty smug tonight,' she said to Hank.

'Am I?'

It was true. Maureen had noticed the look of the cat that swallowed the canary about him but was patiently waiting for the explanation to come from him. She knew how much he enjoyed intrigue.

'Yup,' Betty said. 'Going to say what gives? Somebody die and leave you a bundle?'

'Nope.' He glanced at Maureen, making sure he had her full attention as well, before turning back to the waitress. 'Today,' he paused, 'I finished my book.'

The girl looked disappointed. 'Oh, hey – great,' she said without conviction before leaving them.

Hank smiled at Maureen. 'She didn't seem impressed.'

'Well, I am. I think that's wonderful, Hank.' Maureen

had begun to think that the novel would never get finished. She had begun to think that it was some kind of life preserver to which he clung. Ending it would take away his focus for survival and set him adrift once more, purposeless.

'At four-twenty-two this afternoon I found myself at the end of the final draft.'

'Couldn't you be more precise?'

'And you know what?' he continued, ignoring her sarcasm.

'What?'

'It is damn good.'

Maureen lifted her wine glass and looked at him over the rim. 'Here's to the novel,' she said.

'Here's to *A Solitary Life*,' he replied.

'What?'

'That's what it's called.' He laughed at her puzzlement. Talking about the novel had been taboo until it was finished. '*A Solitary Life*. That's the point, you see. It's all about families – about being alone in the midst of hordes of those whom we laughingly call loved ones.'

'Here,' Maureen said, raising her glass again, 'is to *A Solitary Life*.'

They drank to success.

'So . . . what now?' Maureen asked.

'Now I have to sell it.'

'A formality,' she said.

'Hardly.'

'Nonsense. I'm sure it will be snapped up and a bestseller as well.'

'What makes you so sure?' Hank was serious.

'Because I know you and if you think it's good then it is good.'

'I find your faith very comforting.' Hank was no longer bantering.

'I'm glad.' Maureen was serious as well.

They looked at each other silently for a moment and Maureen became disturbed by the intensity of the look.

She was fond of Hank – more than fond – and the feeling sometimes frightened her.

'So,' she said, breaking the silence, 'tell me more about this magical moment that occurred at four-twenty this afternoon.'

'Four-twenty-two,' he corrected her.

'*Mea culpa*,' she said teasingly.

'It was so strange,' he said. 'I finished reading it and, you know, it was as if it had nothing to do with me any more. It was there, it was real, it had a life of its own.'

'So,' she said, 'now you know you are a writer.'

'Now,' he said, 'I know I have written a book.'

'I don't understand the difference.'

'I somehow thought I would be someone different – but I'm still me.'

'A good thing too,' Maureen knew that was a frivolous thing to say. She knew what he meant. She, too, had thought, having gained, or rather accepted, her independence, having somehow 'got on in the world' as the saying went, she would be a different person. She looked different. She even behaved differently but basically the sleek (and she was sleek, every time she passed a mirror she approved of the reflection) head of China and Glass at the ultra chic Mendel's was very much the same person who had done as she was bidden in the corner grocery shop. The only difference was that all those with the power to bid her had disappeared and she had been careful that there had been no replacements.

'I thought,' he continued, 'that I would be happy just to get away – be on my own – but . . .' he paused. 'Negatives only leave a void. And I guess I don't really like all that emptiness.'

'But you're not alone,' she said, hoping she was not anticipating correctly.

'No. That's true. It was magic when you walked into my life,' he said. 'I know I couldn't have finished the book without your confidence and support.'

Maureen bristled inwardly. So it was she who had walked

into his life. The male perception of himself as the centre of the universe. It couldn't conceivably be that it was the other way around, that he was an adjunct of her life.

'I think,' she said, 'that the support was mutual.' Her voice was hardening around the edges.

'We are good for each other,' he said.

Maureen nodded. She preferred that assessment of the situation.

'And I don't want to lose you,' he said.

Maureen put her hand on his. 'It's difficult to lose the kind of total friendship we have.'

'Marry me.' Hank said it suddenly.

Although Maureen had feared it coming she was shocked by the actual words. She liked Hank. She liked being with him. She supposed she loved him, whatever that meant. She enjoyed his company and she particularly enjoyed going to bed with him. As a lover he was a constant surprise – sometimes gentle and coaxing, sometimes rough and exciting. Sometimes he was an insecure little boy and sometimes sure of himself and strong. Sex had been a middle-aged discovery for her and she didn't want to lose it. But she was not prepared to keep the pleasure at any price. She didn't want to be married. Not to Hank; not to anyone. But the well-laid foundation of guilt worked its way to the surface. What would he think of her? Only certain kinds of women slept with men whom they had no intention of marrying. All along, she reasoned, he assumed it was only his uncertainty that kept them from the vows. He had presumed that she was just waiting for the moment at which he had finally arrived.

Hank interrupted her silence. 'Don't worry,' he said, misinterpreting it, 'I am sure of this, you know.' He smiled. 'I never thought I'd want to get married again. But I guess I hadn't reckoned on coming across a woman like you. You sure know how to hook a guy.'

22

There was no question about it. Along with the rest of Hollywood the studio was in trouble. Every year since 1946 the numbers at the box office had fallen. There was no up and down. The graph was steadily down. The Chief stared at the figures in front of him, trying to make some kind of sense out of them. The movies were good. They were just as good as they had always been. For years he had been making excuses. It was good weather; it was bad weather; television was causing a hiccup. It would, he told himself, be all right in the end. Everyone would get bored with that little box in the living room. They would be back. But the Chief couldn't even convince himself any longer. He always believed that if you gave them what they wanted the people would buy it – but he began to doubt himself. That was a new experience and an uncomfortable one.

All the storms he had ridden out . . . He thought that had given him a confidence that was unshakeable. In fact he had watched with glee from the sidelines as the big studios – his competitors who had considered his studio small peanuts – came under attack from all sides. The Un-American Activities Committee hadn't touched him, unless you counted the way it smeared all of Hollywood. His studio was squeaky clean – not a red in or under the bed. None of the Hollywood Ten had ever so much as set foot on his lot. Even a few years later when the whole rigmarole had started again none of his people had to take the Fifth. They hadn't even been called to testify. Small could be good. There were fewer people to cause trouble. There were fewer people to pay as well, as everything got more expensive. Small protected him from all kinds of things. He had never had to sell his theatres because he had never had any theatres. The system that had worked so well for the big boys for so long – and, he had to admit, to his disadvantage at the time – was now, for them, just another problem to be avoided.

All over the country Metro, Paramount, all the big guns had had their own theatres, showing their own movies. It had never mattered a damn whether the movies were any good or not. They were there. Then the Supreme Court came down on them, screaming monopoly. Paramount was the first to be made to sell and now Metro's chain had gone to some hotel owners. Sure, that had generated some bucks that helped to pay the bills but what did the jerks do with the bucks? 3-D, that's what they did. The Chief had smelled that turkey from the start. Plenty had said he was wrong. 3-D was the future – but he knew better. The future was not in cardboard glasses that pinched your nose and shaky figures hurling knives into the audience which usually felt dizzy by the end anyway. The only one who had a hope of making money from 3-D was Polaroid Corporation.

Sure, the switch to colour had made sense. Like all the others he had gone over to colour just after the war when that easy Eastman process had been discovered in some German's back yard. He was all for change when it made sense but he wasn't falling for gimmicks. He had, of course, due to the falling receipts and inflation, had to make some cutbacks. The studio now employed fewer hairdressers, props people and lighting men but his economies were nothing like the layoffs at Metro. They were losing their goddamn stars! And all the time, while the studios were getting smaller, the pictures were getting bigger – literally. Take *The Robe* – battalions of Roman soldiers marching across the cinemascope screen. That wasn't his style. Hit them in the heart. That's where the money had always been. You couldn't lose on a movie that left them weeping and feeling good about it.

Fox, he had heard, was now on to an Egyptian epic – trekking around the world looking for sunshine and cheap cameramen. No doubt about it – it would break them. What was wrong with Colbert's Cleopatra? There was no need for another one.

But the figures in front of him told him he couldn't gloat. Something had to be done or he knew he would go the way of RKO and Republic – straight into the hands of the new television boys. So – what were his choices? He couldn't go big – which he didn't want to do anyway; it was too damn much of a chance putting everything you had on to one turn of the cards. Sure you could win big if you were lucky but you could also lose your shirt. The Chief had never been a gambler. He had never been an innovator either. Not for him experiment. The tried and the tested, that had been the success of the studio. Give the people what they want. The trouble was no one knew what they wanted any more. He wasn't going to end up with an Edsel on his hands and egg on his face. So that was decided. No big picture. So what was left?

There were the art houses – showing all those foreign things and doing OK in their small way. But in his guts he didn't really believe that people actually wanted all that kitchen sink stuff. All those unwashed actors talking incomprehensible languages. If they weren't dirty they were depressing. Maybe they appealed to East Coast egg-heads but not to real audiences. No – he couldn't see the future in Bergman and Fellini. It was all so . . . Un-American – and phoney, too, he thought.

So that left the really small screen and he came to the not very original conclusion that if you can't beat them you might as well join them before they swallow you up. Columbia had been working on television for years. Hell, everyone was doing it now. They were making weekly shows, commercials even. It was time he joined them. But, and here he thought how clever he was, he would go

285

them one better. Sure, they let their featured players into people's living rooms but not their big guns. You could tell when they lost faith in a star – they turned up on television. Cary Grant, for God's sake, wasn't selling cars or refrigerators like Ronald Reagan. He would put his biggest stars on television and it would work. Kathleen Thornton and George Pierce were about to become bigger than *I Love Lucy* had ever been. In fact, that was it, he thought – *I Love Lucy* with tears. Pleased with himself, he buzzed his secretary. He would lose no time in setting it all in motion.

Daniel Towski did not like the idea. Even if he had liked it, he would have been against it. But it did give him the opening for which he had been waiting. He had been waiting with increasing impatience. He had made it his business to be a part of every aspect of Kathleen's life. It had been a conscious decision from the moment they had married, although he had at the time no idea of where it would lead. He was not going to be the invalid husband of a film star.

'Isn't she good?'

'Isn't he brave?'

These were not the sentiments he wanted whispered out of his hearing. He would be admired all right, but not because he had been crippled. He would be admired because he accomplished things – big things. At first he had no notion of what these big things would be. After all he was just a kid when he went to war. He was trained for nothing unless he counted basketball which, he thought, not without a nod to the irony of it, would not be a profession to pursue now, given the circumstances. Even if you could make a living from it, which you couldn't, he found wheel-chair basketball ludicrous.

At first his interest in filming had extended only to Kathleen's involvement in it. He needed to be with her all the time to ward off predatory males. He was still unsure of her reasons for marrying him. Although she professed

286

her love constantly and she was good at demonstrating her love, he wondered how much of that was the actress and how much of that was the woman. In bad moments he felt that she only married him because she thought it was the right thing to do. She had promised herself to him all those years ago; he was the father of her children. Kathleen had been brought up to believe in vows – to believe that there was right and wrong. So had he, but the war had changed that. Now he knew that there was only what you wanted. He wanted Kathleen. He had her now and he was going to keep her.

Gradually he relaxed his vigilance, as Kathleen had done nothing to confirm his suspicions, and he began to take an interest in what was going on around him. He had been amazed when he sorted individual activities out from what had at first seemed total and mysterious chaos. Like a sheepdog he nosed individuals out from the herd and discovered that each person on the set had a specific and well defined function. Each activity was a world to itself. The director had at first seemed to be a god controlling it all, as does the captain of a ship with the complete authority that comes from total knowledge of the working of the ship. But, whereas the captain of a ship could indeed do every chore necessary for the running of the vessel, Daniel soon realized that the director was much more like the conductor of an orchestra. He had to know what he wanted from the wind section but he didn't have to know how to produce it. He didn't have to play the bassoon himself – he didn't even have to know how to play it. If the bassoon player didn't come up to scratch he just replaced him. Moreover, it soon transpired that the director wasn't even the one in charge. Although the directors he had seen certainly behaved as if they were. Daniel had believed in their power until the day Bill Compton had not returned to the set. He had been there on Thursday evening playing god and on Friday morning John Aldrich was in the director's chair playing god. Head office had decreed a change and change was accomplished. That was

287

where the power was – in the hands of the producer. The power in film making lay where it lay in all things – in the hands of those with the money.

Kathleen made an enormous amount of money as a film star. Daniel had at first been stunned by the sum. But it was not the kind of money that produced films – at least not the kind that Daniel had, in secrecy, taken it into his head to produce. He followed with keen interest the career of Mike Todd. *Around the World in Eighty Days* – that was the kind of film Daniel wanted to make. A great blockbuster of a film. That was where the future lay. It was the kind of film that would get them off their butts in Indiana and out into the theatre again. He even knew what film he wanted to make. He had read the autobiography of a female explorer who lived in the 1890s and had trekked through Africa, the Indian subcontinent and even made her way through China. The book had everything – suspense, scenery, emotion and the exotic. It would be expensive and he wasn't yet sure how he planned to raise the money but he did know that he had one ace up his sleeve already – he had Kathleen.

Kathleen was uncertain. It wasn't a question of choosing between the two ventures which were proposed to her. She didn't actually like either of them. She was thirty years old, although she was constantly assured she didn't look it – whatever thirty was meant to look like. Anyway, she certainly didn't need gauze over the camera lens just yet. She did, however, feel that at her age she should be more in control of her life – it shouldn't simply be a series of responses to the demands of others. While she was doing what everyone else wanted the twins had nearly grown up without her noticing. They were fourteen now. They had acquired waists, the buds of breasts and developed an absorbing interest in clothes. Where once there had been screams of protest over twice weekly hair washing, now the manes were shampooed and fussed over daily. And their growing presented a problem. Hollywood, Kathleen decided, was no place to be a teenager. Although she hated the idea, it was time the girls began to forge their independence. But she hoped it would be a slow process, and in a city of freeways and pretence she didn't see how that could be accomplished. In another year they would be able to drive a car. Californian children of parents of means took for granted the acquisition of a car on their fifteenth birthday. Kathleen shuddered at the idea. She had seen the teenagers cruising the streets, tops of their convertibles down, with the obligatory bottle of beer in their hands. She had heard the stories of week-end parties at the beach and more worrying even than the tales of sex and alcohol was the threat of drugs. Where once it had seemed to be confined to the Beats, now it seemed to be everywhere. Only the other day she had heard of a sixteen-year-old boy who had fallen to his death from a roof top under the LSD-induced belief that he could fly – and his father was an accountant, for heaven's sake.

Besides, she had grown up too fast herself and that wasn't something she wanted for her children. Wasn't that what all parents wanted? To spare their children the hurt they themselves had suffered? No, high school was looming and Hollywood High was not what she wanted for the girls. Still, even though she didn't spend nearly the time she would have liked with them it was precious time to her and she didn't like the idea of being separated from them. While suburban housewives fantasized about being movie stars and going to exotic parties, Kathleen, who knew the reality of the life and the five a.m. studio call, fantasized about welcoming her children home from school with peanut butter sandwiches and sitting over the kitchen table helping them with their homework. It was true, now that they were older she did see more of them. They were no longer tucked up in bed by the time she returned from the studio. They were there to share supper and a chat about the day. But the time had passed when they wanted to be mothered. The bored glaze only left their eyes when there was some unusually unsavoury gossip to be elicited from

her. Usually they excused themselves from the table and
the beat of Chubby Checker extolling his audience to do
the twist permeated the house before Kathleen and Daniel
had finished their coffee.

The Convent of the Holy Saviour was located in Northern
California, about five miles south of San Francisco. It was
set in a large estate and housed in a building ancient by
West Coast standards. It was run by an order of nuns
founded in France in the nineteenth century by Juliette
de Mansur, the daughter of a wealthy industrialist. She
rejected his capitalist values and devoted herself to the
education of the poor and had only recently been canon-
ized as St Juliette. Over the near-century since the found-
ing of the order which had spread through Europe and
into the western hemisphere, the aims of the community
had evolved far from subtly. Now the sisters were renowned for education of the highest standards and for
producing talented, socially able and refined graduates.
Their pupils no longer came from the families of the needy.
They now came, as had St Juliette herself, from the upper
strata of society. As many immigrant Catholics improved
their position in America and acquired wealth, so had the
nuns moved upwards with them. The convent which would
be the twins' milieu for the next four years, offered not
only Latin, Greek and the most modern scientific labora-
tories as well as an excellent grounding in literature and
the arts, but also horseback riding, tennis coaching, sailing
on their own lake and what was described in the prospectus
as 'training in the social skills'. Their proximity to San
Francisco gave them the added advantage of frequent
cultural forays.
   Despite the multitude of activities engaged in, the
parlour into which Kathleen and the girls were ushered
retained an air of tranquillity bordering on the claustro-
phobic. The furniture was old but unworn, the mahogany
tables were polished to mirror brightness. On first
acquaintance it did not seem a room in which to be

comfortable. A life-sized statue of the Sacred Heart, white robed, arms outstretched, dominated it. Kathleen sat on the sofa – Eileen to the right of her and Geraldine to the left. All three perched uncomfortably on the edge of the cushions and spoke in a whisper. Kathleen, having envisaged a warm cosy atmosphere, full of teenaged laughter wondered if she was doing the right thing. The girls turned apprehensively silent as the sun filtering through the stained glass windows lost its warmth on the way into the room. The silence was broken by the clink of beads as a nun arrived with a silver tea tray meticulously set with bone china. Another nun followed in her wake, bearing a three-tiered dish. Neat sandwiches, crusts removed of course, were on the bottom layer. Slices of fruit cake occupied the middle layer and on the uppermost layer, frosted pastries were encased in white fluted wrappers. The silver gleamed and the linen napkins were embroidered with entwined initials HS.

'Mother Superior will be with you shortly,' the first nun said before she and her companion glided from the room. Kathleen had forgotten until that moment the childhood belief that beneath the folds of serge that reached to the ground, nuns did not have legs like other people. As teenagers they had outgrown that notion but speculated that nuns wore well-oiled roller skates under their skirts – the better to sneak up on you.

These nuns dressed much more dramatically than the nuns of her childhood, who wore black and had their faces encased from eyebrow to chin in harsh, starched white cages which flattened the top of their heads like an egg with its top sliced off perching in an egg cup. Over this a fingertip length black veil floated but did nothing to soften the image. The sisters of the Holy Saviour Convent wore blue and the giant rosary beads which hung from their waists were white, pearl-like; a large white bib collar rested softly, reaching to the shoulders and, although like most of the other orders they gave the impression of being bald, the white headdress soared dramatically, with wide wings.

If the habit had been designed to be unobtrusive, the designer had failed – it was stunning.

Mother Superior swept silently into the room, arms folded inside her capacious sleeves. Automatically the three on the sofa rose until she had seated herself on a hard-backed chair opposite them.

'Welcome,' she said and her smile was devastatingly bright, instantly warming the room where the sun had failed and easing Kathleen's doubts.

She poured tea for the guests and offered cakes, taking nothing for herself. Nuns, Kathleen remembered, were never seen to eat. She chatted easily and by the time they had finished tea Kathleen had relaxed completely. She had made the right decision. She looked at her daughters. The fear had disappeared and their eyes glowed with anticipation. The room which had seemed so oppressive had become cosy.

'Your trunks have arrived,' Mother Superior said, rising, 'and I expect you are anxious to see your room. I've put you in together for the first semester, but we can always make other arrangements later on, if you like.'

The girls bounced up eagerly, following the nun from the room like excited puppies, forgetful of Kathleen who followed.

For the first time since she had arrived in California Kathleen had time to herself that autumn of 1960. There was no movie in production, no movie to publicize, no movie to prepare. There was time at last to do nothing but concentrate on Daniel. Time at last to get to know him.

It had been more than twenty-three years since she had fallen in love with him in the church when she had opened her eyes and seen the angelic altar boy. Twenty-three years – most of which had been spent without him. Since that day in the hospital in San Diego there had not been a time when she was not with him – but all she had learned was that he was an enigma. His mercurial mood swings were puzzling. At first she had accepted them as part of his adjustment. Indeed, the doctors had warned her to expect them. From the flights of fancy, where he floated full of plans and ideas (he had already redecorated the house three times; their lives remained in a constant state of flux as he took control, supervising builders and decorators, replacing furniture, summoning landscape gardeners) he swung to days when he became monosyllabic and even silent as his eyes clouded over and he retreated inside himself – where Kathleen could not reach him. He was a constant contradiction.

He was fiercely proud and independent. He seemed to ignore his disability. Perhaps, she thought, it was because he refused to acknowledge it that he would not countenance an artificial leg which would get him out of the wheel-chair.

He was usually loving and tender when they were alone but had become brash and arrogant to the point of rudeness when they were in company. He was seldom away from her side. At first he had seemed protective, lovingly jealous of her, but more and more she began to feel that he viewed her as a possession – as a commodity which he would use to achieve . . . what was it he wanted to achieve?

That autumn his ambition became clear: a movie project – *The Woman Who Walked the World*. Could he pull it off? She feared that he would and she feared that he wouldn't. Either way, she sensed disaster. She had seen what had happened to people who had spent their lives in movies. Her own studio and all the studios that were left, were in chaos. They were losing money on their releases, borrowing money to make more movies that lost even more money. They were spiralling into bankruptcy. For the first time she didn't know what her next job would be but that didn't worry her. She had invested wisely. She was even in a position to retire if she so wanted. At times the idea was an appealing one. To Daniel it was appalling. She had mentioned it at dinner one night and watched his face cloud, not with despair but with anger.

'You have no faith in me, do you? You see me as a helpless cripple to be petted and pampered. I'm not someone for whom you would consider working, am I? I'm not someone who can be in charge, am I? Not to you. Well, let me tell you something, Miss high and mighty movie star – in case you hadn't noticed, it is me who has been in control. It is me who has protected your career since the day we married. You would be a has-been by now without me. You'd be doing some television rubbish, taking anything just to keep your face on the screen. And let me tell you something else. Your performances were getting very sloppy until I took over – or maybe you're not clever enough to have noticed.'

Kathleen was speechless. His voice was cold, sharp, menacing.

'Of course, darling,' she said softly. 'You've been wonderful.'

'Don't patronize me.' His voice got quieter as his anger rose. 'That pansy made you a star but I kept you a star. You couldn't cross the road without someone to look after you. If it wasn't for me you'd be doing some puny job on television – ruining that great movie star image you are so proud of.'

She hadn't particularly liked the idea of television but there were worse things she could have imagined. Besides, although it was true Daniel had been against it, in the end it had been her decision. The real hesitation she had had about doing television was that the schedules were even more gruelling than movie-making. The sense of urgency permeated everything, filling the set with tension as the small screen monster gobbled up talent with its insatiable appetite. *The Woman Who Walked the World* – what she thought of as Daniel's fantasy – had been a timely excuse. So her contract with the studio had lapsed by mutual consent.

She had planned to use her sudden leisure to get closer to Daniel, but now he was constantly on the phone, working at becoming a producer. So she spent her time getting in the way of Josie who managed the house perfectly well without her or digging in the garden next to Raphael whom she knew very well she intimidated by her presence.

Daniel's outburst subsided as quickly as it had exploded. In bed that night he was again loving and tender. He did not apologize. He just pretended nothing had happened. Kathleen found it difficult to silence the alarm bells the incident had set off.

She was pleased when the call came from Hornbeam. She missed the camaraderie of the studio and she realized when she heard his voice that she had particularly missed the man who had so irritated her the day he met her off the train all those years ago and who now had become the only real friend she felt she had . . . besides Daniel.

'How about a junket?' he asked.

'What kind of junket? I haven't got anything to sell.'

'Wait for it, baby. You're never going to believe this.'

'Try me.' She didn't actually think that Hornbeam could surprise her. But he did.

'Political,' he said.

'Political?' she laughed. 'You? I would have bet anything that you don't even know whether Eisenhower is a republican or a democrat.'

'He's a republican, like Lincoln was.'

'You don't fool me. You only know about Lincoln because you saw Ray Massey in the film.'

'And I saw Charlton Heston playing Andrew Jackson and I saw Jimmy Stewart in *Mr Smith Goes to Washington*. I know acres of stuff about politics, so there.'

'OK, you've convinced me – so what gives?'

'There's going to be a rally for Kennedy up in San Francisco and I'm organizing a Stars for Kennedy contingent. You know – wave some placards, get your picture taken.'

'Kennedy!' Kathleen figured that California was sure to go for Nixon. It was an exclamation but Hornbeam took it, or pretended to take it, as a question.

'Yeh,' he replied. 'Now who's ignorant? Even you must

295

have noticed the good looking one who's running for president.'

Kathleen laughed again. Hornbeam was a breath of fresh air. 'Yes,' she admitted. 'I had noticed.'

She had once seen the Senator from Massachusetts through a restaurant window as he dined at Lock Obers in Boston. She had been embarrassed when he looked at her, staring open mouthed. Not only was he immensely handsome, which she had indeed known from photographs, but even through the glass his sexual magnetism was overpowering. He had smiled and given her a wave and she had moved quickly on, confused by her emotional reaction to someone she didn't even know. She didn't think those qualities were necessarily a reason for voting him in as president but as he and Nixon seemed to be constantly debating what was going to happen to some Asian islands called Quemoy and Matsu she wasn't quite sure how to make any political judgement. But he was from Massachusetts and so was she. He was a Catholic and so was she. There seemed to be no harm in a kind of solidarity. Besides, she could go and visit the girls.

'When is this shindig?' she asked.

'Next weekend.'

'OK.' She was pleased to have an excuse to get away from Daniel for a while after his disquieting outburst. She needed to get some kind of perspective on the situation.

'And we can talk about the television series on the flight. Pierce is still dead keen.'

'Ulterior motives under ulterior motives – you never change.'

'It's what I'm good at,' Hornbeam said.

Even given Daniel's outburst which happily hadn't been repeated, Kathleen could not have anticipated his reaction when she told him about the rally.

'Not on your life,' he said.

'What?' She couldn't believe she had heard him correctly.

'No chance. You can't go. I've got some people coming

over at the weekend. Prospective backers and you've got to be here to charm them.'

Kathleen took a deep breath. She looked at this man – her husband – and wondered what in heaven's name had come over him. Whatever it was, she didn't like it.

'Daniel,' her tone was conciliatory. 'I said I would go. I promised Hornbeam.'

'Well call him up and unpromise. It's no big deal. No one is going to miss you there and I need you here.'

'You don't need me, Daniel. This is your project, remember? The thing you were going to do by yourself. And don't get me wrong. I think it's a great idea.' There was no point in telling him she didn't for a moment believe he would get it off the ground. 'And I'm ready, willing and eager to play the part – but this money business has nothing to do with me.'

'And I suppose politics has,' he said sarcastically. 'Well, I'm telling you, they need to see you.'

'Daniel, there aren't many people who have been to a theatre in the past ten years who don't know my face. If these people you've dug up don't know who I am, then I would be seriously inclined not to get involved with them.'

'Oh, it's Miss high and mighty movie star time again is it? Too grand to mix with the people with the bucks. Well, let me tell you . . .'

There was no point in listening to him any more. He went raving on. There was no point in arguing with him in this state. She just interrupted his invective. 'I'm going to San Francisco,' she said simply and definitely.

His eyes narrowed. He seemed to be studying her face, looking for something. 'I see,' he said quietly. 'Oh, yes, now I see.'

'What are you talking about Daniel?' Kathleen felt a chill. Someone is walking over your grave, her grandmother would have said.

'Political rally hell. That's a good one. You're going off with Hornbeam, aren't you? You're having an affair with the bastard, aren't you?'

Kathleen was dumbfounded. Her eyes widened in amazement at the suggestion. Could he really think that?

'Can't deny it, can you?' he continued in the menacing tone. 'Can't even be bothered to lie to your crippled husband.'

Kathleen's eyes filled with tears. She knelt beside him bringing her face level with his. What kind of torment, she wondered, led him to this fantasy? She reached out to touch him as the tears brimmed over and slid slowly down her face. But before she could put her hand on his arm he raised it and brought his hand sweeping across her cheek.

'Bitch,' he said, his voice full of hatred and, backing his wheel-chair away from her, he turned and left the room.

Kathleen knelt there, her hand on her burning cheek.

The plane was airborne before Hornbeam commented on the bruise which Kathleen thought she had successfully hidden with make-up.

'Oh, it's OK,' Hornbeam said. 'I mean it won't show up in any snaps.'

'Thank God for that,' Kathleen sighed.

'But it's not OK, is it?' He put his hand over hers, which rested on the seat arm between them.

Kathleen thought about lying but she had never been a good liar. And besides she couldn't think of any. Black eyes traditionally resulted from walking into doors. Even though no one believed it, it was a possible explanation and vaguely plausible.

'You're going to say I told you so,' she said.

'Most likely.'

'Oh Phil,' she turned her face to look at him. There he sat behind those ridiculous glasses and his hand tightened on hers.

'Come on, babe, you can tell old Mr Fix-It.'

'I do love him, Phil,' she said.

'But . . .' he encouraged her.

Kathleen was glad at that point that they were interrupted by the stewardess with the drinks trolley. It was a short flight and they had to work quickly.

'Bourbon,' Hornbeam said. 'Neat.'

'Oh,' Kathleen looked dismayed. Decisions were beyond her. 'Tomato juice.'

'Put some vodka in that,' Hornbeam said across her. 'You can use it. And I know you – it won't become a habit.'

The stewardess delivered the drinks and moved on.

'Here's looking at you, kid,' Hornbeam raised his glass to Kathleen in parody of Bogart and she laughed.

'Now, that's better,' he said. 'Come on – out with it.'

'I do love him, Phil,' she repeated.

And again he said, 'But . . .'

'I can't seem to make him happy. He's . . . I don't know. I don't know where his mind is most of the time. I can't get close to him.'

'What about in the sack?'

Kathleen blushed. 'Phil, he lost his leg, not his libido.' She paused. 'No, no problems on that side – except . . .'

'Except what?'

'Well, even in bed,' she hesitated, fearing to be disloyal, 'even in bed there is the constant need to prove himself. There is a performance. I mean sometimes it's as if I'm not even there. I mean me.'

'And why that?' Hornbeam asked, indicating the bruise on her cheek.

She chuckled without mirth. 'You'll laugh,' she said.

'Cross my heart and hope to die,' he said, complete with gestures.

'He accused me of having an affair.'

'The bastard.'

She hesitated before she said, 'With you.'

That silenced Hornbeam. Kathleen had never before seen him lost for words. 'And that,' he finally said, 'is so laughable?'

Kathleen looked at him. He certainly wasn't laughing.

Phil Hornbeam's eyes searched her face. 'No, you don't know, do you?'

Kathleen just stared at him, the realization growing.

'Imagine,' Hornbeam said, 'imagine that nutcase figuring it out. I've always said he was a nutcase. Don't look at me like that. I'm not saying I told you so – well, not in so many words. It's nothing to do with the war, with his disablement. That man never had the capacity to love. Think back – back to the beginning. He was selfish. He was using you then and he's using you now. Some people never learn how to love – it's beyond them. In fact,' his voice lowered as if he was talking to himself, 'I used to think I was one of those people – anyway my wife always said I was.'

'Oh Phil,' Kathleen interrupted, 'you are the kindest, sweetest –'

'Let me finish,' he interrupted her. 'I used to think I was incapable of love, unselfish love – fancy that bastard noticing – until I met you.'

'Phil, I don't think I want to hear any more of this.'

'Even more important than that, babe, I don't think I want to say it.'

23

They were into the second month of filming *The Woman Who Walked the World*. If it's April this must be Morocco, Kathleen thought. Oh, the glamour of being a film star. She sat sheltered from the desert sun under a large umbrella waiting for the trained camels to show some of their education and tried writing a letter to the twins. She hadn't seen them since Christmas and wouldn't be back for their Easter vacation. They were going to spend it with some school friends in Seattle. At Christmas she had been pleased to find how happy they were at school. Eileen perhaps a bit more so than Geraldine – but then she had always been the quiet one. After the first few days of their vacation, Kathleen felt that they were keen to get back to the activities of school. All their friends were now elsewhere, spread all over the West Coast and they seemed to spend most of their time on the phone, when they could wrest it from Daniel who had become symbiotically attached to it as he raised money for his project.

Phil Hornbeam had, as usual, come for Christmas dinner. He had never again referred to the conversation on the plane. She tried to put it out of her mind. It was obviously an aberration. He was a good friend and not one she could afford to lose. Neither had Daniel repeated his accusation. When she returned from the rally he had greeted her warmly as if nothing had happened. Since then he had talked of nothing but the project.

The screenplay was completed by December and she knew Harry Adams had done a good job – despite Daniel's constant interference. Hornbeam agreed with her and even encouraged her to go ahead with it. It was a good part. It was strong and gutsy and a nice change from all those soppy women she had played for the studio. There was a lot of humour in it, too; and, more important, wit.

So Christmas had been relatively peaceful, if tense. Although there had been no further outbursts from Daniel there hadn't been a lot of friendliness either. He talked only about the project and when he wasn't on the telephone he was taking meetings. And then the miracle. He meshed together enough money from a consortium of bankers, oil men and hoteliers on the merits of the screenplay, with her name up front, to begin at last. There was a month of filming in Spain – God, how she had hated the cold of the Sierra Nevada, the donkey rides through the snow, she snickered to herself. The Woman Who Walked the World seemed to spend an inordinate amount of time seated uncomfortably on recalcitrant beasts. It was donkeys in Spain, now the stubborn camels and what next? She dreaded the elephants in India. Somehow when she had read the script it sounded exotic; the reality was just uncomfortable. She half hoped the money would run out before India, but she knew that wasn't fair. Besides, when Daniel had flown home to show his backers the Spanish footage they were delighted and once again opened the coffers, though what they knew about movies Kathleen couldn't even guess. She supposed they knew what they liked.

She looked up and could see Daniel now. He used his wheel-chair as a weapon, darting everywhere aggressively. Even on this rocky terrain he kept complete control of it. And the chair gave him another advantage. Anyone who talked to him had to bend awkwardly to come to his level. It gave him a psychological advantage, like an oriental potentate who decreed that everyone's head must be permanently bent in his presence. Daniel was the most visible producer Kathleen had ever known. There was no sitting about issuing orders from behind a big desk for him. Even the director did not make a move without full consultation. Daniel strangely enough didn't attempt to interfere with her performance, but it was about the only aspect of the filming that he left alone.

Kathleen wondered how much of this would interest the girls. She should be giving them a cultural view of the country, she supposed – but then she had not seen much. The hotel which they had virtually taken over in Taroudant was French-owned and managed and consisted mainly of little individual cabins set in a lush garden. It wasn't the way she had pictured an oasis somehow, having come across the concept only in cartoons which pictured thirsty crawling men coming to one palm tree and a puddle. Here, the tangerines flourished and the olives fell, carpeting the ground. She had seen groups of Berbers, the women dressed in garish colours, floaty dresses embroidered with stiff gold thread. The little girls seemed to be constantly in party frocks. Family groups rode in the open-backed pick-up trucks along the single road, turning precariously off it into the vast rocky nothingness to some mysterious destination. Along the roadside barefoot boys attempted to sell glistening mica-encrusted rocks they had scavenged from the desert's edge. Further south, she knew, the sand dunes loomed. They would come next week. She wondered how Daniel would cope in his wheelchair there amidst the shifting sands. Here, it was just barren, flat and hot.

What else could she tell the girls? She hadn't even been to the souk. Her day started at dawn and finished at sunset when she was just too tired to do anything but luxuriate in the French bath and enjoy the cordon bleu French cooking before falling into bed with the script for the next day's shoot. There was something distinctly unmoorish about the Morocco she had so far experienced.

Kathleen was wrong about the girls. It was true that Eileen was blissfully happy at the Convent of the Holy Saviour. There, all her longings for stability and order, the two qualities she had found missing in her life to that point, were fulfilled. Having had no sense of order imposed from without, despite the ritual established by Nanny, she had taken to ordering herself, and her sister. In that way she felt in control, despite the fact that every morning she had wondered if there would be a new home, or a new mother for that matter. Now she knew where she stood. For four years this would be her home – four whole years of not wondering what was going to happen next. With that worry removed she was free to give herself over to the full-time pursuit of study. She was eager to know everything – to collect facts and to hoard them. Information, rather than learning, was her goal. She determined to have all the answers. Information equalled power.

Geraldine, however, felt more lost than she had ever felt. Before there had always been her sister, an anchor. But now it seemed Eileen preferred school and books to her. She had been abandoned by her father, abandoned by her mother and now abandoned by her sister. She had somehow to attract their attention. Her first instinct was to run away from school – then they would have to take note. But she thought Eileen was so busy she probably wouldn't. Her parents were overseas so they wouldn't notice – and when they were told they would just be angry. She would be a nuisance. And her grandmother! Well, her grandmother seemed to have a very full life in which there was no longer any room for her. That probably hurt her more than any of the other defections. She longed for the cosy woman in an apron who had brushed her hair and told her stories and now that woman had totally disappeared. In her place was a chic lady with blonde hair who talked about sales figures and china patterns. Gone were the lace-up brogues and in their place were stiletto heels that stepped gracefully into a white convertible. And she even had a boyfriend, for heaven's sake. Grandmothers shouldn't have boyfriends. Grandmothers should be grey-haired, make-up-less and cosy.

Geraldine found no pleasure in her lessons, but performed adequately in class. Eileen, of course, was top of the class in every subject but Geraldine was always somewhere in the middle – where no one would notice her. She did, however, enjoy music, which was regarded at the Convent as an extra-curricular activity. It was not a subject on which you got marked as it was meant to be a pleasant diversion and contribute to the girls' general cultural development. Much like flower arranging. In music class she sang enthusiastically while most of the girls barely opened their mouths. And she got noticed.

'Geraldine,' Mother Clemens said one day, 'you have a very sweet voice.'

Geraldine blushed.

'I think,' Mother continued, 'you should sing a solo at the graduation exercises.'

'Oh, Mother,' Geraldine looked down at her feet, 'I couldn't.'

'Now, now, my girl,' the woman admonished her, 'God did not give us talents so that we could bury them in the ground. Look it up in your New Testament. False modesty is the sin of pride.'

Mother Clemens had noticed that the girls in the school, despite their advantages, were often lacking in self-confidence. It seemed to her that the more rich or famous the parents were the more inadequate the children felt. Eileen didn't have that problem but her sister certainly did.

'Come to the music room after supper and we'll go over some sheet music. We should be able to find something suitable for your range – and, indeed, for the occasion.'

'I think,' Eileen said to her sister, searching her memory bank, 'it should be something classical – Schubert I think would suit you nicely. Don't you agree, Mother?'

Mother Clemens looked at the twins – they looked so alike yet were so different you wouldn't even expect that they had come from the same home, let alone the same womb.

'I think,' Mother Clemens said, as gently as possible, 'that Geraldine should make her own decision.'

They were filming in India (the elephants were every bit as bad as Kathleen had feared) when the letter from Geraldine reached them.

'Don't be ridiculous, Kathleen, there is absolutely no way you can go,' Daniel told her. 'We'll be in the Malaysian jungles then.'

'I know, with the tigers,' Kathleen sighed. 'At least I don't have to ride them.' She was exhausted. 'Just a few days,' she said. 'You can shoot around me.'

'Just a few days! Kathleen do you remember how far away California is? You could not make the round trip in under a week and then you would arrive back all jet-lagged and in no fit state to work. Besides, you know there's hardly a foot of film you're not involved in – this is a star vehicle, remember?'

'It seems to me the world is the star – or the animals,' Kathleen said sourly.

'I thought,' he taunted, 'you were supposed to be the professional. Professionals do not stop working and go rushing off at every little domestic drama.'

'It is not a drama. It is a very important occasion for her – look . . .' Kathleen held the letter out to him, waving it in his face. 'It's the very first time a freshman has been asked to sing at graduation.'

'Big deal.' Daniel did not even pretend to be impressed.

'Yes, it is a big deal,' Kathleen countered. 'Your mother was at all your games when you were the big basketball hero, wasn't she?'

'My mother didn't have anything else to do. And she was a very silly woman.' Daniel didn't like to be reminded of his mother – he was still full of anger at her suicide. If he didn't denigrate her he might have to feel responsible. 'This is the real world, Kathleen. Every second in it is costing money. It's all set up – the native extras have all been hired. There's no way I can declare a hiatus so that you can go traipsing off home just because you have been taken with an uncharacteristic bout of motherliness.'

Kathleen fumed inwardly but she knew that basically he was right. She was a professional – damn it. She composed the letter in her head: 'Darling, Daddy and I are so sorry not to be with you . . .'

The Convent of the Holy Saviour graduated only twelve girls each year. The enrolment in the school never exceeded fifty so that a family atmosphere could be maintained (a rather large family, admittedly) and so that each girl could receive the attention which would enable her to achieve her potential. And it was a successful formula. At the graduation exercises in June 1961, the audience was told that ten of the girls would be going on to college: one to Stanford and one to Sarah Lawrence and the other eight distributed among the seven sisters of the Ivy League. Another girl was going to Paris to study art. The assembly was not told that Melanie Andrews was the only one not pursuing higher education. Melanie had always been a problem to the sisters. She was an attractive girl and really rather bright but she had a dreamy quality through which they could not break. They regarded her lack of response as a failure on their part but still, Mother Superior told her community, they maintained an admirable standard of success and you couldn't win them all.

The graduates sat on the stage in the auditorium, poised in cap and gown, legs crossed at the ankles as they had been taught, and listened as their considerable achievements at the convent were inventoried. The Valedictorian rose and praised the sisters for instilling in them the values by which they promised to live their future lives. She thanked them and the parents of the graduates for giving them the tools to use in their pursuit of success as they journeyed forth on their different paths from this commencement.

Melanie tried to listen but could not hear above the voice in her head which shut out the real world. The voice had spoken to her for years but usually when she was alone at night or in the chapel. Recently though it had become more insistent. The time was coming near. At first she hadn't known whose voice it was – only that it came from God. Then he told her who he was. It was the archangel Gabriel, the same messenger whom God had sent to Mary to tell her she was to bear his child. Gabriel told her that God required a sacrifice and that he had chosen her as his instrument. She would die and the angel promised her that because of her sacrifice Cuba would be released from Castro's communism, Khrushchev would be converted and world peace would be accomplished. She knew she was a small sacrifice for such a miracle. She didn't want to die, but how could she refuse. It was necessary. Had not President Kennedy said, 'Ask not what your country can do for you but what you can do for your country.' She was sad to be dying but proud that God had chosen her.

As Geraldine rose to sing *Ave Maria* the angel spoke once more to Melanie – his voice was loud, his instructions clear. It must be done today and there at the convent. She would not be going out into the world with her classmates.

Geraldine faltered nervously over the first few notes but recovered quickly and her voice soared pure and clear. The audience was enthralled and the atmosphere electric. Mother Clemens, at the piano, was delighted by the effect Geraldine's voice was having and at the same time Geraldine somewhat surprised herself. She had never sung so well, so confidently. The audience seemed to draw more from her than she had known she possessed. When the music finished the silence was tangible and then the hall burst into tumultuous applause. Geraldine blushed at the standing ovation. She had never in her life been so happy. They noticed her. They liked her. No, it was even more than that. They loved her. All those strangers, yet she could feel it – they really loved her.

A buffet lunch had been arranged out of doors on the lawns. Long tables covered in crisply starched white linen were laden with lobster, rare beef and a multitude of salads. The china was embossed with the entwined HS. The sun shone. It was a beautiful day. Geraldine would have thought it perfect if only her mother had been there to hear her sing – and to hear the applause. But she understood. Work came first. And Grandmother was there. That was something.

'I'm so proud of you,' Maureen hugged the child. She had never before seen her so alive, so sparkling.

308

'They liked me, didn't they?' Geraldine was sorry it was over. She wanted to start again. She wanted to feel that wave of love from the audience.

'Gerry, you know very well they adored you.'

A couple approached. The woman held out her hand to Geraldine. 'Congratulations,' she said. 'Your singing was . . . celestial.'

'Thank you.' Geraldine said it shyly but once again felt a warm glow.

'Have you seen Melanie?' the woman asked. 'We can't find her anywhere.'

Geraldine shook her head. She hadn't seen anything. She was in a delightful daze.

'I saw her going down towards the boating lake,' Eileen said.

'Oh, how strange, thanks.' The puzzled couple moved off and their place was taken by a steady stream, all full of praise for Geraldine.

'That was great, Sis,' Eileen said, clapping Geraldine on the back. 'Except for the wobbles at the beginning.'

Trust Eileen to be absolutely factual, Maureen thought.

'I've decided we should drive down the coast instead of flying home,' Maureen told the girls. 'We can drink in some of that legendary scenery and take a look at San Simeon.'

'Don't you have to get back to Mendel's?' Eileen asked.

'Nope – I've left.'

'What?' The girls were shocked in unison. Mendel's was their grandmother's life.

'Retired?' Eileen asked.

'Not at all. Anyway, it's a long story. I'll tell you all about it on the way home. Let's get some lunch before it has all gone.'

'I don't think there is any danger of that,' Eileen said. 'Mother Superior is an excellent hostess.'

The night Hank had proposed marriage Maureen began to think seriously about herself – about her future; about what she wanted to do. She realized she had slipped back into the old habit she thought she had broken when she handed the children back to her daughter. She had gone back to her established mode of reacting rather than choosing. But she had to admit that lately everything that had happened to her made her happy. California, her job at Mendel's, Hank. It was true that she had transformed the China and Glass department at the store. She did her job very well and the department now showed a bigger profit than any other, including designer fashions. The manager had lately begun treating her with what could only be called respect. But the job itself had just fallen into her lap. She had not chosen it. So, indeed, had Hank. He, too, said that she had transformed him, but Maureen was not so sure about that. His male ego had been badly dented when she told him as gently as she could that she did not want to marry him.

'Why not?' He was incredulous. 'What's wrong with me?'

She laughed and put her hand out, caressing his cheek. 'There's nothing wrong with you, you silly man. I just like being not married.'

'Bullshit, if you'll pardon my French. All women want to be married. Every woman wants a man to look after her and care for her.'

'I hoped you did care about me.'

'I do, Maureen. That's what I'm saying. That's why I want to marry you.'

Maureen shook her head. 'I'm sorry, Hank.'

He hadn't taken it well. In fact he stormed angrily out of her apartment and she heard him slam the door of his own next door. She tried to stifle her sobs so he wouldn't hear them through the thin shared wall.

He hadn't spoken to her again and a week or so later she noticed he had gone when she returned from work. There was no sound at all from his apartment that night and none the next morning. It was a few days before she managed to casually mention the vacancy to the super.

'Yup,' the super said, cigarette firmly clenched in his

mouth. 'Goin' back East, he said he was. Strange kind of guy I always thought.'

No, Maureen thought. A regular kind of a guy, a lovely kind of a guy. Though she sometimes regretted her decision, especially at the magical hour of four in the morning when the earth and everything in it is shrouded in doom, she knew it was the right one.

'I'll be moving on myself soon, I think,' Maureen said.

'You goin' back East too?'

'No, no I don't think so.'

'Well, you please yourself, Mam. You know the deal – a month's notice or a month's rent.' He pulled a cigarette from the pack in his breast pocket, lit it from the stub of the one in his mouth and flicked the stub off into the brown grass.

'I'll let you know,' she said.

Maureen found a maisonette in a square white block. It had a number of advantages. It was gleamingly new, she could actually furnish it herself and it was close to Mendel's. But what really sold her on it was the spiral staircase with a shiny chrome handrail that wound from the living room up to her bedroom. She loved that staircase – it was something Ginger Rogers could have floated down in her hey day. Maureen took a long lease and furnished it exquisitely and totally from Mendel's, taking for the first time full advantage of her substantial staff discount.

It was six months after Hank's precipitous departure when Shirley approached her diffidently at the store. Maureen was at the antique desk with a young girl and her mother. They were drawing up a bridal list and it was difficult. The girl, Maureen thought, had excellent taste while the mother tended to favour the fussy, over-decorated designs. The older woman reminded her of herself and her first foray into purple satin cushions. Maureen was a not-impartial referee in the dispute.

'Excuse me, Mrs Thornton.' Shirley's tone was reverential. How Maureen wondered had she inspired that?

'Yes, Shirley?' She was glad of the interruption.

'There's a call for you.' She pointed to the phone as if Maureen had been previously unaware of its existence. 'It's personal,' she whispered.

Maureen's heart leapt. Had something happened to Kathleen? Or the twins? With as much composure as she could muster she excused herself from the battling pair and made her way a few yards to the phone. Only a few yards but she was breathless with anxiety when she picked up the receiver.

'Maureen Thornton,' she said.

'Thought you would get away from me, did you?'

Maureen was shocked by the voice she had never expected to hear again.

'Well?' he prompted.

'Hank, what a surprise.' She bit her tongue at the inanity of her remark.

'You've moved out of the old apartment.'

'Yes, I've got a maisonette now.' She didn't add that she couldn't go on being constantly reminded of his absence.

'Well, are you going to give me the phone number or not?'

'Yes, of course.' She rattled it off. What was all this about?

'And what about dinner tonight?'

'Hank, where are you?'

'I'm at the airport. Just got in. I've got news.'

'Good news?'

'I think you'll like it.'

'What time?'

'Meet me at the old place, seven o'clock?'

'Make it seven-thirty.' Maureen wanted to shower and change from her working clothes. Chic as they were, she wanted to wear something bright tonight.

'OK. I'll try to contain myself.'

'See you at seven-thirty.'

'Maureen . . .' Hank interrupted her goodbye.

'Yes?'

'I feel like a teenager going on a first date,' he said.

Maureen understood. There were butterflies massing in

her tummy. 'I know what you mean,' she said. 'See you soon.'

Hank was sitting in their usual booth when Maureen arrived to join him.

'You look wonderful,' he said, taking her hand across the table.

'So do you,' Maureen replied.

Betty seemed pleased to see them. 'Well, hello stranger,' she said. 'Long time no see. What'll it be? The usual?'

'Why not?' Hank said, looking across to Maureen for confirmation.

She nodded. He had come a long way from that first night when he had ordered without consulting her at all.

Hank couldn't believe how beautiful she looked, as if by some kind of magic she was actually growing younger rather than following the normal course of the flesh.

'So tell me,' Maureen said, 'what is this news?'

'I have,' he said slowly dragging it out, emphasizing each word, 'sold . . . the . . . book.' He hadn't wanted to tell her on the phone. He had wanted to be there, to see her eyes light up. His delay was rewarded.

'That's wonderful, Hank!' Maureen said. 'But I knew it would be easy.'

'Well,' Hank laughed, 'easy is not quite the word I would use.' And over the steak and Californian red he outlined the last six months of his life, structuring the story as a novelist would, lending drama and suspense, mounting to a climax – and then over the home stretch to the happy ending.

It had started smoothly enough with lunch at the Oak room of the Plaza with a fellow he had known at Harvard who had become a high-flying literary agent. Richard Maxcroft had willingly agreed to read *A Solitary Life* but made no promises of representing Hank.

'Fair enough,' Hank had said, and spent a sleepless night awaiting Maxcroft's judgement. He was delighted when Richard rang him the next morning, full of enthusiasm. Hank couldn't believe how easy it was. But then came the disappointments, as publisher after publisher turned it down. The rejections were all very polite. They would be, as no one wanted to offend the agent who had the power to deliver to the most favoured publisher the next blockbuster which would make a lot of money.

The reasons for rejection were conflicting. So conflicting that through his despair even Hank had to laugh sometimes. It was too literary; it was too low brow; it was too long; it was too short. He thought probably the most honest one said that their marketing men had no idea of what the target readership should be. The book did not fit neatly into an established genre. Then, at last, came the happy ending. The Algonquin Press, Fred Wood to be precise, absolutely loved it.

'And the first hardback print run is to be fifty thousand copies. Phenomenal, I am assured, for a first novel,' Hank concluded.

'Am I allowed to say I told you so?' Maureen was very excited – in a way proud as if somehow she had contributed. 'I always knew you would produce a best-seller,' she said matter of factly.

'Ah, now there's the rub. We've still got to sell them. Imagine fifty thousand unsold copies stacked up in a warehouse, with a picture of me on the back with a silly smile on my face.'

Maureen sighed. 'The eternal pessimist,' she said. 'You never know, Hank, unless you are very careful something nice might just happen to you.'

Hank smiled his little boy lost smile.

'How long are you in town for?' Maureen asked him.

'Just a couple of weeks. They want me back in New York for the proofs and to plan the tour.'

'Tour?'

'That's how they sell books now – morning television in downtown Detroit and midnight radio phone-ins in Kansas.'

'Where are you staying?'

'I checked in at the Beverly Hills.'

Maureen scarcely hesitated before she said, 'Well, let's

go and check you out. Wait till you see my new apartment – you'll love it.'

First a copy of the book arrived. Then almost immediately daily clippings from local newspapers spread across the States came in. There were reviews – all of them good. Maybe, Maureen thought, he only sends the good ones. And there were interviews with him in which he managed to remain discreet and enigmatic. The interviews were always accompanied by the shyly smiling publicity photo. She didn't think he looked silly at all. When her desk became buried under the newspaper footage she bought an album and began pasting them into it. She watched the best-seller list, holding her breath as *A Solitary Life* made its zig-zag climb to the top.

Some ideas of her own were percolating in the back of her mind – gently bubbling like a coffee pot on a slow burner. Her job at Mendel's had lost its challenge. It had become automatic and she felt restless. But what could be her next move? Realistically, she knew that at fifty-three she had left it rather late to pursue a career that would take her to the top of the retail trade even though she had more than demonstrated her aptitude for management. She wondered occasionally if Mr Morris had ever made it to Chicago – to the top floor and the top echelon of the company. He must, she mused, be close to retirement age – if not already retired. She had never told Kathleen about him. She sometimes wondered if she should. But everything about that time had so quickly become like a dream that even she could believe that the love-making under the pines had been all in her imagination.

His tour finished, Hank took Maureen on vacation in Mexico. The success of the book had done little but make him unsure of his ability to write another one. He needed a rest, she assured him, and they rented a hacienda for two weeks in Acapulco. It was there that by talking to him she gradually began to understand the ideas that she had been unable to formulate on her own. The most difficult task at Mendel's, she found, was co-ordinating. Getting just the right table linen to go with the china, matching the cutlery to the plates, flower vases to crystal glasses.

'There should be,' she told him, 'some way of co-ordinating the whole shebang. Getting the various manufacturers' designs together.'

They were eating papaya for breakfast on the patio overlooking the sea. 'Look,' she said by way of illustration, holding up a spoon, its handle tapering to a sharp point, 'if this were curved how much more it would complement the curve of the plate. But it's so time consuming hunting down the right shapes . . . and colours are even more difficult. Look,' the yellow swirls on the china plate caught the yellow of the tablecloth – but not quite. Not exactly. In fact the lack of perfection only drew attention to the fact that an effort had been made and that success had eluded whoever had made the effort. And, Maureen reasoned, she was a professional. How much more difficult, virtually impossible, it was for those who had families to raise or other careers to pursue.

Hank could not quite see the problem. It looked fine to him. But he could see that Maureen was serious about this and he respected her judgement.

'Why don't you do it?' he said.

'Do what?'

'Design your own range of . . . whatever it is you call that stuff. Get it manufactured and sell it.'

'What? China, linen, crystal, silver – the lot?'

'Why not?'

'I wouldn't know where to begin.'

'I think you would.'

He had disappeared after breakfast without telling her where he was going and returned in a few hours laden down with artist's pencils, water-colours and a pad of drawing paper.

'Begin here,' he said, dumping them all down at her feet.

'. . . And so,' Maureen told the girls explaining her reason for leaving Mendel's as they drove south along the coast, 'the designs are finished.' And, she reminded herself, they were good. They had all seemed to come so naturally. Maybe, she patted herself on the back, it was from me Kathleen inherited her talent. 'And I'm off to find the right manufacturers.'

She had decided, having studied the goods she worked with, that she would find what she sought in Europe – most probably England. The textiles, the china, the silver produced there were of the highest quality, although she found the designs too fussy – old fashioned. Besides, she had always wanted to see Europe. Perhaps, she admitted, she was trying to go too fast. It might have been sensible to stay at Mendel's and begin in a slow way, one step at a time. Hank, however, had told her to jump in with both feet. And it was what she wanted to do. She wasn't, after all, getting any younger.

'I'll back you,' he said, writing out a cheque that flabbergasted her. She had tried to refuse it.

'It's an investment,' he said. 'I know a good idea when I hear one. Don't forget I used to be a lawyer. I'm not worrying about getting my money back.'

Maureen had insisted on a formal contract but she had to admit that the timing was perfect. *The Woman Who Walked the World* was moving on to location shooting in England and then into studio work in Pinewood.

'We shall spend the summer in the old country,' she told the girls.

Eileen thought her grandmother had a screw loose. Yet another screw in fact. She should be at home knitting, not racing around the world trying to organize things at her age. But she, for once, kept her thoughts to herself.

Geraldine was elated. The prospect of summer in Europe was exciting enough. Add to that the prospect of being able to watch the filming and it was overwhelming. But most important was that she would be with her mother. There was so much she wanted to talk to her about. She needed her advice. No, that was not true. She wanted her mother's approval. Geraldine knew what she wanted to do.

24

The chancellor of the exchequer, Selwyn Lloyd, announced an austerity programme the day Maureen and the girls arrived in London. His emergency budget was meant to improve the nation's trade deficit. Maureen could not imagine how the country could possibly be more austere. After the vivid Californian landscape the watery sun of London seemed to be liquefied further by the misty grey of buildings drowned in centuries of soot. The people seemed equally grey – colourlessly dressed. Yet, despite, or maybe because of, the sluggish pace of the city Maureen found her first impressions as they drove from the airport reassuring. It seemed familiar and cosy. Piccadilly Circus was a 1930s movie come to life. The large black taxis had featured in countless frames and the red doubledecker buses were as they should be.

They checked into a large hotel just off the south side of the circus and she was thrilled by the top-hatted porters with their scarlet coats and the way they addressed her as Madam, with a slight but deferential inclination of the head. The bedroom, she felt, was like stepping into an Agatha Christie novel with the heavy, dark mahogany furniture and the satiny eiderdown on the bed, but she was less than happy with the clanging pipes that drizzled a meagre flow of water into the chipped and undersized bath.

Maureen kicked off her shoes and sat on the edge of the bed, listening to the dispiriting dribble from the taps through the open bathroom door. She noticed, as she reached for the black Bakelite telephone, that it had no dial. It took minutes before the operator responded to her clicking. Finally, connected to the production office of *The Woman Who Walked the World*, she learned that the company was filming on location in Kensington Gardens that day.

London was her last scheduled location and Kathleen couldn't be happier about that. Considering the modes of transport she had been required to adopt, this one was a piece of cake, but after four hours in the drizzle, seated in the back of a landau, memories of camels and sunshine acquired a certain charm. Descending rather stiffly to have her make-up retouched, Kathleen could only hope that the whole thing wouldn't turn out to be a fiasco. What would that do to Daniel, who was completely immersed in the project? It had to be a success – for him. During the past months they had barely spoken to each other except about the movie and since their arrival in England she had seen him only on the set. And there she recognized him less and less. The burning ambition, the quick tempered reactions – there was nothing she liked about his behaviour, but she reasoned that was because of the pressure. When it was all over, and, pray God, successful, he would have proved whatever it was that needed proving and then her husband, the man she loved, would return. She missed him now. She missed him even more than she had all those years she had thought him dead. He seemed more unreachable now that she could see him every day.

Kathleen could see him now, manoeuvring his chair round the camera. Lisa, his assistant, clipboard in hand, had to struggle to keep up with him. Like a nurse to a surgeon, Lisa was expected to be constantly within reach, supplying him with whatever it was he wanted: schedules, view-finder, coffee. He held out his hand and she read his mind. If by chance she read it wrongly his wrath descended upon her. Kathleen felt sorry for Lisa and couldn't understand why she tolerated it, but tolerate it she did . . . and with a smile. Lately Kathleen had taken to reserving her

319

own smiles for the camera but she found one came naturally when, on the edge of all the activity, she saw three figures – how the girls had grown in a few months! Quickly she negotiated all the obstacles and gathered her mother and daughters into her arms. They all began to speak at once and then, laughing, just held each other.

The girls were content just following the filming. Eileen was storing up information about the techniques of production which she thought could be useful. Although she couldn't imagine the circumstances in which they might be, she felt you never could tell. Geraldine watched the performers – the way they moved, timed their dialogue, subtly changed a delivery as take followed take. She still hadn't talked to her mother about her decision. Although Kathleen was obviously glad to have them there, she seemed, to Geraldine, to be sad – and she felt that their father had something to do with that. He was so distant – and usually angry.

'Nonsense,' Eileen had said when she mentioned it, 'she's just tired.'

Maureen haunted the stores just in case her scheme had already been accomplished on this side of the Atlantic, but from Harrods in Knightsbridge to Selfridges in Oxford Street and the exclusive Goodes in South Audley Street she found the problem of co-ordination still existed. So, from Euston Station she travelled north to keep appointments with linen manufacturers and potteries. She was terrified. It was an extremely grown-up thing she was about to do. She could be about to lose a great deal of money – most of which wasn't hers. But she reassured herself on the journey by studying her sketches, colour charts and, most importantly, her projected balance sheets. It could work if she could negotiate the right contracts. She had to keep her head about her despite the rush of adrenalin to the brain. There would, after all, be no need of any major retooling or remodelling of machinery in the factories. Her concept was based mostly on colour – and as for the silver, well, the changes would be minimal. She convinced herself she would be successful. Her dollars would be very welcome. Wasn't Lloyd banging on about exports?

It was finally the last day of shooting for Kathleen – at the Tower of London with the Beefeaters and ravens. The set-up was just inside Traitor's Gate. Despite the sky, which was constantly grey, there seemed to Kathleen to be something intrinsically photogenic about England. Not just what she considered the set pieces, the Tower, the river, Windsor Castle, the mews houses of Belgravia, but also the countryside, and even the semi-detached houses in the suburbs around London seemed planned with a camera lens in mind. All of it was not beautiful, but even what in any country could be called slums, crumbling terraced houses on bleak roads without the tidy gardens of suburbia or the flowering window boxes of Mayfair, had their own essential reality that was easily captured on film.

She felt a bit guilty about neglecting the girls while she worked. And she wasn't much fun in the evenings either as after a quick supper she fell exhausted into bed. Still, they seemed contented enough. Even as she prepared for her scene she could see Eileen questioning the continuity girl with the concentration she seemed to bring to every encounter. And Geraldine seemed happy enough sitting on the fold-up chair behind the camera – just watching. Anyway, this was it – the last day.

'Kathleen, we're ready,' the third assistant called.

Kathleen adjusted her long skirt and moved into camera range. This is it, she thought again – get this in the can and then we can go home. It had been a long, and not particularly happy time, being The Woman Who Walked the World.

Kathleen breathed a sigh of relief when she and the girls were greeted by Raphael at Los Angeles airport. Daniel and the long suffering Lisa had stayed on to get some scenic footage in the can, but as far as Kathleen was concerned the film was finished. There was bound to be a bit of post-production dubbing but otherwise it was all in Daniel's hands now. And she knew he intended to stand over the editor as tenaciously as he had the director. She would now have time to devote to the girls. Although there was only a week until they returned to school she would make sure she was exclusively theirs. And then . . . and then? She knew what she wanted to do as she handed Raphael her portfolio of sketches to be stowed in the trunk of the car along with the luggage. There were paintings to be done. When she thought about them she felt really excited for the first time in years. Excited as she could never be about movies. She looked at the girls. Eileen had taken charge of the suitcases and was instructing Raphael as to their disposition, while Geraldine stood in some world of her own. Poor child, Kathleen thought. Nonetheless, she reassured herself she had made the right decision when Geraldine had told her she wanted to leave the convent and concentrate on singing and dancing. At first she had reacted with a dismissive amusement. She deemed it a teenage fantasy and when Geraldine had not pursued the subject she thought it was forgotten – like last week's pop song. But gradually Kathleen realized, in the moments she had snatched with the girls during her gruelling schedule as they struggled to finish the film on time, that her daughter had been hurt by her attitude. She had retreated into her shell. Kathleen blamed herself for her insensitivity. It might, from her viewpoint, be a teenage fantasy but it was real to Geraldine and should be treated with respect. She would put that right. There was no way she would allow her to leave school at this stage, but she would explain her reasons and Geraldine would see the sense in it. She was, after all, a sensible girl.

There was an unspoken gloom permeating the Convent of the Holy Saviour when the girls returned. Geraldine thought it was merely a reflection of her state of mind. Mummy doesn't understand, she told herself. She has tried but she doesn't understand. If she realized how unhappy

I am she couldn't be so cruel. She would try to help me, not stand in my way.

At mass, the first morning, Mother Superior had tears in her eyes when she asked them all to pray for the soul of Melanie Andrews. There was a shocked buzz through the chapel.

'*Requiescat in pace,*' the priest intoned.

'Amen,' came the whispered response from the girls.

Through the rest of the mass Geraldine could think of nothing but Melanie. She could see her. How could she be dead? She didn't look sick. She was young. It wasn't fair. She was just about to start out on her life – not just school, but the real thing. It must, she decided, have been a car crash. That's what young people died from – car crashes. It could happen to her. It could happen at any time. She was fifteen and a half and she might, like Melanie, be dead when she was seventeen, having done nothing that she wanted to do. It wasn't fair.

She was in the room she shared with her sister, sorting out her uniform and home clothes and stacking her books, but thinking of nothing except how to get on with her life, when Eileen entered.

'You missed breakfast,' Eileen said.

'Wasn't hungry.'

'Come on now, Sis, have to keep your strength up.'

'Oh, Eileen,' Gerry turned to face her, tears streaming down her face. 'How could you eat?'

'Hey, what's up?'

'What about Melanie? Do you think she was sick and nobody knew? Do you think she knew?'

'They say it was an accident,' Eileen said, implying by her tone that she didn't for a minute believe it.

'Then it *was* a car crash.' Geraldine didn't know whether she would prefer her death to come from a mysterious illness which had a touch of romance about it or from a sudden dramatic accident.

'Nope. They fished her out of the lake on graduation

day. We were all probably still around when they found her. But they kept quiet about it.'

'How could she have drowned? She was a good swimmer. And what was she doing at the lake anyway?'

'Sarah heard she did it on purpose.'

'What?'

'That's what she heard. Just plunged right in, cap and gown and all and did an Ophelia.'

'But why would she do that?'

'Went a bit looney I suppose. Probably couldn't face being sent out into the big bad world. They do rather harp on the difficulties to be faced when we leave these hallowed halls.'

A bell rang down the corridors.

'That's the first class of the new semester. How exciting!' Eileen said sarcastically. 'English composition.' Eileen found the class altogether lacking facts. 'Come on, slow coach, or we'll be late.'

Geraldine followed, mystified by her sister's matter-of-factness about everything. She wondered if she would ever get used to it.

Daniel moved out of the house to be nearer to the studio where *The Woman Who Walked the World* was being edited. Kathleen found his absence lent a peace to the atmosphere that she had never before experienced in the house. Even before Daniel's jealous outbursts there had always been a tension – a walking on eggs – that was now gone. She set up her easel and began working twelve hours a day, barely stopping for the snacks which Josie urged on her. She saw no one and the months passed, marked only by the growing pile of canvases she had filled. She showed them to no one, afraid that others would not share her satisfaction with them.

The girls returned for Thanksgiving. Phil Hornbeam was coming too and in a brief conversation on the phone Daniel said of course he would be there. Kathleen looked forward eagerly to his return.

324

Phil and Kathleen were in the sitting room, Phil with a highball and Kathleen a dry sherry. He was trying to make his adventures as amusing as possible but since the run-down of the studio he had taken on private clients – each job separate, individual, but in a way mechanical. He used his experience but not his heart. He missed the continuity the studio had given him. Suddenly he stopped in mid sentence, staring beyond Kathleen towards the doorway. She turned to see what had mesmerized him. There, framed in the lintel with the aid of two canes, stood Daniel. He smiled a rather self-satisfied smile.

'I'll be rid of these, too, in a month or so.' He indicated the supports as he made his way to the sofa and with an almost graceful movement sat down, putting them to one side.

Kathleen was speechless.

'Don't look so surprised,' he said and knocked his knuckles on his artificial leg. 'They do great work these days – expensive but good.'

'But you said you would never –'

'Changed my mind,' he interrupted Kathleen. 'Entitled to change my mind, aren't I? Or don't you approve? Prefer me in a chair?'

'Oh, my darling.' Kathleen went to him and, kneeling on the floor in front of him, embraced him.

'Still hanging around my wife, I see,' Daniel said to Phil, over Kathleen's head. 'Never mind,' he continued, not giving anyone a chance to speak, 'as it happens you're just the man I want to see. I expect you'll be available to do the publicity for *The Woman Who Walked the World*.'

'I thought you took care of everything yourself,' Hornbeam said.

'Phil,' Kathleen looked up and cautioned Hornbeam with her eyes as well as her voice, 'I think it would be great if you took it on.'

'Well, Hornbeam,' Daniel continued, as if the exchange had not taken place, 'I've got virtually the whole campaign in my head. I just need someone to organize it – you know, the nitty gritty.'

'Then you don't need me,' Hornbeam said, trying, for Kathleen's sake, to control the deep irritation he always felt in Daniel's presence. 'All you need is a good assistant.'

'I'd rather you did it,' Daniel said. For two reasons which he didn't enumerate: it pleased him to have Hornbeam as his employee and secondly he had never publicized a film before. Just as he knew he couldn't direct on his own, he knew he needed Hornbeam's expertise in getting it to the public.

'So would I,' Kathleen said, her voice calm and decisive but her eyes pleading.

Hornbeam saw the look. 'Well, I think we can at least discuss it.' He remained cautious.

'But not now. No business today,' Kathleen said. She wanted to go into the kitchen to check the finishing touches of the meal with Josie but was loath to leave the two of them alone. The antipathy which would be aroused would not bode well for the rest of the day. And it was probably going to be difficult enough. Geraldine had been in a most uncharacteristic fug of gloom since she returned. Eileen reported that she had been like that for most of the term. She had said she didn't want to talk about it, but Kathleen knew it would have to be faced. Just, she hoped, not over the Thanksgiving lunch. Daniel's patience was not renowned and since he had been working on the film it was non-existent.

The silence between the two men was beginning to loom oppressively when Maureen and Hank arrived. Saved by the cavalry, Kathleen thought. Always happy to see her mother, Kathleen on this occasion, because of her relief, reacted with excessive effusiveness, hugging her with gusto. She nearly winded her mother and, leaving her breathless, turned her attention to Hank.

'Hey, steady on, girl,' he said laughingly, disentangling himself from her grip. 'A man of my age can't take that kind of attention from a movie star. It might just go to my head.'

'Congratulations on the book,' Phil said to him, extending a hand. The paperback was now number one on the best-seller lists and had remained there for a number of weeks. 'Sold the movie rights yet?'

'Can't bear to – even for the kind of money they're offering for options.'

'Why not?'

'Well, to be honest, I don't really need the money.'

'No one,' Phil said, 'ever has all the money he needs.'

'I do,' Hank said. 'If there is one thing I've learned in my advancing years it's to know when you have all the material things you need.'

'But it would make a great movie,' Kathleen said.

'Yeh, it could, but probably wouldn't. I feel . . . I don't know . . . I mean, it's my baby and I couldn't bear the idea of Robert Redford or Paul Newman taking over the character. It just wouldn't feel right. Besides, it is well known, even to neophytes like me, that the Hollywood guys buy a book and proceed to rewrite it. An author is lucky if the title remains intact, let alone the spirit of the thing or, God forbid, the plot.'

'Hollywood guys don't exist any more,' Phil said. 'Haven't you heard? We're living in an airport lounge. Everyone in Hollywood is now in transit, waiting for the next location to come up on the board. Besides, if you're so worried you can always do a deal to write the screenplay yourself.'

'I'm not a screenwriter, I'm a novelist.' Hank still loved the sound of the word. 'And anyway – what's a screenplay? By the time it's gone through the hands of the actors, directors, editors and God knows who else it might as well be a Sears catalogue – everyone takes just what he wants.'

'Anyway,' Maureen said, '*A Solitary Life* is finished. If Hank went back to it now it would just interfere with his new novel's germination.'

'Germination!' Kathleen laughed. 'You make it sound like a cauliflower.'

'Honestly, Kathleen, stop being so . . . literal. You know what I mean.'

'I know. The slowly sprouting seed of the next novel. So how's it coming?'

'Very slowly with the sprouting at the moment,' Hank said.

'What's it about?'

'Ah, to talk about it would, if I may continue the tortured metaphor, tend to nip it in the bud.'

'A difficult task if it hasn't even sprouted.'

Daniel watched the exchange in brooding silence. All these very important people seemed to ignore him, as if he wasn't worth their attention. Well, when the picture was the enormous success he knew it was going to be then it would be a different story. They wouldn't be able to ignore him any more.

Throughout the bantering Kathleen had kept one eye on Daniel. She wanted to bring him into the conversation but he was off in some world of his own. A world she was increasingly afraid to invade.

'How's the editing going?' Hank asked him, as if he hadn't noticed that Daniel was not with them in spirit.

'OK,' he replied succinctly.

'And what's this?' Maureen had just noticed the canes and her eyes went to Daniel's leg.

'I should think that's obvious,' Daniel said, lifting first one shoed foot and then the other. Now, he thought, they are about to patronize me.

'Isn't it wonderful?' Kathleen said. 'He just walked in as if nothing had happened. It was a total surprise.'

'Hey, that's great, Dan, boy,' Hank said. 'I really admire you. It must have been some challenge.'

'Not such a big deal,' Daniel said. 'Lots of people walk. I used to do it myself, all the time.'

An uneasy silence followed the sarcasm.

'I think you should tell them your news,' Hank said to

Maureen. 'Or had you forgotten?' he teased affectionately.

'Forget? How could I?' She gave him a playful slap.

'What is it, Mum?' Kathleen wondered if she had finally agreed to marry Hank. It would, she thought, be a very good idea – she hated to think of her mother alone.

'Well,' Maureen said coyly.

'Come on,' Kathleen said, 'if you must be coaxed, I'm coaxing.'

'The samples of table linen arrived last week,' her mother blurted out, running her sentences together, 'they're gorgeous. And I'm expecting the china and silver in about ten days.'

'Oh,' Kathleen was disappointed but Maureen was so excited she failed to notice.

'So, by New Year I'll be on the road – all geared up to go out there and sell. You can't believe it, can you? I can't believe it myself. The linen is just perfect, isn't it, Hank?' She did not wait for a response from him. 'It's exactly what I wanted, right down to the last thread. It will all begin slowly of course. I'm sure Mendel's will take the range and I thought I'd go for Neiman Marcus in Dallas, Bloomingdale's in New York – don't you think? Just one outlet in each major city. Probably Jordan Marsh in Boston. You see, if I can offer them exclusivity it should work better, don't you think?' She fairly rattled on.

Hank looked on in admiration. 'I've been trying to convince her to deal directly herself. I see a chain of Maureen Thornton shops in the best streets – Fifth Avenue, Rodeo Drive, Boylston Street.'

'Oh Lord, I couldn't cope with real estate as well,' Maureen said, but sounded as if it was not an idea she totally rejected.

Eileen appeared.

'Come in, honey,' Kathleen said. 'Your grandmother is just telling us how she's going to make her first million.'

Eileen looked at her grandmother, who was flushed with excitement, like a teenager in love. She kissed her on the cheek. 'You are amazing,' she said, still thinking that her grandmother's behaviour was unseemly.

'How's school?' Maureen asked her. She had been so busy with her own plans that she hadn't been in touch with them since their trip to England.

'I think it's absolutely fine, but Gerry doesn't.'

'Oh really?' Maureen looked around. 'Where is your sister?'

'Upstairs. Still sulking,' Eileen said. 'But I think she'll honour us with her magnificent presence for the turkey.'

Maureen looked at her daughter. 'Is something wrong?' she asked.

'Oh, it's a long story. Nothing serious,' Kathleen said.

'She thinks it is serious,' Eileen said, 'and I think something should be done about it before she sulks to death.'

'What is this all about?' Maureen asked. She felt guilty. She didn't put enough time into the family.

Kathleen shrugged. She didn't really want to go into it. It was just a notion that she hoped would pass.

Eileen had no such hesitation. 'My sister has decided she wants to be a star. Right now.'

Typical, Daniel thought. He looked at Eileen. She had all the confidence, nay arrogance, of her mother. And so had her sister. How could he have thought the twins were his children?

'She wants to be an actress?' Hank asked.

'Not especially – just a star. She wants to leave school now instead of what she calls wasting time. And that's just what she's been doing for the past couple of months. She's off somewhere all dreamy-eyed, worrying about dying before her time, and not doing any work at all. If you ask me, you should let her get on with it.'

'Did you know about this?' Maureen asked her daughter.

Kathleen tried to treat it lightly. 'It's just a phase. You know what teenagers are like.'

'I know what you were like.' Maureen recalled her daughter's quiet determination to follow her own course.

330

Kathleen blushed. 'This is different – different circumstances altogether. I told her there would be plenty of time to think about a career when she finished school – and there will be.'

'What do you think about it, Daniel?'

He looked at his mother-in-law coolly. 'I don't see that it is any of my business.'

'Well, you are her father.'

'Really?' Daniel said. 'Prove it.' He hadn't meant to say that. He was thinking it and it just slipped out. He didn't want to antagonize Kathleen. He couldn't afford to because he needed her. She was after all his star. There was selling to do. Without her help and co-operation, *The Woman Who Walked the World*, no matter how good – and he knew it was good – might just bomb out. He needed her there, smiling at the festivals, doing the interviews. So he laughed at the stunned silence his remark had caused. 'I think I should rephrase that. I mean, look at the girls. They're young women really. You can't think I could have control over them – they're people now, not children.'

'Is she talented?' Phil asked.

'She has a lovely voice,' Kathleen answered him quietly. She knew that Daniel had said what he meant the first time. More than once he had faced her with that accusation.

'Mother Clemens said her voice is extraordinary,' Eileen reported.

'Well then, maybe we should do something about it,' Phil said.

'Like what?' Kathleen asked.

'Maybe we should have some people listen to her – advise her properly. She would probably take the advice of professionals better than that of her prejudiced parents.' Phil purposefully included Daniel in his statement. How dare he treat Kathleen the way he did.

'What if they advise her to give up school?' Kathleen asked.

'Well, that's unlikely, isn't it? But it's a chance you would have to take.'

'I do wish that you wouldn't discuss me behind my back.' Geraldine had come in unnoticed.

'Darling,' Kathleen said, embarrassed. She knew what Geraldine meant. For so many years she knew she had been the absent subject of studio negotiations, only to be faced with a *fait accompli* when others had made their decisions.

'Phil was just saying he knew some people he thought could be helpful to you . . . in your decisions.'

'I thought,' Geraldine said, 'I wasn't allowed any decisions.'

'Come on, Sis,' Eileen said, 'it's going to be OK.' She knew she had got the ball rolling. 'Cheer up.'

Josie appeared from the kitchen. 'It's ready,' she reported, to everyone's relief. The conversation could now centre around the succulent juiciness of the turkey, the sweetness of the chestnut stuffing, the perfection of the vegetables . . .

25

The limousine met them at Nice Airport. The air conditioning was redundant that May. It was warmish in the south of France, but far from hot; although that didn't stop the starlets from romping topless on the sands for the benefit of the paparazzi. They drove smoothly along the wide, palm-tree-lined Boulevard des Anglais to the Westminster Hotel where a suite awaited them and, indeed, a press conference, which Kathleen dreaded.

Daniel anticipated it eagerly, although he was exhausted from working day and night to get *The Woman Who Walked the World* in the can in time for the festival. Still, his adrenalin kept him on edge, for he knew the hardest part was just beginning – the publicity which could make or break his project. He knew the film was a blockbuster. Now it was necessary to convince the distributors, the critics and the public.

Cameras flashed at them as they made their way up the hotel steps and lit their way through the lobby. Kathleen, grateful for the shade of the elevator, shook her head to disperse the coloured globules that floated in front of her eyes. Once more she wished that Daniel had not insisted they catch the connecting flight from Paris to Nice. She had wanted to rest after the Trans-Atlantic journey. She knew she could not possibly be looking her best and dreaded the photographs which would appear. At least their entrance had been swift. Daniel now used his single cane with a flourish. His gait, though stiff, was sure, steady and quick. Kathleen was prouder of that achievement than of the film, but he would not discuss it, complaining that she was patronizing him if she even mentioned it. The movie, and how to sell it, was all he would talk about.

Phil Hornbeam was waiting for them in the suite. He had been sent ahead to oversee all the arrangements. The room, furnished in Louis Quinze style, was overflowing with flowers, and enough fruit to feed a zoo. Kathleen thought that appropriate, as for a week she would be expected to be a performing monkey.

'I've put the conference off till the morning – eleven o'clock,' Hornbeam told them.

'Oh, you angel,' Kathleen embraced him and kissed his cheek. Then she looked at her watch. 'At least ten hours of glorious sleep . . . or am I still on LA time?'

'You what?' Daniel shouted.

'Isn't it great? Oh, how wonderful to have a professional around. With any luck I won't look like a washed out rag bag and my mind might just connect with my mouth.'

'I specifically wanted to make the morning papers,' Daniel said.

'Let them wait,' Hornbeam said. 'It's better that way. They're really happier if they think they got a concession from us. Must never appear too eager . . .'

'I suppose,' Daniel said, unconvinced by Hornbeam's argument, 'that it's too late to do anything about it now.' He was furious. How dare this man contradict his plans. And Daniel knew it had nothing to do with strategy. What it was about was pleasing Kathleen and annoying him. Hornbeam did not take him seriously. No one took him seriously, even now, but they would. 'What other plans have you rearranged?' he asked.

The antagonism between the men was more palpable than ever but Kathleen hadn't the energy to intervene. A bath and then bed was all she could manage. She left them bickering over the logistics of the publicity campaign. In the morning she would do her best to be everything they expected her to be, but without sleep she would be useless to them.

334

The next three days merged into a blur of faces, questions, smiles and flashbulbs. Kathleen, Hornbeam at her side, dealt with the press, answered the same questions dozens of times, on each occasion pretending to be surprised by the interrogation and searching for a reply.

Daniel moved from meeting to meeting, hotel room to restaurant, talking money and distribution. They barely saw each other until the evening of the screening of *The Woman Who Walked the World*.

Kathleen dressed for it meticulously and, she thought, a tiny bit over the top – but this was, after all, Cannes and they expected glitz. Daniel held her hand and they made their way through the throngs, smiling like young lovers. She squeezed his hand. It was good to have him back. She looked forward to all this being over. They would have a vacation, just the two of them. Hawaii maybe, or Mexico . . . They would lie in the sun and eat and drink and make love and nothing else.

The idea sustained her through the ordeal she was about to face. She hated to see herself on the screen. She hated being watched. As they took their seats she looked to Daniel for reassurance, squeezing his hand. His eyes refused to meet hers, darting nervously away. Poor Daniel, she thought, he's not as confident as he pretends he is. She prayed that they would like the film, not for her sake but for his. As the lights dimmed and titles came up on the screen, she squeezed his hand again in a loving gesture but he let go of hers and clasped his hands in his lap once the lights had gone down.

The movie swept over her to such an extent that she forgot that woman up on the screen was herself. The action was well paced, well timed, the scenery magnificently shot and the music was overpoweringly beautiful. It was a good film, a wonderful film and the audience burst into spontaneous applause before the credits rolled. As the lights came up again once more, Daniel took her hand and looked at her adoringly – but Kathleen noticed he was merely looking in her direction. His eyes still avoided hers.

Hornbeam had hired a yacht that was moored in the Croisette for the celebration party. It was huge – an ocean-going boat – but once aboard, the number who had been invited and all the gate crashers for which Cannes was noted, made the space seem confined. Kathleen could not escape the kisses, the embraces, the congratulations, the general press of flesh. The film would walk away with all the honours, she was told. It was magnificent, compelling, enthralling, a tour de force. How much of it was true, she wondered. Had her own enthusiasm not been coloured by the fact that it was very important to her that this movie should succeed? Because it was so important to Daniel. If a tenth of what she heard was sincere, they had a winner – but that percentage of sincerity would be phenomenally high in these circles.

At last the dawn threatened and the last champagne-bloated guest walked down the gangway.

'Raise the anchor,' Kathleen said to Hornbeam, 'and set sail for the nearest desert island.'

'It was a good performance,' Phil said.

'Thanks. Which one?'

'Both of them, on screen and off. He sure as hell doesn't deserve you.'

Kathleen could feel the intensity of Phil's affection. It had to be defused. 'To where,' she asked, 'has the boy genius disappeared?'

'He left about an hour and a half ago,' Phil said. 'With Lisa.'

'Oh, what for – yet another breakfast meeting?'

Phil hesitated, keen for his own sake and he thought probably hers too, to tell her the truth. But he knew he was being selfish. Kathleen had enough to deal with at the moment. 'Yeh, something about the French rights.'

Kathleen looked at him. He seemed to be holding something back. Probably, she thought, just as well.

'Now,' she said, 'what's the schedule for tomorrow?' Then she looked at the sunrise. 'I mean today.' It would be the last day of the circus for her. She figured she could just about manage one more day before folding her tent and creeping away.

'Today is the opening of the exhibition,' Phil said.

'What exhibition?'

'Yours.'

'Phil, what on earth are you talking about now?' She began to think the stress of the job was finally getting to him.

Again he hesitated. Either she would be delighted or there would be an explosion. She had shown him her paintings at Christmas. Wonderful large oils she had conjured from her sketches. And Phil had been amazed at how good they were. She had always been dismissive of her talent. 'Just a Sunday painter,' she always said. Without her knowledge and with Josie's connivance he had had them flown in – and just before the screening he had supervised the last of the hanging. He hadn't been able to rent a proper gallery but had a conference room in the hotel stripped of furniture and, with all the professionals around, it had not been difficult setting up the lighting. They looked wonderful. He reasoned that she couldn't help being pleased – when she got over the shock.

'Look, Kathleen,' he explained. 'It's too good to miss. It's a great publicity coup. All those locations you captured so perfectly. It's a great tie-in. It's different. Just different enough to create a buzz. The papers will eat it up – and . . . ' he had saved the *pièce de résistance*, '*Newsweek* is doing a whole section on it – with colour repros.'

'My paintings?'

Hornbeam nodded, grinning. It was going to be all right.

'My paintings are here?'

He nodded again.

'On show?'

'From eleven o'clock this morning.'

Kathleen looked at him. She stared, trying to fathom his mind. How could he? He knew her painting was private, personal. He was supposed to be her friend and for another publicity angle he was about to make her a laughing stock.

She was not a professional painter, not trained. Her work was clumsy. She did not subscribe to the theory that any publicity was good publicity. How often had she been told 'just count the column inches, honey, never mind the words'? Oh, she might just get away with it. If she was lucky the critics would be politely patronizing, but they would be laughing at her behind her back.

'I suppose,' she said quietly, blinking back the tears, 'it's too late to do anything about it.'

'Kathleen, it's going to be boffo – you'll see.'

'No, I won't see. I'm not going near it. Phil, you have gone too far.' She turned around and calmly walked out. Even her anger at what she considered a betrayal didn't overcome her need to present a composed façade.

Kathleen hired a Citroën whose engine whined like a Greek chorus as it laboured up the hill away from the sea, away from Cannes, away from the circus. She could have made her escape in style in one of the limousines but that would just be a part of it all – no real escape. She had only gone a few kilometres and already the air freshened. It was, she decided, the lack of hypocrisy that made each breath seem clean. Was there no one she could trust? No one she could rely upon? She wanted her mother, her daughters. Even a bit of honest disapproval would be welcome. But if she couldn't have them she preferred to be alone.

She really wanted to be alone with Daniel. But not the Daniel she now saw. It would however, she reminded herself for the millionth time, be all right when the picture broke all box-office records known to man – oh, please God it would, she prayed. Then Daniel would have proved whatever it was he needed to prove to himself. He would know he was important. Important! Such a stupid concept. He was more than important, he was everything to her. He always had been. That wasn't enough for him though. He needed that thing called success. Well, that was all right too.

She was tired. She was very tired. When he got the

338

success she would be able to stop. Leave it all to him. And then all would be well. All would be as it should be. There would be no question about who was head of the household. That, after all, had always been her dream. Father, mother and children. Pity the girls were just about grown-up. But she was young enough. There could be more. They could start a family all over again – and he would be there this time. She mulled the dream over and over in her head as she drove through the green fields. She knew she was just reestablishing conclusions she had long harboured. Reassuring herself.

She reached the village of Grasse and parked the car under a tree. The fields of flowers that would be harvested for their scent and delivered to the perfumery were just beginning to blossom. She sat outdoors at the single café and lunched on crisp warm bread and pâté. Passing villagers nodded and smiled at her – a stranger. The light was wonderful. How wonderful to paint here, she thought. But that thought only reminded her of the perfidy of Hornbeam. There was a man she thought she could rely on. Well, she wasn't going anywhere near that exhibition. They could have their fun without her.

After lunch she wandered through the lanes – down dirt tracks, amongst the flowers . . . They could live in one of those stone houses that stood isolated among the fields . . . No more pictures, no more Hollywood – just real people, in a real world.

She drove back to the circus, feeling guilty. It had been a lovely day.

'We missed you,' Hornbeam said, 'but your pictures were a more than adequate stand-in.'

She looked at him suspiciously.

Hornbeam smiled. He had taken a chance and it had worked a million times better than even he had hoped. 'Honey,' he said, 'believe me – they think you're Da Vinci.'

Kathleen and the girls were helped into the gleaming white Ciga boat at Venice airport and as they sped around

Murano into the lagoon, they settled at the back, Kathleen contemplating the spray the speedboat threw up, Geraldine contemplating the handsome navigator, his deep tan contrasting romantically with the uniform as gleamingly white as the boat, and Eileen straining for her first glimpse of the fabled city. The Venice Film Festival, Kathleen hoped, would be very different from Cannes. Although, two, nearly three, months later that circus had taken on a slightly rosier glow in retrospect. She had, after all, been presented with the silver palm for her performance.

The girls came home almost simultaneously with her return from France and while Eileen spent the summer with her horse and her tennis companions, polishing her competitive instincts, Geraldine, as had been promised at Christmas, began her intensive vocal and movement training. Her path to stardom. Kathleen had hoped the rigorous schedule, promise of which had convinced the reluctant Geraldine to return to school, would prove too demanding, but she had not counted on her daughter's almost frightening ambition. It had been difficult to persuade her to take a week's break to come to the festival, but in the end Kathleen had prevailed.

'You never know who you might meet there. It could be useful,' she told her daughter and that clinched it. Geraldine dreamed of being discovered. She didn't know how, but somehow it might just happen across a crowded room.

Eileen on the other hand had been delighted with the idea. It was not so much the festival which appealed to her as the chance to explore Venice and she had spent weeks poring over books, planning a cultural onslaught.

Daniel and the ever-present Lisa had gone on ahead and of course Hornbeam, whom Kathleen had forgiven. They had been in Venice nearly a week now and Kathleen left it all to them, willingly. She was planning on as much of a family holiday as circumstances would permit. There was no question but that the girls were now going off in their own directions. They would be returning to school

340

as soon as they got back to the States and Kathleen would miss them. She was missing them even now, although they were with her. They were no longer children, they were young women and she was jealous of missing out on so much of their childhood.

If the truth be told, and Kathleen had to admit it to herself, she was broody. A baby wouldn't be a replacement for the girls, she knew, but rather another chance to be a mother – and perhaps a better mother the second time around. She found herself thinking about the possibility all the time. But there had been no opportunity to raise the subject with Daniel. Even if there had been time he was not in a receptive mood. *The Woman Who Walked the World* was still his consuming passion. All summer had been spent travelling the country. He planned a Gala Première – but where? Chicago? New York? Atlanta? Where, he asked himself, would the most publicity be generated? Kathleen had told him that was Hornbeam's job, but Daniel was determined to suss it all out himself. He had, for some reason Kathleen could not fully fathom, decided on Boston. Something, he explained, to do with a new chain of movie houses there. That would be the second week of September and then, she breathed a sigh of relief at the thought of it, that would be the end. *The Woman Who Walked the World* would be on her own. Then they could think about having a baby.

The boat sped across the lagoon. Eileen was kneeling up on the banquette to get a better view of Venice across the water behind them. She was delighted as a misty sun haze made it look ethereal, mysterious – just, Eileen decided, as it should be. Geraldine had gone to the front and stood beside the sailor. They were talking and laughing. Kathleen couldn't hear above the roar of the engine what kind of conversation was being carried on in broken Italian and pidgin English but she could recognize sexual bantering.

As the sun fell on her face and the wind blew her hair, Kathleen thought her daughter's pretty teenaged face had

341

the potential for real beauty – especially now, as her eyes gleamed in excitement. Maybe she would achieve her goal. Maybe she would make audiences respond to her as she felt this man was. But Kathleen feared that the response of an audience would prove as disappointing as that of this obviously professional seducer. Kathleen knew that even if Gerry managed to charm audiences, she would in the end be disappointed. They were not steadfast. They were as fickle as this sun-tanned Adonis. Easily swayed by a new adventure. Always on the lookout for a new conquest. Gazing over your shoulder even as they proclaimed love, afraid of missing something on the horizon. The love of the audience was a romantic fantasy – like the sailor.

They turned into a small canal, Geraldine laughingly ducking her head as the sailor patted it playfully and they glided under two low arched bridges which spilled over with purple and white flowers.

As they docked and tied the boat up to candy-striped poles, the boatman, one foot on the boat and one on the pier, handed them out on to the red carpet. His grip on her hand was firm and the other hand held her elbow. Kathleen noted that he held on to Geraldine a fraction longer, a bit tighter, and her daughter blushed.

It was such a contrast to her arrival in Cannes. There were no crowds, no photographers – all was serene. There was simply the boy who couldn't have been more than thirteen, his highnecked white uniform, with gold buttons that seemed a shade too big for him, giving him a waif-like appearance, who led them along the carpet under the canopy, through a tunnel and up some steps to the reception lobby of the Excelsior. He was solemn and silent. The walls, Kathleen noted as she passed were hung with her paintings. She had now got used to the idea of the travelling exhibition, but still walked quickly, dreading hearing unfavourable comments from spectators. She had in fact been pleased by the *Newsweek* piece which treated her seriously but she refused to let Hornbeam know that. She wouldn't give him the chance to say 'I told you so.'

'Ah, Signora Thornton,' the man behind the desk was in black with crossed gold insignia on his lapels, 'welcome to Venice. Pleasant journey, I hope.'

'Very pleasant, thank you.'

'And the signorine, welcome.'

The girls blushed in unison. The heat, the beauty, the effusive Italian greetings combined to make them feel light headed.

The pace and atmosphere of the Venice Film Festival, proved as Kathleen had hoped, to be totally different from that at Cannes. France seemed to be about money; here it was about movies. While a truly Italian chaos reigned, the hysteria came in lightning flashes rather than rolling on, wave after wave. Only the Adriatic, sparkling in the sun did that. The press here talked about art and style rather than bust measurements and living arrangements, and the photographers were keen to take shots of Joe Losey rather than topless frolickers. The only thing that was identical was the reception given to *The Woman Who Walked the World*. They loved it.

Apart from one hectic day when Kathleen was interviewed constantly in a variety of languages and one truly spectacular thunderstorm which blacked out the Lido for three hours, it was a peaceful week. Kathleen and Geraldine lay by the pool and talked. Really talked for the first time in years. Maybe, Kathleen thought, for the first time ever. She even began to doubt the wisdom of her insistence that her daughter stay on at school. She was so obviously frustrated and eager to get on with her life. It was the typical impatience of the young. Kathleen tried to point out that there was no rush, she was a child still, there was plenty of time. But deep down she realized that the argument was specious. The look on the faces of the boys who caught sight of her daughter told her that at sixteen her daughter was a woman. At sixteen Kathleen reminded herself, she was already a mother. Still, maybe it was because of that – she wanted what every mother wants, to spare her children pain. She wanted to protect them not only from others but from their own folly. Was that possible? Should she perhaps just give Geraldine her blessing and let her get on with it? Kathleen felt desperately alone in that decision. She wanted to share the responsibility with someone – a particular someone. Their father.

She had hoped that now Daniel had an assured success, well, as assured as the movie business ever gets, he would calm down. But still he flitted from meeting to meeting, doing God only knows what, Kathleen thought. It was as if the film would disappear if he stopped for a minute. Eileen, she realized now, took after her father. She, too, was full of nervous energy. She was busy first thing in the morning, gathering boats, churches, museums with the enthusiasm of a Victorian butterfly collector. She wanted everything pinned down neatly and classified and she possessed the solemn determination that not a single aspect of Venice should elude her. How different the girls seemed, Kathleen thought, or perhaps Geraldine had that enthusiasm too, but she was denying it expression. Eileen's activities seemed fitting for a schoolgirl; Geraldine's desires did not. Not for the first time, and surely not for the last, she reckoned, Kathleen regretted the years she had missed with the girls. Perhaps if she had been there for their first words, their first steps – perhaps she would understand them better and know now what to do. It would not happen next time. She would not be an absentee mother again. Who was it who said have another baby if you wanted to baby someone – don't baby the grown-up children you have. A new baby would, she supposed, give her a truer perspective on the girls, as well as giving herself another chance.

Besides, despite the crowds and the work, she was lonely. A feeling of aloneness in the midst of people. Daniel was so wrapped up in his work she didn't recognize him and he certainly gave no indication of needing her presence for anything other than publicity. It was as if he saw her only as strangers did – as a star, a commodity, no as a person and certainly not as his wife. Still, she thought, the film in the long run would be good for him. She had never seen him so happy, despite his preoccupation. He was on a high, a success trip, and she couldn't deprive him of that. He deserved it. But she longed for the dust to settle. She longed to be back home in California where she knew it would be all right – and possibly for the first time. Although she had always loved and respected him, he hadn't loved himself. Certainly not since the war and probably, she thought, since he had single-handedly won the State championship basketball game when he was seventeen. She remembered how his face glowed with pride in his achievement. How she had loved him – from her seat among the spectators – just one more adoring adolescent. He hadn't known of her existence then – but now she was his wife. The success of *The Woman Who Walked the World* would give him back his confidence – all the confidence her love could not give him. And a new baby would cement it. He, too, deserved a second chance at being a parent.

The day of the Gala presentation of *The Woman Who Walked the World* arrived and despite its reception at Cannes, Kathleen was nervous. Too nervous to relax by the pool. She had to take her mind off the forthcoming ordeal and with the girls took a boat into San Marco. Eileen had mapped out their itinerary – one so laden with sights that it would not leave a moment for the fears to creep back into her head.

Daniel, too, was nervous of the reception that would greet his film. Venice, he thought, was so much more serious than Cannes. The Italian critics were intellectuals who expected symbolism and metaphor not simply a good story well told. Whereas the French, although quite happy to recognize and applaud the seriousness of the New Wave directors, were equally happy with a snappy Jean Paul Belmondo cops and robbers flick.

Daniel wanted to take his mind off the evening ahead and had taken Lisa to his bed, not for the first time but

perhaps with the most intensity. In the cosy warmth of the
aftermath of passion, as she lay back drowsily, he leaned
above her, his elbow on the pillow, his head supported in
his cupped hand, and looked down on her serene face,
wondering at her composure. Only minutes before she
had been contorted in spasms of pleasure. With his index
finger he traced a line from her unfurrowed brow to her
chin and she snapped, nipping at his finger.

'Bitch,' he said softly, and playfully tapped her cheek
with his fingertips.

She giggled, childlike, and he thought it was the sweetest
sound he had ever heard.

'I love you,' he said.

'I know,' she answered, 'and I adore you.' She reached
up, twining her fingers in his hair and forced his head down
until once more their lips met and the love-making began
again. But it was different this time. The ferocity had gone
and it was gentle and quiet.

Afterwards, Daniel sat on the edge of the bed and began
unselfconsciously strapping on his artificial leg. He realized
that this was something he could never do in Kathleen's
presence. It had never bothered him that Lisa was a witness
to his handicap. She, after all, had known him no other
way. She had fallen in love with the person he was now,
not the person he had once been.

'When are you going to tell her?' Lisa was still lying
naked in the bed behind him and addressed the question to
his back. It was a question that Daniel had not anticipated.
What had Kathleen to do with this? This was a part of his
life in which she had no share. Why should she need to be
told anything? Kathleen was his wife. She would always
be his wife. He pretended he hadn't heard the softly voiced
question.

'Come on, lazy bones,' he said, turning to her and
tickling her tummy. He enjoyed watching her innocent
squirms. 'Get your beautiful ass out of bed. We've got a
big night ahead of us.'

'You've got a big night ahead of you, oh most important

346

one. I, as the lowliest of the low, will only be a witness to it from the farthest reaches of the upper balcony.'

'You'll be with the girls,' he said, but that thought did not seem to cheer her up. 'Are we feeling sorry for ourselves?' he teased her.

'Just a teeny bit,' she said.

This time he heard the catch in her voice.

'Lisa, you know I couldn't have done this without you. But I couldn't have done it without Kathleen either. And I need her for the publicity just as I needed her for the movie.'

'You just needed a star – like any producer needs a star. Doris Day would have done just as well. And you wouldn't have to hold her hand at all the premières. The picture is yours not Kathleen's.'

Daniel was taken aback. Was that true? But more importantly did Lisa really believe it?

'You reckon?' He said it casually, as if everything didn't depend on her reply.

'I don't just reckon, I know. Stars are made – and there's a new one around every corner. Producers make stars, not the other way around.'

She knelt up on the bed behind him and ran her fingernails down his back. 'You don't need her,' she said softly kissing the back of his neck.

Spotlights played on the long, low, white festival building as Kathleen and Daniel, led by a girl from the festival office, walked the short distance from the hotel. Turbulent crowds around the entrance were only half-heartedly being controlled by police who behaved like fans themselves. The people closed in, forming an obstacle as impenetrable as a brick wall. The guide who had been detailed to them was young, petite, in awe of the celebrities and terrified by the crowd which defeated her as she tried, with timid *permessos*, to carve a path to the door for her charges. Flashbulbs popped and bits of paper were thrust at them for autographs as they inched their way slowly through the mêlée. Kathleen, too, was frightened by the crowds but when she took Daniel's arm it was more to support him than for herself.

'I'm not a cripple,' he hissed at her through clenched teeth and aggressively moved ahead of her, shoving and elbowing his way into the building. She followed quickly in her wake and as she stood in the foyer trying to regain her composure she heard him berating the poor girl who had failed in her task. Luckily, Kathleen thought, the girl's English was not good enough to get the full import of his anger, but the tone was unequivocal in any language.

'I'm sorry,' Kathleen interrupted his flow. 'I didn't mean –'

He refocused his anger. 'I know exactly what you meant,' he said. 'You would rather I were still in the wheel-chair so you could totally control me. Come on, smile – there's an audience waiting.'

They walked down the centre aisle hand in hand, shyly acknowledging the applause which greeted them. They took their seats and the lights dimmed.

He's just nervous, Kathleen told herself. It will be all right when all this is over. She put her hand on his arm in the darkness and felt him draw away from her.

❧ 26 ❧

Once more it was autumn, although the sun blazed in Boston in a sweltering Indian summer – and once more Kathleen was at the Ritz Carlton. It was sixteen years since that hotel had been her alternative to death by drowning and fourteen years since she had stayed there when opening at the Colonial in *Friendly Enemies*.

Like herself, she thought, Boston had changed – some good changes, some bad changes. The shell of the Prudential Tower was rising, set to dwarf the John Hancock building which for thirteen years had seemed itself too tall for the city. Scollay Square had been bulldozed, making way for the Government Center but the bars and the winos had simply moved along Tremont and Washington Street to form a new combat zone where women did not walk alone and seldom walked in groups. The once tranquil Back Bay apartments were sprouting deadlocks and chains as the Boston Strangler frightened any woman who lived alone. It was, however, now possible to dine after seven o'clock at night somewhere other than Chinatown, which was now bisected by a highway. At the enormous Pier Four restaurant at the harbourside, Kathleen had looked out on to the sea and found it indistinguishable from the Pacific.

She and Daniel had a suite at the hotel – two bedrooms were joined, or separated depending on your point of view, by a huge sitting room. Despite the return of summer, the time of year dictated that a well-tended fire greeted them in the marble fireplace.

Daniel had planned a Hollywood-style United States première for *The Woman Who Walked the World*. Search-lights would pierce the night sky, all the local dignitaries were invited and a huge black-tie gala was laid on at the Armoury. And he had chosen his location well. In the midst of a rebuilding programme which would change the face of the city, the locals were pleased by the novelty. Californians would be blasé, New Yorkers too sophisti-cated to respond, but Boston lapped it up. The local television stations were delighted by the chance to go for a nice light-hearted story and the national networks found it a good excuse to cover the controversial urban develop-ment programme as well as to get some pretty faces on to the evening news.

A city of contrasts, NBC reported, as the cameras swept through the Roxbury slums and returned to Georgian Louisburg Square. A city of the old and the new, they reported, and showed Fanuil Hall contrasted with the rising skyscrapers. A city of culture and glitz they said, letting their cameras wander from the university buildings to the première site.

Kathleen was thoroughly sick of *The Woman Who Walked the World*. She was sick of smiling, she was sick of being enthusiastic, she was sick of watching it. But she performed for the cameras when asked. She poured tea for journalists in her sitting room and turned this way and that at the request of photographers. Surely, she thought, this can't be the way Geraldine wants to spend her life.

She was pleased to escape to the Public Gardens which, she noted, mercifully had not yet changed. Her bench, newly painted it was true, was still there. And her tree had not succumbed to age. She sat, sketching its growth and found it as absorbing as she had all those years before. Her worries were now different worries but she still needed intense concentration to shut them out of her mind. It will be all right, she told herself. It will be all right when all this is over. She turned her mind to the sketch pad and to the tree. She could not envisage the future and it was painful to look into a void.

David DeCosta walked along the path. He didn't like the heat. It was oppressive. It wasn't a proper autumn. The air should be crisp and clear as it had been, how many years ago, he wondered. 1947. The year of the Marshall Plan, the House Un-American activities committee, the Polaroid Land camera and the first Tony awards. The year he became a playwright. The year of *Somewhere in France*. He nearly smiled to himself remembering how afraid he had been that autumn. And how afraid he had been of all the wrong things. How young he had been. There were so many things about himself that he hadn't known, and maybe, he thought, it was just as well. If that autumn he had been able to look into the future he would have been crushed by it. Would he have done things differently? He doubted if he would have been able to do other than what had been done. The future to him now – his personal future – held no terrors. It held no terrors because now he knew himself completely . . .

But that was the distant future. He wasn't afraid of life any more, or indeed of death. Like Peter Pan he thought of it all as a great adventure. The immediate future was not so comfortable. There was a problem in the second act of *Streak of Sunset* which was about to open. It was a small problem – a few lines of dialogue that he just couldn't get down to his satisfaction. Every time he heard Paul speak the lines they upset him. They simply weren't clear enough. They didn't say exactly what he meant. If he had known at the beginning that writing only got more difficult, he would probably have opted for his family's construction business. He often told himself that – especially before first nights – but he knew it was a lie. There was nothing else he wanted to do. Nothing else he could do. The trouble was, as usual, every time opening night approached he wondered if he could still do it. That first play took on a rosy hue through the haze of time. How much easier it had been then when he had nothing to lose. Now his reputation preceded him. With the clutch of long-running plays behind him, not to mention the triad of Tonys for heaven's sake, and with *Somewhere in France* being studied by college students, he had ruefully to admit that he was now competing with himself. And it got harder all the time. The more he learned about writing plays the more difficult it got to translate his ideas to the stage. Besides, he knew there was a new generation of critics who were only too keen to make their names by dismissing an established playwright as no longer up to scratch.

The grass by the path was scorched from the intense sun. The flowers wilted in their beds, parched. Their time was over anyway, David thought. The autumn frosts would soon finish them off. Only the trees remained stoically green in the blazing weather. He had never lost the awe Kathleen had given him for trees. Before her, in common he supposed with most of the population, he had just never thought about them. But since her enthusiasm had communicated itself to him he noticed them. He never failed to notice them – in the city standing singly and majestically, in the country in ranks. He noticed their individuality and regarded them with admiration. He had happily planted trees in his Connecticut garden – apple trees, flowering cherries and even oak and elm which he would not live to see mature. As the path curved, he thought there is the tree where it all started – the tall elm.

He stopped. He stared. It was as if he had crossed a time zone. The years fell away as he saw a girl on the bench, pencil poised above a sketch pad, lost in concentration as she studied the elm. The sun glinted in her deep auburn hair and David was young again. He shook his head to dispel the mirage but the scene remained unchanged. He approached quietly although he knew that a rumbling herd of buffalo could pass unnoticed when Kathleen was occupied. He stood over her. There was, he knew, no way he could pass by as if she wasn't there. He didn't know what his reception would be – had she forgiven him? He had often wondered about that and at this moment he had to speak to her.

'Hello, Kathleen,' he said quietly.

Slowly she looked up and he saw the expression of annoyance at being disturbed leave her face. In its place he saw shock and then, yes, it was pleasure. How easy it was now for him to read her face. Before it had been inscrutable. She had been an enigma to him. But it was he who had changed, not her. Her expressions, he realized, had always been there for him to read but the language had been foreign to him.

'David.' She put her sketchbook down on the bench beside her, the pencil neatly on the top and stared at him as if she too was frozen in time.

'May I sit down?' he asked.

'Sit?' she shook her head as if to clear a daze and then laughed, patting the bench beside her. 'Of course; sit.'

They were silent, motionless, reassuring themselves that neither of them was imagining the encounter. David took her hand, holding it tightly, looking into her eyes.

'I never said sorry, did I?' he finally said.

She shook her head. 'You did but it never needed saying,' she responded. 'There are things that aren't in our control.' With a few words she closed a chapter of her life, satisfactorily. 'I've been reading about you,' Kathleen said. 'You've got a new play opening.'

'At last,' he said.

'But you never stop.' Kathleen knew that after Hollywood it had been years before his name was back on Broadway again. She could imagine that they were difficult years – but he had come through them and produced good work.

'It only seems like that – it's taken me two years to write this one. And tomorrow is going to be a disaster.'

'Still a pessimist,' Kathleen patted his hand. 'Or are you just trying to make the gods look the other way?'

'A little of both, I suppose.'

'How's Paul?' Kathleen asked.

'Well, as usual he was fine until rehearsals began and now he's as jumpy as a cat. But he'll settle down. He's good.'

'And good for you?'

'Yes.'

'Still got the house in the village?'

'Yup. And we bought a farmhouse in Connecticut. It's beautiful countryside. Got a little pond – well, a pretty big pond really. You'd love it there. Lots of old trees. And some young ones too. I planted them myself.'

'Good for you. Ah, the New England countryside. I miss all that in California.'

'But you've been traipsing around the world lately. I read the papers too, you know – and you seldom seem to be out of them.'

'Ah, yes, don't remind me. *The Woman Who Walked the World.* I've come out here to get away from her.'

'Première tonight.'

'And I hope that will be the end of it, as far as I'm concerned.'

'How are the girls?'

'Grown-up. You wouldn't recognize them.'

'And beautiful as their mother?'

'Much, much prettier. Geraldine wants to go on the stage.'

'Poor child.'

'I know. I've tried to tell her but –'

'It's no use,' David interrupted. 'And Eileen?'

'Bossy as ever. That girl could organize the world and probably will.'

'And are you happy, Kathleen?'

'Me? Of course I'm happy,' she replied, as if it were the most ridiculous question. Why on earth shouldn't she be happy?

'Daniel is everything you hoped he would be?'

'He is marvellous. I'm so proud of him. He's walking again. And he has worked his heart out on this picture. It has to be a success – for him. He deserves it.'

'It will be, I'm sure. You seem to attract success, Kathleen. Or do you inspire it? Even your mother . . . I've seen her stuff at Bloomingdales.'

'Isn't that amazing? Who would ever have thought . . .'

'We must be getting old, Kathleen, all this nostalgia.'

'We go back a long way, David.'

'Sometimes it seems a whole lifetime ago and sometimes it seems only yesterday.'

'I know what you mean.'

As Kathleen dressed for the première that evening she thought about the afternoon meeting with David and was glad it had taken place. Often over the years she had thought about him, wondering if she had unwittingly caused him as much pain as he had caused her. It was, she figured, pretty evenly distributed as relationships went. Fault did not come into it on either side. It was just the way it was. And even at the beginning of the end, when the wounds on her soul were as painful as the blisters on David's body, she knew she had a lot for which to be grateful to him. She looked at her surroundings now. If it hadn't been for David, would she still be cleaning these rooms, she wondered. How much had she contributed to David's life? She had perhaps given him confidence, reassurance at a time when he needed it. But David was always a playwright. She had nothing to do with that. And he had given her life a new direction. Still, she reckoned, it was never possible to balance the scales.

She remembered the dress he had bought her to wear at the Broadway opening of *Somewhere in France*. It had been the most beautiful dress she had ever seen – a star's dress. She had worn many equally beautiful outfits since then, but that one held a special place in her memory. How bizarre it was, she thought, to measure out your life in clothes. But it is true that what you wear can affect not only the way others see you but your own view of yourself.

Perhaps nudists had the right idea. Although if everyone was naked she was sure people would begin painting their bodies. African tribes had done it. Indians did it. Instead of couturiers there would be designer body painters. She giggled as she let her mind wander over the idea. Fidel Castro vibrantly decorated in red hammer and sickles. She let him keep his beard and his cap. Khrushchev could be covered with even more symbols. Well, he had more body surface. He could keep his shoes to bang on tables. President Kennedy would be done in red and white stripes and she mentally removed his wife's chic suits and painted her blue with white stars. Side by side the first couple could add up to an American flag. Jackie's pill box hat could be the little round ball on top of the flag pole. Tribal sides could be delineated as evidently as the Chinese proclaimed their allegiance to Mao with the uniform jacket.

'What are you laughing about?' Daniel, already dressed in his tuxedo, was standing in the doorway. 'Aren't you ready yet?'

Kathleen jumped out of her reverie. 'Oh.' She hadn't realized that she was laughing out loud. 'I just had the funniest idea –'

'There's no time for that. The limo is waiting,' he interrupted.

'Nearly ready. Just give me a tick.'

'Get a move on,' he said, retreating to the sitting room where she could hear him pacing in his uneven gait. It became like a metronome ticking off the seconds and she fumbled nervously with her zip. She mustn't, she knew, do anything to upset him. If he was upset he could explode – and there would be too many witnesses tonight for an explosion. He was jumpy already. After a quick twirl in front of the mirror to check her image from every angle, she joined him.

'Ready,' she announced, twirling for him too. She would have liked to see admiration in his eyes. She didn't really expect him to verbalize it. But she got no reaction at all. He barely glanced in her direction as he headed for the door. She hurried after him.

* * *

Kathleen and Daniel had been home for nearly a month and it wasn't going according to Kathleen's plan. *The Woman Who Walked the World* was showing in selected theatres across the country – not in continuous performance, but three times a day and mostly to reserved seats. It was more like the live theatre. This contributed to the audience's sense of occasion and got them briefly away from their television sets.

Now that Telstar was in operation and there were live transmissions from Europe, and now that colour had taken over the small screen there seemed to be even more reason to stay at home, even if the Federal Communications Chairman, Minnow, had called television a 'Vast Wasteland'. 'I invite you,' he told a convention of the National Association of Broadcasters, 'to sit down in front of your television set when your station goes on the air and stay there. You will see a vast wasteland – a procession of game shows, violence, audience participation shows, formula comedies about totally unbelievable families . . . blood and thunder . . . mayhem, violence, sadism, murder . . . private eyes, more violence, and cartoons . . . and, endlessly, commercials – many screaming, cajoling and offending . . .' Hollywood, or what was left of the film industry, rejoiced at the speech and the nation went right on watching television. Still, they could go out and see *The Woman Who Walked the World* and still be home in time to watch Johnny Carson.

It had outgrossed any previous film in its first week – but then the movie houses were charging a phenomenal admission fee on the grounds that if the price was high enough everyone would conclude it was something special. In the Midwest the average was $1.50, but in the big East and West coast cities people were actually paying two dollars and more a head to see it. Kathleen remembered when fifty cents was considered the absolute top. In its first week of release the movie had reached the top of *Variety*'s poll and stayed there. Now, Kathleen thought, at last Daniel can relax. He's done it. He's proved himself.

357

God knows, he should know that there was nothing he needed to prove to her. There never had been. But he was as irritable as ever, locked up in his study, going on mysterious outings, snapping at Josie. Ignoring her.

The girls had flown home for the weekend and he had managed to find something important to do elsewhere, away from the house, except for Sunday lunch. She had begged him to stay for that and he had grudgingly agreed and remained morose and uncommunicative. The girls talked on, full of school and gossip and plans, and seemed not to notice. They still seemed perfectly content as Kathleen drove them back to the airport on Sunday evening so that they could catch the short flight back to San Francisco. It amused her to think how different their lives had been from her own. They hopped on and off planes with more ease than she had ridden on street cars.

'See you at Thanksgiving,' she said, hugging each girl in turn. They were both taller than her now and in her flat shoes she had to reach up to kiss them.

'Look after yourself, Mummy,' Geraldine said. She was suddenly very serious.

'Of course, darling.'

'I think you need a vacation,' Eileen said in that authoritarian tone she had developed.

'That would be nice,' Kathleen said. 'I've been trying to talk your father into going to Mexico – but he is so busy . . .'

'I don't mean Daddy,' Eileen said. 'I mean you.'

'Maybe you should get away from him for a bit,' Geraldine said. 'You've been in each other's pockets through this whole thing.'

'I don't know what you mean,' Kathleen said. She thought the girls hadn't noticed the trouble.

'Mummy,' Geraldine said. 'You look so sad.'

Kathleen was speechless. She hugged her daughter again.

'Come on.' Eileen prodded her sister. 'We'll miss the plane and Mother Superior will be furious.'

'I love you, Mummy,' Geraldine said.

'She knows that,' Eileen said. 'Don't you, Mummy? You know we both love you, no matter what.'

Kathleen drove home speculating on what the girls had said. She had assumed that they were so engaged in their own lives that they hadn't given a thought to hers. Theirs, she reminded herself. She and Daniel had a life together, but, despite the common work on the movie, they had moved further apart than ever.

His car was gone when she returned. She had to talk to him but there was no point in waiting up. Kathleen heard him most nights, or rather early in the morning, when he came in, creeping into his room as quietly as he could manage – which wasn't very. He hadn't shared her bed since their return and she hadn't dared approach his. She just didn't understand anymore. He had everything he could possibly want. They were together again after those ghastly years of separation – and now he even had his success. Tonight, whenever he returned, they would both be tired. That was no state of mind in which to sort anything out. But she determined that it was no good putting it off any longer. It wasn't just her imagination. The girls saw it too. The next day they would bring it out into the open. No matter what obstacles he presented, no matter what excuses he gave. Tomorrow they would talk.

Kathleen sat at the breakfast table. She was drinking her third cup of black coffee when at last she heard Daniel approaching. She picked up the newspaper, feigning interest in the words which were but a blur in front of her eyes. She had been awake since six – had washed and dried her hair, applied her make-up with special care and rejected outfit after outfit before deciding on a simple pink dress. She had worn pink on that first date with Daniel.

She stayed hidden by the newspaper until she heard Daniel sit down across from her and pour orange juice from the jug into his glass. Then, carefully, she folded the paper and put it to one side.

'Oh,' she said, as if surprised by his presence, 'good morning, darling. Sleep well?'

'Why shouldn't I,' he countered.

She looked across at him. The sun shining through the window behind him turned his blond hair into a halo. His deep blue eyes were clear but full of anger. She loved him very much. What had she done to anger him?

'I just thought,' she stumbled. 'I wondered if there was any trouble. You were so late . . .'

'I'm sorry,' he said, clearly not meaning it. 'I didn't know I needed to apply for a late night pass.'

'Darling,' she reached across the table for his hand. 'I didn't mean . . .' She searched for the words. This was not what she had planned.

He let her hand lie on his for a moment before pulling away. 'Well, I won't disturb you tonight,' he said. 'I'm going away for a few days.'

'Away? Where to?' There had been so much travelling.

'Do I need permission for everything?'

Kathleen tried to laugh but the sound died in her throat. 'Of course not. It's just . . . what if I need you?'

He was standing now. 'Need me? Why should you? You've never needed me for anything.'

Kathleen was stunned by his exit.

At the convent the girls had all crowded into the television room. There was to be an important television broadcast by the president – at seven p.m. Washington time but at four o'clock in California. The room had never been so crowded. Television watching was discouraged generally. Mother Superior, it seemed, agreed with Minnow.

Some girls sat on the floor, huddled together. Others perched on the arms of occupied chairs. The presidential seal appeared and a solemn-voiced announcer introduced the President of the United States. There was a collective sigh as John Kennedy appeared. A buzz hummed through the room. He was so handsome. But the girlish giggles were soon silenced as they realized the importance of

360

the message. There were nuclear weapons in Cuba.

'The purpose of these bases,' he continued in terribly calm tones, 'can be none other than to provide a nuclear strike capability against the Western Hemisphere.' He called it 'a deliberately provocative and unjustified change in the status quo which cannot be accepted by this country if our courage and our commitments are ever to be trusted again by either friend or foe'.

There was now a deadly silence in the room as the girls tried to comprehend what he was saying and hoped at the same time that they were not understanding properly.

He outlined what he termed would be the 'initial stages' of the operation he intended to carry out. There would be a quarantine on all offensive military equipment under shipment to Cuba; intensified surveillance of Cuba itself; a declaration that any missile launched from Cuba would be regarded as an attack by the Soviet Union on the United States, requiring full retaliatory response upon the Soviet Union; an immediate convening of the Organization of American States to consider the threat to the security of the hemisphere; an emergency meeting of the UN Security Council to consider the threat to world peace; and an appeal to Chairman Khrushchev 'to abandon this course of world domination and to join in an historic effort to end the perilous arms race and to transform the history of man'.

The President's voice was still and calm as he came to the end of the terrifying news – 'My fellow citizens,' he concluded, 'let no one doubt that this is a difficult and dangerous effort . . . No one can foresee precisely what course it will take or what cost or casualties will be incurred . . . But the greatest danger of all would be to do nothing. Our goal is not the victory of might, but the vindication of right – not peace at the expense of freedom, but both peace and freedom, here in this hemisphere and, we hope, around the world. God willing, that goal will be achieved.'

Mother Superior picked her way through the girls to the

front of the room and switched off the set. There was an eerie silence and no one moved. Then she saw Mary O'Connell (Mary was only twelve, a new girl that term) waving her hand wildly in the air.

'Yes, Mary,' Mother said.

'Please Mother, does that mean there is a war? Will we all be blown up?'

'Nonsense, dear,' the nun replied trying to keep her voice from cracking. 'The President is a good Catholic man. He'll look after us and God will look after him. Now I think we should all go into the chapel and say a few prayers for him.' She wished she was as sure as she managed to sound.

'That's it,' Geraldine said to Eileen. 'We're all going to be blown to smithereens any minute.'

'Don't be so hysterical,' Eileen said. 'That was just rhetoric. He's playing poker and I'll bet he plays better than Khrushchev.'

'The stakes are too high and Khrushchev holds all the cards.'

'But he doesn't know that.'

'I don't see how,' Geraldine said, 'you can be so calm.' Her stomach was churning.

'It's not to anyone's advantage to drop the bomb. It's just not logical and besides, governments are run by committee and in committees it is pragmatism that prevails. All the emotion gets talked away. Bureaucracy has much to recommend it.'

Sometimes Geraldine found her sister's lack of emotion daunting. At that moment she found it ridiculous. Eileen would still be convinced of her arguments as the mushroom cloud rose above them.

Kathleen switched off the television set, numbed. Well, that's it she thought. What was it Bogy said to Ingrid Bergman? 'The troubles of three little people don't amount to a hill o' beans in this crazy world.' If the world survived the confrontation she supposed she would survive as well.

It would be difficult but she would work it out with Daniel. He was exhausted, that was all. He needed time to himself.

In Buenos Aires Billy Graham preached vociferously about the end of the world to ten thousand people preparing to meet their maker.

Hank was in New York. He was scheduled to dine with his publisher but had delayed his departure for the Four Seasons to watch the broadcast. It scared him. It reminded him of his mortality. He picked up the phone and dialled Maureen's hotel room in Chicago. It had been six weeks since he had seen her as she roamed the country. He missed her. They talked every couple of days and when the conversations ended he missed her even more. He was jealous of her enthusiasm for designing and marketing. It gave her so much pleasure. He knew it was selfish but *he* wanted to be the source of her happiness, not some goddamn china. And he was frightened. Every time she left his presence he feared she would disappear from his life. He needed her. He wanted a visible bond. He needed that security, but every time he asked her to marry him she sidestepped the question. The first time he had been flabbergasted. It had taken him a long time to work up the courage and he hadn't even been sure then that that was what he wanted. He had just wanted to please her and surely, he had thought, all women wanted marriage. Her refusal had been a blow. But since that time he had learned a lot. It was he who needed the reassurance of a legal bond. He wanted a name to put in that space in his passport that said 'next of kin: please notify in case of accident'. It had been blank for too long. And he wanted it to be Maureen's name.

The hotel operator put the call through to Maureen's room. He listened to it ringing. After twelve rings the operator came back on the line.

'Sorry,' she said, 'there doesn't seem to be any answer.'

Hank thanked her and put the phone down. The first

rush of fear that something had happened to her turned into a cloud of jealousy. Where was she, he wondered. And with whom?

Maureen had switched off the television and proceeded to the bathroom. The world might end tonight, she thought, but there was nothing she could do about that. If it was still there in the morning she had a very busy day ahead of her. She stepped into the shower and failed to hear the phone ringing in the next room.

The buggers are at it again, Daniel thought. War. The images came flooding back to him. The blood-soaked beaches, the bodies in the water. He began to shake uncontrollably. Lisa held him tightly as he sobbed.

'It's all right,' she cooed, more frightened by his reaction to the broadcast than by the implied threat to the human race.

While the politicians and diplomats in Washington and Moscow were in a frenzy of activity, the rest of the world held its breath. The largest invasion force since the Second World War massed in Florida. A U-2 surveillance plane disappeared over Cuba. News teams reported everything they could find out. The behind-the-scenes activities were mostly off limits to them, so toy ships were displayed on the evening news to chart the course of the Russian ships as they approached Cuba. On Thursday a Soviet tanker entered the quarantine zone. This is it, the public collectively thought. On the East Coast a number of young people headed north for Canada, hoping to be out of range of the Cuban missiles which were bound to be let loose when the tanker was forcibly stopped and searched. It was irrational but at least it was activity. And stopping a tanker was an aggressive act. An act of war in anyone's book. But lo and behold, the tanker was allowed to proceed unmolested. The nation sighed its collective relief. One more day's reprieve.

Then, at the week-end the miracle came. The little toy ships on television, mimicking the real ones, turned around and headed away from Cuba, quietly, like a cat pretending it hasn't even seen a bird it has no hope of catching. On Sunday night Kennedy was once again on television. He looked tired but also relieved. He had pulled it off. The missiles were being dismantled. But he wasn't being smug. That was part of his strategy. He didn't smile but the tension was gone from his face and his voice. He spoke solemnly of 'Chairman Khrushchev's statesman-like decision' and as if no one had noticed he added that the conflict had pointed to a 'compelling necessity for ending the arms race and reducing world tensions'.

'You see,' Eileen told her sister. Unlike the president, she did not eschew smugness.

'Pure luck,' Geraldine said, 'and the luck of the Irish can't last forever. So, I've made up my mind.'

'About what?'

Geraldine had spent the week fearing that every day would be her last. And she hadn't even begun to live her life – the life she wanted to live. 'I'm leaving school at the end of the semester,' she declared flatly and the tone in her voice indicated that her decision was no longer open to negotiation.

'Mummy's not going to like it,' Eileen said.

'Well, I'm sorry about that. Truly I am, but honestly, Eileen, we'll be seventeen in January and we haven't even begun to live.'

'I certainly have.'

'Oh, you know what I mean. To do what we really want to do.'

'I am doing what I want to do. And when I've finished here I'm going to Stanford and then into politics.'

'Just like that?'

'I've got it all planned. State politics and then on to Washington.'

'You aim pretty high.'

'Why not?'

'And if you don't get into Stanford?'

'I will – and you know what else?'

'What?'

'You'll be a star.'

'If I'm lucky.'

'I keep telling you, Sis, luck has nothing to do with it.'

Kathleen had spent the week in the house, watching the news and waiting for Daniel's return with equal trepidation. The good news on the Cuban front did not do a lot to relieve her anxieties on the home front. Finally she decided her inactivity was doing no one any good – particularly herself. She got out her paints and tried to work but it was no use. To create she needed to look inside herself as well as out into the world and inside she was just a chaotic jumble. She didn't know what Daniel wanted of her and she couldn't give it to him if she couldn't figure it out. She needed a more structured occupation to take her mind off her failure and that meant working on a movie. Since the studio had dissolved around him, Phil Hornbeam had become an agent as well as working in public relations. She phoned him and they agreed to meet for lunch.

The Bistro-tecque was the newest fashionable Los Angeles watering hole and having put it on the map by steering well-known faces there, Phil had a permanent luncheon table. It was one where he could see rather than be seen. Kathleen had demurred at the thought of being put on display, but he assured her that would not be the case – beyond her entrance. She dressed suitably and after she had put on make-up for the first time in a week, she felt better than she had for a long time.

The maitre d' grovelled appropriately when she entered and led her to Phil's table.

'You are looking magnificent,' Phil said, taking her hand and kissing her cheek.

'Thanks,' she said, sitting next to him. 'I wish I felt great.'

'What's the matter?' He was genuinely concerned. He knew what the matter was, but he wondered what her perception of it was.

'Oh, just a lack of activity, I suppose. After all that *Woman* hype I came down with a plop.'

'What about your painting?'

'I seem to have hit a fallow period.'

Although he admired her greatly as an actress, Phil knew that for Kathleen real satisfaction lay in her painting.

'You'll get over that,' he said confidently.

'I hope so.'

'You know, Kathleen, you really should consider a selling exhibition.'

'Selling? What nonsense. Who would pay good money for my stuff?'

'Stop being so coy. You read the critics – although I know you pretended not to.'

'What I really need is a part to play, Phil. I'm fed up with being myself.'

Phil was not looking at her but towards the entrance. She noticed and her eyes followed his gaze. The maitre d' was leading a couple to the far corner of the restaurant. She blinked and looked again. One member of the couple was her husband – and the other was . . . Lisa. Lisa without her clipboard. It was perfectly obvious to Kathleen that this was not a business lunch. They were so wrapped up in each other that they noticed no one else in the room. Kathleen watched as they sat side by side. Lisa whispered in his ear and he nuzzled her cheek with his lips.

'Phil,' Kathleen said at last, 'how long has this been going on?'

'Since the beginning of the film,' he replied succinctly.

Through Europe, through Asia, through all that publicity! In Cannes, in Venice! All that time Kathleen had put his obnoxious behaviour down to pressure. All the excuses she had made for him. She felt humiliation burning in her cheeks.

'As openly as this?' she asked.

Phil nodded.

'And, classically, the wife is the last to know.'

Phil nodded again.

'Why the hell didn't you tell me?' She blinked back the tears. Tears of sorrow; tears of anger.

'You wouldn't have believed me – would you?'

Kathleen shook her head. That was true. She wouldn't have believed him. There was something too special about her and Daniel. There was God and Fate and all that. No, she wouldn't have believed him.

'When is he going to ask for a divorce?'

'I've heard,' Phil said, 'that he has no intention of getting divorced. And he is convinced that you will never leave him.'

Kathleen could never have imagined leaving Daniel. He was her past and her future. He was her world. But Kathleen could not deny the information she was gathering with her own eyes. What would she do without Daniel? She was muddled. But, slowly, out of the muddle a picture began to emerge. Was it just possible that her mother had been right? Had she invented that world herself and simply slotted a compliant Daniel into it? Had she loved a creature of her own making? Had she, indeed, constructed a cage in which she was determined to keep two imaginary love birds?

'Phil,' she said evenly, her voice in control. 'I think I would like a large margarita, some guacamole, and chili enchiladas.' That was as close as she and Daniel would ever get to her dream of a Mexican second honeymoon. 'And then, after lunch I would like you to find me a real estate agent, an art dealer and a lawyer.'

'In that order?'

'In any goddamn order. I think it's time I tried my wings.'

'Good girl,' Phil smiled at her and called a waiter to the table.